ATLANTIC PYRAMID

Michelle Lowe

BY
MICHELLE LOWE

Michelle Lowe

Cover design by C&S Designs

Michelle Lowe

DEDICATION

To my brother, Jimmy.
Although the birds still sing and the leaves still
change with the seasons, none sound so sweet or look
as bright since you've been gone.

Michelle Lowe

ACKNOWLEDGMENTS

I would like to thank those who have helped make this book possible. First, I'd like to thank my parents, Jim and Janice. To my daughters, Mia and Kirsten, who encourage me to keep telling stories. And to my Aunt JoAnn for always being there.

I want to thank Kate Hallman for her assistance and advice. Thanks to Scott and Colleen Carroll for their generous support. And to the Wolf Pirate Project for their services to inspire writers. Mostly, I would like to give special thanks to May Bestall, who stood by this story for the past year, molding it into the novel it is today. Thanks to programs like The Wolf Pirate Project and people like May Bestall, authors like me have learned so much and have reached new heights.

Michelle Lowe

Chapter One

My name is Heath Sharp. On June thirteenth, I discovered a world within our own and it terrified me.

The horizon glowed white between the ocean and sky. No clouds hovered and there were no strong winds. Gavin Cole was one of my favorite students and not because he was a whiz kid. I'd trained him every Tuesday for the past few months and he'd finally broken out of his shell to fly a few times on his own. I didn't mind his apprehension; patience was just part of being a mentor.

"All right, take the yoke."

"Uh, what's the yoke again?" Gavin asked. He was also a smartass.

I gave him a sideways glance and he shot me a wide grin in return, wrapping his hands around the controls. "Dude, kidding. Just kidding."

"Now, remember, it's not like driving a car," I said, letting go of my wheel. "You don't steer with the yoke. You use the pedals."

"Got it, dude. Yoke pitches and banks; pedals steer the plane."

One of the problems people have when learning to fly is forgetting their driving habits. It's a challenge to help them through the transition from operating a car to flying an aircraft, but I love it.

"Dude, we're at ninety-five knots. Is that too fast?"

I read the LCD screen. The speedometer wavered between ninety-four and ninety-five knots. "No, we're good. Just keep her steady. As for now, the sky is ours."

"I like that."

I have to admit, I did too. Flying gave my students the feeling of being free from the world, where they could leave all their bad memories in the clouds. That was the sensation I'd gotten as a young boy the first time I'd taken to the sky in my grandmother's airplane. I remember the rumble of the runway sliding beneath us before it suddenly became smaller as the plane lifted off the ground. The sky had then opened into a never-ending blue sheet above our heads.

"If you reach high enough, you can touch the stars," Grandmother would say.

She'd taught me how to fly. In gratitude, I'd promised if I ever owned a plane, I'd name it after her—and I had. I'd named my Cessna Skyhawk *Gypsy Girl.*

"Man, I like these screens you got in here," Gavin said, tapping the LCD displays. "Can we get HBO on 'em?"

"You think it's funny acting dumb?"

"Yep, it passes the time." When I grinned, he added, "What's this called again?"

I looked over at him. His thin lips were as straight as a paper's edge. "Nah, really, I'm not acting dumb this time. Honest."

With a deep sigh, I turned back to the horizon. "It's a G1000. What we're sitting in is called a glass cockpit."

"I bet it's easy to teach people how to fly in one of these, huh?"

"You'd think," I grumbled.

"The sight of all these gadgets in an old instrument panel would downright terrify me. I always liked change. Change is a good thing—change in the weather, clothes styles, *lovers*. Anyway, I *do* know what kind of cockpit we're in. I'm not a complete dumbass. I just suck at remembering numbers. Just about anything with numbers makes me as empty-headed as a senile person in a guessing game."

"You did well on the written test. Few people get the part about the altimeter on the first try."

"I hated that section," he bemoaned. "If the small hand is just over the one, how many feet are you? If you're cruising at nine thousand feet MSL, how many feet is that in AGL?"

"And the answer is?"

He bit his bottom lip.

"Damn it, if you've forgotten the answers already, I'm gonna throw your ass out of this plane."

He went from biting his lip to drumming on his front teeth. "Er . . . eighty-two hundred feet?"

"And what does MSL stand for?"

"Mean Sea Level."

"And?"

"And if the small hand is over the one, you're at a thousand feet."

"Good job."

"Whew, I'm glad I didn't complain about *every* test question or this would be one hell of a scary flight. Dude, maybe that's how you instructors should do the tests. Know what I'm sayin'? Bet you'd get a lot more people studying their asses off the night before if they knew they'd get thrown out of a soaring airplane for missing a question."

"Bet you're right."

11

He pressed on the right pedal to bank the plane in the other direction. "I have a cousin livin' in Weed, California. Maybe I'll visit him. While I'm there, I'll check out that reservation your dad lives on."

"Weed is a bit far from Whitethorn,"

"What tribe are you again? Wichita?"

"Wailaki. My father is full-blooded but my mother is white."

"That would explain those pretty green eyes of yours." He laughed. "Don't worry, dude, I'm not hittin' on ya."

I shook my head. "You're stupid."

"That's pretty cool, though. Not many people can say they have Wailaki blood in 'em. Most people say they're Cherokee. It's funny, 'cause they claim their great-great-great-grandmother was a Cherokee princess. Not only would there have to have been a lot of Cherokee princesses back then, but there would also have to be such a thing as a Cherokee princess. What's the reason for people thinking that, anyway?"

"The Trail of Tears," I said, surprised that Gavin even knew the Cherokee princess claims were bullshit. I'd heard people—mostly from white women—say the same thing about their great-great-great-grandmother when I mentioned my Native American heritage. Whenever some bright blonde number told me that, I felt compelled to help piece together her family tree and teach her something about believing everything she'd been told.

"Everything's lookin' good," Gavin said, turning on the XM radio. "Looks like blue skies from here on out."

As he turned up the volume, Don McLean's song *American Pie* came on.

"Eerie," I murmured.

"What, the song?"

"Yeah. Don't you know why McLean wrote it?"

He was quiet for a moment. "Oh, yeah. 'Cause of that band that died in a plane crash. Think it's a bad omen? Should we turn around?"

"It's just a coincidence. Don't worry about it." I leaned back in the leather seat and checked the instruments. "Fuel gauge looks good, knot speed same, and the plane is level with the horizon. You're doing great."

I stared off into the big blue sky. Not a puff of white anywhere, just a clear view of light blue on the dark.

* * *

"Mayday! Mayday!" I yelled into the radio. "This is Cessna 2B-Golf, requesting assistance! We've run into a squall!"

The plane shook violently in the winds. The windshield wipers couldn't push away the sheets of rain fast enough. I looked over at the map on the display screen. "Our coordinates are—"

I stopped myself when I noticed our location. The map had to be wrong. "Wait, how did we fly twenty miles past Nassau?"

Both screens turned to snow as a constant beeping came from the stall warning indicator.

"Shit!" I yelled as static came over the radio. "Steve, are you there? Mayday!" I waited for a response but got none. "We've lost communications!"

"We're stalling," Gavin shouted, pointing to a red light. "Oh, my God, we're gonna crash!"

"Shut up!" I barked. "I'll get us out of this."

I gripped the control stick and pulled back, lifting the nose while using full throttle to build up speed.

"What's wrong with the screens?" he asked. "Oh God, what's happening with the instruments?"

I did my best to steady the jerking plane. The entire backup system went haywire. The compass, speedometer, airspeed indicator, and altimeter spun wildly. All around us, the sky had turned nearly pitch black, while the rain pounded so hard it was as if we were flying through a waterfall.

I couldn't understand it. One second, we were flying through crisp open skies with Miami at our backs, the next, I was fighting to get out of a storm that had literally dropped down on us. I couldn't see anything. I didn't know how high we were or if the plane was even level. All the instruments either beeped or flashed. Both dials on the altimeter went in different directions and the compass spun so fast I couldn't make out the letters.

"Get us outta here, dude!" Gavin shouted, clutching anything he could as another gust pounded the plane.

I white-knuckled the wheel and stomped on the left pedal, trying to turn the plane and head back the way we'd come. My body pressed against the door as the aircraft made a sharp change in direction. It was dangerous going against the wind, like a surfer going against a big wave. The storm was like a playground bully and the plane a geeky kid taking one pulverizing blow after another. I couldn't tell which direction the wind came from. It seemed to come from everywhere at once, giving me no sense of whether I had done the right thing or not.

I gritted my teeth as the wheel violently shook in my sweat-drenched hands. When the plane turned, a rush of calm washed over me. If I could overcome the wind and circle around, there was a chance we might pull out of the storm.

Then the engine died. Darkness shadowed the inside of the cockpit as both screens went blank. The control panel lights shut off. The buzzing of the propellers went silent when the blades stopped.

"Jesus!" Gavin cried. "What happened?"

"We just lost power."

I tried the magnetos to jolt power into the engine, while working to crank the throttle, but the propellers wouldn't turn. The plane was dead. My stomach slid into my throat as the nose cone dipped.

"We're losing altitude," I said, trying anything to regain power.

"Fuck! We're gonna crash!"

I wanted to reassure him that I was going to get us safely out of this, but I said nothing. He was right. We were crashing.

A gust of wind suddenly flew under the right wing, spinning us as we plummeted. Even when I shut my eyes, I couldn't escape the feeling that I was riding the Sizzler at a carnival. Pressure pushed against both sides of my head. Gavin screamed so loud I didn't know if he heard me yell, "Hang on!"

I gripped the wheel so tight my fingernails dug into the handles. I could see nothing outside as we tumbled through blackness. Soon everything went dark.

When I regained consciousness, everything around me was quiet. I was surrounded by dim, blurry objects. The pounding in my skull answered the question of whether I was alive or dead. With a groan, I slowly raised my head. The safety harness still held me in my seat. My dark bangs draped my eyes and I brushed them back with a shaky hand. When I did, my palm came away soaked in sweat.

That wasn't the only part of me that was wet. My feet were submerged in water. My eyes suffered from a hazy cloud shrouding me but my nose told me it was seawater. My first presumption was that the plane had somehow miraculously stayed afloat. I took off my sunglasses and looked at the bent frames until my vision began to clear.

"Gavin," I said weakly, "we have to get out of here before the plane sinks."

Gavin's head lay on the control wheel, facing me. His safety harness had broken and his face had slammed into the aluminum wheel. I tugged on his shirt sleeve. "Gavin, wake up, man. We have to go."

He didn't stir. I slipped his sunglasses off and saw he was dead. His brown eyes were wide and unblinking. Thick streams of blood slid down his face and dripped from his chin. To be on the safe side, I checked for a pulse but found none. There was even a strong stench of urine. I didn't judge him for it. I had only been seconds away from doing the same.

I looked at the control panel. Both displays were blank and one was cracked. I tried the radio and called for assistance, but there was nothing. *Gypsy Girl* was as dead as the woman she was named after.

I pulled out my cell phone but it had no power. I searched through Gavin's pocket and found his, but it was dead as well.

Outside was a gray fog. The rain had stopped, but there was a strange lingering mist in the wake of the storm.

I needed to deploy the life raft before the plane sank. Unbuckling my safety harness, I eased into the back area of the plane, happy it didn't sink any deeper. Maybe we'd landed on a coral reef. If that was the case, perhaps the plane would stay put long enough for me to reach shore. I could then send someone to load the plane onto a ship and tow it back to Miami.

I was ashamed to find myself thinking more about my aircraft than about Gavin. I wasn't an insensitive or materialistic person, but a dead plane seemed more real to me than a dead man. In a way, thinking about the plane's future allowed me to focus on my own. I didn't have time to mourn Gavin. It would make me weak and weakness might do me in.

I found the life raft floating like an orange block in the back. In a wall compartment were two flare guns in a tin box. Since it was so dark and would only get darker, I grabbed a flashlight before strapping on a life vest and making my way back to the front.

Gavin remained motionless against the control wheel, his eyes staring blankly forward. I glanced at him for a moment as I squeezed between the seats and sat down. Then I checked the side window. The water reached only to the lower portion of the door.

I saw a dark, shadowy shape through the glass. It was a solid object close to the plane but I couldn't make it out. I grabbed the door handle. Although I wasn't sure why, I looked back at Gavin and said, "I'll be back in a sec."

I wasn't worried about water rushing into the plane and taking it under, but the thought did cross my mind. The mysterious surface the plane sat on couldn't be more than five feet underwater. Even so, I held my breath as I pushed the door open. It proved to be a bit of a challenge, since the hinges were broken and the water was like syrup. But I used all my strength to push it just enough to squeeze through. Then I threw caution to the wind and leapt out, sinking only waist-deep in water.

The ground was bumpy and hard. What I stood on wasn't coral, it was muddy rock. I was surprised it hadn't torn the plane apart upon impact.

I was glad the ocean temperature near Miami was comfortable. However, the fact that I wasn't able to distinguish anything that might be lurking beneath the surface made me edgy.

I set aside my apprehension and made my way to the nose of the plane to assess the damage. My chest felt tight every time I breathed, as if my lungs had collapsed. I was a bit light-headed from the thick smell of gas. I noticed a sheen of it coating the surface. I thought it came from my plane, until I saw what I'd seen through the windshield of the cockpit—the wing of another aircraft. Its end was underwater but I could still see a white star inside a blue circle with red-and-white stripes painted on the side of its body. A World War II insignia.

"What the hell?" I muttered.

To keep my flare gun and flashlight dry, I placed everything back on the seat of my plane, then climbed the wing of the World War II aircraft. The fog wet my face like sea spray.

Judging by the wing's length, I estimated the plane's wingspan to be at least a hundred and eighteen feet. The wing was tilted enough to give my New Balance sneakers a challenge with traction. It wasn't long before I came across the propellers and a canopy.

I stared at it, trying to catch my breath. The air didn't help but the fog started to thin, like a theater crowd at the end of a show.

I'm a history buff at heart. If I'd gone to college, I would've taken history as my major. One of favorite subjects I took an interest in was planes and ships. I suppose it came from my love for flying. So when I saw the WWII aircraft, I knew exactly what I was looking at.

A much larger Navy symbol was visible on the side of the plane under its canopy. It was a PBM Martin Mariners patrol aircraft. In War World II, battles had raged in the Pacific months after the war had ended in Europe. Planes such as this one had been used by the Navy for long overseas flights. They were nicknamed flying gas tanks because they carried so much fuel. This plane's tank must have cracked and the gas had spread like glossy butter on the water.

Amazing. I was standing on a piece of history.

As I turned, I found that *Gypsy Girl* and the PBM Martin weren't alone. In the field of water around me, numerous planes and ships were scattered about, some clustered together, others by themselves. It was hard to tell in the fog, but I could have sworn they came from several different eras.

Chapter Two

From where I stood, I saw a 1947 C-54 airplane, three yachts, two sailboats, other Cessnas, and one Piper Cherokee. In the far distance, blurry silhouettes of more planes and ships faded into the fog, some larger than the ones near me.

What the hell had I crashed into? I'd traveled all over the world and experienced many strange things, but nothing like this. When I was a kid, my mother and grandmother had taken me to the Mystery Spot near Santa Cruz, where people could walk up walls and pool balls would roll upward on planks. It had been my first taste of the bizarre. In my later travels, I'd seen even more exotic and extraordinary things, but nothing compared to what I witnessed now.

It appeared that I'd crashed at the edge of a mysterious landfill. Behind me, there was nothing but mist and dark water. I turned back to the abandoned ships, both air and watercraft, cupped my hands around my mouth, and yelled, "Hello! Is anybody out there?"

Silence.

After a few minutes, I decided to explore the PBM. The plane was tilted sideways, its wing acting like a kickstand. I walked up to the canopy and looked in. It was dark inside but objects were visible beyond the thick glass. I half expected to find the skeletal remains of the pilot.

No dust coated the equipment. Other than the dented and scratched exterior, the entire plane was in pristine condition. No rust had eaten away at its black metal or the propellers. The stars and stripes on the side were crisp and clear, as if they'd been painted on yesterday. I wanted to go inside but the door was too far down the tail section and nothing was available for me to climb on.

Judging by the wide-open door, it appeared as if the crew had survived and abandoned the plane. Even so, the PBM had gone down several decades ago, so I didn't expect to find them. There were more recent vessels and aircraft with possible survivors I could look for. I needed to find someone. I needed explanations.

The trip off the plane proved more challenging than the trip up it and my sneakers slipped out from under me. I landed on my back and slid along the wing like a water slide, all the way into the ocean. I was underwater for less than a second before my life vest brought me back to the surface. There, I stood on the muddy surface and slid my hands back to pull the hair out of my face. My heart knocked against my breastbone as I waded back to my plane to retrieve the flares, flashlight, and life raft.

When I reached the open door, I looked behind me at the gray horizon. No wrecks sat out there. The water was flat and dark, and as I strained to see through the fog, several chunks of what appeared to be ice drifted by.

Ice in tropical water?

As the ocean swirled around me, the floes liquefied. I waded a few steps to my right, my arms outstretched, until the muddy bottom suddenly dropped out from under me. My life vest kept me afloat but it didn't keep me warm. The subfreezing temperature raced through my body and ate into my bones.

21

How could I be in water so cold that ice floated around me? My limbs were numb and my heart rate slowed. I frantically thrashed my arms to keep afloat. Although it was difficult to do the backstroke with my vest on, I kept kicking until a wash of warm water swept over me. My feet found the ground and I stepped back onto the ledge, shivering.

The irony of it was overwhelming. If I'd crashed just three feet farther away, my plane would've sunk in that frigid water. It was an amazing stroke of luck to escape death twice in the same plane crash.

As I counted my blessings, something bumped against my side—a floating wine bottle with a piece of paper rolled up inside. I popped the cork and managed to pry it out. It was handwritten but in Spanish. I shoved the note back inside, stuffed the cork in the opening, and hurled it back into the ocean.

As feeling returned to my body, I waded over to my plane and pulled the cord to inflate the life raft. Tossing the flare guns, flashlight, and oars into it, I took a last look at Galvin's lifeless body.

"Sorry, but if I find help, I'll come back for you."

It didn't seem strange to make a promise to a dead man. After all, I'd yelled at the living, screaming Gavin not long ago.

I clambered into the raft and started my quest to look for survivors. The journey was more difficult than I anticipated. Everything was surreal. I didn't know what was out here but I needed to keep moving. I had to find someone—anyone—who might give me answers.

I hadn't been rowing more than ten minutes before a sharp, jagged piece of metal snagged my raft and tore a hole in it. I didn't have any patching supplies, so I jumped ship. Drowning was the least of my worries. I'd been captain of the swim team in high school and now wore a life vest.

I should've known the water would be full of hidden debris on the bottom or floating around, and I cursed myself for not thinking of it before ruining the raft. To prevent my legs from getting sliced, I tried leaping from one wreck to the next, until I came upon something my mind couldn't wrap itself around.

I climbed onto the deck of a sailboat, heading toward another plane, when a massive blob stopped me in my tracks. It was a living mass with veins and tentacles, and it stretched over the side of the boat to curl around the mast. Its suction cups—each the size of my palm—had fish bones and broken bits of crab shell stuck to them.

If it was an octopus, it was the biggest goddamn one I'd ever seen. I'd heard about giant octopuses in the North Pacific, but this looked as if it could swallow a car whole. Its glossy black eyes stared at me as it heaved short breaths. I retreated slowly, not knowing if it would envelope me in its huge tentacles. But it didn't. It just breathed heavily, as if gasping for air.

After carefully wading through the water, I stopped to rest on the wing of a Piper Aztec. I was surprised to find a number of other octopuses lounging on ship decks and planes like sea lions. But it was another massive silhouette that caught my attention. Curious, I carefully jumped to another Cessna before leaping onto a speedboat and then stepping into the water. As I drew closer, my mind screamed, *This can't be real! I can't be seeing this.*

It was the underbelly of a massive wooden ship tilted at a seventy-degree angle. The hull was infested

23

with barnacles, and as I looked closer, the white shell of one opened. Something spiraled out, nearly licking my nose. The barnacles were alive, despite being out of water. How the hell did they survive that way?

I waded along the edge of the huge vessel until I could climb to the top of a 1979 Beech Musketeer. There, I stood in silent awe of a thousand-ton Manila galleon warship. It was the oldest and largest vessel I'd come across so far. I'd seen a couple of Grumman T9F-2 Panthers from World War II, at least twenty Chris Crafts, three schooners, several Piper planes spanning three decades, a handful of yachts, and a 1942 TBF Avenger, but the galleon went back two centuries, although it appeared to be in pristine condition.

None of the vessels had been eaten up by the elements. I came across two Lancer wooden boats and a Catalina yacht, all as perfect as the day they'd been made in the fifties. How was it that every one of them seemed unaffected by the humidity and salt water?

Like the other vessels, the galleon looked ready to go. Sails hung in the still air on their masts, along with an American flag on the mizzen topsail. Why the galleon hadn't capsized confused me, until I noticed what it rested on. Crushed beneath the side of the great vessel was another long wooden ship with carvings on its side. The damage done when the galleon had come to rest against it prevented me from distinguishing its artwork.

I caught sight of something else—a long plank extending from the unfortunate vessel to a half sunken sailboat. I wanted to stay out of the water, which meant leapfrogging from one craft to the next. I jumped onto another aircraft, then onto the back of the sailboat, where I studied the plank, which turned out not to be a plank at all, but a wooden sculpture of an ancient dragon.

"A Viking ship?" I muttered, my eyes following the carving to the crushed ship it was attached to.

The head of the dragon nearly reached the sailboat's bow. I took a chance and leapt onto it. The thick wooden construction held my weight but not without some rebellious creaks. I scrambled over the dragon's neck, where a long ladder hung down. I wondered if the crew had placed it there to escape the ship.

I climbed the ladder, but halfway up, the air seemed to squeeze my lungs, making it hard to breathe. I stopped to rest and took advantage of the sights. The fog remained thick but the planes and boats were still visible. It seemed like a dream, and in a way, I was excited about this strange world around me. I loved experiencing new things. When I'd left home to explore the world, I'd journeyed far off the beaten path to discover what most tourists avoided. But hanging out with headhunters in a jungle couldn't top the mystery I now faced.

Near the end of my climb, I found myself face-to-face with a porthole door. When I raised the heavy wooden flap, the mouth of a cannon stared back at me. By the time I reached the deck, my lungs burned like a fifty-year-old smoker. The ship was in perfect condition, with smooth, untarnished floorboards and ropes hanging from shrouds that were neither broken nor frayed.

I climbed one of the stern side staircases to reach the helm. The ship's wheel was polished and turned with ease. I could hear the rudder sliding back and forth behind me.

I'd never been on an actual galleon before. The closest I'd come to that was the Galleon Swinging Ship pirate ride at American Adventures. Like a kid high on imagination, I played with the wheel for a while before going below. There, I peered into the dark captain's cabin. I clicked on my flashlight but it wouldn't work.

"Damn it!" I shook it as if that would help. I'd just changed the batteries.

After my eyes adjusted to the dark, I could make out a small table. The gray light filtering in through the doorway and large windows gave enough illumination to find some matches. An oil lantern hung from a column beside the table. I struck the match and dipped it inside the glass. To my relief, the wick sprang to life.

I expected spider webs and a blanket of dust, but the corners and surfaces were clean. The floor, though, was littered with fallen items. It appeared as if the ship had been caught in a massive storm, throwing everything that wasn't nailed down to the floor.

"Hello?" I called, looking around. The cabin smelled of body odor mixed with a hint of smoke, as if every candle in the room had been blown out only minutes before. "Is anyone here? Anyone?"

I touched one of the flare guns tucked under my belt. I didn't like the idea of using it as a weapon. Shooting someone with a flare would be like shooting them with a ball of fire. I'd use the aluminum flashlight over the flare gun if it came to that.

I scanned the room but there was no reply to my call. I kept my guard up, just in case.

An oak table sat in the center of the room with a scroll on it. I set the lantern down next to a map pinned on each corner by a Mora knife. It was a map of the

Atlantic Ocean, although many Caribbean islands were missing. There were over seven thousand islands in the area but the map showed no more than two hundred. Even the Gulf of Mexico—the ninth largest body of water in the world—was missing, and Cuba was listed as *Isla Juana*. The date in the right-hand corner read 1804.

If the ship and everything on it was really over two hundred years old, why did it all look relatively new?

There weren't many other things in the room. Anything worth taking, the crew had probably carried off with them. Even the mattress on the small bed was gone. I hoped to find the captain's log to give me clues as to what had happened but I couldn't find any trace of it.

I left the cabin and went down to the gun deck, where cannon balls were scattered about. The smell of gunpowder permeated the air. I knelt, placed the lantern and flashlight on the floor, and picked up one of the cannon balls. It was no larger than a coconut but weighed enough that I couldn't hold it for long. When I dropped it, it landed with a thud and rolled across the floor.

As I walked through the ship, I passed several empty barrels. I searched for other artifacts until I found a second staircase.

"Hello? Anyone down there?"

I warily descended to the next level. As I crept down the steps, another strong whiff of body odor struck me. When I stepped off the staircase, I found the source of the smell—a man lying in a hammock.

"Oh shit!" I exclaimed, startled.

The man wasn't disturbed by my expletive.

"Are you all right?" I asked.

He said nothing. He appeared to be asleep, although I thought otherwise.

Several oil lanterns hung from support beams. Playing cards and coins were scattered around, as well as three human skeletons. At first, the skeletons startled me, but I quickly recovered and continued my search around toppled chairs. I found another skeleton lying behind a table. Each was dressed in nineteenth century clothing and armed with weaponry from that era. The bodies, except for the one in the hammock, seemed to have been involved in a struggle before they'd died. It wasn't long before I noticed bullet holes in the walls and one column.

Unlike the others, the man in the hammock looked as if he'd died not long ago, yet he was dressed in the same fashion. He had a single bullet wound to the temple. One of his arms hung down, while the other rested beside him. On the floor, next to a brown stain, was a pistol.

I wondered when he'd died. It couldn't have been any later than that day. His body smelled of BO, not decay.

A note lay on his chest. Nearly every word was misspelled, but at least it was in English—my first real clue. After reading it twice, I was able to grasp what the letter meant.

To my captin, Jon T. Sherbrik,

I writ tis to xplain wat hapined. Onc you red tis, you wil understan an not condem me for the achins I hav takin. Dekhand Pal Roy, canon comandor Joshuy Walkor, secint-in-comand Mastor Richerd Troi an my self had com bak to the shep Thrs day nit to play cards

whin Mastor Walkor acused Mr. Roy an Mastor Troi
of cheeting. To my sham, ech man had ben drinking
hevly an thar mind set was most ineproprit. Harsh
words wer xchaned betwen the men an gun fir eruptid.
Mr. Roy was shot in the gut an fel ded, an Mr. Walkor
was wondid. I saw the devel in his eyes, captin.

Mastor Troi trid takin Mistor Walkors pistel whin
Mr. Walkor tok owt his sord an sunk it strait in to
Mastor Trois bely. I trid to sav him. I puld my gun an
fird, kilin por Mr. Walkor. It was to lat for Mastor Troi
an I fownd myself alon wit my ded shep mats. I didt
want to be hanted by Mistor Walkor, captin. Ater tirty
yers in tis God forsakin plac, we al no wat hapins win
we kil. I codnt liv that wa. I kiled Mistor Walkor an
cold not hav him arownd, tantin me til I go mad. So I
hav kiled myself, captan. Ma God show mursy on me.
Tomas
Febuwry 4ᵗʰ 1836

A tide of questions arose in my head. It wasn't
just the misspelling that confused me. If the men's
death had happened on the same night, how could it be
that all but one—Tomas—had long since decomposed?

"There's no freakin' way this guy died in 1836," I
said out loud, as if to someone else in the room—
someone with a pulse.

I collected some of the coins strewn across the
floor. They were old and American. I saw no other
kind of currency, which wasn't surprising if the
incident had taken place in 1836, since paper money
hadn't been issued in the United States until the Civil
War.

My head was spinning and not just because of the
strange quality of the air. I wondered what Tomas had

meant when he'd said he didn't want to be haunted by the man he'd killed. I placed the note back on Tomas's chest and went topside.

I continued in the same direction I'd been heading before boarding the galleon. After climbing over wreckage and wading through dark water, my heart lurched into my throat. A pale fin drifted across my path. I stopped as it made a U-turn and headed straight toward me.

"Oh shit!"

I fought my way toward a nearby plane rudder. Even though the water was only waist deep, I knew I wouldn't make it to safety before the shark reached me.

I spun around, pulled a flare gun, and fired. I missed my target but it scared the shark long enough for me to reach the plane. I grabbed hold of the rudder and started up. The shark came back and hitched its teeth into my life vest, yanking me into the water, thrashing. I unbuckled the vest and slipped out of it, then grabbed the rudder again, hoisted myself up, and flopped onto the tail of the plane. Breathing heavily, I watched as the shark glided just beneath the surface. It was a baby great white, an inexperienced hunter. That was the only reason I was still alive.

Once it realized I wasn't in the water anymore, it swam off. I lay on the tail section for a long time, collecting myself before I stood up and crossed over to a 1950s Grumman F6F-5 Hellcat. As I neared the cockpit, I saw another dead body. The canopy window had shattered, sending a large shard of glass into the pilot's left eye. Like Tomas, the pilot's body showed no sign of decomposition.

Somehow, the vessels and aircraft—and most of

the bodies—remained perfectly preserved. I became more confused by the second, but it was getting late and I had to find a dry place to sleep.

Just as it almost became too dark to see, I caught sight of a blotchy dot—another galleon. Light came from torches lining the railing and through the window of the captain's cabin. I climbed onto a yacht and read the distant ship's name on the stern: *The Pride*. A moment later, I heard gales of laughter booming from inside.

Chapter Three

Voices eventually replaced the laughter. It sounded like a party.

Even so, I wondered if I should make myself known or do a little investigating first.

I didn't have time to decide before a man from above yelled, "Ahoy! Friend or foe?"

Even though the only light came from torches, someone had spotted me. He must have been wearing night vision goggles.

"Friend, I guess."

"You guess, good sir?" the invisible man asked with an English accent. "What's that you hold in your hand?"

"A flare gun."

"A what?"

Before I could repeat myself, another voice said, "He says it's a flare gun, Master Judson."

"Aye, captain," the first voice said humbly.

A shadowy figure approached the railing between two torches. "When did you arrive?"

"Today," I replied.

"Today? Well, then, I'm sure you're full of inquiries, *non?* You better come up and have a drink. Believe me, you'll need it. Lower the plank! We have a guest!"

I went to the yacht's starboard side, while a pair of crewmen slid a long board gently into the water.

"Hurry up, *señor*," one of them called. "Get on before the sharks come."

The thought of getting back in the water frightened the hell out of me, especially when it was now inky black. Nevertheless, I wasn't about to look like a fool in front of a band of sailors. I climbed down from the yacht, waded quickly through the water, and stepped onto the plank.

Unlike the first galleon, *The Pride* was tied to other ships and planes by thick rope, keeping the vessel upright. As I walked up the plank, I wondered who these people were and what they were capable of doing. Common law most likely wouldn't apply in a place like this. I reminded myself that I was on a quest to find people—people with answers—and perhaps I'd found what I was looking for. Even so, it was best to stay vigilant.

The deck was decorated with a web of lights strung overhead. Some were solar-powered party lights of various colors. Others were little square glass lamps, each lit by fire. Torches tied to the railing provided the most light. Why fire and no electric lights? Probably because an old ship like this had no way to charge batteries.

Once I was on the deck, a pale man with short bristly hair and a dense mustache greeted me. He was dressed in denim bell-bottoms but no shirt. "That flare gun you have, I'll need it—and any other weapons you have." His accent was English and he wasn't wearing night vision goggles as I'd thought.

"I think I'll keep it. Don't worry. I'm not going to try anything."

He held out his hand. "Trust me, lad, you don't want to kill anyone around here, even accidentally. Hand it over. It's for your own good."

I didn't understand what he meant, but I handed

both my loaded and unloaded gun over. He didn't take my flashlight, which I held as casually as I could so as not to draw any suspicion to it.

Other men appeared on the deck—five black, four Spanish, and three Caucasians. Each was dressed in clothing from different eras. One Spaniard and one of the Caucasian men wore dirty white Royal Navy sailor uniforms. One of the black men wore only a brown vest and trousers. Another Caucasian was dressed in baggy denim shorts and a long white T-shirt, reminding me of a wannabe thug. None of them was over five-foot-six. I was six feet tall and towered above them, but I was outnumbered and needed to keep my guard up.

"Hi," I said sociably. "I'm Heath Sharp."

"I'm Judson," the bristly-haired man said.

Before anyone else could introduce themselves, a voice from the staircase said, "And I am the captain."

A man dressed in a blue captain's coat with *Windfall* sewn in gold thread on the breast pocket walked down the steps. He wore an admiral's hat and white pants that were cuffed over his brown loafers, as well as a Hawaiian shirt. His hair was dark, wavy, and shoulder-length, and his eyes a piercing black. One hand was tucked into his pants pocket, while the other held a clay pipe.

"Oh, the questions that must be running through your head, *monsieur*," the captain said as he reached the deck, his voice laden with French tones.

I said nothing as he approached. His graceful movement was mesmerizing. When he was about two arm's length away, he stopped to take a drag off his pipe. His black eyes never blinked.

"Where are you from?" he asked as he exhaled

34

gray smoke into the night air. His lips then froze in a slight grin, as if he loved hearing the sound of his own voice.

"California, originally," I replied.

He took another puff off his pipe and studied my face. "You have a unique look about you. What did you say your name was?"

"Heath Sharp."

He moved closer. "*Bonsoir,* Monsieur Sharp, I am *Capitaine* Jean Lafitte."

My eyebrows rose in confusion. I'd heard that name before and my mind quickly backtracked through my memory. The name reminded me of New Orleans, which reminded me of the magazine *The French Quarter: An Informal History of the New Orleans Underworld.* I'd read a copy years ago when I'd visited the city, of an article about Jean Lafitte.

"Jean Lafitte, the pirate? Didn't Jean Lafitte die of fever in Teljas in the 1800s?"

The captain frowned, his eyes narrowing. "I was no pirate. I was a *privateer.* And no, I did not die of a fever."

The man was probably insane. This guy, who dressed like Mr. Howell on *Gilligan's Island,* told me with a straight face that he was one of the most famous pirates in history. I couldn't help but show my skepticism. "So, where's Blackbeard?"

"Unless you want to spend eternity in the brig, *señor,*" one of the Spaniards sneered, "I suggest you watch your tongue before I cut it out."

I instinctively gripped my flashlight a little tighter.

"No, Amado," the captain said, "he is confused, much like the rest of us were when the hurricane brought us here." The captain extended his hand to suggest that I follow him. "Come, let us sit together like gentlemen and I will clear your perplexity as best I can."

I wanted answers so I followed him to his quarters, my shoes squeaking like mice in hysterics along the way. I was exasperated and wet. In his quarters, I asked, "Could I trouble you for a pair of dry socks?"

The captain snorted. "It would seem that you need more than dry socks, *mon ami*."

True. I needed an entire new wardrobe, but my wet feet irritated me the most.

"You may borrow my robe for the night," he said, plucking a long fluffy one off a hook on a wall. "Undress and we'll hang your clothes outside to dry, provided it doesn't rain."

I peeled off my clothes except for my boxers. I wasn't going to get totally naked in front of a man I didn't know.

The room was well lit by a number of candles, even a cylinder shaped star lamp displaying tiny stars on the ceiling and walls. The firelight inside it made the little dots flicker from time to time. The room was also adorned with all types of things from the past and present. A strong smell of tobacco smoke hung in the air. Heavy chairs surrounded a large oak table, much like the one I'd seen on the other galleon. The table was littered with naked pinup girl playing cards, coins, paper money, and chips, as well as wine and rum bottles. I must have interrupted a poker game.

To my left was a bookshelf filled with novels, comics, and reference books. A handful of paintings hung on the walls but I paid them little mind. Instead, I examined several crude sketches of the captain, crew, and the planes and ships surrounding the galleon. A strange triangular shadow hovered in the background but I dismissed it as just another plane or ship in the sketches.

"Is it always so foggy around here?" I asked as Lafitte poured two glasses of wine.

He turned slightly and said, "Indeed. From time to time, it thins out, but it always lingers. It's like a bad joke." His tone became somber. "I do miss the sunshine and the crystal-clear ocean."

His expression was the saddest I'd ever seen, as if he'd been committed to life in prison. "I also miss the bayou and my kingdom in Barataria." He let out a mournful sigh and approached me with a wine glass in each hand. "But life always has a way of surprising you, *non?*"

"For an ancient pirate, you've accumulated a lot of modern things," I said, draping my sopping clothes over a chair and tying the robe around my waist. I still didn't buy that I was in the company of such a historic figure.

"I told you," he said sharply, handing me a glass, "I am no pirate. I'm a privateer. And just because I was born in the nineteenth century doesn't mean everything I own has to come from that era. Especially when we're surrounded by such wonderful new treasures. I only wish most of them worked."

As I accepted the glass of wine, he continued. "You like my drawings, *non?* It was my hobby until I ran out of paper."

I pointed to the odd triangle. "What's this object in the picture?"

He lowered his glass and studied where I pointed.

"That is the SS *Marine Sulphur Queen*."

He thought I meant the ship next to the shadow. There was a jagged crack running down its keel. "It looks like it's been badly damaged, like it snapped or something."

"The *Queen's* captain explained to me that such cargo ships weren't structurally sound. When his was caught in the storm, she snapped in half. You'll see her tomorrow. She's not too far from here, and a ship that large is hard to miss, even on the saddest of days."

"Saddest of days?"

"*Oui*, when the fog is at its heaviest, it can be quite gloomy." He took a long drink. "You will soon come to realize that for yourself."

"You really believe you're Jean Lafitte?" I asked, looking him squarely in the eye as if searching for the truth within his face.

He sighed again. "I understand your confusion and disbelief, *mon ami*. I myself once had the same doubts as you. Come, let me show you some things that may lessen your disbelief."

He turned on his heel and approached a redwood wardrobe in the back corner. I finally took a drink before following him to the closet. It was good wine, some of the best I'd ever tasted, although it left a tart aftertaste in my mouth.

Inside the wardrobe hung a long red coat, a black cape, and breeches. A pair of scuffed boots sat on the floor. Hanging from a hook on the back of the door was a black brim hat with a gray feather. A pair of musket rifles and a scabbard were propped against the inside wall.

He slipped off his jacket, tossed it onto a nearby chair, and pulled out the velvet coat. He put it and the hat on, then turned to face me as he buttoned it up. While the coat was majestic and a perfect fit, it didn't go well with his Hawaiian shirt or brown loafers. Its slender sleeves hugged his arms but gave his wrists some freedom. The wide white collar sat flawlessly around his neck. The entire ensemble seemed tailor-made, and even the hat sat on his head as if it was part of him.

"I haven't worn this in over a decade," he said, swinging the cape around him.

"This is how you prove you're Jean Lafitte?" I asked. "By putting on some old coat?"

"No, I want to show you what I wore when this portrait was painted." He moved over to a framed picture of a man in a red coat hanging on the wall and posed like the image on the canvas. "Before coming here, the portrait sustained some salt air damage, but can you see the similarity?"

I studied the painting before shifting my eyes to the captain's same stern expression. The man in the portrait was the spitting image of him.

"The amusing thing about this painting is that it's the original."

"Why is that funny?"

"Because scores of people have told me that the copy the artist made before giving me this one is the original. The year 1814 was a chaotic one. I received a letter from King George III, asking me to fight in his Royal Navy against the Americans. I still have the letter, if you'd like to see it."

Before I answered, he slid open the top drawer of a nearby desk. There was something on the desk covered by a green velvet cloth. "What's under there?"

"Just something I collected from a spiteful little

39

man. Would you like to see it?"

He pulled the cloth back. What lay under it made my stomach turn inside out.

"Jesus!" I gasped, gaping at a severed arm submerged in a yellowish liquid in a ten-gallon fish tank. "Is that thing real?"

"*Oui,* it belonged to Captain George Saxon. He's no one famous. Just another unfortunate louse to get caught in this place."

"What happened between you two?"

"Hard feelings," he said, lowering the cloth over the tank. "Let us leave it at that." He turned and held out an envelope. "Would you care to read the king's letter?" Seeing my pallid expression, he asked, "Are you all right?"

"It's the air," I lied.

"Ah, don't fret, *mon ami,* you will soon get used to it and breathe it as well as the air in the natural world. Like being constantly exposed to a bad smell. Eventually, you won't notice it anymore. Come, let us sit and talk. There is something else I would like to show you."

In spite of myself, I began to believe what he told me. Could he actually be Jean Lafitte?

We sat across from each other at the table. The robe's fabric prickled my skin. It wasn't as fluffy as it appeared.

"Okay," I said as he reached into his shirt pocket and retrieved a small leather pouch. "If you are who you say you are, what does that make you? Immortal?"

He withdrew a pinch of tobacco and stuffed it into his pipe. "That is precisely the case." He struck a match. "My crew—and everyone else trapped here, including you—are now immortal."

40

I sat back in surprise. "Are you saying I'll never die?"

"Oh, you can die," he said, puffing on his pipe. "Death's bony hands can reach far, *mon ami*, even in this place. You can kill yourself or be murdered, or die accidentally. Just not of old age."

"What *is* this place?" I asked, leaning forward again.

He exhaled through his nose, the smoke looming in the air. "It's the Bermuda Triangle. Or the Devil's Triangle. Call it whatever you wish."

I blinked. "The Bermuda Triangle? As in the area where ships and planes vanish?"

"Haven't you seen enough evidence today to confirm that?"

I rubbed my forehead. "But how is that possible?"

"Anything is possible."

"Apparently," I mumbled. "Okay, if that's true, answer me this. I saw dead bodies today inside a ship and one of them looked like he'd died just before I found him."

The captain's eyes widened as he stood. "You didn't disturb his body, did you?" Not waiting for my reply, he asked again, this time more insistently. "Did you?"

"Who? The dead man?"

"Yes, you fool, did you disturb it? Touch it? Move it?"

I gave him a questioning look as I shook my head. "No, I only read a suicide note, but I returned it."

"And you didn't touch the body?" he asked, still anxious.

"No, I didn't touch it."

He sighed deeply, lowering himself back into his

chair. "Well, that should be all right, then."

A moment of deep silence settled over us as he took a drag from his pipe. I waited for him to explain his outburst, but he didn't and I became impatient as he casually took a sip. "What the hell was that all about? I tell you about some dead guy and you nearly shit yourself."

He slowly lowered his glass to the table, sliding his eyes over me. "I do not wish to travel far into the subject. My sole advice to you about the dead is to leave them be."

"Why?" I asked, utterly confused.

"Just do as I tell you and let us now talk of other things."

"Like what?"

"You were asking how this was possible."

"Yes, how is it?"

He twisted his fingers around his long goatee. "I know not. It just is."

It was like having a conversation with the Caterpillar from *Alice in Wonderland*. I sighed in frustration and snatched my glass from the table. "How many people are here?"

"Hundreds…thousands. I am not sure anymore. I don't leave the ship very often. There are some out there, the British especially, who continue to hold a grudge against me for my part in helping the Americans defeat them in Louisiana."

"Is that what happened between you and Captain Saxon?"

"Let's talk about you," he suggested, changing the subject.

I put my glass down. "What about me?"

"Your physical appearance is intriguing. Tell me,

42

what nationality are you?"

Again with my appearance? I'd inherited my father's Native American cheekbones, nose, and dark hair, but I had my mother's bright green eyes, which stood out against my olive complexion. I had to admit that seeing a Native American with green eyes was a bit like coming across an albino.

"I'm half white and half Wailaki Indian."

"Indian, you say? You're the first Indian I've seen since we arrived. I must say, your skin color is very light for an Indian."

"I'm only half Indian."

"And from whom did you inherit those electrifying green eyes?"

"My mother."

"Ah, how times have changed. People of your time can breed with another nationality without prejudice and fear of death, *non?*"

"I wouldn't say without prejudice, but at least you don't get put to death for it."

"What year is it?"

I tried to ease myself into the reality of this surreal moment. I told him the year and he stared at me a moment before lifting his glass to take a drink. "Well over a hundred years," he muttered.

"What does that mean?"

He lowered his glass, resting both elbows on the arms of his chair, slouching, his legs crossed. "Nothing."

I let it go and went on to another topic. "How did you come to end up here?"

He took one last draw from his pipe before placing it on the table. "My life took a turn for the worse in 1821. Despite my loyalty to the US Navy, they still viewed me as a threat and drove me out of Galveston. In retaliation, I set my entire empire ablaze so the government couldn't claim its spoils. I meant it as an act to bring me more power but it caused my downfall. After losing two of my ships when I refused to attack a Spanish merchant vessel, I was reduced to nothing but a common thief. I tried to rebuild my militia but failed. After five years of living like an outcast in the country I'd fought for, I went to Teljas to enjoy wild hunts with the natives. I then left for Puerto Rico to buy slaves, but a hurricane set upon us.

"When the storm ended, we found ourselves here. There were other ships trapped here, as well, but not nearly as many as there are now. Over time, more ships came. Then strange flying machines began to fall from the sky." He chuckled. "I thought I'd seen everything. Then I saw my first television, although it didn't work. Nothing that requires batteries or electricity can operate here."

"Why not?"

"No one knows."

That explained why neither my cell phone nor flashlight worked. "What about that body inside the ship? The suicide note I found said he died in 1836. If that's so, why hasn't he decomposed?"

"Nothing from the outside rots here," he explained. He twisted his fingers around his goatee again. "Everyone is preserved in the same manner they were when they arrived, even after death. Machines and ships stay as they were. Metal does not rust and the water does not eat at the wood." He untangled his fingers. "And flesh does not decompose or wither away."

"Why?"

"I do not know."

"You don't know? You've been here all this time and still don't have a clue?"

"I told you, I don't leave the ship often. And frankly, I no longer care."

I decided to try another route. Perhaps it was because I still didn't fully believe he was who he claimed to be. "Before you came here, you say you were a slave trader?"

"*Oui*," he answered without hesitation.

"So, those black men on the deck are slaves?"

"I understand in your time the thought of slavery is inconceivable. But in my time, slavery was a part of everyday life, like tying a witch to a stake and burning her to death. Yes, I sold salves, even owned them. We're all guilty of the wrongs from our own eras, *non?*" He took a drink. "And yes, they were slaves. They once belonged to me, but shortly after we arrived here, I set them free. I gave them the option to leave or stay. At first, they wouldn't leave the ship. Like the rest of us, fear kept them planted here—especially the sounds at night."

"Sounds?"

"*Oui*. Torturous shrills with the ability to cease the beating of even the stoutest heart. Fortunately, they're not as common now as they once were. As time went on, some of the crew and slaves left, but those who remained here have become my friends. My equals, if you will."

"Didn't you say you wanted to show me something?" I asked.

"But of course. Wait right here."

He went to the other side of the room, where he rummaged through his belongings. As he did, I

45

glanced over at the green sheet covering the severed arm. If I didn't watch my step, I might end up losing a limb.

When Lafitte returned to the table, he carried a large wooden chest. With a mighty heave, he hefted it onto the table, knocking over several bottles and sending them crashing to the floor.

"It's not another arm, is it?" I asked nervously.

He smiled. "How well do you know my story?"

"Not well."

He reached into his shirt pocket for a handkerchief. "I see," he said, pressing the cloth against his forehead and drumming his fingers on the lid of the chest. "When I left home, I took a substantial amount of treasure with me."

My eyes widened when he raised the lid, exposing silver and gold coins, pearl necklaces, rubies, and uncut diamonds. It was a typical pirate treasure—enough to make Bill Gates drool.

"Holy shit!" I said, reaching into the chest and plucking out an uncut diamond. I held it up to the light to study the stone. It was heavy, with rough edges, and about the size of a prune. Once cut and polished, the clarity would be clear enough that it would be worth more than my plane.

"It's all real, *mon ami*," he said, pulling the stone from my fingers and tossing it back into the chest. He closed the lid. "Everything is real. And so am I."

I sat back as the reality of the situation washed over me. Lafitte laughed as he retook his seat and rekindled his pipe. Blowing a perfect smoke ring, he said, "Tomorrow, I will show you where you must go."

Chapter Four

I had difficulty sleeping that night. Too many questions were left unanswered, giving me a headache. Lafitte had urged me to rest and given me a couple of sleeping tablets. I didn't take the pills. I was afraid of what strange shit might happen while I was knocked out.

The hours crept on and I was still tossing and turning on the upper deck. Finally, I drifted off to sleep. As I slipped into unconsciousness, I began to accept that I was actually on the pirate ship *The Pride* and Jean Lafitte was alive and well. I couldn't explain how it was possible but I vowed to find more answers as soon as I woke up.

I don't know how long I was out before I heard a familiar voice. "Heath, you gotta get me outta this, man."

I opened my eyes but saw only the colorful lights overhead. Thinking the voice was part of a dream, I closed my eyes again.

"Heath! Damn it, get your ass up! I need your help!"

I sat up but saw no one. "Who's there?"

I liked to consider myself a brave soul and a disembodied voice in the dark wasn't too frightening, but when someone stepped out of the shadows, I nearly screamed.

"Hey, man, it's me!"

Gavin? He looked exactly as he had when we'd gotten into the plane for takeoff. He wore the same jeans, gray T-shirt, and worn boots. The only thing different was the blood on him.

"What's the matter, man?" he asked in his familiar southern accent. "I ain't that grotesque, am I?"

Gathering my senses, I stammered, "Y-y-you're dead. I checked your pulse before I left the plane. And you have blood running into your eye."

"Blood? Oh, this thing?" He bent over slightly to show me a gash near the top of his skull. The wound was no larger than a ping-pong ball but it bled profusely. "It hurts like a bitch, man. Itches too."

"You can't be here," I said, shaking my head. "You're dead."

"Okay, ya got me there. I'm as dead as the wood on this ship, but I'm here all right and I can't leave till you help me."

"Help you?"

"Yeah, I'm stuck. I need you to dispose of my body. I don't want to be left in the plane, marinating in piss."

"You're stuck? What do you mean?"

"I dunno."

"Then how is it you're talking to me?"

"What do you think we are? I mean, what we're made of?"

"I don't know, seventy percent water?"

"Energy," he corrected. "Our bodies are just meat, but inside, we're pure energy. I'm talking to you now 'cause I'm focusing my energy squarely on you."

"When did you become a scientist? Do we get smarter when we die?"

"No," he said, a little petulantly. "I'm just able to channel my energy through your own energy. You know, like a magnet."

I didn't understand what he was saying, and it surely didn't sound like Gavin. He'd never struck me as the philosophical type. Even so, I pressed for more information. "What do you want?"

"I already told you," he snapped, wiping blood from his eyes. "I need you to dispose of my body."

"What do mean, *dispose?*"

"Bury it, burn it, put it on a raft and push it out to sea, I don't care. Just don't leave it out there, man."

I couldn't recall him ever calling me *man* before. He'd always called me dude, which I hated. "I don't understand. Why can't you leave if your body stays where it is?"

"Look," he said, continuing to wipe away trickles of blood, "I'm not sure how I know anything, but I think it's a rule around here."

"A rule? What's that supposed to mean? What do you know that I don't?"

"I can leave my body if I'm speaking to you, but only for a short time. I can't fully explain it, but for some reason, my body keeps me latched to it. I've been told the only way to be free of it is if my body is rightfully taken care of."

"You've been told?" I inquired. "By who?"

"Other ghosts. They're all around us. There are more bodies out in the ocean than you know about. You think things are strange? You ought to see what it's like on my end."

"I rather not. But I'd like a more in-depth answer."

"Maybe next time. Right now, I'm out of time."

He walked over to the railing and floated onto it as if he was weightless, then twisted around to me. "I'll be back later. My head is killing me. Ha! Killing

49

me—that's a good one!"

He stepped off the railing and dropped like a stone. I rushed over to where he fell but saw nothing—not even ripples in the water.

It was getting brighter, the black sky fading into gray. Morning was coming and I was glad, even though I'd gotten very little sleep. After Gavin's visit, I wouldn't be able to go back to sleep anyway.

As I leaned against the railing, I wondered what he meant by out of time. Did he have some ghostly curfew?

My ruminating soon vanished when I noticed the fog was gone. Everything became clear and visible, and for the first time since my arrival, I could see the vastness of the wreckage. It was a museum of transportation, displayed like toys in a gigantic bathtub. Masts of other galleons and schooners poked up in the far distance. Planes, sailboats, and yachts were strewn about in the shallow water. The *SS Marine Sulphur Queen* was exactly as the captain had sketched it.

"My God," I whispered.

"God isn't here," Lafitte said, coming up beside me. "I stopped believing in him years ago. Nothing but mystery resides in this place."

"The fog is gone," I pointed out.

"*Oui*. Every morning at this time it dissipates. Don't get excited. It'll return in a matter of minutes." He lit his clay pipe. "We should reach the island in good time."

"What island?"

He pointed behind me. "Over there."

I twisted around. My eyes widened as I stepped across the deck to get a better look. It was truly remarkable. It was the mysterious triangular object I'd asked about in the sketches. How the hell could I have missed it? The island was at least a mile high, covered with lush trees and heavy fog hovering around its peak. Below the hills was a coffee-colored beach. "It kind of looks like a—"

"A pyramid," the captain said, finishing my sentence. "*Oui,* a lot of us thought the same thing. We call it the Atlantic Pyramid. Fitting, *non?*"

"And people live on it?"

"*Oui.*"

I studied the island a bit longer, before the sky became overcast and the fog rolled in. It was as if someone had switched on an oversized smoke machine.

"What the hell?" I muttered, turning back to Lafitte.

"I told you. Now, get ready to go ashore."

I quickly put on my clothes, which weren't completely dry, then followed him and two crewmen, Judson and Amado, through the open water and pockets of wreckage. Judson, shirtless and with my flare guns tucked into his belt, was incredibly pale. Vampires had better skin color than him. Had he been sick before he'd arrived here? He seemed healthy enough.

The journey to the island was easier than what I'd endured going to Lafitte's ship. Planks had been placed between the wreckage of planes and boats, creating narrow but sturdy bridges. After a while, the planks stopped, forcing us to leap from one wreck to the next. The captain, his pipe in hand, didn't wheeze one bit as he made catlike jumps.

"How can you chain smoke like that and not be

dead?" I asked, trying hard to keep up.

"I told you, everything here is preserved. My lungs were in perfect condition when I arrived, and they still are today. I can smoke a can of tobacco every day and my body will react to each puff as if it was the first. But beware, you can become ill by fault of the island, so try to stay healthy."

I glanced back at Judson. If what Lafitte said was true about the health of someone when they arrived here, wouldn't it be the same for someone who was sick?

"Don't you ever run out of supplies?" I asked.

Lafitte jumped onto the tail end of a small plane. I was in mid-leap when I realized he'd stopped. I tried to avoid bumping into him, but my foot slipped and I fell in the water.

"What are you doing down there?" he asked as his crewmen laughed.

I stood up, angry. "I was trying not to run into you, since you apparently felt the need to stop like that."

"Oh, my apologies, I was about to answer your question."

"And?"

"Yes, of course we do. Run out of supplies, that is." With that, he turned and resumed walking, talking to me as he went. "That's why we trade or grow our own things. I have a tobacco garden on a vessel not far from my ship. And I should show you our vegetable garden."

I grabbed the plane rudder and pulled myself up. "Trade? With who?"

"Villages."

"Villages?" I teetered from side to side, my arms

out to maintain my balance.

Lafitte continued strolling along, as if he was on a flat surface. "Of course. Where else are people going to live?"

A simple explanation, I'll admit, but it took me by surprise. "But—" I started, until I was cut short when I almost lost my footing again. "Okay, new question. Why aren't there any planks for us to walk on anymore?"

"To keep any threats of the island from coming to my ship. Come, come, it can't be that difficult. We're almost there."

"What kind of threat? People from the villages?"

"No, people I can handle. It's the monsters that worry me."

I let that remark pass. I could finally see the shoreline as Lafitte stepped off the nose of the plane, onto one last plank at least twenty feet from the beach.

My eyes never left the island as I sloshed through the shallowest part of the water, onto the sand. I was dead tired of nearly breaking my neck just trying to get from point A to point B, and the thrill of having my feet on solid ground sent shivers up my spine.

"Master Judson," Lafitte said, patting his pipe against his palm to dump the ash. "Give him back his flare guns."

Judson handed the guns to me without a word.

"Thanks," I said, to which Judson nodded in reply.

"Don't go into the forest," Lafitte warned. "It's safer to stay on shore."

I slid my eyes up the island's steep hillside. "I'm not in the mood for climbing, but why not? What's up there?"

"The monsters I mentioned, they're Vikings gone insane."

"Vikings? Are you serious?"

"Very much so," he said gravely.

"How did they get here?"

"Just like the rest of us. They wandered off the beaten path."

"So why do you say they're insane?"

"Too many years trapped on this island, I suppose. In my time, there were over a dozen of them. Some were women and children, but they never seemed to stay together. In fact, they hunted each other."

I slapped at the back of my neck, at a hungry mosquito. "What do you mean they hunted each other?"

"That's one of the reasons why my crew and I stay onboard *The Pride*. For some reason, the Vikings turned on each other. Whatever happened to them in that forest made them worse savages than they already were. I can only image how bad things got after they started killing each other."

My question about what happens after death once again came to mind, but he continued before I could ask it. "After years of picking each other off, their numbers dwindled to only four. There are only three males and a young girl left. Professor Inglewood captured the girl."

"Whoa, hold on. Professor *who* captured *what*?"

Lafitte smiled at my confusion. "Professor Inglewood captured the young Viking girl."

"This is getting too weird."

He snorted. "You haven't even begun to experience weird, *mon ami*. Come, I will walk with

54

you a little way before you go off on your own."

We strolled along the misty beach while his men stayed behind, and Lafitte spoke gravely, "I wanted to talk to you alone and give you some hard facts."

"Like what?"

"Like you shouldn't expect to leave this place. There is no way out. If you get bored, you can pass the time by trying to escape, but that's all you'll be doing—passing the time."

"Why'd you have to tell me this alone?"

"My crew doesn't like to hear such things. They stubbornly hope there'll be an end to this miserable place."

"Is it really so bad here?"

He paused. "It depends on how you perceive the situation."

"Lafitte," I said, addressing him by his name for the first time I, "something happened to me this morning. I was visited by my student pilot."

"Did he die in the crash?"

"Yeah."

He stopped to give me a grim look. "Go on."

"He told me he's stuck and I need to dispose of his body."

"You told me you hadn't touched any bodies."

"I didn't. I mean, shit, I checked his pulse. But what does touching the body have anything to do with what happened to me this morning?"

"And you say he asked you to dispose of his body?" he asked, seemingly avoiding my question.

"Yeah."

He sighed as he stuffed his pipe. "What I'm about to tell you is in the strictest of confidence, understood?"

"Yeah, sure."

He reached into his pants pocket for a book of matches and lit one. "I had a similar experience myself."

"You?"

"*Oui.*" He puffed on his pipe until the tobacco caught fire. "When we were first marooned here, some of my crew and I took a longboat to explore other ships we'd seen. The sharks attacked us when we jumped out, mortally wounding my first mate. I managed to get him out of the water and onto a crow's nest that sat just above the water of a completely capsized vessel. Despite my efforts to stop the bleeding, he died anyway. I escaped by walking over the mainmast and finding another longboat. The following morning, my first mate woke me and said I had to retrieve his body and give it a proper burial."

"What did you do?"

"I refused to go back. But he insisted, then vanished."

"That's exactly what Gavin did. He just disappeared."

"I told none of the crew because they would have thought me mad. Morning after morning, my first mate came to me, pleading for me to bury his body. I never did."

"What happened?"

"Eventually, he faded away and never returned."

"Is that what I should do? Ignore him so he'll go away?"

"Don't tell anyone about it. Ignore the situation completely. It'll be over before long."

I wished that was the case with all my problems. Just ignore them and they'd simply disappear.

"And don't listen to the urge," Lafitte added.

"The urge?"

"To do the dead's bidding. It will pull at you to fulfill their request."

"Is it really Gavin?"

"I've given you all the advice I wish to give," he said shortly. "I won't discuss it any further."

I knew no amount of prodding would help, so I asked, "Should I continue going this way?"

"*Oui.* Stay on shore and you should reach the village by afternoon."

"Village?"

"*Oui.* Where else did you think I'm sending you? Now go, and if you ever feel like having a drink, come see me. Farewell, *mon ami.* Good luck."

Lafitte watched as I headed down the beach. I looked back every once in a while, hoping he'd change his mind and come with me, at least until I reached the other people he'd spoken of. I was wandering into the unknown and I was afraid. I'd crash-landed in some otherworldly place where there were unique dangers to be wary of. It was like being a character in a novel written by a twisted author who could play me like a puppet. Whether or not insane Vikings were out there waiting, I had to keep moving. I needed to find more answers than what Jean Lafitte had provided. How was it that people could live without growing old? And what was up with the dead?

That last question brought goose bumps to my skin. The dead didn't decompose, but why not?

I kept walking, slapping at mosquitoes, until I noticed that no waves washed up on the beach. I stopped and studied the ocean. The water seemed completely motionless. It was yet another mystery—

one I would have an eternity to understand, if Lafitte's words were true. It had only been a day and I already missed home.

I'd seen many dangerous things in my lifetime. Whether it was freezing to death on Mount Everest, being kidnapped and held for ransom in México, or contracting food poisoning in Peru, I at least had some idea what to expect. That wasn't the case in this wretched place. What lurked in the shadows of the forest? I felt like a frightened Boy Scout after a night of horror stories around the campfire.

My thoughts were interrupted by a rustling in the nearby underbrush. I turned away from the ocean and stood motionless for a minute while reaching for the loaded flare gun in my belt.

A minute later, eight shapes emerged from the forest, walking hunched over. At first, I thought they were apes in ragged clothing. Their hair was long, even the children's, and matted like dreadlocks. Their faces were distinctly human, but not like any human I'd ever seen. Their foreheads were small and furry, with a protruding brow shielding their eyes. None of them, not even the full-grown males, were more than five feet tall, but they had the muscle mass of a gorilla.

It was one of the children—a young girl—who spotted me first. She called out to the others, making a sound in no language I'd ever heard before. As they shifted their attention to me, my grip on the flare gun tightened. They stared at me like wax figures, and for the life of me, I couldn't think of what to do.

There was a long, uncomfortable silence. Then one of the females yelled at a male wearing green flip-flops. He grunted in acknowledgment and approached me, carrying a musket like a spear. As he drew closer,

I could see a dark fuzz on areas of his body I never thought could grow hair. He had gray eyes, a large fat nose, and a mouth full of crooked, chipped teeth.

He shouted and waved his hand, shooing me away. I took a step back, but then decided to hold my ground. When he realized I wasn't going to back down, he took the musket in both hands and trained the bayonet on me. Again he shouted, but I refused to move. Were these the people Laffite wanted me to find?

The man approached again, more aggressively than before, leaving me with no choice but to react. I raised the flare gun and pointed it his way. He stopped and cocked his head, as if he was confused by the sight of it. Then he came at me again. I was about to pull the trigger when I glanced at the rest of the group. Whoever they were, they appeared to be a family. I'd never killed anyone in my life and wasn't about to start now, but I had to do something.

I raised the gun and fired into the air. In a burst of bright red sparks, the flare shot into the sky, leaving a trail of smoke behind it.

The advancing man stopped abruptly and nearly tripped over himself to run the other way. The others took off as well, women pulling their children who stood watching as the flare reached its peak and exploded into a fiery bright light. The adults didn't even look back as they raced into the forest.

I composed myself from the strange encounter, building enough courage to continue down the beach. After twenty minutes, another group appeared. I stopped and held my empty flare gun tightly. After some time, they came closer. I was pleased they seemed more advanced than the first group. Even so, I kept my guard up.

"Was dat you, mon?" a black man asked with a Jamaican accent.

"Yeah," I said, holding the flare gun at my hip like a lame version of an old-time cowboy.

"You just get here?" another man asked with the Queen's English.

"Yesterday."

"You'd best come with us," said an older woman. "This area isn't safe."

Chapter Five

I studied the people I was now among. The Jamaican in an army-green shirt, with ragged shoulders where the sleeves had been cut off, was thin and a few inches taller than me. He had short hair and a long braided goatee. His skin was dark, almost pitch-black, and he had light brown eyes and high cheekbones. The woman's hair was shaved on both sides and only a bit longer on top. Gray bangs hung over her blue eyes. Although she was short and stocky, she carried herself with a don't-underestimate-me attitude. She wore Converses, calf-length denim shorts, and a black T-shirt reading: IF I COULD BE SOMEWHERE ELSE, I WOULD BE.

The five-and-a-half-foot Englishman had dark blond dreadlocks and russet eyes. He, too, had a long goatee and a well-trimmed mustache, and was dressed in a Union Jack T-shirt, torn jeans, and black sandals.

"What do you mean it isn't safe?" I asked.

"This area is where the Ancient Ones live," the woman said, turning in the other direction. "Come on, we can walk and talk."

"The Ancient Ones? Like the people I ran into a little while ago?"

"What did dey look like?" the Jamaican asked.

"Like they'd just come off the *Quest for Fire* movie set."

The Englishman gave me a confused look but the woman said, "That's them, the Neanderthals."

"Neanderthals?"

"You lucky, mon," the Jamaican said. "Dey be da least to worry 'bout."

I stopped and slapped at a mosquito on my arm. "Are you serious? How the hell are there Neanderthals here?"

The others took a few more steps before stopping with me. It was the woman who asked, "Do you know anything about human history?"

I wiped the blood from the mosquito on my shirt. "Sure, do you know yours?"

"Great, a funny man," she said. "Then you outta know that tens of thousands of years ago, tribes spread out from Africa all over the globe, searching for other lands. How do you think they ended up on Easter Island, and in Hawaii and Cuba?"

"Are you telling me those people drifted off the mainland and ended up in this place thousands of years ago?"

"Yep."

"Sucks for 'em, eh?" the Jamaican said, slapping at a mosquito. "I'd much rather be in Hawaii."

"Never been, mate," the Englishman said. "From my understanding, those islands were discovered two years after I arrived here."

It was a lot for me to take in. Just the day before, I'd gotten out of bed, had breakfast on my porch, and showered in my bathroom. I'd spoken with my mother about nothing important, then gotten into my car and driven to the airport. I couldn't have imagined a turn of events like this, not in a billion years. Even death was more plausible than this.

"I'm Travis Livingston," the Englishman said, extending his hand.

I shook it and replied, "Heath Sharp."

Travis smiled.

"Khenan Evans," the Jamaican said.

"Nice to meet you," I said, shaking his hand as well.

"Marissa Agnew," the woman said over her shoulder, keeping ahead of us. "Tell us, Heath, what's the day and month?"

"Tuesday, June fourteenth."

"Whatcha you know? Ole Inglewood got it right," she said.

"Inglewood? Professor Inglewood?"

"Aye," Travis said. "How did you know?"

"Lafitte told me to ask him about the Viking he caught."

"Ah, Lafitte," Khenan said. "Da gentleman pirate. 'aven't spoken to 'im in years."

"Yeah, well, the old fool better watch his ass if he doesn't want to get tortured again," Marissa said.

"Tortured? Is that what happened between him and that guy, Saxon?"

"Aye," Travis confirmed. "Saxon has a dark loathing for pirates, especially Lafitte. He got his hands on him once when Lafitte came ashore looking for help to pull his ship upright. Saxon knew he couldn't kill him, so he spent a week torturing the poor sod."

"Jean got 'is revenge, dough," Khenan said with a grin. "One night, 'e got loose and chopped off Saxon's arm wit 'is own sword while 'e slept."

"Lafitte warned the bloke that if he ever bothered him again, he'd cut off his other arm," Travis added.

"What happened after that?" I asked.

"Lafitte went back to his ship like nothing ever happened and ole Saxon went back to his village."

63

"Saxon didn't have any men with him?"

"Nah, mon, 'is sailors were the superstitious sort. Dey believe da island to be cursed and dared not wander off dere ships until the villages were built. Some still 'aven't left."

"Bloody shame about the Ancient Ones, really," Travis said. "Some haven't evolved at all, like the lot you encountered. They've been here thousands of years, give or take, and act like we're wicked gods out to get them."

Marissa cleared her throat loudly.

"Oh, and wicked goddesses," Travis added with a smile.

"Are there a lot of people here like that?"

"Not as many as there used to be," Marissa said. "They're out there, though, living in a village on the other side of the island."

"How many villages are here?"

"Three, so far," Marissa said. "The assholes who built their village on the other side of the island are called the Obsoletes."

"Obsoletes?"

"They hate it when we call them that. They know it means they're archaic."

"Aye," Travis said. "They're thinking the exact same way they did when they arrived here."

"You mean like the Neanderthals?"

"Kind of, only those chaps choose not to let go of the past. Their beliefs don't apply to modern folk."

"They're a bunch of sexist, bigoted sons of bitches," Marissa spat. "They think women should be subservient to men and people like Khenan should serve them hand and foot."

"They were in control for a while," Travis

64

explained. "At least up until the sixties, when they were outnumbered by the newer generation and those who'd had enough of their shallow-minded ways."

A brief silence came over the group and I took advantage of it to soak in what I'd learned. Then I rotated my head around to Travis. "How long have you been here?"

"Since 1777," he said as if I'd asked his age. "I was a Royal Navy gent, sent to fight in the Revolutionary War. We were supposed to go to Savannah, but our bloody drunk steersmen took a wrong turn and we ended up a little ways down from the port. The next thing we knew, we were caught in a hell of storm and, well, here we are. I was twenty-three then. Pity I never got to see America, even if I was only going to get meself killed."

I turned to Khenan, and he waved his hand at me. "I 'aven't been 'ere nearly dat long. I was on da *Jamanic K.*"

Before I could ask, Marissa raised her hand. "Piper Cherokee, 1994."

"Passenger?" I asked.

"Pilot."

"What'd you come in 'ere wit?" Khenan asked me.

"Cessna Skyhawk."

"Where in da junkyard is it?"

"The junkyard?"

"That's what we call the water around the island," Marissa explained, "on account of there's so much junk out there."

Referring to something as wild and beautiful as the ocean to a junkyard saddened me, but I was interrupted by a shriek from overhead. A flock of pelican-sized birds soared out of the forest and circled over the ocean. Their shrill cries were punctuated by clicking sounds, as if they were sucking their tongues against the roof of their mouths.

"Well, if it isn't the Shark Hunters," Travis said. "Looks like they're hungry."

"What are the Shark Hunters?" I asked, shooing away the mosquitoes.

"Watch dis, mon."

Marissa rolled her eyes. "He'll have an eternity to see this shit. We need to get back."

The word eternity struck me hard, giving me chills. I'd only been here a day and I was nowhere near accepting that I'd be here forever.

"They're making their formation, lad," Travis announced excitedly. "They've spotted one!"

Dozens of birds glided in pairs thirty feet above the ocean, as if following a drill sergeant's order. Then they did something I'd never seen birds do. The first ten dove straight into the water like torpedoes. Minutes later, a rush of water erupted. Mixed in with the salty foam was a fountain of blood from a thrashing shark. The birds had latched onto its head and were picking at its skull with sword-like beaks. It was the same kind of shark that had attacked me the day before.

A second wave of birds dove in for another assault, allowing the first batch to fly off. Among those fleeing was a bird in possession of one of the shark's eyes. The bird jerked its head back and sent the eye down its long, slender gullet. The rest of the birds tore at the shark's flesh. Their quick action and organized technique helped them avoid its snapping jaws. After several strikes, the thrashing stopped and the only sound was the shrieking and clicking of the birds.

Travis nudged me with his elbow. "That was bloody marvelous, eh, mate? Watch what happens next."

A minute later, the birds emerged from the water, dragging the lifeless shark onto shore. It had to weigh five hundred pounds, but together they managed to drag it onto the beach. It reminded me of a theory that dinosaurs were descendants of modern day birds and that certain herds killed large pry, some bigger than themselves.

The eye eater sat on the sidelines, not helping the others, just shrieking and clicking. It was larger, with burgundy feathers and a black line running from the top of its head down its back. Its claws were off-white, unlike the others' black ones, and its banana-shaped beak was speckled with white spots. It had to be the flock's leader.

When the shark was completely out of the water, a feeding frenzy began. Birds ripped off large chunks of flesh and flew off to perch on trees or rocks. They stood on one leg, eating the meat from their other foot. The leader finally waddled over to the carcass and plucked the other eye out.

"They'll have that whole bloody shark picked clean in minutes," Travis said.

When the leader spotted us, it expanded its wings and shrieked loudly.

"All right, Bongo, we're leaving," Travis called to the bird.

"Bongo?" I asked as we moved on.

"Dat's da stupid name some idiot gave 'er," Khenan said.

"Aye, but no worries, lad, the Shark Hunters might be intimidating, but they won't bother you

67

unless you bother them."

"They're more like our allies," Marissa said. "The sharks are a threat to us and the birds are a threat to them."

"I was nearly eaten by one yesterday," I grumbled. "Do the birds usually kill baby sharks?"

"No, that was a full-grown one," Marissa said. "They're small in size but they're dangerous all the same."

"I've never seen birds act like that before."

"That's because they're nowhere to be found on the outside," Marissa said.

On the outside? She made it sound like we were in a fishbowl. "Are you saying this place has its own species of birds?"

"Wildlife in general, chum," Travis said.

"Really? You mean animals have gotten trapped here too?"

"More like born and bred, mon," Khenan said. "Da animals 'ere have been around since da island developed. Unlike us, dough, de're not eternal. Dey grow old and die like da way it outta be."

"Coming through the junkyard, I'm sure you noticed the octopuses," Travis remarked.

I remembered the heaving octopuses lounging on the sailboat. "A few."

"Scary, eh? But they're harmless. You can actually go up and pet them."

"The first one I came across didn't seem very friendly."

"Aye, they tend to get nervous, especially when they're pregnant. But the only thing deadly about them is if you eat them. They're poisonous."

"Which sucks," Marissa grumbled. "'Cause

they're easy to kill."

"Dat's why dere ain't too many of 'em left. People used to kill 'em for fun."

"How is it that people trapped here can live forever?" I asked.

"We don't know," Marissa said, maintaining her steady stride. "All we have are theories."

"Such as what, aliens? Atlantis?"

"How did you know?" Travis inquired.

"I read *Limbo of the Lost* when I was in high school." I waved my hand at his confusion and added, "Sorry, that was way after your time."

"I'd like to see what the world is like today. What it has become in the last two hundred plus years. We've had updates from new arrivals, but I'd like to see it with me own eyes."

"When was the last time anyone other than me arrived?"

"Some young bloke named Gibbons," Travis answered. "He arrived with his girlfriend on his father's yacht last year. He'd snuck the yacht out while his dad was away."

"And he acts like he's cock of the walk," Marissa added.

"Aye, that he does," Travis agreed. "He's a real wanker, that one."

"What about people?" I asked. "Are there any humans native to the island?"

"If there were, I'd hate to meet them," Marissa replied. "I can only imagine what they'd be like."

"Dere ain't no people 'ere but us, mon," Khenan added.

Chapter Six

We continued for a while longer before signs of human habitation appeared.

"Home sweet home," Travis said in a less than enthusiastic tone. "Heath, lad, welcome to North Village."

His attitude was downright melancholy, which brought my own mood down a few notches. Then he threw an arm around me and said, "Aw, it's not all that bad. Think of it as a permanent getaway from everything you hate on the outside."

My spirits fell when I realized I'd never enjoy the things I loved again.

About a hundred yards from the village, tucked away behind a few palm trees, was a square stone and mortar building with five slim windows and a flat roof. "What's that?"

"That's our jail," Travis said dismissively.

"Oh," I replied, not wanting to press. As we moved on, I saw at least three hundred round stone huts, some perched on the island's steep hillside, with many just twenty paces from the shoreline. Each was fifteen feet tall and thirty feet wide, with pointed roofs and two windows in front. Narrow spaces between them had stairs leading to the beach. A wharf wide enough to drive a tank on stood on six-foot columns. It ended at the steep hillside, where it turned into stairs. Piers branched off from the wharf, all lined with huts.

The mountainside huts were of the same design as the ones on shore. The only difference was the

70

width of the walkways, which were narrower and had railings. Four paths branched off from a set of stairs leading up the hillside, one above the other. The highest path was the shortest, the bottom the longest. Huts lined one side of the walkway against the mountain, overlooking the beach. Above them was a larger hut partially hidden by trees.

"Does your leader live up there?" I asked.

Khenan looked to where I pointed and shook his head. "Nah, mon, no one's really in charge around 'ere."

"So, who lives in that hut at the top?"

"No worries, mon, you'll meet 'er soon enough."

"Hey!" Marissa shouted to a group of people standing by the ocean with fishing rods. A few waved half-heartedly before returning their attention to the water.

"Who are they?"

"Folks who got caught here on their way to the fishing grounds," she replied.

"Is a sad story, fer sure," Khenan added. "All dey do, day in and day out, is stand out dere an' fish."

"Do they ever catch anything?"

"Not much."

"Then why do they do it?"

Khenan shrugged. "No one really knows. It's just da way it is."

When we reached the end of the wharf, we climbed some steps to where a pale elderly man sat on a patio chair reading *Naked Lunch.* Chickens pecked at the ground around him.

"Hey, Carlton," Marissa said, "isn't that the hundredth time you've read that book?"

Without looking up, Carlton said, "And I'm still

trying to make sense of it, Miss Agnew." He shifted his eyes up to me as I climbed the steps behind Khenan. "Newcomer?"

It was a simple question but I didn't know how to answer it. The term sounded like what prison inmates called new arrivals. The irony didn't escape me. It was exactly how I felt.

"Yeah," I said gloomily.

Carlton went back to his book. "Welcome to the world beyond."

I didn't know what to make of that, but I had other things on my mind.

Every hut had distinctive features. Some windowsills and doors were painted different colors but were badly chipped. Lawn furniture sat on piers and back porches, where wind chimes and shells hung from the eaves. Potted flowers and vegetables made up gardens. In a way, the village was like a tropical vacation hotspot, a place to escape the pressures of life. But in reality, the village was home to people who couldn't go back to their lives.

Sitting on a bent lawn chair was an obese man. He was shirtless, showing off his large, saggy breasts. It didn't bother me. I'd seen plenty of unhealthy physiques at the beach.

He turned his head toward us and raised a meaty arm. "Hey there, did you find out where that flare came from?"

"Sure did," Travis said, pointing at me. "It was this bloke."

I waved and said hi just as an overweight woman came out of the hut carrying a flower pot.

"This is my wife," the man said as she bent over to place the pot on a short table. "Look at that big ass.

72

She got that from her mother. Our daughter inherited it, too, poor thing."

The woman turned to her husband and pointed to his chest. "That may be, but she inherited her tits from you."

"Ignore those two," Marissa said, continuing on. "They're a couple of idiots."

"Do you get a lot of high tides?" I asked, referring to the wharves six-foot columns back on the shore.

"Nah, mon, dere's no tide 'ere. If dere was, da 'ouses would rest on poles, yeah?"

"Every house has a crawl space," Travis said, which surprised me. "You know, some place to put things."

"If there's no tide, why have the columns?" I asked.

"To protect us from the stingrays," Marissa replied.

"Stingrays?"

"They come outta the ocean at night," Travis said. "They hide beneath the sand and creep toward their prey, till they get close enough to stab with their tail. Their sting paralyzes their victim, letting them wrap their tail around an arm or leg and drag their prey into the ocean. No one even knows it's happened 'cause they eat every last bit of you, bones and all. So stay off the beach at night."

"Does that happen a lot?"

"Unfortunately, yes," Marissa said.

"The plus side, though," Travis added, "is that they're fun to kill and they taste marvelous."

The village was full of people doing all sorts of things—playing Frisbee or volleyball on the beach, doing maintenance on their homes or cooking on small grills, while chickens and goats roamed the pier freely. We approached an old woman in a peach dress sweeping her doormat.

"Hello, Mrs. Truk," Marissa said.

The old woman raised her head and smiled. "Oh, hello, um, what was your name again?"

"Marissa."

"Oh, right, I'll remember it the next time. I promise." When the woman saw me, she added, "Oh my, you're a handsome young thing. Would you like to come inside for some tea?"

Khenan grabbed my arm and pulled me away. "Just got 'ere, Mrs. Truk. We need to show 'im around first."

The old woman's smile faded for a moment but then quickly returned. "Oh, well, how about you, young man? Care for some tea?"

Khenan gave her a contrived smile and waved as he pulled on my arm. "Nah, tanks, Mrs. Truk. Got tings to do."

Again she seemed disappointed, but her eyes brightened as she asked Travis, "And what about—"

"Sorry, love," he said, cutting her off and hurrying by, "loads to do today."

"Well, don't be strangers now," she called as we rushed away. "Come by and see me anytime."

"What the hell was that about?" I asked as Khenan pulled me along. "Why are we running away like a bunch of thieves?"

Marissa giggled but Khenan shot her a look. "Dat wasn't funny, woman."

"It was to me," Marissa said, barely able to stifle her laughter.

"Bloody hell! Why did you have to draw attention to us like that?"

"Oh, stop it, you two," she growled. "Just having a little fun."

"Who was that old woman?"

"Mrs. Truk …" She was unable to continue as another fit of laughter washed over her.

Khenan shook his head, but Travis tried to explain. "There isn't anything wrong with her. Well, not harmful or anything like that. It's just that, um, to put it delicately, she has a taste for…er, younger men."

"She's a sex addict!" Marissa blurted. "She'll take on any young male who's willing."

My eyes widened as I looked back at the sweet-looking old woman still waving at us from her porch.

"She's been like that since her prime," Travis added. "She claims to have eight illegitimate children. I tell you, it's funny to see people looking older than me when I'm a couple hundred years older than them."

"I'm glad that hasn't happened to me," Marissa said.

"You wait."

"What's with the goats and chickens?" I asked. "Where did they come from?"

"They're livestock from ships," Travis replied. "People keep most of the goats as pets."

I thought it was odd that sailors would keep animals as pets when they'd originally intended to eat them. "Why haven't they been eaten?"

No one answered my question but they all gave me strange glances. Finally, Travis said, "We don't kill the outside animals. We trade for meat—things like wild pig and seafood."

"Wild pig? You mean boar?"

"Kind of, but a lot tamer," Marissa said. "Once they're captured, it doesn't take long for them to adjust to captivity. And they breed like rabbits."

As we traveled along the wharf, people approached to ask questions. *What did you come in? Plane or boat? What's your name? When did you get here?* I answered their questions as more people gathered around, feeling a little like a celebrity harassed by the paparazzi.

"Bugger off!" Travis finally shouted. "He'll tell you everything at tonight's Welcoming."

That satisfied the crowd and they stood watching as we moved on. Marissa left us to go inside a hut, but Travis, Khenan, and I headed for the long staircase leading up the mountain.

"Where are we going?" I asked.

"Dere's a vacant hut on da fourth level," Khenan said, pointing to a hut one row down from the top. "Dat'll be your place. It has a nice view."

"Why isn't anyone living in it now?"

The men glanced at each other. "Might as well tell 'im. He's gonna find out once we get up dere."

"Tell me what?"

Travis sighed deeply. "It's because of Tommy Pine."

We passed a red-haired man wearing cargo shorts and sunglasses, holding a tanning mirror to his chest. He sat in a patio chair, resting his skinny pink legs on a wooden crate. He bolted upright at the mention of Tommy Pine.

"You're taking him to ole' Tommy's place, are ya now?" he asked with an Irish brogue. Khenan and Travis didn't answer, but the Irishman laughed anyway.

"Shut it, Paddy," Travis snapped. "It's not bloody funny."

"Oh, yes, it is. Once he sees what you're trying to pawn off on 'im, he'll punch ya square in the kisser!"

"Make yerself useful and get to da tavern an' start making whisky fer tonight."

Paddy continued chuckling as he got up and moved to the edge of the wharf, leaping down to the sandy beach.

"Bloody idiot," Travis said. "I love him like a brother but he's a handful sometimes. He owns Miller's Tavern on the far end of the village. Well, inherited it, I ought to say."

"When did he get here? The same time as you?"

"Nah, he emigrated from Ireland during the potato famine after losing his family. He went to New York but decided it wasn't the place for him. He made his way to Florida, which was insane at the time 'cause the place was overrun with Indians. One morning, he went out fishing and his boat went too far, and, well, here he is."

I started to ask more about this Tommy Pine but Travis cut me off. "It's best if we just show you, lad. If you don't want the place, you can bunk with me till we find somethin' else for you."

It was unnerving that no one wanted to talk about Tommy Pine, but I maintained the patience they requested. As we climbed the stairs, I noticed the mosquitoes didn't bite anymore. We passed a few first row residents standing outside their huts, staring at us.

Travis and Khenan led me to the fourth walkway and a hut on the far right end. "Dis be da place, mon," Khenan said as he opened the door. When I hesitated, he assured me, "It's awright. Da inside is perfectly fine."

I held my breath and stepped into the hut. It was nearly pitch black inside. Travis followed me in and took a match from a jar on top of a single table, lighting a candle. Other than the table, the place was empty. No furniture, no pictures, just an open space. It was the size of a small studio apartment—ten times smaller than my home in Miami.

Even though I lived alone, I had enough room in my one-story home for an entire family. It was a three-bedroom ranch with a wraparound porch and a two-car garage. To see the ocean, all I had to do was step out onto my back porch. Granted, I rented the house, but it wasn't just a place to sleep at night—it was home.

As I looked around the one-room hut, my heart fell. Khenan patted my shoulder. "Don't look so grim, mon. Once ya fix it up da way ya like, it'll grow on ya."

"And over here is the loo," Travis said, opening a small door.

I peeked inside. The room was merely a stall, no more than five feet wide, with a wooden toilet seat on a crate. "Where does it all go?"

"Every hut on the hill has a steel pipe running down into the nearest hole in the ground."

"Hole?"

"Yeah, mon, da hillside is riddled wit holes we been using to dispose of waste fer centuries now."

"What about the people living on shore?"

"They have the same kind of loo but no pipes. They go in a bucket and then dispose of it properly. For those who find that too undignified, there are male and female stalls near the village against the mountainside."

"What about bathing?"

"There's a waterfall that drops off the ledge of the mountain and makes for a perfect shower."

"Fer dose of us who bathe," Khenan said with a sly smile.

"Yeah, well, lots of people take showers. Not me, per se, since I don't give a toss anymore. If ever."

"What about fresh water?"

"It rains plenty, so there are no worries about that."

Again, I scanned the room. So far, I saw nothing suspicious or creepy. "All right, what's the catch?"

Khenan sighed heavily. "Come dis way."

I followed him out the back door and onto a small wooden porch near the steep slope. Four plastic buckets filled with rainwater sat near the door. Healthy green foliage and large red and purple flowers grew along the stone wall four feet from the back porch, nurtured by the humidity.

"Look down dere," Khenan said, standing by the rail.

I leaned over the railing and instantly wished I hadn't. Lying about fifteen feet below, in a narrow crack, was the body of what I presumed to be the previous occupant, Tommy Pine.

Travis came up beside me and shook his head. "Bloody shame, it was."

"What happened to him?"

"It was an accident."

I'd hoped the catch to the house was a leaky roof or infestation of some kind. What I got was a mangled corpse.

79

Chapter Seven

Tommy Pine had been standing on the railing, trying to pick a flower, when he'd slipped and fell. According to Travis, Tommy had been a jerk, but that didn't change the fact that his body now lay below the hut.

"Can't the body be moved?"

"Nah, mon," Khenan said. "Ya can't mess wit da dead."

What's up with the dead?

"No worries, lad," Travis said, giving me a slap on the back. "He won't smell up the place. He'll just lie there and make no fuss, as long as you leave him be."

I was about to ask why when someone called out in a German accent, "Knock, knock."

"Oi, Dominic," Travis greeted when a man stepped into the hut.

Dominic joined us on the back porch. He was about my height, with strong facial features and large dark eyes.

"You my potential neighbor?" He extended his hand. "Dominic Flank. I live next door."

"Heath Sharp," I said, shaking his hand, which felt like a vise.

"Nice to meet you, Mr. Sharp. Have you met Miss Houghton yet?"

"We were about to go up and talk to her," Travis said, leaning against the railing.

"While you do, I help set up for the Welcoming."

Dominic spoke in broken English, but had he known the language before or after he'd arrived on the island?

"What's the Welcoming?" I asked.

"Eleanor thought it up ages ago," Travis said. "It's a gathering we have for newcomers."

"I get things started," Dominic said.

"Cheers, mate," Travis said as Dominic disappeared into the hut. "That's half the work done."

"It sounds like a big deal."

"No worries, mon," Khenan assured, "Travis is just lazy. We do dis fer anyone who wants to live in Nort' Village."

"Do a lot of people live here?"

"Some live on their vessels," Travis replied. "Like that rich little bugger, Neal Gibbons. Lives on his dad's yacht 'cause our village is too primitive for the likes of him."

"How does he get ashore when he needs to?"

"Rowboat," Khenan said. "But Eleanor suggested we build a pier fer da ships to dock. We need it, 'specially after da cruise ship arrived. Dat way no one 'as to go into da water."

"Cruise ship?" I said in surprise. "Are you talking about *The Ramón?*"

"Da very same. Dat fat couple you met befah was on da ship."

I couldn't believe it. In August 2010, *The Ramón* had left Key West, headed for the Bahamas. It had disappeared after a few hours at sea. No trace had ever been found and no distress call had ever been made. At first, people suspected pirates, but after weeks of no ransom demands, authorities had considered other possibilities. I'd laughed at the flakes who'd blamed the Bermuda Triangle for her disappearance.

"D'ya need to get anyt'ing from yer plane?"

I thought about it a moment. "Actually, I do."

"When yer ready to go out dere, let us know and we'll go wit ya. We don't have anyt'ing else to do."

I had no intention on taking him up on the offer. I felt I could manage well enough on my own, plus I didn't need anyone around that could slow me down.

"Okay. Thanks."

* * *

I stayed in the hut to give myself time with my thoughts before the Welcoming. I also needed a bath. I was sticky and reeked of the ocean.

As I walked around, I felt a bit like a prisoner contemplating my escape. It was impossible to believe people couldn't leave this place. What could keep them here? Maybe I could get my plane working and fly out. Or get on a boat and sail away. We weren't hundreds of miles from land. How could so many people be trapped on an island, yet no one had found a way to escape.

I stepped out onto the back porch to look down at Tommy Pine's lifeless body. Was there a way to cover it up without stirring up bad juju?

It suddenly struck me what I was thinking. I was considering how to conceal a dead body so I didn't have to see it every day. Unbelievable. Then again, so was this entire situation.

I went through the hut to the front porch, where I leaned against the railing and gazed out at the ocean. To my dismay, fog blocked the horizon and most of the junkyard. The haze was a strange thing. Was it the

82

reason why I couldn't breathe comfortably? My brain was bogged down with questions and I hoped to get some answers at the Welcoming.

As twilight settled in and the ghostly sky shadowed into darkness, fireflies appeared by the thousands. They moved in a hypnotic dance, drifting up and down, and offering me a mild distraction from my questions.

"I brought you some fresh clothes, lad," Travis said when he returned. "Hope you don't object to wearing another man's undergarments."

"I won't object at all. These clothes are stuck to me."

He handed me cutoff shorts and a gray T-shirt. "How are you holding up?"

"Okay, I suppose. I've just been watching the fireflies."

He turned toward the thousands of glowing dots. "Aye, they're a sight, all right. It's the blasted mosquitoes and bees I hate."

"I haven't been bitten by any mosquitoes since we reached the village."

"That's 'cause every home is protected with pesticide lamps. A cargo ship got stuck here a while back, carrying tons of chemicals. It's been a real treat, believe me."

"After being eaten alive today on the beach, I can believe it. Are you usually that lucky?"

"When a ship's captain and crew realize we need what they're carrying, they usually donate it. Building materials, food, clothes, cleaning supplies, toiletries. We have to stretch it thin at times, though."

"Dang."

"Are you going to take the hut?"

"I suppose. But I have to find a way to cover Pine without disturbing him."

"There you go, lad! Out of sight, out of mind, eh? You'll see it ain't so bad. You'll just get put off a bit when you don't see much sunshine. You'd think a bloke like me would be used to overcast skies, being from Britain, but I do miss the warm touch of sun on me face."

"What do *you* think is happening here?"

"Don't really know, mate, though I've often wondered about it. There've been countless discussions about it, so you're bound to hear loads of theories."

"No one knows for sure about the real story behind this place?" I asked grimly.

"Not even the people who've been here longer than me."

"Damn."

There was a brief silence before Travis spoke in a serious tone. "Would you like to know the deep dark secret about the dead?"

My expression alone gave him my answer. "You know?"

"Aye, everyone knows, but no one wants to talk about it." He raised his T-shirt to reveal a long nasty scar across his side. "See this? I got it from a deckhand on me ship one night during our first month here. It took ages for this to heal up, it did."

He lowered his shirt and stared off into the void. "One of me shipmates and a deckhand got into a drunken scuffle. I tried breaking it up while everyone else, including the captain, did nothing. The deckhand slit me open with a dagger. When me mate saw that, he grabbed the dagger and stabbed the deckhand in the neck." Travis crossed his arms and paused a moment. "The crew carried me away, but I didn't know what had happened till after the doc had patched me up."

"What *did* happen?"

"They sent Tucker to the brig for killing the deckhand, which was a joke, 'cause the captain had done nothing to prevent it. As soon as I was on me feet again, I paid him a visit. I thought he'd gone mad. He was pacing back and forth, holding his hands over his ears. I asked him what was wrong, and he screamed, 'You can see 'im, too, can't you? Tell me you can see 'im!'"

"What was he raving about?"

"There wasn't anyone else in the cell with him and I told him that. But he told me as soon as he killed the deckhand, he saw that bloke standing over his own dead body. Tucker claimed the wanker had been tormenting him ever since, cursing him for stabbing him to death."

"Do you think he was telling the truth?"

Travis stayed quiet a beat. "I didn't want to believe him. We all thought he'd gone daft, but he got worse. The captain was afraid to let him out of the brig. Tucker cried night and day, begging the deckhand to leave him alone. Other times, he cried for death. After a while, I couldn't bear it anymore. I brought a pistol to the brig and gave it to him."

"You gave him a gun?"

"Tucker saved me life. I owed him that pistol. It was like giving water to a thirsty man. He grabbed the gun and put it to his head."

"I still don't understand."

"No one really understands," he said, shaking his head slowly. "All we know is that when someone dies, we leave 'em exactly where they lay. If anyone moves them, they come back, but only the person who moved them can see and hear them."

"Will the bodies decompose if they're disturbed?"

"Aye, that they do."

I stared at Travis, trying to figure out if I was the victim of a cruel joke. But Travis's expression was dead serious. "It's true. The souls of the dead will come after you."

"Can they hurt you?"

"It depends on the spirit and your relationship to the person. I've been here a while and I've seen too many blokes who didn't heed the warning. If you murder someone—or even kill someone by accident— it doesn't matter if you move the body or not, they'll come to you anyway. "

"What about people who die on their own?"

"They sleep."

That took me by surprise. "Sorry?"

"Like little ghost babes. Only those lucky sods can rest in peace. But if anyone disturbs them, it can get nasty."

"Jeez," I muttered. What he said made me think about Gavin. He'd died in the crash, so why was he visiting me? Had it been when I'd touched him? "Laffite told me that all someone needs to do is ignore them and they'll go away."

"That's very rare, lad. Most ghosts don't vanish when they're ignored. It only makes them angry. I've only heard about a ghost vanishing once since I arrived. Lafitte told me about his first mate, who told him to do something about his body. He ignored the specter and eventually it went away." Travis chuckled.

"Though the bugger told me when he was so drunk, he doesn't remember telling me now."

"It just happened to Lafitte?" I said despairingly. "No one else?"

"There was one other case like Lafitte's. Irving, George's co-pilot. George is a dead WWII chap out in the junkyard. Irving claimed George wanted his body disposed of."

"George? The one with the glass shard in his eye?"

"Aye. You came across him then, eh? Anyway, Irving said George wanted his body disposed of."

Maybe if I could talk to this Irving guy, he could shed more light on my problem. "Is Irving going to be at the Welcoming?"

Travis shook his head. "Nah, he died long ago. A sad story there."

Damn it.

Khenan approached us. "Dey've got everyt'ing set up down dere. Come on and meet everyone."

I gradually stood, my nerves on edge at the prospect of meeting new people, most who probably should've been dead years ago. I didn't know what to expect. I only hoped I wouldn't have to walk on hot coals or eat a beating pig's heart to be accepted.

Tiki torches and pesticide lamps lined the wharf. Colorful lights, like the ones on Lafitte's ship, crisscrossed overhead. Travis and Khenan led me to the center of the wharf, to a long table created from several smaller tables pushed together, covered with food and drinks.

As we walked among the crowd, I was introduced to the crew of eighteenth century warships, passengers from Flight 441, people who'd tried to catch fish on the beach earlier, and many others. But one stood out among all the others.

"Hello, sport," a soft-spoken young man said as he enveloped my hand in a strong grasp. "Charles Carroll Taylor. Pleased to meet you."

Chapter Eight

Lieutenant Charles Carroll Taylor shook my hand.

"Taylor? As in Charles Taylor, the leader of Flight Nineteen?" I asked.

Taylor smiled, and when he did, his upper lip vanished above perfect teeth. He had kind eyes, long dark hair tied back, a beard, and mustache. He wore blue jeans, a button-down short-sleeve shirt, and no shoes. "I'm afraid so, my friend."

I couldn't find my tongue, which prompted him to say, "Don't believe that rumor about us crashing into some ole' swamp in Georgia, sport."

I don't know why I was so surprised about meeting the leader of the legendary Flight Nineteen. I'd already met three hundred-year-old pirates and a tribe of missing links, yet I was star-struck, as if I'd met Clark Gable's ghost.

"Maybe you should sign an autograph for him, Charles," a sweet southern voice said. "Something he can hang on the wall."

I turned in the direction of the voice and saw a beautiful woman with bewitching blue eyes.

"Hello," she said. "I'm Eleanor Houghton."

Her glowing face and deep Mississippi accent instantly distracted me from Taylor. I swallowed and said, "Hi. I'm—"

"Heath Sharp," she interjected. "So I've been told. Come, sit over here with me and two others you're familiar with."

As she led me to the end of the table, I hoped I didn't have to sit at the very end, where everyone could stare at me. It was like being the new kid at school and having to be introduced in front of the whole class.

To my relief, Eleanor took the chair at the end. I was even more relieved when Travis sat directly across from me with Khenan beside him.

"Where's Marissa?" I asked, taking a seat.

"Don't know," Travis replied. "Most likely, spending the evening with her girlfriend."

"Oh."

Eleanor pointed at someone behind me. "Mr. Sharp, this is Carlton Malone, from Texas."

I turned to a man I recognized as the guy who'd been reading *Naked Lunch*. I couldn't explain it, but Carlton's appearance seemed odd. He was a short, round man with skin as white as paper. He reminded me of Judson, his bushy gray eyebrows nearly touching each other and his earlobes hanging low enough to reach his shoulders.

"I remember you," Carlton said, shaking my hand vigorously. When he let go, he made his way to the table and sat down.

"And this is Professor Inglewood," Eleanor said.

I turned my attention to an average-sized man wearing a brightly colored Hawaiian shirt. He took a seat next to Travis. As I sized him up, I couldn't help wondering how someone with his skinny physique had managed to capture a brutal and insane Viking.

"I've heard of you," I said. "Jean Laffite mentioned you."

"Oh, did he?" the professor said with an Aussie accent. "Good things, I hope."

90

I didn't want to tell him the reason Laffite had talked about him, mainly because I didn't want to appear eager to see his Viking, like a tourist looking to visit an attraction. I chuckled a bit just to be polite. That response was as old and stale as a hundred-year-old piece of toast.

Everything on the table was familiar, but with odd variations. Directly in front of me were steamed shellfish that reassembled lobster, but instead of having two antennas and claws, antennae covered their backs and additional claws protruded from their torsos. Steamed oysters and crabs filled a large bowl. The crabs had four hind legs and two large claws, and were in the shape of a star. The oysters were pink instead of gray.

"I know," Eleanor said, noting my confusion, "it looks a bit strange, but believe me when I say they taste exquisite. Have some wine."

Before I could say anything, she poured some into my cup. The dishes were old China with blue flowers around the edges and one large rose in the center.

"These dishes have been around since the eighteen century," she said. "We use them only for a Welcoming."

"I'm honored," I said, examining the sterling silverware. "You really didn't have to go through all this trouble for me."

She laughed as she poured wine into her crystal goblet. "Don't be silly. We do this for everyone on their first night in the village. It's a way for a newcomer to get to know everyone."

"Yah, mon," Khenan said, "it's just a one-time ting. Tomorrow, you'll be just anot'er face in da

91

crowd."

I was relieved to hear that. I didn't want to be an anomaly among this bunch of lost souls.

"And I'm sure you have many questions," Eleanor said. "But first, fill your belly and drink some wine. We have all night."

I took her advice and ate before making any inquires. I was hungry and longed for the comfort of food.

Everyone served themselves. Some said prayers before eating, while others went right into stuffing their faces. I filled my plate with pink oysters, four-clawed lobsters, steamed vegetables, and shark stew, the latter just out of spite.

Eleanor was right. The food was exquisite, and although it had its own unique flavor, it tasted familiar. The wine, which left an aftertaste of citrus and kiwi, made my tongue tingle, as if it was made from a grape that had yet to be discovered.

The feast was punctuated by lively conversation. Words were exchanged as often as platters of food. People looked over at me, but when my eyes met theirs, they turned their attention elsewhere. I detected no threat from anyone. I was the new guy and it was only human nature to be curious. They were no different than the people I used to pass on the street, except that most should be dead.

After I finished eating, I caught Eleanor looking at me. She blushed and turned away as soon as our eyes met.

"So, Mr. Sharp," Inglewood said, "tell us about yourself."

Everyone stopped talking and looked my way.

"Yes," Eleanor said, placing her elbows on the

table and resting her chin on her hands. "For starters, where are you from?"

I took a drink of wine. It was my fourth glass and felt like it. "Well, I'm originally from San Francisco. I…travel a lot."

I had no idea what to say, even though I'd lived an adventurous life. Being on the spot felt like studying all night for a test, only to forget everything the second the test hit my desk.

"Forgive me for asking," Eleanor said, "but what nationality are you? You have beautiful eyes, but they don't quite match your features."

I didn't know how to address her question. It sounded like a compliment, but only about my eyes.

"Don't get me wrong, darling," she chortled, "I'm not indicating that there's anything displeasing about your face. It's just that you look like an—"

"A Native American," I cut in.

She gave me a look as if I'd spoken a foreign language. Then I realized she must've come from a time where there was no such thing as political correctness. I smiled and added, "An Indian."

She brightened. "Really? What tribe?"

"The Wailaki. My father is a full-blood Wailaki and my mother is white."

Her smile grew wider. "How did your parents meet?"

I finished my drink, then poured myself another. "As kids. Every year my grandmother took my mom to the annual Weaving Connections near King Range National Conservation Area. My grandparents took my dad. My parents later kept in touch through letters." I took another sip. "They fell in love when they were teenagers. When my grandmother took Mom to the

Weaving Connection that year, Mom and Dad…well, they decided to…um…hook up."

She gave me a perplexed look. I didn't want to elaborate.

"He means they fucked," Travis translated, his mouth full of food.

"Young man," Carlton snapped, "your choice of words is as ugly as your face."

"Don't you be talkin' about mi face, ghost man," Travis shot back.

"That's so romantic," Eleanor said, ignoring their argument.

"I guess, but what happened next really wasn't romantic at all. My mother got pregnant and my father's family wasn't happy about it. My dad's father wouldn't accept an interracial relationship. He wanted his son to marry a Wailaki. He threatened to disown him. My father wanted to marry my mom and they made plans to elope."

"Did they?" Travis asked.

"No, my mom's mother talked them out of it. She told them that if they ran off, it would cause a rift between the two families. She told my paternal grandfather that she and my mom would raise me and we'd continue to attend the basket weaving so my dad could see me."

"What was she like?" Eleanor asked. "Your grandmother."

I took another drink. "She was a realist, but also a free spirit straight out of the sixties. She marched with Martin Luther King in Birmingham and burned her bra on her college campus as a statement for equal rights. She even lost an eye during a riot."

"Oh my," Eleanor said. "How awful."

"She found it amusing. Sometimes she'd rub her glass eye until it fell into her hand, then say, 'Oh dear, Heath, I lost my eye.'"

Travis laughed while Khenan shook his head. "Jeez, mon."

"The first time she did it, it scared me shitless. But from then on, I thought it was funny."

After talking about myself, it was time to learn more about these people and the island. "What about the rules around here? How do things work?"

"It's really quite simple, darling," Eleanor replied. "Everyone pitches in. Each of us has a talent that proves useful. Some of us do repair work and others sew clothing. There are people who garden, while others fish. We trade with South Village for things we need. To live here, you must contribute, not be some hunk of useless meat for everyone to provide for."

"Sounds like a hippie commune."

"We're just trying to survive. One important rule is to never disturb the—"

"Dead," I finished. "I know."

"So you've heard," she said softly.

"Yeah," I said, looking at Travis. "It's been explained to me. If you kill someone, their soul follows you as their body decomposes. If someone dies all on their own, their soul sticks with their body and sleeps." I said it out loud for my own benefit, just to make sure I remembered it.

"Correct," Eleanor confirmed.

"What about suicides? What happens to them?"

"The rules are simple—and complicated. In the case of a suicide, the soul stays attached to the body because there's no living person to attach itself to."

"They linger around the place where they died?" I asked. "How far can they go?"

"Not very far, we've been told."

"Told by who?"

"From the others that are bound to the living."

My courage teetered on the edge. I suddenly understood about Tomas and the skeletons. Tomas had killed himself so his body stayed where it was, unlike his murdered crew mates, whose corpses decayed because of the way they'd died.

"That's weird," I said.

"It gets even weirder," Khenan replied. "Da same applies to animals. If you kill an animal, its soul attaches itself to you. Pets are more tolerable than people. Dere's a lady who lost 'er German Spitz and she brought it back. Dere're been cooks from old ships with livestock with 'em. And, believe it or not, an old sea captain from the 80s has a ghost parrot."

I was confused. "What about all this food? Isn't someone going to be haunted by all these creatures?"

"It doesn't apply to the island's animals," Inglewood joined. "They're perfectly safe to kill and eat. Anything native to the island is exempt from the rules."

"What are the theories for why that is?"

"Maybe it's magic from the city of Atlantis," Carlton joked.

"There are plenty of theories," Inglewood said, giving Carlton a disapproving look.

"What kind of theories?" I asked.

"There's a theory that the island is some kind of base for extraterrestrials."

"I don't doubt it," I said. "But have you ever seen spaceships?"

Inglewood shook his head. "No, there's nothing we've seen or heard of that would support that theory. But dozens of people on the island assume aliens are keeping us here—and immortal."

"Why wouldn't aliens want us to age?"

"For shits and giggles, most likely," Travis said. "Maybe these are the kind of aliens that go bloomin' mad for entertainment."

"Some have suggested that ancient tribes built a pyramid on the island to connect the ley lines," Inglewood said. "That's what we've named the island, the Atlantic Pyramid."

"The ley lines?" I inquired. "Aren't they supposed to be some kind of energy pathway for aliens to travel?"

"In theory, yes," the professor replied. "Perhaps this very spot is a broken section of their juncture."

"What do you mean broken?"

"Not structurally sound enough to hold a ley line, or perhaps too primitive."

"Like a forgotten highway exit?"

"Exactly. Although it may not be in use, the electrical impulse is still here, holding us to it."

"But other pyramids don't suck people in and trap them there."

"Those pyramids were built for other reasons," Inglewood went on. "In my personal opinion, we're in the middle of a doorway to another dimension, caught between two worlds. That could be the reason why we're not seen by anyone from the outside."

If I hadn't experienced what I had in the past forty-eight hours, I would've thought the professor was off his rocker. "Why hasn't anyone from the outside seen the island? It's pretty big and obviously been around a while."

"We don't know the answer to that," Inglewood said with a shrug. "We've heard planes flying overhead, especially when the cruise ship arrived, but they never seem to see us."

"Have you tried getting their attention?"

"Of course," Inglewood said. "We've fired flares, lit bonfires, but it seems as if we're invisible to the outside world. In my personal opinion, we're in the middle of a doorway to another dimension, caught between two worlds. That could be the reason why we're not seen by anyone from the outside."

"I heard about the Vikings," I said, changing the subject.

"That's just one of the many black marks of our past," Eleanor said grimly.

"What do you mean?"

She brushed her long dirty-blonde hair away from her face. "This isn't a perfect life, Mr. Sharp. When I said we're trying to survive, I mean just that. People have gone mad or gone into deep depressions, which results in numerous suicides. We've lost so many, especially children, to sharks and stingrays. We've also had our share of rapes and murders."

"We have a prison for those offenders," Carlton added, his droopy earlobes wobbling.

"A prison?"

"Aye," Carlton said.

It was odd that he used the word *aye* instead of a hardy Texan response like *yup* or *right you are.* When I'd passed through Texas during a cross-country drive to Miami, I'd heard a lot of that sort of talk.

"The prison is on the *Southern Districts.* It's the ship farthest from the island. If someone gets out of line—"

"Or goes dangerously insane," Inglewood supplied.

"That too. We put them on a boat and take them to the ship. The area is surrounded by sharks, which keeps anyone from escaping."

"A floating prison, huh? How do they survive?"

"We give them plenty of supplies," Eleanor said. "Livestock, seeds, and soil. Even fishing equipment. The rest is up to them."

"How many people are out there?"

Eleanor looked at Carlton, who supplied the answer. "I lost count years ago. Luckily, we haven't had to go out there in a while."

Eleanor set her sights on me then. "Carlton was a chief of police before he came to this place, so it made sense to appoint him judge."

I turned my head to Carlton, who said in mock seriousness, "That's right, boy, don't mess up or I'll put your ass in a sling!"

"Oh, Carlton, stop it," Eleanor said with a laugh. "No need to scare him out of his wits. Don't fret, Mr. Sharp, only the worst offenders go to the *Southern Districts*. Minor crimes like stealing are dealt with differently. We have a jail on the island."

"Most of the time, people go there overnight to cool off after getting drunk at Miller's Tavern. It's laid-back here, but not without its flaws."

"Why hasn't anyone escaped the island?" I asked. "Why not just row away?"

"You mean out trough da boundaries?" Khenan posed. "I tried a couple of times and almost died."

"What happened?"

"I went out to da edge of da shallows in a life raft,

where da water drops off. Da cold nearly killed me. Den a storm came up. It was fierce, mon, an' nearly took me under. Da wind blew me right outta da boat an' I swam fer my life back to da shallows. I'd figured da storm was a fluke, so I tried again a few days later."

"Aye, only this time, the bloody bloke got me to go with him," Travis threw in. "I'd done it meself with some crew mates and almost died when the same kind of storm came up. I figured I'd give it another go, but before I knew it, I was back in the shallows, licking me wounds."

"Yah, mon, da storm happened again exactly like before, except dis time, it took away me raft."

"What happened to it?"

Khenan shrugged. "Dunno. I remember hearing stories on da outside about ships an' life rafts being found adrift wit'out passengers. Maybe dey were da vessels of dose who tried to escape dis place."

"Just ask the crew on the *Ellen Austin,*" Inglewood said. "She's the only ship that went out and brought in a second lot."

A wave of cold washed over me. I turned my attention on the glowing firelight. "I've been told there's no electricity."

"Yeah, and it sucks!" exclaimed a woman sitting farther down the table. "Radios are useless and every goddamn battery might as well be a paperweight!"

"She's right," Eleanor said. "Every piece of electrical equipment here is immediately drained of its power. We've been using gas from planes and ships, along with propane and any lighter fluid that comes our way for lanterns and cooking grills."

I thought on that. For years, pilots had reported their equipment going haywire while flying over the

Bermuda Triangle—compasses spinning crazily, radars going blank. Some pilots became so disorientated they couldn't distinguish the sea from the sky.

I took a drink and returned my attention to Eleanor. "What about you? When did you get here?"

"I arrived in 1864. I was on a steamboat that belonged to my fiancé. He loved boating, and even though the water made me ill, he insisted I go with him. We went on a family cruise to the reefs off the coast of Jupiter. Within an hour of sailing, a storm came up. He and I were the only ones who survived the storm. Many of the crewmen, God rest their souls, drowned, including my future mother-in-law." She smiled coyly. "I must confess, I wasn't too stricken by her loss."

There was a moment of silence before she continued. "My fiancé and I were able to stay in our longboat until we made it ashore, where we met many young sailors."

"Including yours truly," Travis said, taking a bite of crab.

Eleanor grinned at him.

"What happened to your fiancé?" I asked, trying to sound nonchalant.

"He lives with the Obsoletes. Before we met, Darwin had struck it rich in California after years of panning gold. He moved himself and his widowed mother east to Mississippi. He always had to have everything he wanted—until we got stuck in the Bermuda Triangle. He lost his mother, whom he dearly loved, and his ship, which he'd paid handsomely for."

I should have left it alone but I asked, "What's he like?"

"He's an asshole, mate," Travis replied, as if the

question had been directed at him.

I thought Eleanor might stand up for her fiancé, but she didn't. "He is indeed."

I thought she wouldn't go any further into the matter, but she did. "The villagers on the other side of the island refuse to believe anything outside their own era and won't accept that the world has moved on. They live a structured lifestyle, set in the old ways, and can't relate to the other two villages. To them, living so freely is distasteful, if not sacrilegious, and they want none of it. They initially wanted to thrive and continue building up the village, but as the years went by and new people arrived, the ones who no longer wanted to live such a disciplined lifestyle moved away."

"And you were one of them?" I asked.

"Yes."

"Oh, tell him about Mrs. Chancier," Travis said excitedly.

Eleanor shook her head. "I rather not go into it."

My curiosity piqued, and when she noticed my expression, she set her glass down. "All right. When I lived there, Doctor Chancier's wife hung herself from a tree in their backyard. She was a dreadfully sad soul. I was surprised she lasted as long as she did. Doctor Chancier now has to see her every day, unless he moves out of that house, which he'll never do. He's a stubborn old fool, like the rest of them."

Eleanor didn't look like she wanted to continue, so I said, "Travis told me there's going to be a dock built for people who want to live on their boats."

"Yes," she beamed. "In fact, we plan to get started tomorrow. And the docks are just the beginning, although we have to figure out a way to haul the ships through such shallow water. It'll be like when I designed the layout of the village."

"I didn't know women in your era did things like that."

She gave me a surprised look. "Why, darling, you sound shocked. Surely, if a woman can create life in her womb, she can create buildings."

"Way to put yer foot in yer mouth, mon," Khenan scolded.

"I guess I'm good at that. Sorry, I didn't mean it that way."

"Don't fret about it, darling. You're right, of course. Until forty years ago, being a woman was like being a pet, obligated to obey her master."

"Aye, those were the good ole' days," Travis said facetiously. When Eleanor shot him a look, he added, "I'm joking, love. Only joking!"

She turned back to me with a sigh. "I've always had a fascination with designing things. I wanted to be an architect since I was a child. Unfortunately, in my time, it was considered a man's trade. It wasn't until I was stranded here for some time that I was able to express my lifelong desire." She reached out and gently patted my hand. "Tomorrow, I'll show you around the safe areas. And you can meet the professor's Viking."

Chapter Nine

The wine made me drunk faster than I expected. Before I said anything stupid, I excused myself and stumbled back to my hut. I felt uneasy sleeping so close to the late Mr. Pine, but I made myself as comfortable as possible on an outside patio chair.

"Why haven't you done anything about me yet?"

The question rang so clear in my sleep it sounded as if it had been spoken directly into my ear. "What?" I mumbled, unaware if I was awake or asleep.

"I said, why haven't you done anything about me yet?"

I snapped awake and whipped my head in the direction of the voice, which came from the darkness. Then a face appeared, startling me so badly I fell out of the chair. I shot to my feet the instant I hit the ground.

Gavin stood at the railing, looking out over the sea. "Nice view you got here. You should really look at it."

I tried to regain my composure. "What are you doing here?"

He turned toward me, his head still bleeding, but not as profusely as before. "I've come to remind you that I'm still out there. So, what are you going to do about it?"

"Nothing," I said bluntly.

"Nothing? You mean you're going to just leave me out there forever?"

"I don't know much about this place, but I've been warned about one thing—never disturb the dead."

"You're damn right you don't know much about this place," he snapped. "Most of those shitheads don't know the half of it."

"How the hell would you know? You just got here yourself."

"But I have an advantage," he said with an ironic smile. "I'm dead. That means I can see things the living can't."

"What kind of things?"

He grinned at me slyly. "Show me yours and I'll show you mine. First, say you'll get me outta that foul-smelling plane."

I was new to it all but I sensed something wasn't right about what he said. Suffice it to say, I wasn't easily duped. "They say the dead come back to haunt you."

Gavin snorted. "What the hell d'ya think I'm doing right now?"

He had a point, but I had no intention of ignoring warnings from people who'd lived on the island for centuries. "No. Until I know the lay of the land, I'm not going to move your body."

Gavin's expression turned sour but he said nothing. Instead, he headed inside the hut. I followed him with my eyes only until he vanished.

The brightening sky pulled my attention away from the hut. I noticed a pattern to Gavin's visits. He always seemed to appear while I was exhausted and too hazy in the head to get a grip on his presence. But I couldn't understand why his spirit haunted me. I wished Lafitte had given me a better explanation.

The morning sky was vibrant again, just as it had been the morning before. Without the fog, the view was clear, but as soon as the sun began to peek over the horizon, the fog arrived, covering the scene with a gloomy gray mist. Yet I saw tanker ships on the horizon, some tilted sideways, others capsized. The massive white sails of galleons reached toward the sky. Hundreds of boats and airplanes lay scattered about. Calling it a junkyard was apropos.

I heard loud clicking noises as the Shark Hunter flock flew over the village. I expected them to swoop down for another kill, but they made a circle before landing on the beach. Their clicking and shrieking was ear-piercing, like thousands of spoons tapping against ceramic dishes.

Paddy emerged from his hut, shouting, "Shut it, you damn birds! Get the hell outta here!"

The Irishman jumped over his porch railing and threw stones at the flock. He didn't frighten the birds. Instead, he was forced back to his hut when a group flew in his direction. He screamed, flinging his arms to block their attack.

I wanted to assist him but I noticed a man standing by my own railing. For a split-second, I thought it was Gavin. I jumped back before I realized it was Dominic, who also watched the show.

As Paddy ran toward his hut, Dominic murmured, "Ah, Paddy, you certainly have the luck of the Irish in you."

Paddy bolted into his hut but emerged a moment later, swinging a broom at the birds. Dominic watched for a few minutes, then turned to me and said, "*Guten morgan, Herr* Sharp."

"Morning."

"How was your first night?"

"Actually, it was my second, and it was fine, thanks."

A horrendous scream interrupted our conversation as Paddy was chased back inside by one of the birds he whacked with the broom.

"Paddy sometimes lets his emotions outweigh his good sense," Dominic said.

I took his word for it.

"I overhear you speaking to someone a little while ago," he said, leaning against the railing. "Is someone with you?"

"No," I replied evasively.

"So, you come in a plane?"

"What? Um, yeah, a Cessna Skyhawk."

"I come on the freighter, *Anita,* in 1972. The storm brought us in, like it bring everyone else in. We end up on other side of the island. I didn't care for the people there, so me and the rest of the crew go to South Village. Some stayed, but others come to North Village. Miss Houghton welcomes us here. She's a wonderful woman."

He lapsed into silence and I decided to change the subject. "My boss, Jason Starr, flew Hawk jets during the Gulf War."

"Starr had been a good man and a good friend. He insisted that we call him by his last name—not Mr. Starr, just Starr. He'd loved to tell stories about students vomiting in flight or discovering their fear of heights during their first time in the air. He was also prone to mood swings, which sometimes got us into trouble in bars. Even so, I wished he was on the island with me."

"You miss this friend?"

"I guess, even though I haven't really started missing anyone yet."

"That's because you don't accept that you not

going anywhere."

His words stung. I hadn't yet accepted that I would be stuck on this island forever. It didn't seem possible. After all, the fog wasn't a wall and there were no guards to force anyone to stay. If I was really immortal now, I had plenty of time to figure out a way to escape. I was determined to explore every option before surrendering all hope.

"Have you ever tried getting out?" I asked.

"Nearly everyone does, and by the looks of you, I am sure you will too. Just do not get killed when you do." He set his sights on my hut. "You decide to stay here, even with Mr. Pine down there?"

"There's nothing I can do about it."

"You could put a plank over him and then set potted flowers on it. That is how many people handle their dead." He turned to go and said something that sent chills up my spine. "This place can take a toll on a man. If time don't do it, the things living on the island will."

I climbed down the long staircase, heading for the beach. My mouth felt grainy. I really wanted to brush my teeth, but I had neither a toothbrush nor toothpaste. I had a bag of toiletries on the plane but I didn't look forward to going back to retrieve them. I cursed myself for not bringing them with me.

I thought about what Dominic had meant when he'd said *by the looks of you*. Was he referring to my youth or had he been on the island long enough to spot a dumbass? I was an energetic young man, a big kid, really, unable to sit in one place for any length of time. Because of my active lifestyle, I was in great shape. Maybe that was why Dominic assumed I'd eventually try to escape.

As I passed Paddy's hut, he peeked out the window and called, "*Psst!* Hey, new bloke, are those bleedin' birds gone?"

I looked to where the flock was clicking away at the waterline. "They're down on the beach. I think you're safe for now."

His head vanished from the window. A moment later, his front door swung open and he emerged holding a candle. He had scratch marks on his shoulders and arms, and bled above the left eye.

"Are you all right?" I asked as a goat followed him out.

"Aye, it was just a little scuffle."

He plopped down on his patio chair, reached into the pocket of his cargo shorts, and brought out a pouch of tobacco. He began rolling a cigarette in a brown leaf. "I guess I should've known better than to mess with them bloody birds, but I never did have much sense." He pointed his chin to the other patio chair nearby. "Have a seat, lad."

I sat while Paddy rolled his cigarette. He lit it with the candle. "Want one?"

"No thanks, I don't smoke."

He exhaled and patted the goat's head. "If it's your health you're worried about, it won't make much difference here." He took a drag, looked me up and down, and added, "It's a good thing you and I came here in our prime, unlike some poor buggers, like ole' Carlton. He's gonna be in that old, wrinkled, fat body forever. Can you imagine?"

"Was he sick when he came here? Is that why he's so pale?"

Paddy scratched his chin. "Y'know, I really can't say."

I shuddered at the thought of being locked inside such a body for eternity, especially in a place loaded with so much danger. But living in a community like North Village gave him a better chance.

"'Course I wouldn't want to be a kiddy forever, either."

"What about women? Can they get pregnant?"

"Nah, lad, the way you came in is the way you stay." He examined a wound on his arm. "There've been a couple of cases of women who've arrived pregnant. Sad story there."

"Why? What happened to them?"

"The first was at the turn of the century. A lady sailing with her husband on their yacht when the storm got 'em. She was two months pregnant and always sick. The baby never grew. She threw up and felt fatigued for a solid year. She couldn't stand it anymore and forced herself to have a miscarriage."

"How did she do that?"

"With a stick. She survived but was miserable for years afterward because she kept seeing the fetus everywhere she went. She now lives with her husband in South Village."

As the goat wandered away, I asked, "Is that your goat?"

He shrugged. "I guess. She keeps coming here. I think she likes me, but I want none of that."

"What about the other pregnant woman?"

"She arrived with her mum and dad on their yacht back in the seventies. Nice girl, barely out of her teens. She was eight months pregnant when she arrived. Her child didn't grow but she didn't want to get rid of it. About eight years ago, she hung herself."

"Really?"

"Aye. She was melancholy after being pregnant for so long and never able to see her child. It's just another sad story in our history book."

I sank into my chair. Paddy slapped me on the arm. "Don't look so miserable. Here, let me get you something to drink."

He went into his hut and came back with a glass bottle. I assumed it was water and gulped it down. It was alcohol and burned my throat like hot coals. I coughed as tears filled my eyes, my faced flushing.

I handed the bottle back to him, and it was several minutes before I was able to choke out, "What the fuck is that stuff?"

"Good whiskey, eh?" he said, laughing loudly. "Made it meself. Since inherited Miller's Tavern after the man got himself killed some time back, I've taught myself how to brew. Ol' Miller had built his own brewery in the basement of the tavern." He snorted. "Funny, I didn't want the place, but s'pose someone's gotta take it, why not the Irishman, eh?"

"I've never tasted whiskey like this before."

"That's 'cause the ingredients I use here are different from those on the outside. I'm sure you noticed a strange aftertaste in the wine."

"I did."

"It's the same with other alcohol. Same with tobacco and food. It tastes about right, but different. That's just the way the island works. We have to make do with what we've got."

I rose unsteadily and made my way to the end of the pier, where I stepped onto the beach. The dark grains of sand felt good beneath my bare feet. The anglers already stood beside the still ocean, each holding a pole. I stopped next to them but not one of

111

them acknowledged me.

"It might help if you put some bait on your hooks," I suggested to the woman closest to me.

Each of them turned their heads in my direction and stared before returning their attention to the ocean. I decided to stroll farther down the beach and eventually reached a spot where I could stand alone and gaze out over the misty water and nearby wreckage. As impossible as it seemed, given everything that had happened since my arrival, there was only one thing on my mind at that moment. Eleanor.

Although I'd just met her, she'd captivated me in a way I hadn't felt in a long while. She was interesting to talk to and intelligent. I looked forward to spending the day with her to learn more about the island—and about her.

I wondered if I should visit her at her hut, but it was still fairly early. I also thought about going back to my place to wait for her there. I feared if she didn't find me at home, she might change her mind about showing me around. The dock construction would start soon and she might have a lot to do before it began.

Just as I turned, a figure appeared. I stood motionless as Eleanor's shapely form drew closer.

"Ah, Mr. Sharp, there you are," she called happily. "Are you ready for your tour?"

Chapter Ten

Eleanor led me around the village and told me about some of the people. There was Joshua Slocum, from Mount Hanley, who'd sailed solo around the world before he ended up on the island. He still lived on his boat, *The Spray*, not far from shore. Eleanor also indicated a hut where the captain of the *S.S. Marine Sulphur Queen* lived near the end of the pier with his new wife, a woman he'd met on the island a few years earlier.

A little farther up, she pointed and said, "That's where Mrs. Buckner lived before she went into the forest and came back insane. She murdered poor Mr. Gerald, who'd been a passenger on a Douglas DC-3. We had no choice but to send her to the *Southern Districts*."

"She went insane after going into the forest? How?"

"There are strange things out there, stranger than anything on shore. That's why we live on the beach. In the forest, people either run into the Vikings or vanish altogether. And sometimes something eats at their minds." She paused a moment, then added earnestly, "You mustn't ever venture too far into the forest, darling. It is very rare people have come back unharmed."

"Do people go out often?"

"Seeing what could happen discourages most from ever leaving the shoreline."

I glanced over at the hut. "Is everyone who goes

insane violent?"

"In most cases they're harmless and can still function in our community. They can perform simple tasks, like painting and prepping food. Some even help in the gardens."

"It sounds like you use them as work drones," I said, then regretted my words.

She didn't seem the least bit offended. Fingers crossed, maybe she hadn't understood what I meant. Before she could mull it over, I said, "It's good that you give them something useful to do."

As we strolled through the village, a young woman stepped out of her hut, carrying a guitar. She sat on a rocker and began to play.

"That's Mrs. Jones," Eleanor said softly. "She and her husband got stranded here in the early seventies. Mr. Jones died, and although she knew about the dead, she buried him anyway."

"Didn't she believe what you told her?"

"She did, but she wanted him with her. She told me later that the two of them had discussed it and promised if one of them had died, the other would bring them back so they could always be together. After he passed, he taught her how to play his guitar, and now she plays beautifully."

As we moved on, I recognized the song: *Stairway to Heaven.*

"It was their wedding song," Eleanor explained.

Next, she showed me Miller's tavern. It was built like the huts, only with a wraparound porch and torches outside. A counter circled the single room so the bartender could serve from the center. More chairs and stools sat around the open bar, shaded by an extended eave. I knew I'd visit it soon.

After the tour around the village, we set off down the beach in the opposite direction from where I'd come the day before. Eleanor took me to a very large garden spanning out from the shoreline, with a huge mosquito net covering it like a circus tent. There were grapevines, tomatoes, cabbage, broccoli, and peppers, each surrounded by sizeable plank cubicles.

"We dug into the beach and poured soil inside to grow these crops. Since there are no tides, we don't worry about them washing away."

My chest felt tight the longer we walked. I hoped Lafitte was right about getting used to the air and that I'd eventually be able to breathe normal again.

An Asian woman with a worried expression appeared from behind the garden, carrying several small tools. "Have to get things done. Things to do," she muttered, scurrying along.

"That's Aiko," Eleanor said as the woman slipped through a slit in the netting. "She went into the forest ten years ago and came back like that. We put her on garden detail because the crops need constant tending. She works the entire day until she gives out from exhaustion."

"Jeez, how does she eat?"

"She picks things from the garden whiles she works. That's another reason we put her here, so she'll eat."

"Where did you get the seeds to start the first crops?"

"We managed to find different kinds of them throughout the years."

A short time later, I spotted the shower stalls Travis had told me about and the waterfall dropping off the ledge. The water ran off in dozens of directions, its flow looking more orchestrated than natural. It fell into the stalls and formed a soapy stream leading out to the sea. A small bridge spanned the brook. Even though there were many stalls, a long line of people had accumulated.

"Who are the people in South Village?" I asked.

"Soldiers, mostly. They're good hunters, but they're impatient when it comes to farming. We trade fruits and vegetables for seafood and meat."

"What about the village on the other side? What does it look like?"

"The Obsoletes? The people there are less than desirable," she grumbled, "but their homes are quite beautiful."

"Do they really live according to the old ways?"

"Yes. It's actually good that they stay on their side of the island. They keep to themselves and we don't go over there." Her attention was then diverted to something. "Oh, look! I want to show you these."

I followed her to a patch of brightly colored flowers, almost like the ones growing on the rock wall near my back porch. They were highlighter-yellow in color, with brown stripes on their petals.

"Watch this," she said, stomping on the flowers, twisting her foot from side to side.

"Are they dangerous?"

"Not at all," she said with a smile. "Watch what happens now."

She stepped back, and as I watched, the flowers slowly resumed their original shape.

"They're very durable. Nothing seems to kill them."

"Apparently not," I said in awe.

"Oi! Eleanor!" a voice called.

I looked to see Inglewood trotting toward us. Eleanor waved and said, "Hello, Professor." To me, she added, "We're just in time."

"For what?"

"The professor always leaves at this time to feed his Viking."

I'd completely forgotten about the Viking girl.

When Inglewood reached us, he smiled amicably, panting a bit. In one hand, he held a bag. "Well, then, up early, are we?"

"I'm giving Mr. Sharp a tour."

"Oh, that's right. She doesn't do that often, you know."

I turned to Eleanor to see her face flush. She cleared her throat and said, "Shall we, then?"

"Of course. Let's go see Sassy. I'm on my way to bring her some breakfast."

"Sassy?" I asked.

"Trust me, young man, the name suites her. Come on."

As we walked along the misty beach, the only sound was the occasional clicking of the Shark Hunters. I had no doubt that Inglewood was intelligent, but he didn't seem capable of capturing a Viking, even if she was a little girl. "How did you catch her?"

"It wasn't easy, I'll tell you that. I had to use a number of traps to snare her."

"Why did you want her?"

"I didn't really, but she kept coming to the village, harassing people and vandalizing property. We tried befriending her, but she was too wild to tame."

"Sassy has been a constant nuisance," Eleanor added.

"I tried many ways of catching her," he went on.

"I set ankle nooses and made a cage to fall on her while she devoured a carcass I left as bait, but she either cut her way free or avoided the traps. I even followed her to her lair once, which was nothing more than a hollow in the mountainside. I'd brought another carcass with me, dosed with ten grams of Zolpiden."

We came up on a sign in the sand with a warning: DANGER! BEES. It was repeated in four different languages. I didn't ask about it. I wanted to know more about Inglewood's Viking. "Wasn't that dangerous?"

"It wasn't enough to kill her, and I'd rather not have a spirit from the likes of hers haunting me."

"No, I mean following her to her home. What if she'd seen you?"

He shrugged. "Most likely, she'd have butchered me, but I managed to follow her without being detected. I waited until she fell asleep, then set the bait at the entrance. In the morning, she ate it, and when she passed out, I carried her down the mountainside."

"Where do you keep her?"

"I built an iron cage in a nice little area up ahead."

"You did that all on your own? Why didn't anyone help you?"

"We offered to help," Eleanor said, "but he refused."

"Why?"

"It was a challenge," he replied. "I've always enjoyed a good challenge."

We walked a few minutes longer before there was a buzzing off to my left.

"Be careful," Eleanor warned. "Our bees are kept over there."

I looked into a clearing, where a bee colony

118

rested on a cliff fourteen feet above the ground. Like the cliff where water fell onto the shower stalls, it was a flat surface with man-made stairs leading up to it. The bees buzzed so loudly it sounded as if they were amplified.

"They're like bumblebees," Inglewood said. "They won't sting you unless you antagonize them. However, it doesn't take much to infuriate them and their toxin is quite deadly. That's why we put the colony up there. They generally don't fly too close to shore because the pollen is scarce down there. Our beekeepers go up there once a week to collect the honey."

"Is that all you keep them for? Honey?"

"That and beeswax," Eleanor said. "We use that for candlesticks and other things."

"How much honey can they make in a week?"

"Loads," Inglewood answered. "These bees can produce twice as much honey as any on the outside. Which is good, since we're always in need of honey and candles."

"How long does it take for the toxin to kill you?"

"If it's not sucked out, you'll die in a day or two, very painfully. In a way, that's a good thing, since it keeps people from trying to use the bees to commit suicide."

Inglewood led us to a path leading into the forest, and not long into the trek, we reached iron bars, like the bars on an eighteenth century brig. The cage was some forty feet in diameter and abutted the mountainside, where there was a cave entrance. The whole thing was covered by a roof of bars, while the ground was carpeted in lush grass. The mountain went straight up and thick brush afforded some privacy.

Lamps stood at the corners of the cage.

"I really need to go in there and cut that damn tree down," Inglewood grunted.

The tree he referred to was inside the cage and its trunk was bent against the ceiling.

"The cave goes back several feet," Inglewood explained, "and before I got her in there, I had this area cleared of stones so she couldn't throw them at me. She's smart enough to dispose of her own waste so she's not living in filth." He reached into his cloth bag and brought out a plate of cooked food, similar to what had been served at the Welcoming. "I feed her twice a day, and sometimes I bring her gifts."

Toys were scattered on the ground inside the cage—dolls, toy cars, wooden blocks, and an inflatable pool.

"She's intelligent and perfectly capable of taking care of herself," he said, sliding the plate through a narrow opening. "Which makes it all the more painful to keep her caged."

He took an eight-foot pole from a nearby tree and used it to push the plate farther into the cage. Then he returned it to the tree.

"Sassy, daddy's here, sweetie. Come get your breakfast."

I waited for the mighty Viking girl to appear. A moment later, a figure emerged into the yard, clutching a doll in her arms. She was very small and had the face of an eight-year-old. This wasn't the killer I'd been expecting.

"Isn't she beautiful?" Inglewood said fondly.

"What happened to her parents?" I asked as she tentatively approached us.

"They probably died when the tribe turned on

each other."

Sassy crouched at the plate of warm food, holding the doll to her side. She studied the meal. Then, with her free hand, she picked up some and threw it with little grunts.

"I suppose I've spoiled her," Inglewood said. "She's a picky eater now. Every day, I try feeding her vegetables, but she always tosses them away."

"I feel bad for her," Eleanor said sullenly. "I always have, even when she stole from us. I wish she could learn things. You know, evolve."

"Yes," Inglewood agreed. "I've tried to teach her English and how to read, but she's incapable of grasping anything beyond what she learned during her lifetime. She's lived a hard and terribly long life."

I studied the girl as she plucked bits of vegetables off her plate. She wore a red dress with spaghetti straps, camouflage pants, and no shoes. She had silver scars carved into pale flesh and her unkempt hair fell to her tiny waist. Her pastel skin was dirty and she had dark circles under her blue eyes.

"I hate keeping her locked up," Inglewood moaned. "I wish she could interact with the other children. The clothes she's wearing belonged to children who've died over the years."

"It's hard keeping the children safe," Eleanor admitted softly.

After Sassy cleared the vegetables from her plate, she stood with it, then shouted at us before she stomped back to the cave.

"I like to think she's saying thank you," Inglewood said.

Eleanor took my hand. "Let's go back to the village, shall we?" She turned to Inglewood. "Are you coming?"

"Not right now. I think I'll stay for a while and read to her when she comes back out."

As Eleanor led the way back to the beach, she asked, "What do you think about the Bermuda Triangle?"

She held my hand and I enjoyed her touch. "I think it's dangerous as well as interesting."

She smiled. "I suppose that's the best way to describe it."

"Do you miss home?"

"I miss Mississippi and going on riverboat rides."

"I thought sailing made you sick."

"Rivers are different, even a river as big as the Mississippi. The ocean is so vast and stretches hundreds of miles into nothing. I guess I'm afraid of the unknown. Which is ironic, considering where we are."

"What else do you miss?"

"My mother, although she's been dead a long while. All she ever wanted was for me to be happy. It thrilled her to no end when a wealthy man asked for my hand in marriage. He promised to give me everything I ever dreamed of."

"Did he? Give you everything you dreamed of."

Her expression dampened, but it did nothing to quell her beauty. "Darwin Bradford loved to be in control. He always had to be, especially when it came to women." She paused a moment. "In his defense, it wasn't completely his fault. That's how most men treated their wives in our day. Yet, even after we arrived here, he continued to keep me under his thumb, demanding absolute obedience. He forced me to wear all those useless Victorian clothes, even in this heat.

He talked down to me as if I was a helpless child." Her eyes found mine, her expression straightforward. "If I hadn't left the Obsoletes, I probably would have ended up swinging right next to Mrs. Chancier."

I'd never met Darwin Bradford but I didn't like him. If Eleanor asked me to go to his village and beat him senseless, I wouldn't hesitate.

"And I also miss the stars," she said fondly. "Since childhood I was always fantasized by all those twinkling little lights. I would sneak out on warm summer nights to stare at them in our yard and allow myself to drift away into my own imagination where I would have marvelous adventures in other worlds."

The depth of emotion she expressed when speaking about stars told of her longing to relive what was most likely the happiest moments of her life. It made me feel obtuse for I had always lived under light polluted skies, only experiencing patches of star-filled nights in certain parts of the world, so I hadn't taken notice of the stars' absence. Thinking on it, I assumed the fog blocked them completely out from the islanders.

We continued toward the village in silence. I wanted nothing more than to stay by her side.

Chapter Eleven

The village slowly came up to meet us. Soon Eleanor and I walked over the long pier, heading for the steps leading up the mountainside.

"Do you have any plans today?" she asked, breaking the silence.

"Actually, I need to get some things from my plane." I became self-conscious about my breath, having not used toothpaste in a while. "Unless you need help with the docks."

"No, there are plenty of people to get it started. You go gather what you need. When you come back, you're more than welcome to help."

"Of course," I said, climbing the stairs with her. "Don't think I'm the type of guy who won't lift a finger."

She smiled. "I never thought that for a second. Do hurry back, though. I'm sure to miss you." She let go of my hand and continued up the steps. I stared at her, unaware that I now stood beside the row my hut was on.

"'Allo," Khenan called from behind, ascending to my level.

I returned to watch Eleanor as she headed on. She glanced down, as if she knew I was watching her, while Khenan came up alongside me. "Ah, she is beautiful, eh?"

"Um, sure," I said, quickly heading for my hut, aware of how obvious I was in my gawking.

"Sure?" Khenan said, following me. "You is

smitten."

"All right, let's not make this into some high school romance thing," I grumbled, entering the hut to grab my socks and tennis shoes.

"Are you going somewhere?"

I stepped out and sat on the patio chair. "I'm headed to my plane to get a few things."

"Let's get Travis. I tink 'e isn't trilled about starting on da docks, any'ow."

"I think I'm good on my own," I said, slipping on a shoe. "I survived once, I'll be okay."

"Don't tink dat be wise. Out der you're surround by dangerous tings. It be best to have other 'round far protection."

Damn it, I thought. I didn't want to be a dick with someone who only offered to help, but I wanted to go get my things without worrying about anyone getting hurt on my account. At the time, I didn't feel I needed anyone to watch my back and that I was more than capable of taking care of myself.

"Trust me," Khenan urged.

"All right," I huffed while lacing up my sneakers. "Let's jet."

We went down to the shore, where we found some people preparing breakfast on their grills, while others headed for the waterfall with small bags. The smell of simmering meat flourished everywhere. Unlike yesterday, when everyone had gathered around me, I now received only a few greetings and waves. Most simply ignored me. It was exactly as Khenan had predicted. I'd become just another face in the crowd.

"Hey, guys," Marissa said, standing next to her grill, "where are you heading off to?"

"My plane to get some things."

"Oh."

"Wanna come wit us?" Khenan asked.

Great, more company. I thought grimy.

Before Marissa answered, another woman stepped through the open doorway. She was younger than Marissa, at thirty or so, wearing a tank top and short pajama bottoms, with long silky hair and dark freckles across her fair skin. Her round face didn't quite match her petite frame.

"Hey, Khenan."

"Hey, Tammy."

"Is this the guy you told me about?" she asked Marissa. "The one you found yesterday?"

"Yep," Marissa replied, scooping scrambled eggs from a hot pan with a spatula and sliding them onto a plate. I wondered where the eggs came from. The Shark Hunters, maybe.

"You're cute," Tammy said with a grin. "For a man."

"Thanks."

"They asked if I'd like to go to the junkyard with them," Marissa said.

"For what?"

"To get some stuff from his plane."

"You're not going out there, are you?" Tammy whined. "Not with those sharks."

Marissa placed the spatula in the pan and used her free hand to grasp Tammy's face. She puckered her lips and said in a babyish tone, "You're so damn adorable when you worry. Yes, you are."

"Stop that," Tammy said, slapping her hand away. "I hate it when you do that."

Marissa grinned and leaned over, her lips puckered again. Tammy leaned in and gave her a kiss.

When they drew away, Marissa said, "I think I'm gonna sit this one out, boys. We've got a lot of work to do today and I'm sure Eleanor is gonna need all the help she can get."

"All right," Khenan said, "see you 'round."

"Bye," I said, leaving with Khenan. "Nice meeting you, Tammy."

"Bye," she said sweetly.

As we walked away, Marissa said, "Stop flirting."

"I wasn't flirting," Tammy countered. "I just said bye. Jeez."

Travis lived in a hut at the end of the last walkway, closest to the sea. When Khenan knocked on the door, he responded from inside, "Who is it?"

"Is me, idiot. I got Heat wit' me."

"Come in, lads."

Nailed to the inside wall of Travis's hut was an oil painting of a pinup girl leaning over a tombstone in the middle of a graveyard. The only furniture was a cot across from an oak dresser and a night stand. Bottles of alcohol sat on the dresser and bedside table, most with melted candles wedged into their mouths.

Travis had a collection of handguns, rifles, and spears hanging from bent nails on the wall. He used the skin of a stingray as a curtain, the tail reaching all the way to the floor. The hide was beige with dark spots. It was thick enough to blot out the light, although there wasn't much light to block. It was the first time I'd seen a stingray from the Bermuda Triangle, and judging by the size of the thing, I could understand why they were a threat.

On the table was a plate sprinkled with crumbs and a half-filled wine bottle with what I assumed was water beside it. A large Union Jack draped the back

127

door and we had to move it to the side to get to the back porch. There, Travis sat in front of a round vanity mirror that was propped against the railing, shaving with a disposable razor. Aside from one rectangular line racing down his jaw, the lower half of his face was covered in shaving cream. His dreads were also missing.

"Mornin', lads," he said as he slid the blade slowly across his face.

"Cut yer 'air again, mon?" Khenan asked, staring at the pile of golden locks on the floor.

"Nah, it just fell out."

"Smart ass Englishman," Khenan snorted.

"Aye, I guess me arse is smarter than me head," Travis said jocularly. "Ready for a long day of tree chopping?"

"Actually," I said, leaning against the rail, "we're going out to my plane. Want to come along?"

Travis turned his head slowly to me. "Aye, I forgot about that."

"Den make 'aste and shave yer face, princess," Khenan urged. "We need to get."

"You know I bloody well hate it when you call me princess," Travis said, sliding the blade across his lower jaw, then rinsing it off in a basin beside the mirror. "It's *Mr.* Princess, all right? How many times do you need reminding of that, eh?"

I smiled at their banter, then turned my attention to the mountainside, where Eleanor's house sat above other homes. Although I'd be back in the morning, I'd miss her. I couldn't remember feeling so strongly about any of the women I'd known in the past. I'd always been on the move, searching for new and exciting experiences. I'd never given Heath the family man much thought. I hadn't even lived in one place for more than a year until I'd moved to Florida and gotten a job as a flight instructor. I wasn't the type who slept with a woman and then split on her, especially after having been raised by two headstrong women. Even so, I'd never found the right woman to share my adventures with.

"Heath," Travis said, interrupting my thoughts. "Hello, Heath?"

I snapped my head around to him. "What? Did you say something?"

"Bloody hell, mate, I asked how far in the junkyard your plane is."

I was about to answer when Khenan cut in. "'e don't 'ear you 'cause 'is mind be on Eleanor."

"Oh?" Travis said, raising his eyebrows. "Fancy her, do you? She's a sight, eh?"

I flushed with embarrassment, feeling like an adolescent having to admit to a crush.

When Travis finished shaving, he washed the remainder of foam off his face, changed his clothes, and brushed his teeth. He then packed some bottles of water into a small backpack, along with a loaf of bread and meat to make sandwiches.

"We ought to bring guns in case we run into sharks," Travis suggested, plucking two World War II rifles from the wall and handing them to us.

"Why these particular guns?" I asked as he took down another rifle for himself. "Why not newer ones?"

"'Cause there are more bullets available for these, lad. During the war, Liberty ships got stranded here with whole cargos full of ammo."

I held an M1941 semiautomatic rifle. My grandfather on my mother's side had owned one just like it. I was thinking that firing it might be fun when Travis said, "At least we won't be using the guns from *my* time. Trust me when I say that reloading a musket during a life-or-death situation can turn your hair gray in seconds."

We slung the rifles over our shoulders, along with lengths of coiled rope. I didn't look forward to seeing Gavin's dead body but I was excited. I was really in the Bermuda Triangle, on an island no one knew existed. Most of the islanders were people from the distant past, a handful of them from an era that existed before the first civilization.

As we walked along the beach, Travis grumbled, "Bloody hell, look who's coming."

"Good morning, common people," a man said as he drew nearer. A beautiful young woman carrying a tote bag walked beside him. "Going hunting?"

"Yeah, for bloody wankers named Neal Gibbons," Travis said sarcastically. "Looks like our hunt is over."

"Very funny," Neal sneered, stepping directly into Travis's path. "Why don't you take your act on the road?"

Neal looked to be in his twenties, with light blond hair and hazel eyes. He wore no shirt, showing off his six-pack abs and firm biceps. He had a beach towel draped over his shoulder and a small toiletry bag. To me, Neal was nothing more than a spoiled, cocky little bastard. I disliked him immediately.

"Ain't no road here, love," Travis returned. "Why don't you do something useful and build one, eh?"

"Speaking of building, I hear your little Doozers are planning on building a dock for the ships."

"That sounds awesome," the young woman said

130

breathlessly. "When will it, like, y'know, be done?"

"Give your mouth a rest, Sandy," Neal snapped.

"We could use an extra 'and," Khenan said flatly. "After all, it concerns you too."

"I'm not risking my life for an idiotic project like that," Neal snarled. "It's all Eleanor's idea, and I like my yacht exactly where it is—away from the likes of you."

"You know," Travis interjected firmly, "you act like you're something special just 'cause you beat out all the other sperm your pappy pumped into your mum. I got news for you, lad. That's a race we *all* won!"

"You must be the new guy," Neal said, shifting his condescending gaze toward me.

"Yeah."

"Why wasn't I invited to the Welcoming?"

"Assholes aren't invited," Travis said bluntly, making Khenan laugh.

"Whatever," Neal dismissed, not even bothering to look at them. To me, he added, "Word is you're an Indian."

"Half Native American," I answered grudgingly. "And half Caucasian."

Neal raised his hand. "How, half-white man."

My eyes narrowed. I didn't waste my time explaining how offensive his remark was.

He threw up his hands. "Whoa, no need to get pissed. I don't want you scalping me or something."

Sandy giggled. "That's so funny!"

"Bloody hell, Neal, what are you doing here, anyway?"

"Just came to bathe, chump," Neal said derisively. "Would you like to watch?"

"Blimey, that's a ghastly image."

Neal said nothing in reply, but as he and Sandy continued toward the pier, Khenan said, "Don't take what 'e said to 'eart, mon. Neal's like dat wit' everyone."

"Aye. He needs a good kick in the arse, he does. He thinks he's bloody well better than everyone else."

Neal's insults had angered me but I wasn't going to let him get under my skin. To elevate my mood, I raised my eyes to Eleanor's house. Neal's insults faded and we resumed our walk toward my plane.

Chapter Twelve

The fog grew deeper as we made our way across the wing of a plane and started our long and dangerous journey through the wreckage. We used Lafitte's planks to move across the ocean, while the sky became dark with storm clouds. They eventually shed heavy drops. When the planks ended, we were on our own.

"Bloody hell," Travis complained, struggling to maintain his footing on the slick surface of a C-19 tail section. "We're gonna get ourselves killed. You picked a marvelous day to go out to your plane, lad."

"Sorry, but I didn't get a chance to watch the Weather Channel." I leapt off the wing, onto a small fishing boat.

"Travis be right, mon," Khenan said. "Da rain stirs tings up in da water. Look down tere."

I steadied myself and looked over the edge. A shadow glided just beneath the surface. It was soon joined by another, then another.

"Shit," Travis swore, kneeling down and holding onto the rudder. "They're surrounding us. At some point, we'll have to go into the water, and when we do, it's off with our legs. We ought to do this another time."

I hated to retreat, especially after just starting out, but Travis had a point. It wasn't worth dying for a toothbrush and a change of clothes. I could hardly see a foot in front of me. Yet something urged me on, pulling me toward the junkyard.

I looked around for possible transport, then

133

realized I was standing on what I needed—a fishing boat. I reached down and grabbed the motor cord. "You guys can head back if you want, but I'm going on."

I hoped they would. Instead, they watched in silence as I pulled the cord a few times, but the motor refused to come to life.

"Won't work, mon," Khenan said. "Remember, nuttin' mechanical operates 'ere."

I tried a few more times, yanking the cord in frustration, then rose to my full height. "Damn it," I grunted, giving the motor a kick. "I'll have to find an oar."

"For Christ's sakes, if it's that crucial, I'll give you one of my toothbrushes," Travis offered. "I've got several. I'll loan you some clothes, too, and throw in some mouthwash. There's no need risking your arse over toiletries, lad."

"Where you get mout'wash?" Khenan asked.

"I swiped it from ole' Gibbons a while back, when he and his puppet came ashore."

"Wicked."

I thought about Travis's offer but I couldn't shake the compulsion that pulled at me. For some reason, I needed to reach my plane. It was more than just gathering my things. There was something else— something that tugged at me to continue into the dangerous sea. "I have to go out there."

"You *have* to go?" Travis inquired. "That sounds interesting. Okay, I'm in."

"Ah, so dis be some kind of mystery mission, eh?"

"I don't know." I suddenly felt silly, even more than when I first realized I was about to risk my life for supplies. "I just…it's…well, it's hard to explain, but I have a strong feeling that I'm supposed to do something. Does that make any sense?"

"Nope, but I'm in just the same," Travis said.

"Me too. We won't let you go alone. But how are we gonna git past da sharks?"

"No worries, lads." Travis slung his rifle around. "I'll get these bastards off our backs."

He fired into the water several times before pegging a couple of sharks. The remaining ones went wild and tore into the dead and wounded.

"If we can get to a galleon, we can pull down a longboat," Travis suggested.

While the sharks were distracted, we scrambled over some wreckage, leaving them to their feast. In a short while, we stumbled upon a boat covered in lounging octopuses. Travis and Khenan proved there was nothing to fear by petting one. I didn't want to look like a wuss, so I touched one's smooth skin. It breathed heavily but did nothing. Travis explained that they used to lie on the beach until people started killing them, then they found new places in the junkyard to inhabit.

I led the way, hoping we were going in the right direction. The fog and steady rain made it difficult to distinguish any of the planes or ships I'd seen on my way to the island, but my plan was simple. We'd go straight until we reached the end of the junkyard. If that didn't lead us to my plane, we'd follow the edge until we found it.

The sharks followed us, even after shooting a few more. Yet we kept out of the water as much as possible.

"I say, Heath," Travis said from the nose of a

Grumman F9F-2 Panther, "what's your take on this bloody place?"

I struggled to make my way up the slippery wing of a Star Tiger. "I don't really have a theory."

"You said you traveled da world," Khenan said. "'ave you ever seen anyt'ing like dis before?"

I grabbed a propeller blade and extended my hand to pull him up. "Nope. And I hope there's no other place like this anywhere else."

Travis jumped on the wing and tried to maintain his hold. "I wore the wrong bloody shoes for this. I should'a worn me boots."

I tossed a rope down just as he lost his footing. He fell flat on his stomach and slid toward the murky water below, toward a pack of sharks.

"Travis!" Khenan shouted.

I thought about going after him but I'd end up in the ocean as well. Travis's shoes screeched as he struggled to slow his descent, but they were unable to gain traction on the slick metal. Just before he hit the water, he leapt like a cat, propelling his body over a three-foot space to latch onto the nose of the Panther. The nose dipped under his weight, but he kicked his legs in the water to bring himself up.

I handed Khenan the rope. "Tie this to the propeller."

I swung my rifle around and took aim.

"Whatcha doing? You gonna shoot 'im!" Khenan cried.

"I'll do my best not to."

"Bloody hell, this isn't the way I wanna go!" Travis hollered as an aggressive shark pounded against the plane, trying to knock him off.

I squeezed the trigger and felt the rifle kick hard

against my shoulder. There was a loud explosion first and then a spark next to Travis as the bullet bounced off the plane's exterior. It startled the sharks enough to drive them back.

"Who are you shooting at?"

I aimed as a shark reappeared. It went for Travis's foot but clamped onto the plane instead. Travis screamed and kicked at it, but its teeth were stuck in the metal. As it thrashed, Travis struggled to stay on the nose cone.

I pulled the trigger and hoped for the best. There was another loud blast, then silence. The shark went motionless as blood trickled from the back of its head.

Travis quickly stood up. "Bloody bugger." He gave us a salute. "Cheers, mates. I got it from here." He aimed his rifle at the water and began firing. "Get away from me, you bloody bastards!"

Fins of several more sharks gathered for another feeding frenzy. As they tore at the body of the hanging shark, Travis pinwheeled his free arm to maintain his balance. If he fell in the water now, he wouldn't last a minute.

Khenan tossed the rope down to him. "Jump, Travis!"

I held my breath as Travis leapt back onto the wing and caught the rope before he slid down. As we pulled him up, the rope burned my hands. When Travis came close enough, Khenan and I each took a hand and pulled him the rest of the way up.

"Are you okay?" I asked, holding his arm.

"Aye, I'm fine." He heaved deep breaths. "Thanks, lads." Then he looked up at me and said sternly, "You almost shot me, mate." He patted me on the shoulder and continued climbing the plane.

Travis almost getting killed for tagging along with me was one of the reasons I wanted to do this alone.

We rested for a few minutes, gathering our strength and senses. I was about to call the whole thing off when Travis looked to our right and said, "Oi, lookie there."

My eyes followed to where he pointed and I saw the tall masts of a nearby galleon.

"It's not too far off," Travis said. "Maybe there's a longboat onboard."

As we climbed over a PBY Catalina, I noticed the galleon wasn't alone. Leaning next to it was another galleon. The two ships held each other up in the shallow water. Their great masts mingled together, looking like two lovers.

"Are either of these ships yours?" I asked Travis.

"Nah, me ship ran aground on the other side of the island. These are warships from the 1800s."

"It looks like they arrived at the same time."

As we climbed onto the deck of a sailboat, a gunshot rang out, forcing us to duck behind a railing at the stern.

"Shit," Khenan whispered, squatting beside me. "Who'd be out 'ere?"

I swung my rifle around. "I have no idea."

"What if there's more than one of them? They could be surrounding us right now," Travis said fearfully.

Before I could reply, a voice demanded, "Reveal thyselves!"

"Travis," Khenan said, "dat voice sounds old, like you. You talk to 'im, eh?"

"What do you mean I should talk to 'im?"

Before Khenan could speak, another shot rang out and a puff of smoke rose from a cannon window of one of the galleons.

"I said reveal thyselves!" the voice thundered.

"Talk to da mon," Khenan insisted.

"You think he'll calm down just 'cause he might be from the same time as me?" Travis protested. "He could be an American soldier who hates Brits. Did you think of that? Why don't you talk to him?"

"I got a cannon aimed on the boat you're on," the voice shouted. "I suggest you start talking!"

"He's gonna blast us to bits!" Khenan cried. "Damn it, Travis, say someting."

I decided to take matters into my own hands and rose to my feet, my hands in the air. "Ahoy there!"

"What's your name, my good fellow?" the gunman asked.

"Heath Sharp, and with me is Travis Livingston and Khenan Evans."

"Is that all? Just the three of you?"

"Yes."

"Are you from the island?"

"Yes."

"Are you friend or foe?"

It was a simple question but it might be a trick. I hesitated a moment as I decided how to answer.

"The answer is *friend,* lad," Travis whispered.

"That depends," I called back. "Who are you?"

There was a long, eerie silence, during which my arms grew tired and my nerves began to crumble. Khenan and Travis got to their feet and stood beside me.

"Where is 'e?" Khenan whispered.

I slowly lowered my arms. "I think he's in the

hull."

"He's probably loading the cannon," Travis said, "while we're standing here like dodo birds."

"Don't you tink it's prob'ly already loaded?"

"I guess you're right on that, mate."

"Ahoy," the man finally called as he appeared on the deck and waved to us. "I'm John T. Shubrick. Welcome to my kingdom."

Chapter Thirteen

"Oh, Lord," Travis muttered, "it's bloody John Shubrick. This is gonna be interesting."

"Wah did 'e say?" Khenan whispered. "Some'ting 'bout 'is kingdom?"

"Shush," I said sharply. I looked at the imposing figure on the boat and called, "Mr. Shubrick, permission to—"

"It's King Shubrick!" the man snapped. "*King* Shubrick, do you hear? I should have made that clear."

The man was obviously insane but we were in his territory. I would call him whatever he wanted me to— Jesus, Pablo Escobar, Santa Claus, it didn't matter as long he didn't blow us away.

"Forgive us, King Shubrick," I said apologetically. "I request permission for me and my comrades to board your vessel."

Shubrick stroked his incredibly long beard, then waved us forward. "Sure, come on up."

"Do you know dat mon?" Khenan asked Travis as we began our approach.

"Aye, but I'm not sure it will do any good. Keep a sharp eye out, lads."

When Shubrick pushed a ladder over the side, we eased into the water and waded toward the galleon. It took two ladders tied together to reach the water, which only came up four feet on the tilted hull.

I led the way, my rifle bumping against my back as I climbed. When I reached the top, the first thing that greeted me was the end of a musket, trained directly on my face. Shubrick commanded, "Keep moving."

I thought about warning Travis and Khenan, but I couldn't think of a way to do that without alerting Shubrick. My only option was to let them find out for themselves and hope for the best.

Once I was aboard, I raised my hands. When Travis appeared and saw the gun, he blurted, "Oi, lieutenant, put that gun away, eh?"

"Do I know you?" Shubrick demanded.

Travis and Khenan joined me, but it was Travis who said, "No, but I remember you from the ole' days. You were the lieutenant of the *U.S.S. Epervier*."

Shubrick ran his hand through his dark hair, looking confused. He seemed to be more of a pirate than an honorable seaman. He was filthy and reeked like a homeless person dipped in sewage. Shells, feathers, and small wooden soldiers were either tied or just stuck in his hair and beard. He considered Travis for a long time before lowering his musket. As the rifle dropped, so did my arms. Only then did I take my first real breath.

Shubrick's expression changed when he asked Travis, "You said you're from the island. How is Eleanor?"

"She's doing well. And you?"

"Always could be better," he said grimly.

"Your crewmen are livin' on the south end of the island."

"Are they? I hope they're doing well."

"You left the village sometime during the twentieth century, mate. No farewell or anything. What happened to you?"

"I wanted to kill myself."

"Oh."

"I didn't want anyone to see my corpse, so I came out here to do myself in."

"I remember you were suffering a bad depression in those last few years," Travis said.

"Indeed. And in truth, I've always been guilt-ridden because I've never been able to carry out my mission."

"Wah mission's dat, mon?"

Shubrick shifted his eyes to Khenan. "To deliver a signed copy of the treaty between the American commissioners and the Dey of Algiers. When the storm came upon us, many of my men were killed and I was trapped here to live with my failure." His voice became even more determined. "I swear, if I ever leave this place, I'll deliver that treaty to the United States."

"How is that you've become a king?" Travis asked with amusement.

"I hadn't planned to go too far out to sea before turning a gun on myself. I just wanted to get far enough away from the village. But the farther I went, the less distressed I felt. I kept going until I arrived at these two ships." He gestured to the *General Gates* and the *Insurgent.* "They reminded me of my own vessel, which gave me a sense of peace, so I stayed here and lived off the sea while I built my kingdom with whatever I could salvage."

"Why didn't you go back to your own ship?" Travis asked.

"An ugly incident that occurred in the lower hull," Shubrick explained. "It became a grave site for some of my crew mates."

John T. Shubrick. I mulled over the name for a moment. It was the same person Tomas's suicide letter

143

had been written to. I'd found Shubrick's ship on the first day of my arrival.

As they talked amiably, I scanned the ship and discovered something unnerving—a number of barrels marked GUNPOWDER. I took solace in the idea that centuries of rain had probably soaked through the barrels.

"I just built a new bridge," Shubrick exclaimed. "Come, let me show you."

We followed him across the deck, over a plank, and onto the other ship, where more barrels sat. There were also dozens of water buckets and shoes hanging everywhere. A herd of octopuses lay leisurely on the deck.

At first, I thought the plank was the bridge he'd mentioned, but when we reached the stern, I realized otherwise. Tied to the railing was a long bridge made from various boards with ropes as handrails. Its other end was tied to the deck of a capsized Liberty ship. It rested mainly on its hull, but slanted all the same.

"Come," he urged, stepping onto the bridge, which creaked loudly in protest.

We looked at each other, then Khenan urged Travis, "You first, mon."

Travis narrowed his eyes and said, "Fine."

He examined the bridge a moment, then crossed himself before stepping onto it. He took one step, looked at Shubrick, and added, "This bridge doesn't exactly seem new, mate."

"No? Well, perhaps I built it a while ago. I can't recall—and since I'm now a king, I prefer that you address me properly."

"Your Highness, where are your subjects?"

"There's no one here but me, young man,"

Shubrick said without looking back.

"Dat's no surprise," Khenan whispered behind me, his words nearly lost among the groaning and creaking of the bridge.

Travis started to say something, but I grabbed his shoulder and whispered fiercely, "Don't, we need a boat and he's got explosives all over the place."

Travis nodded and called out to Shubrick, who'd put some distance between us, "I say, Your Highness, we are in need of a boat."

Shubrick stepped off the far end of the bridge and turned to us. "What do you need a boat for?"

"We need it to get through the junkyard so we can get to my plane," I replied.

"The junkyard? Is that what you're calling it now? Well, young man, it is decidedly *not* a junkyard. The ships out here are valuable pieces of history. Some of them fought for countries and others took people on pleasurable getaways."

I understood exactly where he was coming from. I felt that way about my own plane, *Gypsy Girl.* Every time I sat in her, I felt closer to my grandmother. My plane was more than just transportation to me.

"You're right, Your Majesty," Travis chortled. "Now, about that boat?"

When we boarded the Liberty ship, Shubrick said darkly, "Watch how you speak to the king, sir, or I'll blow you all to kingdom come."

"How?" Travis challenged. "I see no explosives up here."

"The crew left crates of TNT on this ship," Shubrick said in earnest.

We stood on the rail that now served as a floor. It overlooked four floating life boats lined side by side

145

with piles of junk stored in them, one with what appeared to be a poorly tended garden. There were planks leading from the deck to the garden boat. None of them were usable, though.

Shubrick's face brightened as he swept his hand grandly. "Do you need food? I have plenty of vegetables in my garden."

I studied his so-called garden more closely, which consisted of a few scraggly potted plants.

"No," Travis answered, "we had weeds for lunch."

Shubrick gave us a tour of the ship, which meant climbing on rope nets to the nearest hatch. Our strange tour inside the ship included TNT crates in the hull—perhaps to let us know he wasn't joking. He told us stories about his childhood, which sounded suspiciously like the plot of *Tom Sawyer* when he talked about convincing friends to paint a fence and searching for treasure in a haunted cave. Being unbalanced, I could understand how he might entwine Twain's story with his own.

"You may have a longboat," he finally announced in his most regal tone. "Don't worry about bringing it back. I have several. You'll probably need it to return to the island."

When the tour ended, we headed back toward the *General Gates.* None of us spoke as we crossed the rickety bridge. The rain died down but didn't make the journey any less unnerving.

As we got into the longboat, the rain dwindled to a light sprinkle. Before I stepped in, Shubrick grabbed my arm and whispered, "Everything has an ending. I think you're part of something that will one day affect my kingdom."

"I wouldn't do anything to harm your kingdom," I said.

"Do what to what?" he asked, letting go of my arm, his unblinking eyes locked on me.

Before either of us could say anything, Travis interrupted us, "Come on, let's be off, eh?"

"Yah, mon, let's go before da rain 'its again."

I turned, leaving Shubrick to stare after me as I climbed into the boat. He continued to watch as we lowered the longboat into the misty water.

"Things will get very bad before they get better," Shubrick called as Travis and Khenan manned the oars. I sat in front, trying to light a torch Shubrick had given us for the journey.

"Was 'e always like dat?" Khenan asked.

"Nah," Travis replied. "The sod went into the forest and came back completely off his rocker."

"Wat 'e say to you back dere?" Khenan asked me as he leaned into his oar.

"Nothing. It was just gibberish."

"Figures," Travis grumbled. "When people lose their marbles, it can be bloody scary."

We navigated our way through the misty ocean as a light drizzle began to fall again. A few minutes later, the fog lifted just enough to see a few hundred feet ahead of us. We eventually came upon two massive ships and four large commercial planes. The planes were from the same airlines—three DC-3 Into the Blues and a Douglas Dakota.

"'ey, I been 'ere before," Khenan suddenly said.

"Really?" Travis said. "When?"

"Nineteen ninety-five. Look over dere. Is da *Jamanic K.*"

The vessel Khenan pointed out was completely

capsized, with the *Sylvia L. Ossa* resting beside her. Khenan stared at the wreckage in silence.

"Are you all right?" I asked.

"I 'ave a son," he said softly. "'e be a young mon by now." He paused, then growled. "If it wasn't fa dat goddamn ship, I'd be 'ome wit me family. Dat ship took everyting from me."

"Don't blame the ship, lad," Travis soothed. "She's just as much a victim as any of us."

I felt horrible for being the one to bring Khenan's pain back. It had been a long time since either of them had seen their homeland or looked upon the faces of friends and loved ones.

"When I was a child, my brother burst into flames and burnt up right before ma eyes," he said unexpectedly.

"Your brother spontaneously combusted?" I asked in surprise.

"Ya, an' from wat I 'ear, it be genetic. Wat if me own son 'as gone up in flames?"

"He won't, lad," Travis said, as if they'd had this discussion before. "Your son is out there somewhere, living his life in peace."

Khenan took in a deep breath. "I 'ope so."

The rain stopped as we headed toward another cluster of wreckage. The boundary of the junkyard appeared where the water level turned dark blue. Since my plane had crashed on the outskirts, we decided to weave our way in and out of the deep water to bypass any trouble spots. But each time the boat glided into deeper water, the temperature dropped so low I could see our breath.

"Jesus, Mary, and Joseph," Travis said with a shiver. "I forgot how cold it is out here."

"How is that possible?" I asked, rubbing my arms. My skin tingled. Chunks of ice floated around us like white islands, tapping against the wooden longboat. No one answered my question but I doubted if either of them knew. "Was it always like this?"

"Aye," Travis said, "it most likely has been this way long before the Ancient Ones came."

In the distance, bodies floated face down in the water. Before I could ask, Travis said, "Those are some of the unfortunate sods who tried rowing out and didn't make it back."

"Dis place is no Disneyland, mon," Khenan added. "Da rides 'ere can be deadly."

We rode in silence for the next ten minutes, the only sound being the slicing of the oars through the water. Just as I began to worry we'd either missed my plane or were rowing the wrong way, *Gypsy Girl* appeared.

"There she is!" I shouted.

"Bloody hell, mate!" Travis cried. "You nearly scared the life outta me."

"Over there," I said, pointing to my right. "There's my plane."

We crossed into the shallow area, where the air around us suddenly rose to a more comfortable temperature. Khenan tied the longboat off on a propeller blade and jumped out. Travis reached for the open door where Gavin's body stared blankly back at him.

"Jeez," Travis said, disgusted, "it smells like piss in here."

Chapter Fourteen

"Why does it smell in here, mate?" Travis asked as I grabbed the doorway and pulled myself inside.

"My co-pilot pissed himself before we crashed."

"I've been on the verge of doing that once or twice meself. Been that scared, I mean."

I hardly glanced at Gavin's body still slumped in the chair with blood on his face. The stench of urine permeated the air. I hadn't told my companions that Gavin had appeared to me since I'd arrived, just as Lafitte had warned. Instead, I sloshed through the water to the back of the plane, where I raised a hidden lid from the submerged floorboard and reached inside.

"I bet it's something to ride in one of these," Travis said, sitting in the pilot's seat and moving the throttle around. "To see the world from a bird's-eye view. You're both lucky to have lived in the era you did, lads."

With considerable effort, I pulled a waterproof bag out and unzipped it. I always kept my emergency items in airtight bags in case of a crash. I hadn't seen this one for at least a year since I'd packed it. It contained four changes of clothes, a jumbo tube of toothpaste, a toothbrush, a stick of deodorant, a six-pack of soap, and three large towels. I'd also packed beef jerky, canned food, a can opener, lighter fluid, matches, and several bottles of water in it.

"Doesn't it bother you dat you're sitting next to a dead mon?" Khenan asked as Travis played around with the switches.

"Nah, I've seen dead folks before. Blimey, I've seen 'em in worse shape than this."

I zipped the bag back up and slung it over my shoulder. "Let's go," I said dolefully. "I think I've got all I need."

"Are you all right, lad? You look a little green."

In truth, I thought I might vomit. Being inside the plane was like being inside a gas chamber. The air had become toxic.

"I'm okay. I'm just feeling mixed emotions right now."

I could almost hear Gavin's voice pleading for me to take his body out of the plane. I glanced at his corpse. An unseen force drew my hand close to Gavin's body.

"Wat you doin', mon?" Khenan asked. "You don't be messin' wit da dead."

"Stop it!" Travis insisted.

For the life of me, I couldn't pull my hand back. I struggled to regain control of it, but the force beat down my willpower.

"No, lad!" Travis exclaimed, snatching my hand. "That's enough!"

It felt like I was in a trance. Before I had time to think, I moaned, "Get me out of here."

Travis and Khenan quickly helped me into the longboat. My shirt was drenched in sweat.

"You all right, lad?" Travis asked as I took my place at the bow and clutched the bag close to my chest.

"Yeah, fine," I said, staring blankly forward.

Khenan shoved the longboat away from the plane. "Jeez, mon, wah 'appened in dere?"

"Don't worry about that now," Travis said,

beginning to row. "Let's just head back."

Waves of tremors rocked my body. What had been the force that had pulled at me and why had it been so intent on getting me to disturb Gavin's body?

The rain returned, though not as heavy as it had been earlier in the day.

"By da time we get back to shore, we're gonna 'afta run fer da village. I really don't wanna make camp in da woods in da dark."

"We could stay with Lafitte," I suggested.

"Jean Lafitte?" Khenan said, his voice rising. "Might be int'resting. I 'ope 'im 'ave some wine."

After an hour of rowing, I spotted a familiar landmark. I looked back at Travis. He said nothing but his expression told me he wanted to tell me something. I wondered if he held his tongue because Khenan was with us.

We crossed under a wing, heading for a yacht, when a gunshot rang out. Travis jolted forward with a start.

"You say you fought in a war, mon?" Khenan mocked, just as a second blast split the air.

"No, I was on me way to one," Travis retorted as he ducked.

Loud shouting followed the shot. I recognized Lafitte's voice and climbed out of the longboat, onto the bow of the yacht to get a better view.

"Lafitte?" I called.

"*Qui est la?*"

I squinted into the dense fog. "Is that you?"

"*Oui.*"

"It's Heath Sharp, remember me? We met a few days ago. You showed me how to get to the island."

Lafitte made no reply. What if he didn't

remember me? Could his memory be that short?

"*Ah, oui! Bonsoir, mon ami,*" Lafitte said. "*Comment êtes-vous?*"

"Wet and tired."

"Just like the first time I met you, *non?* Are you coming from the island now?"

"No, we went to my plane for some things. Would you mind if we spent the night on your ship?"

"We?"

"Yeah, I'm with two friends."

"No," Lafitte said abruptly.

"Oh," I said, surprised. "Well, all right, then. I guess I'll see you later."

Before I could convey Lafitte's message to Travis and Khenan, an orange-and-yellow glow came toward us. As it drew closer, Lafitte appeared, wearing a bright yellow raincoat and hat, carrying a torch.

"I mean no, I don't mind if you stay the night. But first, help me with this shark I've killed."

I peered over the railing. Below us was a one-man sailboat. I leaped off the yacht and landed hard on the stern. The boat wobbled as I struggled to maintain my balance.

"Oi, Jean!" Travis called from the yacht above.

The pirate looked up at him. "And who are you?"

"It's Travis Livingston. Remember me?"

Lafitte stared at Travis a minute, shaking his head slightly. "I don't recall, but you're welcome aboard my ship, anyway."

As Travis and Khenan leaped onto the sailboat, Travis said, "Captain, you and me drank rum once on the beach when I first got here."

"Rum isn't exactly memory fuel, mon," Khenan said with a chuckle.

153

"Good point, lad."

The journey to Lafitte's ship was short. Travis and I carried the shark. It was considerably smaller than the sharks we'd encountered earlier but heavy nonetheless. I held the tail, while Travis carried the head, its beady black eyes aimed at him.

When *The Pride* came into view, Lafitte called for his crewmen to help with the catch. We boarded the ship and were invited into the captain's quarters. The room looked as if it had been ransacked. Everything that wasn't heavy had been moved and stacked into piles or placed on the table.

"Would you gentlemen care for some wine?" Lafitte asked, taking off his wet rain gear.

"Aye, Captain," Travis replied as Khenan smiled broadly.

"I have dry towels," Lafitte said, walking to his dresser and pulling out the top drawer. He brought several out. "I've been doing some cleaning. Don't be disturbed by the arm."

"Blimey," Travis whispered, nudging Khenan with his elbow. "Look at that. It's ole' Captain Saxon's arm."

"Dat be wicked, mon," Khenan said, paling.

Lafitte handed each of us a towel. "The weather was bad today. What made you go out to your plane to fetch things that could wait for another time?"

"We were gonna turn back but dis idiot refused to."

I flushed with embarrassment.

"Did you get everything you went out for?" Laffite asked.

I didn't quite know how to respond. I'd retrieved my clothes and toiletries, but somehow I felt unfulfilled. "We found the *General Gates* and the *Insurgent,*" I said, avoiding the question.

Lafitte snorted. "So, you met the mad sea king, then? What did he have to say?"

"He said everything has an ending and that things are going to get bad before they get better," I replied, studying Lafitte's face.

Lafitte's expression melted into a stone-serious one. "He told you that?"

I nodded. "Why? What does it mean?"

Lafitte walked over to a cabinet where he kept bottles of wine and brought one out. He popped the cork and said, "I don't know. The only thing I can interpret from that is change. And if change is coming to a place like this, not everyone will survive."

Chapter Fifteen

Travis, Khenan, and I slept in hammocks in the hull. We'd stayed up most of the night, drinking and playing poker with the pirates. I slept so soundly it seemed nothing could wake me—until someone called my name.

"Heath, get up."

I recognized the voice but tried to ignore it.

"Damn it, Heath," Gavin said more insistently. "I know you can hear me. You need to go back to the plane and do something about my corpse. I can't believe you went out there and did nothing but get that stupid bag."

I decided to tune him out. Maybe if I treated him like an unwanted advertisement, he might eventually fade away, like Lafitte's first mate. I turned to the side and pulled the sheet over my head.

"Oh, I get it," Gavin said derisively, "you don't want to take responsibility for what you did to me, huh? You're gonna leave me out there forever, is that it?"

I clenched my teeth. I wanted to sit up and yell at him that it wasn't my fault he'd died, but I kept my mouth shut and threw my arms over my head, pressing my biceps against my ears to block out his voice. I closed my eyes, doing my best to disregard everything he said from that point on, no matter how vulgar or unfair it was.

The golden rays of the morning sun came in through the window. An echo of Gavin's voice lingered in the air, but it faded like lowering the volume on an annoying disc jockey on a radio. When I finally opened my eyes, he was gone.

As Travis and Khenan continued to snore, I got out of the hammock. I wouldn't be able to go back to sleep. I stretched my arms and back, spotted my bag lying on the floor, and decided to do something I'd wanted to do for days—brush my teeth.

I rinsed my mouth with water from a bucket that had caught the previous day's rainwater and spit over the side of the ship. The fog already covered the area. I slid my tongue over my teeth, feeling the minty freshness I'd taken for granted and debated whether to change clothes. But I'd wait until I took a shower at the waterfall.

By the time I finished with my teeth, I was ready to get on with the day. My stomach grumbled and my head hurt from drinking. The leftovers from our shark dinner had been thrown overboard. Unlike dead things from the outside, the flesh of the native dead rotted fast.

An hour had gone by before I went back down. "Khenan," I whispered, "wake up."

He slowly raised his eyelids and groaned. "I got an 'eadache, mon. Is cruel to wake a mon wit an 'angover."

"I wanted to let you know that I'm heading back to the village. Do you want to come or are you going to stay here?"

He closed his eyes for a moment, then slowly rose, his eyes still closed. "I'll go wit' you, but whatcha up so early fa?"

I held my tongue about Gavin. "Just an early riser, I guess."

Smacking his dry lips together, Khenan finally opened his eyes. I went over to Travis' hammock and shook him. "Get up, we're leaving."

Travis didn't stir, just kept on snoring, oblivious to the world.

"Let me 'andle dis," Khenan offered, pushing me aside.

I took a couple of steps back as he grabbed the hammock and yanked it, flipping Travis onto the wooden floor. The thud was so loud it woke a crewman sleeping nearby. He said nothing, only raised his head slightly, looked at us, and sank back into his hammock.

"Why'd you do that, mate?" Travis asked, rubbing his shoulder.

"I wanted to see 'ow far I could flip an Englishmon."

"Apparently pretty bloody far," Travis grumbled, standing up. "You best sleep with *both* eyes open, 'cause I'm gonna get you for that."

We gathered our belongings and left the ship, taking the star lamp Laffite gave me when I asked for it. I led the way to shore, following the planks. On land, we headed north toward the village. I couldn't explain it, but as we got closer, a heavy feeling weighed on me, as if a giant had me pressed under his thumb. It got to the point where the heaviness became so overwhelming it was like I was walking through quicksand. I tried to maintain a normal pace and said nothing about it. I figured it had something to do with the alcohol I'd drunk.

Marissa called to us as we reached the village. "Guys, guess what happened!"

Tammy was behind her, running as fast as

Marissa, her dark eyes wide and cheeks red and glossy.

"Wah?" Khenan asked.

I knew the news would be bad and hoped it had nothing to do with Eleanor.

"Inglewood is dead," Marissa blurted.

Two conflicting emotions shot through me— shock and relief.

"Dead?" Travis echoed. "What the bloody hell happened?"

"He didn't come back yesterday," Tammy said, "so someone went to check on him."

"Didn't come back from where?" Khenan asked, his voice rising.

"He went to feed that Viking girl," Marissa replied. "Y'know how he is, sometimes he stays there for hours at a time, but never all day. This morning they found him by her cage."

"Jesus," I said, "what killed him?"

"*She* did," Marissa said. "She somehow got out of her cage and slit his throat."

"That little thing?" Travis said in disbelief.

"You mean that vicious little thing," Marissa retorted.

"Has she been caught yet?" Travis asked.

Marissa shook her head. "No. She must've high-tailed it into the forest. She'd best not come back to loot our shit like she used to or she's gonna get a bullet in the leg."

Eleanor stood on the edge of the pier, looking in our direction. While the others continued to talk about Inglewood and his killer, I started toward her. She rushed down the steps and ran to me. I picked up my pace, and a few seconds later, I held her in my arms.

"Oh, it's awful, utterly awful," she said, burying

her face in my chest. "He was such a good man. He didn't deserve to be killed in such a brutal manner."

I didn't know what to say, so I held her as she sobbed.

"Heat," Khenan called from behind me, "we gonna go see 'im. Wanna come?"

I wasn't sure I wanted to see another dead body. In fact, I was positive I didn't. But Eleanor loosened her grip and said somberly, "You should go. It'll help you understand the kind of danger this place presents."

Her voice was stern yet gentle, like a mentor teaching a student a hard lesson in life. I didn't argue. I only nodded and followed Khenan and Travis down the shoreline. When I looked back, Eleanor had her arms wrapped around herself, her long blonde hair draped over her bare shoulders, reaching just below her breasts. I wanted to turn back more than anything.

We passed various people on our way. Some cried and others talked among themselves. We said nothing and kept moving until we reached the path leading to the cage. Inglewood's body lay near the feeding slot. As we approached, a man standing near the corpse ran into the woods to vomit. I was certain I didn't want to see.

When we reached Inglewood, Travis crossed himself and gasped, "Lord be merciful."

A powerful numbness dulled my senses. I felt nothing as I gazed at the butchered body, studying it like the Mona Lisa at the Louvre. Inglewood was on his back, with one leg over the other. His arms were above his head, as if he'd been killed during a stickup. The wound across his throat was jagged. A sharp, bloody rock was nearby.

"How did she get out?" Travis wondered.

"Through that hole up there," a woman said, pointing at an opening near the top of the cage. It had been pushed up by the same tree Inglewood had talked about cutting down. It wasn't big enough for a grown person to squeeze through, but enough for a girl like Sassy.

Inglewood must have arrived just as she was getting out and she attacked him before he could stop her. The food dish was empty, but there were vegetables scattered around him. After killing him, she must have eaten what she wanted and fled into the woods.

"Since he was murdered, we can give the poor sod a proper funeral," Travis said.

I realized why Eleanor wanted me to witness this scene. She needed me to see that horrible things could happen in this lost section of the Bermuda Triangle. I had to abandon any sense of security I harbored from the outside. Here, the human race wasn't at the top of the food chain. We were somewhere in the mix. Travis and Khenan knew better, that was why they wanted to come with me out to the junkyard. Being a lone wolf out here was a surefire way to get killed very quick. That made me dizzy.

* * *

That night, we held a wake for Inglewood at Miller's tavern. The people who knew him best said a few kind words and then Eleanor made a toast in his honor. After that, it didn't take long for the mourners to get drunk. As the drinking continued, Mrs. Turk sniffed around for a young man intoxicated enough to take her home. Carlton tried getting in on the action

161

but she wouldn't have it. He was too old for her.

Eleanor was in no mood for conversation after her toast. We shared a table with a few others, and whenever I glanced at her, she smiled, but her eyes couldn't hide her sorrow.

Some spoke about Inglewood, while others continued to drink. The tavern was packed and poor Paddy could hardly keep up with the orders. Finally, the bar was tapped out. What liquor there was worked its magic, and Carlton and Mrs. Turk left together.

Soon afterward, Eleanor stood up. "Heath, I don't want to be alone tonight. Will you come and have a drink with me in my hut?"

It seemed inappropriate but I was delighted. "Sure."

I met her back at her place after returning to my hut. She asked me to wait outside if she wasn't on the porch when I arrived. I waited on her front porch and admired the village lit up in different colors against the endless black sky. When Eleanor returned, she wore a green T-shirt and a long flowing skirt. She held two wine glasses in one hand and a bottle in the other.

As she handed me a glass, I asked, "Is this the same wine I had at the Welcoming? That stuff went straight to my head."

"I'm sure it did. You have to build up a tolerance to the things that grow here. But no, this came from the outside."

I took comfort in that. The other wine had put me on my ass and I didn't want to get sloppy-headed around her.

"What's that?" she asked, pointing to the lamp I held.

"I thought I'd give you stars," I said, handing it

162

over.

With her free hand, she accepted it and studied it a moment.

"Oh, darling, this is wonderful. Thank you."

Her wide smile was all the gratitude I needed.

She sat the lamp near a chair. "Ah." She sighed, sinking into the chair. "This is more like it." She filled her glass with an amber-colored liquor, then handed me the bottle.

Her pale skin had turned golden in the glow of the lanterns. As I poured my own glass, she said, "I've seen photographs of women in string bikinis sunbathing on the beach. If I ever leave this place, that'll be the first thing I do. In my day, a woman would never show so much of herself. Do you like it?"

"Girls in string bikinis?"

"No, silly," she said with a giggle, "the wine. Do you like it?"

"Oh, wait a second." I took my first sip. "It's very nice and sweet."

I found myself hypnotized by her eyes. If she told me to leap off the porch, I probably would, without question.

"It's the last bottle I have. My ex had tons of wine and brandy on his boat. When I left him, I took some for myself."

"Really?" I liked it less after hearing where it had come from.

"He drank constantly after we arrived and I feared he'd do something that would put him in his grave. I disliked him from the start but I never wanted him hurt."

As she stretched her legs, her skirt slid off her calf. She pointed her toes and swung her foot a couple of times before crossing her legs. "The Victorian era was a terrible time for women," she said matter-of-factly. "We wore layers and layers of unnecessary clothing all year 'round. In those days, a man had no knowledge of a woman's body. The law even prohibited the use of female cadavers for medical study. Doctors could touch a woman only in places her clothing didn't conceal, which meant her hands and face."

"That sounds rough," I remarked stupidly.

She nodded and took another sip. "You have no idea. In an ironic way, coming to this place was my ticket to freedom. Here, I've been able to live long enough to benefit from the thoughts and views of modern women."

"Like what?"

"Like life in general. As strange as it may seem, I've learned to enjoy life during my stay in the Devil's Triangle."

She drained her glass, then stood and walked over to me. She came so close our knees touched. Looking down with a girlish grin, her blonde hair framed her face perfectly. One hand rested near her inner thigh, while the other still held her wine glass.

My heart began to pound. I realized what she meant by telling me she didn't want to be alone. After losing her friend, she wanted some comfort. Death heightened sexual behavior in some people, probably because it reminded them that life is short, even on an island of immortals.

"In my time, women weren't supposed to enjoy sex," she said huskily, leaning toward me.

I swallowed nervously. She was a hundred and thirty-five years older than me. That difference far surpassed Dustin Hoffman and Anne Bancroft in *The Graduate*.

"Do you?" I asked, my body trembling.

Her answer was in her kiss. I could taste the sweet wine on her lips. She gripped my wrist, forcing me to drop the bottle. Her mouth pressed against mine and she moved my hand under her shirt, guiding it to her breast. A moment later, she stepped back and raised her shirt above her head. Her long hair dropped gracefully back over her shoulders as the shirt fell to the ground.

I could have sat in that chair and admired her all night long, but she pulled me to my feet and led me inside. At that moment, my thoughts about escaping the island vanished from my mind.

Chapter Sixteen

Eleanor and I sat outside on her round wicker chair with only a blanket covering us, staring at the dots of light glowing through the tiny star-shaped holes of the lamp. The dots of light shone everywhere, on us as well as the porch ceiling.

"Heath," she whispered.

"Yeah?" I said softly, sliding my fingertips lightly over her arm.

"What did you do out there in the real world?"

I still wasn't used to the incarcerating way that sounded, *in the real world*. But at that moment, I didn't care. "I taught people how to fly planes."

"That sounds exciting. Where did you live as a child?"

"With my mother and grandmother in Northern California, until I graduated from high school. Then I went backpacking for a few years, until I went home to live with my father on the Wailaki reservation in Whitethorn."

"Tell me about your tribe."

"What do you want to know?"

Her shoulders moved up on my chest. "I don't know. Their history."

I thought for a moment. There was a story to tell but it took a while for me to remember it. It had been a hell of a couple of days. My mind and body were exhausted, the latter which still tingled with pleasure.

"My great-great-great-grandfather was killed at the Horse Canyon Massacre. He was twenty-two at the time. It was in September and the tribe needed horses for hunting when the winter came. He and sixteen other warriors went to the Round Valley and were shot down by the settlers they tried stealing horses from."

"That's awful," she gasped.

"Have you ever heard about the Horse Canyon Massacre?"

There was a moment of silence. "I think…I think I have…yes, I do remember reading about it in the papers weeks after it happened."

The fact that she'd read a piece of my tribe's history dating back over a hundred years blew my mind. But, instead of getting caught up in the bizarreness of that, I went on. "My father told me the story the same as his father told him." Then I said something I thought I'd never hear myself say. "And someday I'll tell my own children."

Again, silence fell between us. I hardly noticed it, but what I'd said stunned me.

Eleanor sniffed and rose off me.

"Where are you going?" I asked.

"To get us some water." She hurried toward the door. "I'll be right back."

Her words trembled like a 6.0 earthquake. She was distressed about something, but I didn't have time to ask before she disappeared into the house. Still, I got to my feet and caught the door before it closed.

Candles gave me a view of her in the kitchen by a counter. She had one hand cupped over her eyes, sobbing softly.

"Eleanor?" I said from the open doorway. "Are you all right?"

She jumped and turned to me. "I'm fine. Sorry, it's just that there are some things in life we cannot

167

change. Coming here, I broke free from my controlled lifestyle. But it also took something from me."

"Whatever I said, I'm sorry if I—"

"It's not your fault. Making love to you this evening brought me more pleasure than I've ever experienced. It's what we can't gain from it that saddens me. What we can't bring into this world."

My confusion lingered. I was about to ask what she meant when I suddenly remembered what Paddy had said. *The way ya came in is the way ya stay.*

"Kids," I said. "You can't have them."

"And you can't give them," she put in. "In this place, we're unchangeable, like images in a photograph. It's impossible to have a family."

I approached the counter and stood across from her. "If you want to look at it from another perspective, you could see it as a blessing."

"What do you mean?"

I was walking a thin line. "You told me that children don't survive long here. Wouldn't it be unfair to bring a child into this scary place just to die in a terrifying way?"

Her eyes flickered with understanding. "You're right. This place isn't for children—or adults. The way it is around here, few women would even survive childbirth, much less be able to safely raise a child."

It seemed that she said it out loud to give herself comfort. I said nothing else about it. We went to bed and made love two more times before we talked about the work on the dock. That made her happy again. I guess working to build something came a close second to having children. We never discussed children again after that.

I stayed the night with her, holding her close,

even after she fell asleep. Eventually, I drifted off as well, only to wake in what seemed like a second after shutting my eyes.

"Was it good?" Gavin asked. "Was screwing her just swell? Did you enjoy nibbling on her tits? Did her pussy taste like candy?"

I recognized his voice before opening my eyes, yet I sat up to make certain it wasn't anyone else—like Eleanor's ex-fiancé. The dim light from the early morning gave enough illumination to see Gavin sitting on a wicker chair next to the bed.

"I hope you're enjoying yourself while I'm out there suffering."

A creepy feeling came over me just then. Could Gavin watch me throughout the day?

I shook it off. His poetic rant about my sexual experience with Eleanor gave it away that he couldn't. I hadn't performed oral sex on Eleanor.

I turned to her in case she'd overheard Gavin's abrasive words. She was lying on her side, her back to us, peaceful in slumber and deaf to his crude words. At least that was a plus. Until I got rid of this nuisance, I didn't have to worry about someone else acknowledging him.

"You're a real prick, ya know that?" Gavin said.

I wasn't going to fall for it, no matter what he said. I resisted shouting back at him by thinking how crazy I'd look if Eleanor woke up to find me naked and cursing at her wicker chair. Any kind of relationship I might have with her would be gone. If only Gavin's ghost had been solid, I'd have knocked his wise ass to the ground days ago. But there was no sense wasting precious energy if my fist would only go through a patch of cold air.

169

Then again, if he *was* solid, he wouldn't be dead and bitching at me.

I ignored him and rolled over, gently kissing Eleanor on the shoulder without disturbing her. Soon, the morning light grew stronger and Gavin's voice weakened. When the overcast in the sky returned, his ruthless insults went away.

Later, people who wanted to pay their respects to Inglewood gathered around his grave, which was in a cemetery on the mountainside. The rest of the villagers stayed away for many different reasons. Some didn't know him well enough to say goodbye or had already been to plenty of funerals. Or perhaps they didn't care. The village was the size of a small subdivision and one man's death wouldn't affect their daily function. But it was my first ceremony on the island. Yet, I overheard people remark on how nice it was to actually be able to bury someone properly for once.

I stood by Eleanor under tall trees growing on a slope, holding a pesticide lamp to keep the bugs from biting. Her face was somber as a priest read a Bible passage. Afterward, people threw flowers on the coffin and went home.

By the time we reached the village, a steady sound of chopping echoed from the forest. Several trees had already been cut down.

"We should get to work now," Eleanor said as we walked over the pier. "I'm going to change first."

"Are you going to be all right?" I asked.

She looked over her shoulder without stopping. "Life goes on."

* * *

Days went by and hundreds of planks were made. They were stacked in piles on the beach. When thick posts were ready, it was time to piece the dock together. It was dangerous work at first, with the sharks taking notice of the workers digging holes in the ocean floor for the first four posts. To protect the diggers, the best snipers in the village kept watch. The method was effective. Whenever a shark was killed, the others tore into it, culling their appetite for fresh meat.

When the first four posts were in, the frames were nailed in place, creating a box outline for the planks. At the end of the week, over forty feet of dock had been completed.

Eleanor and I spent most of our time together. It didn't take long for people to notice our affection for each other. Being around her made me content. It forced me to look at the bright side instead of focusing on the negative. I didn't have to pay rent or bills. I didn't have to worry about overcharged accounts or late fees. But those were minor in comparison to what I missed, like my parents, flying, and my friends. Eating normal food, the ocean waves, and blue skies were also on my list, but with Eleanor, it was easier to accept.

At the end of the day, evening began to bleed its mark over the island. The workers retreated back to the safety of the pier before the stingrays crawled in. It had been a long day and all I wanted was some quiet time with Eleanor. On my way to her place, the song *Turn the Page* grabbed my attention.

"You're sounding awesome, Mrs. Jones," I said to the widow, just as she finished strumming her husband's guitar.

"Thank you," she responded softly. "I've had a lot of practice."

"Your husband taught you well," I commented cheerfully.

Her expression was anything but. "Yes, we spent many months working together after his death. At first, it was gratifying. Now I'm an expert and we have nothing more between us. We can't make love or hold a conversation because there isn't much to talk about. He can't join in and share his stories with the others. I can be the medium, but it's much better if he tells them. His only real comfort is speaking to the other dead."

That took me aback, but then I remembered Gavin mentioning something about speaking to other ghosts.

"I've always been the shy one." She placed her instrument down. "Sometimes I see him staring at this guitar with such longing. I know he wants to play it so much it hurts. We thought we wanted to be together forever, even if one of us died, but the mistake was considering how long I have to live. He's not a man. He's just a shade who can do nothing more than linger about."

Her sad brown eyes came up to me. "Don't ever bring a loved one back if they're taken from you, no matter how much you want to."

Her words shattered my good mood, but I never forgot them.

* * *

I exited Eleanor's house carrying two empty wine

glasses and a bottle of Barolo with just enough for the two of us.

"This is quite funny," Eleanor said as I poured her a glass. "This is almost how we spent our first night together, only I was the one who brought out the wine."

I leaned over and gave her a kiss, then sat beside her on the patio chair. I was tired and my joints and muscles ached from working all day. I poured the last drop of wine into the glass and set the bottle on a small table between us. For a while, we said nothing, just sat in complete silence like an old married couple. After taking my first sip, I leaned my head against the chair and closed my eyes. The wine tasted good but I wasn't much of a wine drinker. I missed my favorite beer.

Eleanor said something but my exhausted brain didn't register what it was.

"Heath?"

"Sorry, what did you say?"

"I said I appreciate your help today. You worked hard."

"We both did." I looked at the misty sky for a little while before I laid my head back and closed my eyes again.

It was well into the night when I rolled over and noticed Eleanor wasn't in bed with me. I raised my head to see a single light on the other side of the house. Eleanor was at a table, mumbling to herself. I got out of bed and joined her. When she heard me, she turned in my direction.

"Hey," she said sweetly. "Did I wake you?"

"I heard you talking. You don't secretly have a ghost with you, do you?"

She let out a dry laugh. "No, and I'm not going

173

insane, either. I talk to myself when I'm frustrated."

I looked at the dock's blueprints on the table, drawn on actual blueprint paper. The edges were rough and a bit tattered. "What are you doing?"

"Trying to figure out something."

"Maybe I can help."

"Can you tow four hundred tons of ships to shore?"

I leaned back in my chair and rubbed my chin. I needed a shave. "Sorry, this island seems to be built out of Kryptonite. I'm powerless here."

She gave me a puzzled look.

"Superman," I said just to see if she'd understand.

"Oh, I know what you're talking about now. I've read those comics before. They're very entertaining. And you're being a smartass."

"You haven't figured out how to move the ships in yet? I thought you were working on a plan."

She sighed deeply and it sounded as if her soul escaped through her lips. She buried her face in her hands and set her elbows on the table. "No, I should have been, but I've been distracted by you."

"Don't blame me," I said jokingly.

She raised her head and stared down at the blueprints. "The smaller sailboats should be easy to bring in, but it'll be near impossible to tow in the heavier yachts that are farther off. So many other vessels are in the way. I'm afraid people are going to be disappointed."

Concern masked her sweet face. "Hey," I said warmly, stroking her shoulder. "Don't worry about it. We'll think of something. Maybe we can hold a meeting and solve this problem together. You don't have to do it all on your own."

Her lips rose a bit. She allowed another dry laugh to escape. "You're amazing."

"What do you mean?"

"I mean you've adapted to this place fairly quickly. Most of us live in denial. We want to find a way out. You seem at peace with it."

I thought about that for a minute. "I honestly don't know why that is. Maybe I'm just happy."

Another concerned expression came over her face. Only this time, her uneasiness was for me.

"What?" I asked.

She rose from her seat, rolling the blueprints up as she did. She turned to the work desk behind her and opened the drawer where a six-shooter sat. "It's good you're happy, but don't expect it to carry you through eternity." She closed the drawer.

"Don't you get it?" I said, standing up. "*You're* the reason I'm happy."

I thought that would delight her, but her face paled. I immediately went on the defensive. "Is that what this is? Just some fuck and run?"

"Fuck and run?" she repeated, her sweet southern accent just as beautiful saying the crudest of words. "What are you talking about?"

"Nothing, I'm sorry I said it. But now you got me worried."

"Good, you should always be worried. The longer you stay on your toes, the longer you'll survive. That is, if living is what you want." She leaned toward me and stared me dead in the eyes, her face darkening in the shadows of the candlelight. "In this place, darling, anything can happen, and it's more than you can imagine. Here, nightmares come true."

175

Chapter Seventeen

What Eleanor had said kept me awake the rest of the night. I didn't want to believe bad things could happen to me. No one really did, but it would be naïve to ignore the possibility. Bad things could happen to anyone, at any time, any place, and the Bermuda Triangle was no different.

I went out to the porch to clear my head after she fell asleep and took in a deep breath. The air had become easier to breathe and my chest was no longer tight. I let the air out slowly. Dawn was approaching and I braced myself for another visit from Gavin.

A clear sky stretched overhead as the sun peeked over the horizon. The ships and aircrafts came into view. I'd seen them nearly every morning, but this time I took Gavin's advice and looked beyond them, toward the horizon. Something else was out there, peeking up from the earth. It was too far and hazy for me to distinguish exactly and I wished I had a pair of binoculars. What the hell was it?

"Whatcha lookin' at?" Gavin asked, as if on cue.

I started to turn my head but then kept my attention on the spot. I only caught Gavin's profile from the corner of my eye, but I noticed he'd become less solid and more transparent. When he spoke, his voice sounded hollow, like an echo in the distance. It was working. Gavin was fading away.

I paid him no mind as I tried to distinguish what the dot was, but the fog rolled in, obscuring my view.

"Look, man," Gavin said, "I want to apologize for

what I said to you last week. I wanted you to start talking to me again. What's wrong? Are you mad? Maybe you're upset because you survived the crash and I didn't. We were friends."

Friends? Gavin and I had never been friends. I was just his flight instructor. We'd never even gone out for drinks.

It was strange that he'd refer to himself as my friend. Perhaps he didn't have many and considered anyone who gave him any attention to be his buddy. Yet he hadn't come off that way. He'd never asked me to hang out with him after a lesson and never struck me as being lonely. Alive, he'd been a likeable guy, amusing and fun to talk with—unlike his ghost.

I started to say something, but the words caught in my throat. I retreated back into the house and closed the door, hoping he wouldn't follow me in. I wanted to get some sleep before I had to help with the dock.

* * *

The beach flourished with activity and the air was filled with the sound of hammering. The anglers stood in their usual places, holding their fishing poles, but several others were busy putting together the rest of the dock.

Khenan and I helped put support posts in. It was hard work. Digging in water was as complicated as reciting the Chinese alphabet. Once we had a deep enough hole, we held the post while a couple of guys beat it down with sledgehammers. Every vibration caused my teeth to rattle and I had to trust those banging the top wouldn't miss and bash my head in.

When the posts were set, we screwed the stringers

177

on and with the workers keeping up with nailing in the planks behind us, we completed almost the entire length by late afternoon.

"This outta be done by the end of the week," Carlton told Eleanor as they supervised the work.

"I can't believe it's almost complete."

Carlton turned his massive head to her. "You don't sound excited."

"It's not that. It's just…I still have no idea how to bring the ships in."

"So?"

"So?" she said in surprise. "How are we going to get them to the docks?"

"I dunno, but we've got plenty of time to figure it out yet."

Travis suddenly drew my attention when he said, "Get off it. There ain't no way a doctor can do an operation without cuttin' the poor bloke open."

"It's true," said Sam West, a doctor from Jacksonville, Florida. He helped nail on the decking. "All we do now is drill a couple of holes into the heart and zap, zap, we create new vessels for the blood to flow through."

"Using a tiny instrument?" Travis said in awe.

"Yep."

"Blimey. I know you're a heart doctor but d'you think you could do something about me choppers?"

"I don't know. Let me see."

Travis clenched his teeth, curling his upper lip back and lowering his bottom one. He looked like a snarling dog. West studied his yellow teeth, some of which were missing, then whistled and shook his head. "I'm afraid there isn't much hope for that mess."

Everyone laughed, but Travis wasn't pleased. "It

isn't that bad! Bloody hell, I didn't even start using toothpaste 'til the 1960s. No one in mi day and age had good teeth!"

Khenan and I laughed—until Travis suddenly raised his rifle and shouted, "Incoming, lads!"

I spun my head to see a fin heading for the dock. Travis was one of our sharpshooters and kept his rifle handy in case another shark showed up, even though no one was in the water. He steadied his aim and pulled the trigger. Water sprayed where the bullet hit the ocean, but the shark kept coming.

"Damn!" he swore, ejecting the spent cartridge from the chamber. It fell with a heavy *tink* on the planks as he aimed and squeezed the trigger again. A pool of red swirled in the gray water and the body rose to the surface. "Hoorah! We'll be eatin' shark tonight!"

A minute later, Neal Gibbons called out, "Haven't you guys got that thing built yet?"

"Shit, mon," Khenan groaned, "it be 'is royal 'ighness."

Neal rowed toward us in an orange life raft. This time, he was alone.

"What are you doing here, Gibbons?" Travis asked coldly.

"I want to stake my claim."

"Tought ya were 'appy weh ya were," Khenan said.

Neal stopped near the dead shark. "I decided it would be easier for me if I brought my yacht over so I wouldn't have to use this piece of crap whenever I need something from the island."

"Sorry, lad, but the docks are for those who actually lifted a finger to help," Travis said.

"How about this finger?" Neal said, giving him

the bird.

Travis cocked his head sideways, studying the gesture. "I don't care how small your wanker is, chum. Why doncha stick that back up your arse where it belongs?"

Neal's face turned as red as the blood in the water when everyone laughed. "You know, you can be a real asshole, Travis!"

"Please don't use stupid insults on me. I've got two hundred years of experience on you."

"One day, Travis, I'm gonna—"

"Going to what, Mr. Gibbons?" Eleanor asked from behind us.

"Nothing," he grumbled. "Listen, Eleanor, I want to move my yacht to the end of the dock. That way I can still have privacy. Has anyone claimed it yet?"

"No, but it will be awhile before any ships are pulled in."

He looked confused. "Why's that?"

"We haven't figured out how to do it yet. Large vessels like yours will be more difficult because the keel will tear off if we try to drag it. Then there's the matter of—"

"You don't know how to bring the ships in?" he interrupted with a scowl. "Why are you building this in the first place?"

Her eyes narrowed. "Don't take that tone with me, Mr. Gibbons. We'll find a way to bring nearby boats in, but it'll take time."

"Listen, bitch," he spat, pointing at her. "I'll talk to you in any tone I want. No one tells me what to do."

He acted like the spoiled brat he was—a kid who'd always gotten what he wanted, whenever he wanted. He'd obviously never been taught the value of respect.

I jumped into the water and started toward his raft.

"Get away from me, Indian man!"

He raised an oar to swing, but I caught it and jerked it out of his hand, then punched him in the face. Travis laughed hysterically as I threw the oar back into the raft and growled, "Don't you ever talk to her that way, you little bitch."

Neal's face was drenched in tears and blood. I doubted he could see anything, but he could hear me. I waded back to the beach, raising my chin to Eleanor, expecting a look of disgust, but she smiled.

"You bastard!" Neal screamed. "You didn't have to break my nose!"

"I think you outta go now," Carlton said. "You're no longer welcome here."

"To hell with you, old man. To hell with all of you!" he cried as he picked up the oar and rowed away.

Travis shouted, "Incoming!" He raised his rifle, aimed in Neal's direction, and fired. A hole appeared in the raft and air wheezed from it. Neal scrambled to escape the deflating raft. As he leapt onto a plane's wing, Travis cried, "Hoorah!"

The entire dock burst into applause as Neal screamed from the wing, "You're all a bunch of assholes! There's gonna be payback for this!"

As Neal slowly went into the water to wade back to his yacht, Carlton said, "With this kind of entertainment, I need to get out of the house more."

* * *

That night, the villagers gathered to come up with a solution for bringing the ships to port. Some suggested a pulley system, while others recommended alternate ideas. The debate went on until everyone grew tired and left, leaving nothing solid established.

Eleanor was upset with the lack of results. I tried to comfort her as we lay in bed. "It'll take some time, but we'll figure it out."

"I know," she said, stroking my chest. "In a way, I'm glad we haven't come up with anything. It'll let the older folks feel useful again, offering ideas."

I caught something in her statement. "You planned it this way, didn't you?"

She rose a bit. "What do you mean?"

"This—the docks, the ships—it's all going exactly how you want it to go. You want something for people to do, so you came up with the dock idea."

There was a long silence, then she smiled coyly and slapped me playfully on the chest. "You know something, Mr. Sharp? You're a very perceptive man."

I snorted. "Why were you keeping it a secret?"

"I didn't want anyone to think they were being pitied. I wanted to find something to occupy their minds. A lot of people suffer from depression after being here for a while and having nothing useful to do. Many have committed suicide as a means of escape."

"If that's true, where are all the bodies?"

"Some went out to sea, like seagulls do when it's their time to die. Some go into the forest, and others just dug their own graves and laid in them before turning a gun on themselves." She took a breath. "Most try one final escape attempt. It's a joke that when someone goes missing, there's no point looking for them because they're probably already dead."

"That's crazy. I hope I never get like that."

"Me too."

I kissed her gently. "You're really something, the way you watch over people around here. That's awesome, especially when they don't even know you're doing it. You're as clever as you are beautiful."

She kissed me again. I looked deep into her eyes and said, "I love you."

She ran her hand through my hair and whispered, "I love you too."

Chapter Eighteen

It was afternoon when Eleanor and I went back out to assist with the docks. Nearly three dozen trees had been cut down and only a handful more were needed. We'd hardly made a dent in the dense forest.

I'd gone into the forest with the other lumberjacks to cut the last of the trees for the boardwalk. After chopping for a good half hour, I really began to miss gas-powered tools.

"Excuse me, sir," a man said as he came up the hillside. "I'm looking for a Mr. Heath Sharp. Would that be you?"

His appearance was peculiar, dressed as he was in a long-sleeved shirt, vest, pinstriped trousers, and narrow-toed shoes. He looked like he'd just walked off an old southern plantation.

"Yeah," I answered between pants.

"Um," the man said, nearly slipping on the steep incline. His shoes weren't right for the terrain. He stopped and swiped sweaty hair from his blue eyes. "So, you're the new beau, eh? I just wanted to congratulate you, man to man."

"Who the hell are you?"

"Just a friend. Good day."

He turned and hurried down the hillside, onto the beach.

"Well, well," Travis said, walking toward me. "Look who it is."

"It's Darwin, isn't it?" I said.

"Aye. Come to see Eleanor, no doubt. What did

184

he say?"

The acid in my gut bubbled with concern. "How the hell did he know my name?"

"We'll investigate that together," Travis said as he followed me down the slope.

On the beach, Eleanor stripped bark off a long tree trunk. When she looked up to wipe the sweat from her brow, she saw Darwin approaching—and she wasn't pleased.

I felt a little like the insecure boyfriend spying on them, but I decided to stay out of the way. Travis and I hid behind a support beam under Miller's Tavern to watch.

"What are you doing here, Darwin?" Eleanor asked hotly.

"Ah, Miss Houghton," Darwin said with a formal bow, "it's a pleasure to see you again."

"What do you want?" she snapped, folding her arms. "I'm very busy and I have no time for foolishness."

Darwin rose to his full height and said nothing for a moment. Then, "You are looking well, my dear."

"And you," she said lethargically. "Now enough with the pleasantries, you've yet to indulge me with an answer."

"I have come to say farewell, my darling. I am leaving."

"Leaving?" she asked in confusion. "Did you find a way out? Are you going to try for the boundaries again?"

"No," he said somberly. "But I am leaving, nonetheless. I just wanted to say goodbye to the loveliest person who ever came into my life."

I rolled my eyes at his line.

185

"Goodbye, my dear." He turned on his heel and walked away.

She ran after him. "Darwin, wait. Please."

"Let him go," I murmured.

As she ran to him, he smiled. But that quickly disappeared when he turned to face her.

"What are you talking about?" she asked with concern. "You're not saying what I think you're saying, are you?"

He turned his face away, hiding it from her. But I was in a position to see another sly grin.

"I don't like the looks of this," Travis said next to me.

Darwin faced Eleanor with a somber expression. "I cannot live like this any longer. Even if I could escape this God forsaken place, the world outside is not my world anymore. I wouldn't be happy in it, any more than I am here."

Judging by her wide expression and sharp gasp, she caught his meaning. "Before you do anything rash, let's go to my place and talk."

Darwin said nothing, only followed her to the pier. A sick feeling boiled inside my stomach. "Travis, distract them for a while, 'kay?"

"Oi, no problem, mate."

As Travis ran off, I rushed from under the pier and headed for the steps. By the time Eleanor and Darwin entered the house, I was already there.

"Honestly, I don't know what's gotten into Travis," Eleanor said as they stepped onto the porch. "He's been obsessing about his teeth lately." They went into the house, where I awaited.

"Oh, Heath," she said with a start. "I thought you were cutting trees."

186

"I just came to use your first aid kit. I accidentally cut myself," I lied. I showed her a small gash I'd made on my hand.

She rushed to me. "Oh, you poor thing, let me have a look." She took my hand and studied it. "The wound isn't deep but it'll take a very long time to heal. Heath, you have to be more careful."

"What are you talking about?"

"Wounds have to age in order to heal," she explained. "And since we don't age, neither do our injuries."

Shit! I thought. *I wish someone had told me that before I'd cut myself. I would've used another excuse to get into the house.*

"Wrap your hand and I'll get you something to put on it in a little while," she said. "It's a salve that comes from the island and will help."

I smiled at her. "Thanks." I caught a snarl on Darwin's face. "What's up, Darwin?"

"You two know each other?" Eleanor inquired.

"We met briefly," Darwin replied. "I should be going. I see you're busy."

"Bye," I said.

"No, wait," Eleanor pleaded. "Don't go."

The alcohol I used to clean my injury no longer burned after she beckoned him back. She turned to me and pleaded with her eyes for me to leave.

"I'll be out on the porch," I said, picking up the first aid kit. I went outside and sat on the chair closest to the door, which I left partially open. I had no intention of leaving her alone with him.

"Would you like something to drink?" Eleanor asked Darwin.

"No, thank you, I'm fine."

187

I peeked in to see what they did. Eleanor poured water into a ceramic mug.

"I remember that mug," Darwin said.

"It's a different one. You hated the other one, along with most of the china my mother gave me," she spoke harshly, no doubt feeling the anger toward his oppressive ways.

"Yes, your mother," he said slowly. "At least here I'm granted the small favor of never having to see *that* woman again. Honestly, I can't believe this is the kind of person you've become. Living with people God himself wouldn't spit on. Interacting with a man outside your race and wearing such revealing clothing."

I now understood why she'd once been on the brink of killing herself.

"Let's be civil," she said in return.

I finished wrapping my wound and listened intently.

"I am civil. It's you who's become an animal."

"Are you really planning on killing yourself?" she asked bluntly. "Have you finally become so disgusted with yourself that you feel the need to end your life?"

I smiled at her boldness.

"The way you speak to me crosses many lines," he returned. "Just look at how you hold yourself."

I peered through the window again. Eleanor leaned against the counter, her arms folded over her chest. Not a big deal in my book, but I guess Darwin didn't view her as being ladylike.

"You look like a whore on a street corner waiting for her next John to lift her skirt."

I was about to go in and stop his verbal bashing when she yelled, "Answer my question!"

"Yes, I've decided to take my life," he said, approaching her. "Life means nothing to me now." He turned his back on her and poured himself a glass of water. "I heard you were in love."

"Who told you that?"

"It doesn't matter," he said, bowing his head. He sank his hand into his pocket. "Is it true?"

"Yes, it's true. And we've slept together, if that's your next question."

"I must confess, although I no longer wish to live, I want nothing more than to be with you."

His dark tone turned my blood to ice water. He took something out of his pocket and placed it on the counter top. I didn't catch what it was as I reached for the door.

"I'd hoped we could talk like human beings," she said, "but I was wrong. I think you should go now. Go back to your village and do your best to stay afloat."

"Stay afloat?" he said, his voice growing louder. "I'm drowning! All I wanted was a respectable life with you, and you had to leave me!"

When I entered the house, he turned on me. I didn't expect him to charge me like he did, but I suspect he'd spoken the way he had just so he could lure me back in. I raised my fists for a bare-knuckle fight, but he pulled a knife from his other pocket.

"Get away from him!" Eleanor shouted as Darwin and I fell onto the back porch.

"I'll cut your eyes out," he cursed, putting the tip of the blade to my face.

I held his wrist, trying to push the knife away, but for a short man, he had power behind him, backed by anger. Blood seeped through the gauze on my hand and slid down my arm. Sharp, hot pain bolted through

189

my forearm. It weakened me as the blade sank into my cheekbone. I screamed so loud I felt the vibrations in my chest.

"Get off him!" Eleanor demanded from inside the house.

Blood spurted from the side of Darwin's head as a shot rang out. He fell on top of me and I pushed him off.

Eleanor was quiet. The smoke from the flintlock pistol she held hovered around her in a hazy whiteness. The smell of gunpowder was overwhelming.

"Oh, no," she said, dropping the weapon.

I got to my feet when I noticed what she'd done. "Eleanor," I said in a whisper.

She looked up at me with teary eyes. "Quick, help me get rid of it," she said in a panic.

"Get rid of what?"

She went to Darwin's feet and lifted them. "Hurry, before he comes. Out of sight, out of mind, right?"

I knew what she meant but I didn't see how hiding the body would help.

"It just happened," she said timidly. "Maybe if we get rid of the body, he won't be able to come back."

She wasn't making sense. Shock and panic screwed up her thinking. But I was in just as much shock and almost agreed with her so-called logic.

Before I could help lug the body out, she dropped Darwin's feet. "No, we won't be together forever. Leave me alone!"

"Eleanor?"

She started pacing with her hands over her ears. "Stop it! Shut up! Leave me alone!"

Darwin's spirit was with her. I could only imagine what he was doing to her.

"Heath," she said, her face soaked with tears. "Help me, he's here."

I approached her when she screamed, "No!" She retreated from me. "Stop it, please. I never wanted to spend my life with you!"

"What's going on?" Travis asked, running into the house. "We heard a gunshot."

"She was protecting me," I said, pointing to the body.

"Bloody hell," he said. He took a step toward Eleanor. "Ellie, darling, it's all right, love. It's me, Travis. Everything is going to be fine."

"He keeps saying I belong to him and that I won't be able to get away from him now. Tell him to stop! Tell him to go away!"

"Ignore him," Travis said. "He has no power over you."

Her eyes turned in my direction but she wasn't staring at me. She was staring at the spirit of her ex when she said angrily, "Leave me be, Darwin. There's nothing left between us."

"Eleanor, I'm here," I said soothingly. "He can't drive me away. We'll get through this together."

I approached her again to take her into my arms. She stepped forward, shaking, wanting so badly to fall into my embrace. Then she covered her ears and shouted at the top of her lungs, "Shut up! You bastard, you planned this, didn't you?"

The pieces came together then. Darwin had somehow found out about us and come here to force her to do him in so his soul would attach itself to her. Even if I hadn't been here, he would have somehow

191

provoked her to use the pistol he'd placed on the counter top.

Eleanor began hyperventilating.

"Jesus, what's he saying to you?" Travis said.

"He says as long as I'm alive, we'll always be together," she said somberly.

I took hold of her and whispered, "It's going to be all right. Whatever we have to do to get through this, we'll do it. You won't be alone in this."

"There's nothing you can do to help me," she said. "Things will only get worse as long as he's around." She shut her eyes tightly before more tears slid down her face. "His words hurt so much. He won't ever leave me in peace."

She fell on my chest and I held her. Her body trembled against me for a long while, jolting once or twice. I imagined what that bastard said to her. Then she relaxed and said softly, "He's gone."

"What?" Travis asked. "He's gone?"

She pried herself away from me, looking up to meet my gaze. "I don't hear him anymore."

"He left?" I asked.

She took a quick look around. "It appears so." Then she gave me a long passionate kiss that made every nerve in my body tingle.

"Huh," Travis said. "Maybe he just vanished for a bit. They do that when they want to. He's still around but not seen."

"Perhaps," she said as she withdrew from me and walked away. "Maybe it is only temporary, but it'll give me time to think."

I was such a fool. I didn't realize she was lying until she reached into her desk drawer. "Eleanor! No!"

She pulled out her six-shooter pistol, put it to her

temple, and pulled the trigger.

Chapter Nineteen

The nearby window shattered when the bullet passed through it. Blood sprayed the wall and glass.

I blinked once before Eleanor fell, it happened that fast. One second, she stood; then *blink,* she was on the floor. Her body hit hard, the gun clanking on the wood, her hand wrapped around the butt. I stood frozen a moment before rushing toward her.

"No, lad," Travis said, holding me back. "Don't touch her!"

People who'd heard the shots stood on the front porch, looking in. Travis was able to hold me back despite his diminutive stature. His military training kept me in place but his hold was slipping.

"I need some help in here," he called to the people outside.

"Eleanor!" I shouted after I found my voice.

"Get him out of here!"

I reached for her as more hands grabbed and pulled me away. My natural reaction, my basic instinct, was to hold her. In my desperate state of mind, she wasn't really dead, only hurt and needed help. After all, she'd been alive just seconds ago.

"Let go of me, damn it!" I shouted. "Eleanor!"

"She's gone," Travis said calmly.

His soothing tone helped me realize the bitter truth without throwing me into a raging fit. Even so, I wanted to hold her. A part of me hopefully, foolishly, thought she wasn't gone yet, and if I could just cradle her in my arms, she could die peacefully. But I couldn't reach her, not with people dragging me out the door.

After I was across the threshold, she was no longer in view, and they took me home. By that time, I was calm and in zombie mode.

"Wah 'appened?" Khenan asked, entering the hut.

Travis pulled him aside and whispered, "Bad news, mate. Eleanor is dead."

"Dead?"

Travis looked back as the others let me go. "Darwin came by. Things got out of hand and she shot the bugger, then killed herself."

Free from their grasp, I slowly walked out to the back porch.

"We 'ave to keep 'im away from da body," Khenan whispered. "He may wanna try burying her or someting."

"I know. We'll stand by. When he clears his head, we'll have a chat with him."

I was on lockdown. I stared at the odd plants growing from the stone wall directly in front of me. Travis and Khenan talked behind me but they sounded distant. I gripped the railing with one hand and pressed the other against my face as I wept.

"Let's go," Travis whispered. "Give him some space, eh?"

They left, gently shutting the door after them.

By the time they returned, I was sitting out front, my eyes dry from crying.

"How are you feeling?" Travis asked.

"I want to see her," I said.

They looked at each other apprehensively. Travis nodded and said, "All right, mate, we'll take you back. But, remember, you can't touch the body."

195

"I understand."

"First, let's treat that cut of yours." Travis whittled a vine out of its dark green skin, down to a neon green inside. He mashed it in a bowl, then squashed a handful of seeds in before mixing it all together. When he applied this mixture to my cut, it stung, then tingled. This must be the salve Eleanor had told me about.

"This will keep the infection away and numb the pain," he explained. "If you use it every day, the wound will begin to heal itself."

At Eleanor's, we found Neal standing in the hut, looking dirty and worn, as if he'd just fought his way out of the Amazon jungle. He had dark circles under his eyes from the broken nose I'd given him. He said nothing and left.

A short time later, Carlton came in and walked past me, looking paler than usual. He didn't acknowledge my presence at first, until I noticed Darwin's corpse was gone.

I didn't ask where his spirit had gone without a host. I didn't care. Nor did I care about what they did to his corpse. It was no more than a piece of trash to me.

I wanted time alone with Eleanor and asked everyone to leave. As evening came, I lit the star lamp and placed it on the floor near her body.

I couldn't take my eyes off her. She was lying on her side, her head to the left. The entrance wound on her right temple was large enough to fit a finger through, where just a sliver of blood had trailed out. The exit wound was much gorier. A pool of red surrounded her head, as if it rested on a crimson pillow. Her blonde hair was matted with it and the gun was still in her hand.

After some time, Travis and Khenan returned. Travis said, "I know you're dying to do it, but you can't touch her, lad."

"Go away."

"Sorry, we can't do that. At least, not until we've cleared up a few things."

"Like what?"

"Like if you're planning to draw Eleanor's spirit to you, you need to consider what you might be taking from her."

"What do you mean?"

"I'm talking about peace," he said. "She loved this place and now she's bound to it."

"And?" I asked, needing more of an explanation.

"Don't bring 'er back, mon," Khenan said. "If you draw 'er to you, she'll have more limitations den before."

"You two would never be apart," Travis said. "Which might sound grand to you right now, but think about it from her point of view. Wherever you go, she'd have to go with you. The two of you could never interact on the same level again and that would be torture for you both. She'd just be *there*."

It hurt to admit it, but what they said made sense. I remembered Mrs. Jones, who'd buried her husband. She'd said he was just a shade, not a man, and no matter how much he wanted to play his guitar, he couldn't. It was bad enough to be stuck on the island, but not to be able to do the things that gave you pleasure would be infinitely worse.

How could I adjust to never having any physical contact with her? What about personal space? Even couples who are in love need their time alone. Would she and I stay in love if we couldn't touch each other or have time apart? Not likely. Our relationship would eventually turn bitter—an eternal hell for both of us.

"What if it's not like that," I challenged. "What if we could make it work?"

"It's possible," Travis said half-heartedly. "But is that a chance you want to take?"

I turned back to Eleanor. My head was so clouded with grief it kept reasoning at bay. I didn't care about the repercussions my actions would cause as long as I had her with me.

Someone had to talk sense into me. With Travis and Khenan's help, my head cleared a little, forcing me to think twice about what I was close to doing. Perhaps I'd been waiting for clarity all along and didn't know it. Otherwise, I would've already moved her.

I remembered what they'd said about suicides, that the departed were stuck with their bodies. Eleanor might not be able to wander far, but at least she could go about on her own. Having her with me might be like having a second chance, but it would never be the same.

"I won't do anything," I promised. "I just want some time alone with her."

Both Travis and Khenan exchanged glances and nodded.

"All right, lad," Travis said, patting me on the shoulder. "We'll be down at Miller's Tavern if you need us."

"Thanks."

They left me alone in the house. I sat with Eleanor for a long time and wanted so much to stroke her hair, despite the blood soaked in it. But I couldn't. I knew I couldn't. It wouldn't be fair to either of us.

We could no longer feel each other's skin or smell each other's scents. We could walk together, talk for hours, but soon that wouldn't be enough. Our conversations would dry out.

Immortality is a bitch. I thought.

The clouds in my head dispersed and I finally came to terms with where things stood. Eleanor was dead and that was the end of it. I had to treat it as if I'd lost her and didn't have the choice to share her company. That was the real hell of it. It seemed like a test of willpower, saying a final goodbye and meaning it.

* * *

I couldn't sleep that night. Every time I closed my eyes, the vision of her blowing her brains out replayed in my mind. When it had happened, it had taken a split-second and was done. Now that my memory had time to process it, the act played out more slowly, revealing every gruesome detail.

I stayed on her front porch, staring into the dark. It was so quiet out here. The fireflies did their usual dance. I sat there in complete silence for hours until the morning light crept over the heavens, while the darkness made way for blue skies. When everything became visible, I saw the strange formation sitting on the hazy line of the horizon again. It was the same thing I'd seen the week before. There was something in the far distance, just naked to the eye, but I couldn't identify it. I kept my eyes on it, leaning over the railing, trying to distinguish exactly what it was.

"So, she's dead, huh?" Gavin said.

I turned to the vague outline of him. He'd nearly

faded into oblivion, along with his voice, which sounded far off. I was nearly rid of him for good.

"It's a shame. She was the only thing that made you happy. She made you forget about your plans to escape."

I turned my head to watch the sky turn cobalt.

"Now that she's gone, there's no reason for you to stay. Nothing to distract you from your original goal of getting out of here. But there's that little thing about dying to consider." He turned to the ocean and rubbed his chin in deep thought. "If only there was some way you could leave without worrying about gettin' yourself killed." He snapped his fingers. "Ha! I know. I've known it all along. Eh...since my death, that is."

My expression was level. I thought, *fuck it.* "How?" I asked.

Chapter Twenty

On the day of her funeral, Eleanor's front deck was completely covered in flowers. The attendees closest to her stood around her body, listening to a priest read the same Bible verse he'd read at Inglewood's funeral. She remained exactly where she'd fallen, a halo of dried blood still around her head, the gun clutched in her hand. Her body would stay in that position forever, like the statue of a fallen empress, and unless disturbed, it would never decay. The blush of her cheeks would never fade.

I felt so numb I could have lain on a bed of nails with a sixty-pound cinder block on my chest and not felt a thing. The priest's words never seeped into my thoughts. Though I hardly blinked while I stared at Eleanor's body, I didn't see her. My conversation with Gavin and the agreement we'd made ran through my mind as the priest rambled on.

* * *

It was like I'd given life back to him when Gavin had my attention. He'd materialized into solid form, like an image developing on an old Polaroid picture. Once he became whole, he stretched his limbs as if he'd been cooped up in a box all that time.

"Ah, that's better," he'd said in a strong and clear voice.

"I want to bring the others with me."

"Oh, you wanna get them out too? I don't care.

201

Take 'em all outta here."

"How?"

"Before I tell you, you have to do something."

"I'll do anything," I'd said grimly. "But how do I know you won't double-cross me?"

"You have my word. I've been here long enough. I'm ready to move on to whatever else is out there. And I know you are too."

I'd nodded. I'd lost Eleanor. Without her, there was no reason for me to stay. Like a lion in a cage, I wanted to return to the wide open plains where I could run free. Or die trying.

"So, do we have a deal?" Gavin had asked.

"Yeah, what do you want done?"

"Burn my body. Drag it back to shore and bury it. Shoot it into space, it doesn't matter. Just take care of it."

I'd turned toward the ocean with a sigh. "All right, I'll do it. Just leave me alone in the meantime."

It was a desperate act and I knew it. I couldn't be sure Gavin would keep his word and reveal the escape route that only the dead knew about, but I wanted out one way or another.

* * *

I hardly noticed the service had ended. Everyone brave enough to look at Eleanor's body walked by to pay their respects. Afterward, people boarded up the windows and doors and enclosed her in the hut like a tomb.

Travis, Khenan, and I went to Miller's Tavern, where I got shitfaced and later crashed at Travis's place. I didn't want to think. If I could've drunk myself into a state of total oblivion, I'd have done it. Instead, I had to settle for temporary memory loss. The hangover hurt like hell the following day.

No one seemed to care about the docks anymore. It was as if their interest to build them had died with Eleanor. Nothing was done about the logs lying on the beach. They didn't affect the fishermen's daily routine.

Travis, Paddy, Khenan, and I were amusing ourselves with a game of poker in front of Travis' hut when Travis said, "Carlton told me we're gonna get back to work on the docks in a couple of days."

"Good," Khenan said. "I'm ready to do someting constructive. 'ow 'bout you, Heat?"

"What?" I said, barely paying attention. "Yeah, sure, definitely."

When Paddy tossed two hundred American dollars and six British pounds on the table, Travis said, "Are you aware of how much loot you're bettin', mate? The max is twenty."

"So?" the Irishman said with a shrug. "Who gives a toss? It ain't like I'm gonna be buyin' meself a mansion anytime soon."

"Hmm…I suppose you've got a point. I'll raise you."

I folded.

"Call," Khenan said.

Travis laid his hand on the table: a pair of deuces, a three, a queen, and a ten.

"Shit, mon, you shoulda folded," Khenan chortled.

"I was never one to back down."

"A pair of aces," Paddy announced.

"Not enough, mon," Khenan said happily, laying down his cards. "Straight flush."

"Damn it!" Paddy cursed. "Now I'll never get that Mercedes Benz."

Khenan pulled his winnings toward him while Travis collected the cards to reshuffle. His eyes caught something behind me and hiked up. "Bloody hell, is that Sandy?"

I twisted around to see a woman coming up the beach toward us.

"Yep," Khenan said. "Wonder what she's doing 'ere wit'out Neal. She's never come 'ere alone before."

As Sandy reached the stairs, I noticed marks on her face.

"Stepping out of your castle to mingle with the common folk, milady?" Travis said sarcastically.

Sandy approached our table. She wore navy blue sweatpants, a gray T-shirt with a faded Care Bear on the front, sand-covered sneakers, and dark sunglasses.

"You awright?" Khenan asked.

"I . . ." she began, then hesitated. "I have to tell you something. It's about Neal." She removed her sunglasses to reveal a swollen eye. "He's, like, done some bad things."

According to Sandy, after his humiliation at the docks, Neal had gone back to his yacht and taken his anger out on her. The next day, he'd left until nightfall. When he returned, he'd told her that he'd gone to the Obsoletes' village and told Darwin about Eleanor and me to provoke him into coming to North Village.

My face flushed with anger, but it was Travis who asked, "Are you sure about that, lass?"

"Like, yeah," she said in her usual ditzy verbiage. "I've had it with Neal hitting me whenever he gets pissed off."

We went to Carlton and had Sandy repeat her story. When she finished, Carlton said angrily, "Gentlemen, I think we need to pay Neal a visit."

Neal lay on his bed reading a magazine when I pushed the door to his bedroom open.

"What the hell are you doing on my boat?" he demanded before I yanked him off the mattress and hurled him to the floor.

"We just found out what you did, you son of a bitch!" I bellowed, scarcely able to control the urge to kill him with my bare hands.

As Neal staggered to his feet, he stammered, "Wh-what are you talking about? I didn't do anything."

The fact that he denied his actions pushed me over the edge. I grabbed him again and smashed my fist into his face. He started to go down, but I caught him and wrenched his head up to punch him again. "You sent that bastard to start trouble between me and Eleanor!"

Even over my yelling I heard the crack of cartilage.

I didn't wait for a response before I hit him again. If Paddy, Travis, and Khenan hadn't pulled me off, I would've killed him.

"Don't punch 'is freakin' face in, mon!" Khenan yelled, holding my arms tightly.

"That's right," Carlton said from the doorway. "He needs to be tried."

Spitting blood from his mouth, Neal staggered to his feet, but fell due to his injuries. "That's bullshit! I've been on my yacht the whole time!"

"Except when I saw you shortly after Eleanor

killed herself," Carlton accused. "I'm guessing you were returning from the Obsoletes' village. You looked like shit and we all know you're too vain to let yourself go about like that."

Neal narrowed his eyes at Carlton. "You have no proof, old man."

"We have a witness," Carlton returned. "Your other victim."

"What other victim?"

"Beating up women is a criminal offence around here," Carlton said darkly. "I hereby sentence you to the *Southern Districts.*"

"Wait!" Neal said defensively, "you said I was going to have a trial."

"You just did, my boy."

My eyes traveled over everyone. It was a law that a person would be tried before he could be sent to the *Southern Districts*. But in this case, no one would miss a snotty little bastard like Neal. We handcuffed and placed him in a sturdy rowboat.

Khenan and Paddy rowed while Travis sat with a rifle. Carlton was in the back and Neal sat in the middle, pleading for mercy. They didn't let me carry a gun. I assume they were afraid I'd do something stupid.

"Look, I was pissed, okay?" Neal said pitifully. "You can't condemn a guy for anger issues."

"You should've thought about that before you acted," Carlton replied.

Carlton had escorted murders, rapists, and the insane out to the *Southern Districts* for many years since becoming the top dog in law and order here. He said he felt like the Ferryman, carrying the departed souls to the Underworld. No one was ever allowed to leave the prison ship. Many committed suicide there, leaving bodies strewn about the deck that could never be touched. People who'd slipped into insanity were locked away in the brig by other prisoners.

The fog was light and I could easily see the massive ship. It leaned against the belly of a capsized vessel, the *Cotopaxi*. Its nearly upright position was one of the reasons why it had been chosen as a prison. She was secluded from other wreckage, with sharks infesting the area, which kept prisoners from venturing into the water. Ever since the ship had been gutted and converted into a holding facility for criminals in 1962, no one had ever escaped.

When Neal saw it, he cringed and began babbling. "Look, I'll do community service. I'll be a goddamn slave. I'll do anything, just don't send me there!"

I hoped Carlton wouldn't give in to his pleading. I never wanted to see Neal again. I might kill him, and then he'd haunt me forever.

"You know, that might not be a bad idea," Carlton said, scratching his chin. "Humility would do someone like you good. Unfortunately, sending you here wasn't our idea. It was Sandy's."

Neal's eyes widened. "What?"

"That's right. Since you beat her up, we let her decide what to do with you. So, here we are."

There was a long silence, then Neal asked hopefully, "How long will I have to stay?"

"Forever," I said, as if the question had been directed at me.

He turned my way, and I thought he might say something, but he kept quiet. As we neared the ship, prisoners began to call to us.

207

"Come one, come all! The angels listen but it's the devil who calls!"

Inmates gathered at the railing, at least six dozen of them. More faces peered through porthole windows on the lower decks. The sheer terror on Neal's face gave me some silent satisfaction.

The boat finally stopped and the prisoners began chanting, "Jump! Jump! Jump!"

Neal seemed confused and turned to Carlton. "What's going on?"

"You have to swim from here on," Carlton said.

His eyes widened. "Swim? Why can't you just take me there?"

"If we get too close, the prisoners might attack," Carlton explained.

"But what about the sharks?" Neal asked, his voice rising. "They could get me!"

"They might," Carlton said with no trace of emotion. "I suppose you should start praying that Mr. Livingston can shoot them first." His eyes grew cold and hard when he added, "It's time to go."

"I won't jump," Neal said defiantly.

"The hell you won't," I said, rising to my feet.

My move seemed to make Neal a little more compliant. After a long silence, Carlton said, "We can wait out here all day, lad. Trust me, I've done it before."

I made a mental note to ask Carlton why he used British jargon every now and then. In the meantime, he removed the handcuffs from Neal's wrists. Travis pointed to a steel ladder running up the keel of the *Southern Districts*. There was a second ladder welded onto the first one to extend its length. "You see that ladder?"

Neal nodded.

"Good, that's where you want to go. Now get started, mate."

Neal stepped to the edge of the boat as the prisoners chanted even louder. I wished I'd been appointed sharpshooter.

The sharks proved to be impatient. One rammed the boat, forcing Neal to topple into the water. I was afraid he'd try pulling himself back in, but he resurfaced and swam toward the ship.

The swim was a little more than twenty feet to the ladder. The chanting stopped and the world became quiet except for the splashing of arms and legs. A minute later, several fins cut quickly through the water in his direction. The prisoners cheered excitedly.

"Mr. Livingston," Carlton said mildly, "show us your talent."

Travis aimed his rifle and took a few shots at the sharks. For his sake, I hoped he didn't hit Neal.

"Feast! Feast! Feast!" the prisoners shouted.

Neal made two or three more desperate strokes before he disappeared underwater. A second later, he came to the surface, screaming, "They're pulling me down! Help me!"

Khenan and Paddy maneuvered the boat to give Travis a clear shot as Neal continued to scream. But as Travis raised his rifle, Neal vanished again.

"Bloody hell, where did he go?" Travis cursed, still looking down the barrel of his weapon.

Neal resurfaced, but not in the same spot. Blood swirled in the water around him. Shortly thereafter, he was sucked into the murky soup, which churned into a froth by the frenzied sharks.

The water finally calmed as the sharks swam

away, leaving only a dark pool of blood and chunks of flesh floating on the surface. The prisoners cheered.

"Damn," Travis said with an unaffected sniff. "I suppose that's a shame."

Chapter Twenty-one

Twilight loomed when I left North Village, forgetting all about the dangers lurking on the beach after dark. If anyone was in the jail, they said nothing as I passed it. I tried not to think too much about what I was about to do. If I did, I'd probably turn back.

Grief tore into my heart. Even after witnessing Neal's death, I could feel the heavy weight of sadness pressing down on me. With my thoughts on other things, I didn't notice what slid out of the sea until I heard an eerie noise.

I stopped abruptly and looked toward the water. The sound occurred again, a low steady hum that rose in pitch and then descended. A minute later, something moved beneath the sand. I raised my lantern and spotted two slender columns rising in front of me, topped by marble-size eyeballs. The stingray hummed louder than before, alerting others to my presence.

"Shit!"

I bolted toward the forest as mounds of sand charged after me, accompanied by vibrating calls. A stingray reached my heels, trying to snare my ankle with its long tail it used like a bullwhip. I leapt to keep from getting stung. If the creatures brought me down, I'd face a merciless end.

A long mound raced alongside me, trying to cut me off. As its tail sprang from the ground, I had only a split-second to react. I swung my lantern in its direction. The arrowhead stinger crashed the glass box and sliced into the fuel reservoir. I dropped the lantern

211

and it instantly ignited into a fireball.

A sharp scream came from behind me but I didn't look back. I spotted a cluster of boulders ahead and leapt onto them, clambering to the top. Only then did I look down as the sand roiled in the glow of the fire. Long tendrils rose from the beach with eerily glowing eyes glistening in the light as they moved.

I crouched and swung my backpack around to pull out a small torch. Breathing heavily, I lit it to watch as the creatures retreated back toward the ocean.

"Now what?"

My goal had been to reach the area where Lafitte had left his planks, but I was only halfway there. It appeared I wouldn't be able to reach it until morning. I contemplated taking my chances but decided it would be best to stay put. There was no real hurry and I had only a vague idea of the dangers lurking in the forest after dark. My business at sea could wait one more night, even if it meant sleeping on jagged rocks.

To avoid drawing attention to myself, I snuffed out the torch and concentrated on trying to get comfortable.

Morning light filtered brightly through my eyelids and I squinted as I opened them. A snake-like hissing blew into my left ear, and when I turned, the eye of a stingray stared back at me. I thought I was a goner, until the eye splattered, spraying ocular fluid all over my face.

I sat up and wiped it off, while Bongo, the leader of the Shark Hunters, popped the eyeball into her mouth. She aimed her red eyes at me, hissing and clicking as I slowly leaned back, hoping she wouldn't attack me next with her sharp beak.

"Hey, girl," I said as calmly as I could.

I backed away as her beady eyes fastened on me. The pelican-sized bird looked even more intimidating up close. She ruffled her black feathers and spread her wide wings. Hundreds of teeth were lined in three rows inside her beak, with pieces of meat wedged between them. Her spotted tongue looked like a thin strip of pink modeling clay and her breath reeked.

To my relief, she rose into the air, her wings snapping like a wet towel. The breeze they created brushed against me. She landed amid the rest of her flock on shore, which was gathered around something.

I climbed down from my perch and slipped quietly away, moving from whatever the Shark Hunters devoured. But curiosity drove me to at least look and I saw what they ate between their feathered bodies—the stingray that had driven the end of its tail into my lantern.

I hurried along the shoreline as the fog swept overhead, making my way across the ocean to the planks, heading for the boundaries. It seemed easier than before, since I knew what to expect and how to adjust to the unbalanced junkyard. It also helped that it didn't rain, giving me relatively dry surfaces to walk on. I'd borrowed a life raft from a resident in the village, which I carried in my backpack. When the wreckage thinned, I inflated it and paddled the rest of the way out, hoping a shark didn't tear it.

At my plane, I climbed inside and made my way to where Gavin's body sat, exactly as it had when we'd crashed weeks ago. The stench of urine was less intense but still pretty potent. I clasped him on the shoulder, no longer afraid to touch him, and said, "Okay, Gavin, I'll set you free, in exchange for your doing the same for me."

213

I'd brought a container of lighter fluid, which I used to drench the interior of the plane. My original plan was to load his body into a wooden longboat, set it on fire, and push it adrift, but since *Gypsy Girl* would never soar among the clouds again, I decided to put her out of her misery, as well.

When I'd first planned my escape, I'd thought about returning later to reclaim *Gypsy Girl* and restore her to working condition. But coming back to the Atlantic Pyramid for the others would be hazardous enough. To risk my life for a plane would be ludicrous, even a plane as precious as *Gypsy Girl*.

I squeezed out most of the lighter fluid, then stepped out onto the plane's wing. I gingerly settled back into the life raft, where I reached into my backpack and pulled out an empty glass bottle and a piece of cloth. I poured the last of the lighter fluid into the bottle and shoved the cloth into its mouth.

Before I rowed a safe distance away, I spotted Gavin's body in the cockpit. It was the only thing I hadn't covered in flammable liquid.

"This is it." I said, "I hope this brings you peace."

I washed my hands in the ocean before I pulled a lighter from my pants pocket and flicked it to life. I set fire to the cloth and quickly tossed the bottle through the open door. As the bottle shattered, a fire storm roared to life. The flames grew so intense the dashboard began to sizzle and pop.

I hastily rowed into the boundaries before a piece of debris could puncture my raft. I shuddered as I crossed over into them, my breath escaping in clouds of vapor as the temperature plummeted. When I'd reached a safe distance, I stopped and focused on the spectacle, which was about to get much more exciting

214

than I anticipated.

I forgot about the PBM Martin Mariners patrol craft nearby, filled with hundreds of gallons of gasoline. As the cockpit of *Gypsy Girl* burned, the flames eventually found their way to the fuel tank, causing a fiery explosion. Burning debris landed on the sheen of gas floating on the surface of the water and followed it up to the Martin. That burst into an intense fireball, sending debris into the air and pushing the remains of *Gypsy Girl* out into the boundaries, where she sank into the dark, cold depths. Luckily, nothing pierced my raft as debris fell into the water.

When it was over, I sighed. I'd kept my word and disposed of Gavin's body. Now it was time to learn the secret of getting out.

A faint dripping sound pattered on the rubber of the raft. I twisted around to find a charred and drenched man climbing aboard, looking at me.

"You're an asshole," Gavin said.

Chapter Twenty-two

My shock alone rendered me mute. The skin around Gavin's right eye was scorched black and the white sclera was dark red from blood. His left eye was completely contused. His clothing was in rags and dripping wet. His ears looked as though something had gnawed on them and the rest of his face was blistered. The explosion had blown off half of his left arm and broken his back, forcing him to hunch forward, leaning a little to the side like a sand-filled doll.

"Did you hear me?" Gavin demanded. Smoke breezed past his blistered lips. "I said you're an asshole. Look what you've done to me!"

It took a few seconds for any words to come up from my throat. I swallowed thickly and stammered, "Why...why are you here?"

He shrugged, which caused his shoulders to pop. "Dunno, dude. All I know is I was in a kind of dream world one minute, like I was sleeping, and the next, I'm here. But something—instinct, I guess—tells me it's because of you. Wanna explain?"

I was nonplussed. I had dozens of my own questions, but Gavin wanted explanations.

"You told me to do it," I said. "You told me to dispose of your body in exchange for telling me how to escape."

"Why the hell would I want you to burn me up?" His smoky words dissipated completely.

"To put you at peace."

"Does it look like I'm at fuckin' peace?"

"You told me to do it," I repeated insistently.

"I didn't tell you squat!" he fired back. "Like I said, I've been in some other place—and a restful one, at that. I felt safe there. *That's* what gave me peace, not this!"

I couldn't wrap my brain around it. If he was telling the truth, what was it that had visited me every morning since I'd gotten here? It made no sense.

I turned away and ran my hands through my hair, on the verge of a mental breakdown. "What's going on? What's this place doing to me?"

"From my point of view, it looks like you've got it better than me," he said sarcastically, looking down at his scorched body.

"Are you in pain?"

He shook his head. "Nope, don't feel any pain, but I'm a little ticked now that the Elephant Man would have a better shot at getting laid than me."

His words made me think back to when he—or whatever the hell it had been—had first visited me on Lafitte's ship. That entity had claimed its head hurt like a bitch, yet the Gavin with me now mentioned feeling no pain at all, even though he was more severely wounded. I realized everything the other Gavin had told me was a lie. The pain it claimed to have, the promise of telling me a way out, everything. And I'd been dumb enough to fall for it.

"Gavin, I'm sorry. I swear, you came and asked me to do this."

"I'm really gonna scare people lookin' like this," he said miserably.

"Don't worry," I said, my voice heavy with remorse, "no one but me can see you. Well, living people, that is."

217

"Oh? I guess that's a plus." His strange eyes slid up to me. "So, what's next?"

"We go back," I said soberly.

As I made the dangerous journey back to shore, Gavin followed closely. He seemed to bounce everywhere, sort of skipping from one place to another. One minute, he stood on the tail of a plane, the next he was sitting in a small fishing boat. He asked the same kind of questions that had popped into my head when I'd arrived. I answered as best I could, while trying to process my own questions about the other Gavin and why it had wanted me to awaken the real Gavin.

It had been a long day and I decided to visit Jean Laffite onboard *The Pride*, just as I'd done on my two previous trips through the junkyard. Gavin was stoked to see a pirate in the flesh.

"That was quite an explosion you caused today," Laffite said with a grin. "I could hear the boom from here."

"It was bigger than I planned," I said, leaning against the railing. "Gavin promised me he'd show me the way out."

"And I told you to ignore him," Laffite retorted, reclining on the rail next to me. He looked at the soaked gauze around my hand and said, "I'll give you clean wraps for that, but you must apply some salve to your wound as soon as you return to the village. It doesn't take long for an infection to settle in."

Gavin skipped around the deck, taking in everything. He finally stopped to stare at Laffite. "Wow, I've never met a real pirate before. When I was a kid, I wanted to be one. This guy doesn't look much like one, though. Maybe it's the clothes."

"I don't understand what went wrong," I said morosely.

"I don't think anything went wrong," Laffite said. "It seems to me that whatever was planned is working perfectly."

"What's he talking about?" Gavin inquired. "What plan?"

"Shush!" I hissed. To Laffite, I asked, "What do you mean?"

Laffite pulled a gold case from his shirt pocket, clicked it open, and slipped a brown leaf cigarette from it. After he lit the cigarette and exhaled slowly, he said, "It's no secret this place is unusual, but its mysterious elements aren't much different than the world outside."

I chuckled slightly, thinking what a crock that was—until the thought of Bigfoot, space aliens, and the Holy Grail came to mind. Maybe what he said wasn't that far-fetched.

"My first mate's ghostly image vanished simply because I ignored it," Lafitte continued. "Why, I know not. But the ones who cross the borders and disturb the dead are stuck with that soul forever." He took another drag on his cigarette. "Just touching a body in the junkyard seems to be a gateway for false spirits."

"What do you mean false spirits?"

"I mean illusions, *mon ami*. This place is notorious for trickery, so be wary."

A shudder ran through me, as if someone had dumped a bucket of ice water on me.

"But why did it want me to awaken my co-pilot?"

"In my opinion, I believe the island is trying to tell us something."

"What the hell does that mean?"

"I've been here a long time," Laffite confessed.

219

"Not as long as some, but long enough to get a sense of this place—and I sense it changing."

"Changing? How?"

Laffite folded his arms on the rail and said in a whisper, "This place seems worn and tired, like a man who's lived too long and has nothing more to offer."

"Worn and tired? How could this place feel anything?"

"When I first arrived, the air smelled more like the sea, but now it's stale. Granted, this place has always been dark and weird, but in the course of a hundred years, it seems to have gotten more displeasing."

"What do you think it means?"

"It's as if this place is reaching out but doesn't know how to communicate what it longs for, even though it tries. It tried with me and now it's trying with you."

It was a strange conversation, but given the context of our surroundings, it was almost as if we were just two men discussing cars or women. I studied Gavin, who gawked up at the crow's nest like a country bumpkin seeing a skyscraper for the first time. The way he acted was actually more like the old Gavin than the one who'd visited me. The real Gavin was a laid-back hick who could eat raw lemons and say, "At least it ain't a steaming pile of dog shit."

I wished I'd hung out with him more. I would've gotten to know him better, would've gotten more accustomed to his personality. I shouldn't have ignored the things I knew about him before I'd set his body on fire. And I should've listened to Jean Lafitte's warning.

Chapter Twenty-three

I returned to the village the following day, paranoid and hopeless. What Laffite had told me didn't help much. I mean, really, a depressed island? Maybe what he meant was that the island was about to go through evolutionary changes and we needed to stay on our toes. For all I knew, the island was really a volcano gearing up to erupt. That was a scary thought. If the island did blow, everyone would end up as ash statues, like the people of Pompeii.

I wasn't ready to throw in the towel just yet. I decided to risk physical and mental health to go up into the forest.

"You're here!" Travis greeted as I walked past his hut. He sounded relieved to see me, as if I'd just told him he didn't have cancer.

"Yeah, I'm here," I said dejectedly. "Why?"

He hugged me. "We thought the worst, mate."

I pulled away. "What are you talking about?"

His eyes were a little misty as he took my arm. "Let's go over to Khenan's."

"Wait," I said, pulling away. "First, I want to know what happened to that copilot." When Travis looked confused, I added, "You know, Irving, the one who told you about the dead pilot inside the plane in the junkyard."

"Oh, him," Travis said. "He killed himself years back."

"Tell me everything that happened."

"We heard the plane crash and waited on the beach for someone to show up, and sure enough, Irving did. At the Welcoming, he asked if we could help him bury his friend, George. We told him the rules about the dead and left it at that. The next day, he said George had come to him and told him to give him a proper burial. That was the first time we'd heard of such a thing, 'cause the dead don't usually care about their bodies after they're free of them. We asked if he'd moved the body, but he said he'd only touched him."

That's all I'd done to Gavin. I'd touched his shirt sleeve. But, according to Laffite, a touch was all it took.

"We figured he'd done the deed and disturbed the bloke. So, me and some other folks went out with him to the junkyard to bring the body back for burial. When we got to the plane, we were surprised by how fresh the corpse looked. I mean, even just a day and half at sea would've had some effect on it. But he seemed like a sleeping spirit to me. I asked Irving if George was with him and he said no."

"Go on," I urged. "What happened next?"

"I told him to wait a day to see if the body started decomposing. Irving thought I'd gone 'round the bend. A few days later, the body looked the same, but Irving kept swearing George's ghost demanded that his body be buried. He got real scared, but none of us knew what to do.

"We had to restrain him from going back. He lost it more and more every day. We finally put him in jail for his own safety, even though Eleanor hated doing it. We knew something wasn't right and we didn't want him touching George until we understood what was going on. I remembered what Lafitte had told me and went to his ship to ask more about it. But, as I told you,

222

he claimed he was too drunk to remember saying anything about it. By the time I returned, Irving was dead. He somehow got hold of a knife and slit his wrists. We blocked off his cell after that."

Maybe Lafitte was right about the island trying to communicate with us. But what exactly did it want with us and the souls of the dead? While listening to him, I noticed a connection.

"Do these fake ghosts only occur if a person dies out in the junkyard?" I asked.

Travis shrugged. "I guess. Lafitte's first mate died while they were out at sea and ole' George died when his plane crashed out there."

It seemed strange to me that both Laffite and Irving had someone who'd die out at sea and been harassed by phony ghosts the same as me.

Travis rubbed his forehead a moment, then slapped at a mosquito on his arm. "Is that what happened to you, lad? Did your friend come to you? What did you do out there?"

"Let's go to Khenan's," I said with a sigh. "I'll explain everything."

As we approached Khenan's place, we found him sitting on the porch. His surprise at seeing me was evident. "You're alive!"

"Yeah," I said dryly.

"Where'd'ya go yesterday?"

"Why is everyone so damn shocked you're alive?" Gavin asked, standing next to me. "Did they think you were dead or something?"

When I didn't answer, Gavin prodded, "Heath?"

"I don't know," I answered shortly.

"You don't know where you went?" Travis said.

"No. I mean yes, I know where I went. Didn't

223

Michelle Lowe

you guys hear the explosion?"

"Yeah," Khenan said coolly. "We seen da smoke and fire, too, but we just figured it was anot'er suicide." He narrowed his eyes. "We tought it was you, mon."

"I didn't go out to kill myself."

"But you *were* out in the junkyard," Travis pointed out.

"Yes, but I went to…take care of something," I said hesitantly. I glanced at Gavin, flesh bubbles still oozing on his cheeks and lower jaw.

"Take care of what?" Travis asked firmly.

It would be better to tell them everything. They'd eventually catch me speaking to Gavin and I didn't want them to think I'd gone totally insane.

"Okay, here it goes," I began. "Since I arrived, I've been visited by Gavin, my student co-pilot. Only it wasn't Gavin. It was an imposter. It promised to tell me a way off the island if I disposed of Gavin's body, so I did. It wasn't until afterward that I learned I was being fooled the entire time."

"What are we talking about?" Khenan asked. "A fake ghost?"

I never thought anyone as dark as Khenan could pale so fast. I didn't blame him. I'd just realized this myself, and if I put too much thought into it, I'd most likely vomit.

"I'm going to climb the island," I announced, changing the subject. "Do either of you want to come?"

It was the first time I'd asked for their company. It wasn't solely out for the fact that I finally realized going solo would only get me killed in some horrible way, but also these guys had become my friends. We'd

224

come to care deeply for one another and I couldn't think of anyone else I'd trust my life with.

Travis looked at me in silence, his expression uncertain. "All right, lad."

"You out of yo 'ead, mon?" Khenan blurted. "Is it deat yer seekin', 'cause most likely dat's what'cha gonna find up dere."

"I don't care," I said. "I need to find a way out and I don't think it's on the beach or through the junkyard. There has to be something up there, some kind of answer."

Khenan turned to Travis. "And wha's yer reason for going along?"

Travis shrugged. "I've been here for two hundred years. I could use a change, whether it be dying or finding something we've been too afraid to go lookin' for."

Khenan shook his head and took a drink of Miller's home-made whiskey.

"Come on, mate, what else is there to do 'round here, eh? Finish building the docks?"

Khenan turned his gaze to me. "What'cha expect to find up dere, mon? What'cha tink you'll find dat ot'er idiots 'aven't been able to?"

"That's what I want to find out."

Although I could sense his apprehension, Khenan asked, "When ya wanna leave?"

"Tomorrow morning."

"We should get some others to come along too," Travis suggested. "Some blokes with fighting experience."

"Like who?"

Khenan took another drink. "We'll go to Sout' Village."

* * *

I slept on the floor of my hut for only the third night since the keys had been handed to me. I missed Eleanor's soft bed and I woke to the sound of banging.

"There's a lot of hammering going on down there," Gavin said. "What are they doing?"

"They're building a dock," I said with a yawn.

"Oh. What's with those people standing on the beach with fishing poles? I saw 'em yesterday doing the same thing."

I rose, expecting him to be at the front window. Instead, he was sitting on the back porch railing, looking at his hand. I walked out and leaned on the rail next to him. "They just do that."

"Things are really weird around here."

"That they are."

I prepared myself for the sight of him. When I looked his way, he was hardly recognizable. Nearly every inch of him had been burnt by the fire. His back cracked every time he moved and water dripped from his body. I wondered what he'd look like if his corpse hadn't fallen into the abyss with my plane. Would he have come to me as a talking pile of ash?

It seemed as if the water had become a permanent fixture on him, like his torn clothes and burnt skin. It dripped off but vanished before hitting the floor. Gavin continued to study his only hand, which was nearly fleshless. His expression was melancholy, though it was nearly impossible to tell through his deformity.

"Gavin, I'm sorry," I said sullenly. "I should've left your body alone and—"

"Yeah, ya should'a," Gavin interrupted angrily. "I could've done without looking like a piece of

226

overcooked meat. Know what I'm saying?"

"I do, and I'm not asking for forgiveness, but—"

"Good," he snapped. There was silence before he said, "Since I don't sleep anymore, I've had time to think about things these past couple of nights."

His voice sounded cold and dark, and I shuddered. Gavin was dead but he was still capable of doing things—horrible things. And I was the only one he could do them to.

"I thought I ought to hate you for this," he said intensely. "I thought I ought to get revenge or some shit. Maybe find a way to keep you from sleeping every night till you went nuts, or talk really loud whenever you talked to somebody."

"Would you do something like that to me?" I asked, straining to keep from sounding nervous.

A deep and uneasy silence followed my question. Gavin kept looking at the ash-white finger bones showing through the holes riddling his skin. "I understand why you did it and I think I would've done the same." He raised his head, his neck popping loudly, his movement jagged. "I don't know what the hell's going on. After the crash, it was like I fell into an endless dream. Then, the next thing I know, I'm here with you, lookin' like I'd give Satan the heebie-jeebies. I've had an overwhelming need to follow you around like a goddamn dog or something, but you did what you did 'cause you wanted outta here, not to hurt me. I just want you to know I understand."

The corners of my lips raised, relieved to hear him say that.

"I wish I'd survived the crash with you," Gavin continued. "At least then I wouldn't look like this! D'ya think I'll be like this forever?"

227

I wanted to tell him no. I wanted to say that one day he'd move on and be free to do whatever he pleased, in any form he wished, but I didn't know that for sure. For all I knew, he'd be with me forever, like a string balloon tied to a child's wrist, forced to tag along no matter how much it tried to float away.

That was the reason I couldn't bring Eleanor back. I couldn't do that to her. But I'd done exactly that to Gavin, even if it had been unintentional. It pained me that he'd possibly stare at his deformed hand forever. How long would he continue to be understanding before he finally reached the breaking point? Whatever happened, it would be ten times worse if I spun him a story about a better future that never came.

"I hope not," I said delicately, "but maybe we'll find answers once we reach the top of the island."

* * *

Khenan took care of the food, mostly vegetables and bread, which could last longer on our journey. Travis was responsible for the weapons. Before meeting them, I took a much needed shower at the falls and had breakfast with Marissa and Tammy. They gave me one of those fingerless black leather biker gloves to protect my wounded hand. I dressed my wound with salve and wrapped more gauze around it, then put on the glove. After taking my dirty clothes to my hut to wash later, I grabbed my pack and headed out the door.

"Where're you going this time?" Carlton asked, standing on my front deck.

I nearly jumped out of my skin. Gavin laughed as

I said, "Jesus, Carlton, you trying to scare me to death?"

"Hell's bells, son, it'd take more than a start to bring down a strong man like you." He took a couple of steps toward me before he stopped. "I envy you, boy. I wish I'd been thirty years younger when I got stuck here."

I was lucky in that respect. To always live in a young body was truly a gift. On the other hand, being trapped in a body close to its expiration date would be hell.

"Why do you want to know where I'm going?" I asked defensively.

The old man threw up his hands. "Just curious. And a little worried. I'm sure you miss Eleanor something fierce."

Having Eleanor ripped so senselessly away tore at me. The only thing keeping me sane was going on my self-appointed missions. As long as my mind stayed occupied, it kept the clock in my soul ticking.

"Son, she would've wanted me to make sure you're all right. I thought I'd check in on you."

"I'm fine, thanks. If you must know, I've decided to climb to the top of the island."

"That's very risky," he said sternly.

"Does everyone go crazy up there?"

"Most of them."

"Why?"

"If we knew that, we'd all be living in flats on the mountainside."

"In flats, huh? You know, you use quite a bit of British lingo."

"Do I?" he said, thickening up his Texan drawl. "Guess being 'round all those English folks has rubbed off on me."

I didn't see that as a credible excuse, considering there weren't many Brits on the island. "Are you really from Texas?"

Something flashed in his hazel eyes. I'd touched on something.

"Don't get your hopes up, son. It's mighty dangerous up there. Watch out for them holes. Some of them are pretty deep and you don't want to fall into one."

I didn't ask him for any more information. I shook his hand and left to meet my friends.

* * *

"It'll take us a while to reach the village," Travis said.

"You think they'll help us?" I asked. "The soldiers."

"I don't see why not. Most of them don't have much else to do."

"Do they have a leader? A commander?"

"Not really," Khenan said. "But dere's a famous sea captain living dere you might've 'eard of. Dey call 'im da Cyclops."

"The Cyclops?" I repeated. "You mean Lieutenant Commander George Worley?"

"One and the same, lad," Travis moaned. "But don't get too excited till you meet him. He can be a right proper arse most of the time."

"Is he going to be an obstacle?"

"Nah, he'll just be himself. And trust me, that'll be enough."

Our walk to South Village took nearly an hour,

and by the time we reached it, my feet hurt.

"Jesus," I said in amazement. "Look at this place."

A heap of old planes and ships stood twenty or so feet from the shore. A dock, starting at the beach, wrapped itself around the heap where people fished. We walked past pigsties built on a short platform covered in mud for boars to wallow in. A man near the back of a small slaughterhouse was in the process of skinning one. As we drew closer, someone yelled, "Halt!"

A man in cutoff khakis emerged from the thicket, holding a rifle against his shoulder.

"Oi, Salinger!" Travis called. "They got you on guard duty again, boy-o?"

"Yeah, it's sinks," Salinger complained. "All I do all damn day is sit around scratching my balls."

Salinger was definitely a soldier. Although short, he had the muscle mass of an athlete. The World War II eagle tattoo on his broad chest dated him.

"What's with the gear?" Salinger asked. "You boys going somewhere?"

"We're gonna climb the island," Travis explained.

"You're going up the mountain? Jasper and Tony went up not long ago. Haven't seen 'em since."

His cavalier manner made it seem like people vanishing into the woods was a common occurrence.

"Ya wanna come wit' us, mon?" Khenan asked hopefully.

"Hell no!" Salinger decried. "I don't have a death wish."

We left him at his post and headed for the massive pile of steel. In the distance, I could see the

231

U.S.S. Cyclops, the vessel that had three hundred and nine souls onboard when she'd vanished without a trace, making her one of the world's greatest Bermuda Triangle mysteries. She wasn't hard to spot. Her massive body was tilted on its side like a beached whale. She didn't appear a century old. She looked fresh and ready for battle.

The heap of ships and planes actually seemed organized, as if they'd been crammed together deliberately. As we got closer, I realized we approached a village made of steel and iron. When I asked about it, Khenan said, "It be Worley's doin'. Over da years, 'e an' 'is crew took ships and planes apart and 'auled dem near shore to build da village."

"As more unfortunate blokes came," Travis added, "the village expanded. Goes to show what a band of bored soldiers can do over the course of a hundred years, eh?"

"You 'elped 'em build part of it, remember?"

"I rest my case," Travis said with a smile.

"Maybe they can help us bring the ships to our docks," I suggested. "At least it would give them a new project to work on."

"That ain't a bad idea, mate," Travis said. "I'll suggest it to ole' Carlton."

"How long did you live here?"

"Not long. A bunch of me ole' crew mates are still around, though. I suppose soldiers like to stay close to each other, no matter what time they're from. I just got sick of all the bollocks we'd put up with when Worley was in one of his moods."

I wanted to ask about Worley but we were close to the village. Travis wasn't shy about speaking his mind, and if someone related ill words to Worley, it might jeopardize our mission or make for an uncomfortable encounter.

Several people recognized Travis and Khenan and greeted them by name, but they didn't ask mine. I didn't care. I wasn't here to make new friends. Travis asked someone wearing a World War I cap where we could find Worley and we were told he was at his place.

The dock spread out like a spider's web, branching off in different directions like a maze. Each plane and boat had been renovated to serve as a house, shop, or pub. Doors had been added to the sides of U-boats, and there were patrol boats with army green or camouflage tarps over them to serve as roofs. Warplane wings sheltered other boats. No plane was larger than a B-24 and all were bolted together, keeping each craft upright and securely in place.

Travis led the way through the village. We walked through a U-boat with a perfect passageway cut through the middle. A sign above the lintel read: SOUTH VILLAGE, HOME OF THE LOST BUT NOT FOUND.

As we entered the passageway, I began second-guessing my decision to climb the island. After all, a village full of soldiers with all their skills and training hadn't reached the top. Was I leading my friends—and anyone else willing to come with us—into real trouble?

My mood brightened a bit when a far-fetched idea popped into my head. Suppose the people who'd gone missing had actually found a way to escape? Maybe they'd found a portal that took them out of the Bermuda Triangle and back to where they'd come from, with no memory of what had happened. Maybe we'd be searching for a doorway to another dimension,

233

just like Inglewood had suggested. It was a long shot but I needed to hold on to something.

"This is some crazy shit," Gavin exclaimed from behind me. I jumped like a scared cat.

"You awright, mon?" Khenan asked.

"Yeah, fine," I said with a hint of agitation.

"These guys really know how to build a village," Gavin said. "How long do you think it took to build it?" When I didn't answer, he said, "Oh, I see. Can't answer the dead guy, huh? It'd be too embarrassing. Well, thanks for reminding me that I'm dead by ignoring me when I ask one simple fucking question."

I hated to admit it, but he had a point. After all, I was the one who'd turned him into a monster. The least I could do was talk to him in front of others. "I don't know how long it took."

"You talkin' to yer ghost friend?" Khenan surmised.

"Yeah, I might as well get used to it."

Travis had been to Worley's place before. He never broke stride, even when ducking under clothes drying on a line. "Almost there, lads."

The entire village was very animated. People all around kept busy. Some were cooking on grills, while others fished or played musical instruments. A group of children played tag. One woman was even painting. They must have been aboard the cruise ship *Ramón* and thought it best to keep their loved ones near the soldiers for protection.

We came to a short staircase at the end of the village, which led up to a door of an A-10 Thunderbolt.

"Well," Travis huffed, "let's see if the bastard's home."

Chapter Twenty-four

Once we reached the top of the steps, Travis knocked on the metal door. "Worley! Open the bloody door, mate!"

On cue, the door opened, and there stood a man of five-foot-seven with short blond hair and hazel eyes. He wore denim jeans and an unbuttoned shirt with a white undershirt beneath it. When he spoke, it was with a German accent. "Travis, to what do I owe the pleasure of your visit?"

"We're going up the island."

"So?"

"So, do you know anyone who might be willing to go along?"

The man scratched his head, then shifted his eyes to me. "Introductions are in order, yes?"

Travis turned to me, then back to Worley with a sigh. "Worley, this is Heath Sharp."

"Hi," I said with a wave.

"Guten abend."

"Do you know anyone?" Travis cut in.

Worley glared at him. "You should come inside. We have some trading matters to discuss."

I expected Travis to argue, seeing how aggressively he treated the man, but he said simply, "Alrighty."

Worley stepped back inside the plane. Travis grabbed the door before it closed and followed him in. Khenan and I brought up the rear.

"Wow," Gavin said, "is that really George Worley?"

"Yes," I whispered back.

The plane offered little room for four grown men, but amazingly it had been hollowed out and converted into cozy living quarters. There was a cot in the far back with a small dresser. A ceramic bowl rested on top of it and a mirror hung on the wall above. Small nick-knacks sat on metal shelves welded into the walls.

What caught my attention the most were the metal sculptures. By the door stood a tree three feet tall. Thin pieces of metal used to make the tree were twisted in various ways to form the masterpiece. It reminded me of the village itself. A sculpture of a human skull, done the same way, sat on a shelf, and a full-sized person posing like Michelangelo's David stood near it. The works were both impressive and eerie.

On a nearby table was a thirteen-gallon waterless fish tank with sculptures of fish suspended from thin pieces of wire tied to the tank's lid. An octopus rested on the bottom, its tentacles reaching upward. To add to the effect of a real aquarium, fake plants and a treasure chest sat amid colorful pebbles.

Worley went around a small work desk under the cockpit. Gray light drifted through the glass canopy.

"You're not proposing we use currency, are you?" Travis said, dipping his hand into a bowl on the desk. He brought out a handful of silver coins and allowed them to drop between his fingers.

"No," Worley said, sitting behind the desk, "that would be obtuse. I was merely bored." He shifted in his seat. "I need to inform you that I'm raising the price of a pound of our seafood to four pounds of your vegetables."

"Wah?" Khenan exclaimed, stepping past me to

approach the desk. "Dat's two pounds more dan before. Why so much?"

"Because the demand for fresh vegetables is high, now that we have so many more mouths to feed."

Their conversation brought me back to what Eleanor had said about how South Village supplied most of the seafood and meat. North Village traded their main resources, such as fruits and vegetables, for them.

"Fair enough," Travis said. "I'll relay the message to Carlton."

"Splendid," Worley said, pleased. "Ah, I see you're admiring my chandelier, young man."

He referred to me as I looked up at a small chandelier made from the same twisted metal as his sculptures. It hung directly above Worley's desk from the canopy. Melted candle wax drooped from it like stalactites.

"Did you make it?"

He nodded proudly. "From manganese. We were transporting thousands of tons of it. I decided to make use of it." He adjusted again in the creaky chair, propping his bare feet up on the desk. "So, you're going up the island? What for?"

"What reasons would we have, mate?" Travis said.

The lieutenant cocked his head back and laughed. "Oh, another foolish quest to find freedom, eh? What makes you think you'll succeed where others have failed?"

"Heath," Gavin said, drawing my attention away from them, "look at all this stuff over here."

He stood near the wall, looking at metal arrowheads and knives encased in glass frames. I assumed they'd been made by Worley.

"No worries 'bout dat," Khenan said. "We just need a few more strong backs, is all."

Worley said nothing.

"Well?" Travis prodded. "We're kinda in a hurry here, Frederick."

Worley gave him a cross look. "Don't address me by that name."

"What? Johan Frederick Wichman has a nice ring to it, wouldn't you say?"

"You're fortunate, Mr. Livingston, that you were never under my command."

"Ah, shit," Travis cursed. "Here we go."

Worley's face blossomed into a glowing red fireball, his eyes nothing more than slits. He stood. "Go ask around for help. I'm sure you can find fools to go along with you."

There was a long moment of utter silence. Travis and Worley didn't move the entire time. Gavin whistled a tune from *The Good, the Bad, and the Ugly.*

"Alrighty," Travis finally said, walking away from the desk. "Cheers, mate."

"What did he mean by you're fortunate you were never under his command?" I asked after we exited the plane and headed down the steps.

"He isn't too fond of Brits. He hates that a little British sailor like me doesn't have to abide by his rules. But I'm old enough to be his great-great-grandfather, for Christ sakes."

"Or," Khenan cut in, "could be 'cause you called 'im a German sympat'izer."

"Yeah, that too."

"Is he?" I asked as we reached the dock.

"Doubt it," Khenan said. "I mean, da *Cyclops* is

'ere an' not someplace in Germany, right?"

"Then why did you accuse him of being a traitor?"

"To get under his skin," Travis said. "When he first got here, he acted like he was cock of the walk and was nasty about it. I confronted him a few times and we ended up fighting. So, yeah, there's history between us."

I said nothing more about it and we went in search of soldiers. It surprised me how many young, able-bodied men hadn't already gone up the island. Most flat-out refused to go. Twenty-two soldiers had gone up the island and only six had returned. None of them spoke about their journey or what had happened to the other sixteen. In truth, none of them really spoke anything but gibberish. One of them stood in the water and didn't move. Travis told me that others cared for him by bringing food and getting him out of the ocean at night. Other than that, they let him be. A couple of others just walked around, muttering to themselves with wide cherry-red eyes, while another pair sat across from each other, staring down at an untouched chessboard. I was told that if anyone tried taking the board, the two would attack.

The sixth was the most disturbing case. He was completely clothed, gloves and all, which were strapped to him with duct tape. The reason was to keep him from eating his own skin. Travis explained that he and a few of his crew mates had the responsibility to clothe him that way. Back then, they'd only had rope to use, and for years, they'd tied him up so he couldn't hurt himself.

Those six men were the reason why no one went too far into the forest. Hell, it forced me to rethink my

239

plan.

But then we managed to scrape up some players, and by the time we assembled a team, evening had already settled. We decided to stay the night. The volunteers got us a few hammocks and we set them up wherever we found space.

The evening was fairly early. People were still out but the beach quickly became vacant. Travis joined some sailors for drinks and a card game, while Khenan turned in early and I went exploring.

South Village made me wish I had a workable camera. It was one of the most unique places I'd ever seen—and I'd seen a lot. I didn't head in any particular direction, but I soon came to the dock and stopped by the railing overlooking the depressing ocean. Another guy wearing a plan T-shirt and plaid shorts was with me. We stood in deep silence for a long while.

"For the last time, stop bothering me!" he exclaimed. "I don't have any food for you!"

I jumped, snapping my attention to him. "You have a ghost too?"

"Yeah," he said with frustration. "Only they're not men, but goats, chickens, and a pig."

I blinked. "Animals?"

"Yep, several of them, in fact. I used to be a cook onboard *The Wasp,* and before we knew the rules about the dead, I killed some livestock. Now they follow me everywhere."

I found that amusing but tried not to show it.

"They don't bother me too much, save for one goat I call Pest. She keeps nagging me to feed her. I think she was hungry before I slit her throat."

Annoying as it would be to have a goat constantly begging for food it couldn't eat, I'd trade places with him in a heartbeat.

I wandered around aimlessly for a while until I found myself near Worley's home. Even after the time I'd spent trapped in the Bermuda Triangle with all these famous people, it still left me star-struck to stand where the commander of the *U.S.S. Cyclops* actually lived. Hell, I couldn't even wrap my mind around the fact that I'd met the guy. I became overwhelmed by it just to distract myself from the day ahead. I didn't like the idea that I could end up standing in waist-high water for no reason or go barbaric on myself.

I didn't plan to linger long. I wanted to find other ways to take my mind off what I might head into. Maybe I'd join Travis for drinks.

I turned to leave when I suddenly found myself standing face to face with George Worley.

"*Guten abend.*"

"Lieutenant," I said simply. I hoped he didn't think me a weirdo for staring at his house.

He cradled a bag filled with items. "I got some beer. Care to join me?"

How the hell could I say no to what should be a ghost? "All right."

Worley went first up the stairs. "Tell me, how did that British idiot convince you to climb the island with him?"

"Actually, it's my idea."

Worley reached the door and opened it. He looked over his shoulder. "Is that so?"

Once inside, he moved over to his small kitchen area, where a pot of boiling water simmered on a makeshift stove. "Travis mentioned he'd relay the new trading price to Carlton. Why not to Eleanor?"

When I told him of her death, he nearly dropped

the bag before he got it to the table. "She's dead? How?"

I told him.

He looked very upset, almost on the verge of crying. Before I finished my brief account, he collected himself and brought out a beer inside a water bottle. He untwisted the cap and handed it to me. "And the young man responsible was taken to *Southern Districts,* I take it?"

"He died before he made it to the ship."

Worley nodded in approval.

"You knew Eleanor, then?"

"*Ja.* And I'm deeply distressed to hear of her death. Did you know her well?"

I nodded but added nothing personal.

He reached into the bag and pulled out another bottle of beer, only this one was in an old glass Coca Cola bottle. He brought out two more, one in a half gallon milk carton, the other in another Coke Cola bottle, and set them on the table.

"She was a good woman," he said, taking out odd looking crabs. "She helped save many lives, including my own."

He threw the crabs into a pot without a second thought and pulled the cork off the beer inside a Coke Cola bottle. I took a drink of mine. It tasted almost like beer except for a strange blueberry aftertaste.

"It's the hops," Worley explained when I smacked my tongue against my lips. "The ground makes them taste like blueberries."

I took another drink. "How did she save your life?"

"When I first arrived here, I saw myself as I did out there. You know, in our world? I was strict with my men and demanded their obedience every step of the way. And when they didn't comply, I reprimanded them viciously. We tried rowing ourselves out of here, but all we accomplished was getting several men dead.

"I thought myself high commander over everyone, including the ones who'd come here before me. I was put in my place, so to say, and cast out of South Village, which was nothing more than little shacks and tents at that time. Foolishly, I went into the forest."

He said nothing more, only took a stirring spoon out of a jar.

"What happened?" I asked.

"Like you, I went searching for another way out. I climbed the island and encountered...things I wish not to share with anyone."

I wanted to ask—oh, God, how I wanted to ask—but, I respected his wishes and said nothing.

"I'd gone mad. I don't know how it happened or when. Days, maybe weeks later, I ended up in North Village. I was in and out of consciousness. I'd hear the villagers say, 'He's gone crazy. His mind is dead.' Someone even said, 'He's a zombie. Let's send him back into the woods.' I tried to protest but I couldn't talk." He took a drink while stirring the crabs in the pot. Their hard shells scrapped against the tin. "But I didn't have to. Eleanor spoke for me and told them to give me a chance to recover. If I didn't make it back, I could stay there, like the other insane. They helped me, nursed me back to health. Eventually, I began speaking again and my mind returned."

"How did you regain your sanity?"

"I don't know. Many who've gone crazy don't come back to their senses, but there are some who do."

243

I couldn't believe what I was hearing. "No one ever told me that before. Not even Eleanor."

"It's uncommon, *very* uncommon. I can't say how I returned to the land of the sane." He snorted and took a drink. "As sane as any person can be around here."

"You didn't run into the Vikings?"

"No. I suppose I was lucky. Speaking of which, I hope you found some good souls to help you tomorrow. You'll need it."

* * *

I didn't get much sleep, despite the beer I'd indulged in. The horror stories about going insane took me out of my confront zone. I had to admit, I was scared. Physical damage can be tolerated to an extent. The body heals and you're fine, depending on the injury, but a royal mindfuck was something else entirely. But what the hell else was I going to do? Settle down? No, I couldn't live day after endless day reminded of Eleanor's death every time her house came into view. And the only way to escape it was to move out of North Village.

What then? South Village was too cramped, despite how artfully constructed it was. And I'd be damned if I'd unload my luggage with the Obsoletes. The only option was to become a hermit, but from what I'd learned, safety was in numbers.

We gathered supplies—bottles of fresh water, dried fruit and vegetables, and Tupperware containers full of meat and beans. Travis, Khenan, and I sprayed ourselves with insect repellent. The soldiers didn't, but they did bring an arsenal. I thought the guns Travis,

Khenan, and I had would be enough for the trip, but in comparison to how much ammo the soldiers carried, it made us look like little boys with BB guns. The three armed themselves each with four handguns, knives, and two rifles. It was a lot of gear and I hoped it wouldn't affect their ability to climb.

It turned out it didn't. In fact, they climbed better than us. Khenan and I were the ones who lagged behind, trudging up the incline, trying our damnedest to keep up. The climb was steep but there was enough leverage to stand without holding onto something. The foliage was coarse and the fog was ever present. Heavy brush constantly clawed at our legs and large leaves covered dangerous rocks. My toes hurt from striking or tripping over them.

The trees helped with the climb. I grabbed one after the other to pull myself up. I couldn't stop sweating. It got very hot and humid the higher we went. Then there were the bugs. Big ones, and they attacked me like kamikazes. The bug spray seemed to deter most from biting, but the ones that did left a hot sting.

After a while, we reached a twenty-foot-tall stone wall. I call it a wall because though the rock was part of the island, it appeared to rise up from the ground, its exterior nearly smooth. We found no footholds to use, nothing to grab onto other than some twig-like trees growing from the cracks or straggly grass dangling over the top. And there seemed to be no end to it. We walked alongside it for a while, trying to find a way up. I hoped the ground would have swallowed a portion of it during a landslide or something, but we didn't find anything like that and we hadn't brought any climbing equipment. We almost resorted to standing on each other's shoulders for the first man up to find something for the rest to climb onto.

Eventually, we came across a tree. It reminded me of one of those large *Ficus Strangulosa* trees that grow on top of ancient ruins, breaking the building apart with its gigantic roots. This tree's roots followed the wall down like squid tentacles, sinking into the ground by our feet.

"Bloody hell," Travis said, wiping the sweat from his brow. "Would you look at that?"

"Damn," a soldier named Phil said. "This goddamn island grows some peculiar things."

I almost told them about the trees in South America. Hell, I'd even had a picture taken of myself standing by one, but I was too tired. This tree did have one distinctive difference from the others I'd seen. The whole thing, roots and all, was covered in a weird glossy purple substance.

"We can climb this," another soldier nicknamed Point-Blank suggested.

He was the first to go up. Travis, Khenan, and I watched as the two other soldiers climbed the wide roots like panthers. I was about to follow when I touched the roots. The thick goo felt like wet gum. I wrenched my hand back. It smelled pretty bad, too, like worn socks.

I waited for someone to yell girly insults at me but no one did. Another soldier, Eric, yelled at us from the top. "You don't wanna be coming up the tree, fellas."

I raised my face to him and the others. Their clothing was drenched in the shimmering goo. I could imagine how funky they must feel.

"We'll find ya somethin' to climb up on."

"Cheers, mates," Travis called. To us, he said, "Good lads, eh?"

Khenan touched the roots. He made what little he had on him into a web between his fingers. "It's sticky."

I wiped the smelly crud off on a rock. I didn't even want it on my clothes. Travis stayed clear of it altogether.

"Heath," Gavin said beside me, "I dare you to taste it."

I glared at him with a sickened expression.

"What?" Khenan demanded, standing right behind Gavin.

"I wasn't looking at you."

The best part about telling Travis and Khenan about Gavin was that whenever I spoke to him or acted somewhat out of character, I didn't need to pull a quick lie out of my ass.

In no time, the soldiers threw down a line of rope they'd created from vines. The vines had come from another tree and were dry. Travis went first, then Khenan, and finally me. When we reached the top, we decided it was time for a break—far away from the stinky tree. We sat on a group of boulders and the three soldiers stripped off their tainted shirts.

"It's been a hell of a day, eh, fellas?" Eric said, tossing his sticky T-shirt away.

"Have you guys ever been up here before?" I asked.

"Not this far," Point-Blank said, scrubbing his torso with a wet rag. "It's funny, now that I think about it. I mean, we've been here for, what, sixty-something years?"

"I guess after what happened to them boys and

247

Worley, we just kept clear," Phil admitted, shuffling through his bag.

"What made ya wanna come now?" Khenan asked.

"Dunno, really," Phil said, putting on a clean shirt. "Guess we thought it was time to overcome our fears."

"No shit," Point-Blank said, tossing away the rag. "I mean, the boys and I fought at the Battle of Iwo Jima. Why should we be afraid of a little climb?"

After they'd changed into clean clothes, we ate and loaded up for the climb ahead. We didn't get far. About ten paces up, Phil dropped through the ground. He'd been leading and fell right in front of us. We rushed forward and dropped to our bellies.

Phil dangled by his pack strap hooked on a jagged piece of rock. He'd fallen too far for us to reach him. Point-Blank left to fetch a rope. The hole seemed to be bottomless. Loose stones clanked against the wall as they fell.

"Phil!" Eric called. "You all right?"

Phil looked up at us, somewhat disorientated, although he quickly adjusted to what had happened. He reached up for the rock holding his strap. "I'm fine. I just need to get a hold of this rock."

The strap broke and he disappeared into the darkness below. The echoes of his screams followed long after his fall. Eric called after him.

Point-Blank returned with the rope and stood at the edge, looking down with a wide-eyed expression.

"We gotta go after him," Eric exclaimed, getting to his feet. "We have to go down and get him!"

I wanted to tell him what a bad idea that was, but Phil was his friend, a friend he'd fought next to during one of the bloodiest battles of WWII. A bond such as that was as solid as a mountain. But I didn't need to talk sense into him. Point-Blank did that for me.

"He's gone! There's nothing we can do for him."

"We can't leave him down there," Eric argued.

"He's dead, soldier! There's nothing we can do!"

Point-Blank surprised me. I guess it's the stiff heart of a warrior that made him practical. The longer they lived, the more friends they must have seen die.

We pressed on, taking the vine rope with us in case another hole opened up underfoot. When the gray sky darkened, we made camp. Travis made a fire, while Khenan cooked dinner. As I helped Point-Blank set up the tents, Eric stood as a lookout.

"What exactly are you looking for anyway, sport?" Point-Blank asked.

"Answers," I said simply, hammering a pole into the ground. "I want what everyone else wants—to find a way out."

"And you think you can find what others before you couldn't?"

I was growing tired of that question but I understood where he was coming from. His sharp tone underlined his agony of losing his friend. I guess he directed his anger at me because the journey was my idea. He was pissed, so I didn't return the attitude when I said, "I don't know. But living here forever isn't an option for me."

"Rather die fighting than live with a head quietly bowed, eh? I can respect that."

* * *

Everyone but Eric ate. He went into the tent the moment they were assembled and never came out. No

249

one spoke a word. After a while, we turned in. Khenan took first watch while I shared a tent with Travis.

I couldn't say how long I slept before I heard voices outside our tent. It was still dark. When I sat up, every nerve tingled like blood rushing back through a limb after it had fallen asleep. My arm felt heavy as I reached for the tent flap.

"What the hell is wrong with me?" I asked out loud. The question echoed in my head. I pulled the flap back and peered out. Eric was sitting by the fire, talking to himself.

"We should'a gone after him. We shouldn't have left him down there."

At first, I believed his words were repeated inside my head, like my own, but his moving lips told me otherwise. I exited the tent and asked if he was okay.

"Is no use, mon," Khenan said. He was leaning against a tree trunk, holding a pistol by his side. The tree was slightly slanted on the steep incline, allowing him to lean comfortably with a leg propped up on it. "'e's been out 'ere mumbling dat shit fer some time now an' 'asn't stopped."

Something like a twig snapped nearby. I couldn't tell. When I turned my attention to the sound, Point-Blank stood just beyond the light of the fire. His body rocked slightly from side to side, his back to us. In each hand, he held a knife.

"Dun worry, mon," Khenan said, "I been keeping a close eye on 'im. 'e's been like dat fer awhile."

Even with Khenan's calmness about the situation, I was unnerved by Point-Blank's and Eric's behavior.

"I feel strange," I said. At least I think I said it.

"Someting's 'appening to us," Khenan said. "Someting bad."

250

Chapter Twenty-five

The way Khenan said that frightened me. I had a feeling it would prove true enough. Nearly everything was whirling and the slanted ground didn't help the situation. Eric's muttering freaked me out, so I sat down beside the tent and buried my face in my hands. Glowing shapes visible through my eyelids were like a bizarre light show. They spun around, dipped and rose in a coordinated fashion. I thought if I didn't move and didn't fight it, I'd be okay. Maybe I'd be able to come down eventually. *If* I came down. I did my best not to think about it.

"Heath, it's me."

It had been years since I'd heard that voice, but I recognized it immediately and raised my head to find my grandmother sitting in front of me.

"You got yourself into quite a pickle, haven't you?" she said.

Just go with it. "Yeah."

I hoped Khenan couldn't hear me. Although I had no idea what his state of mind was or what the hell he was seeing, he seemed to be alert. I had to believe he'd defend the camp if Point-Blank attacked. I even thought about getting my gun from inside the tent.

"I miss being alive," Grandmother said, rubbing her hands together as she had when her arthritis had bothered her. "Death is boring."

"I'm sorry."

"You just wait. You'll know what I mean soon enough."

251

I didn't want to hear about dying. I didn't give a shit if I could learn the answer to the big mystery. I couldn't handle that kind of heavy trip.

"I don't think you're my grandmother," I said, shutting my eyes tight. "She wouldn't talk like that. She'd encourage me to stay alive."

I opened my eyes, hoping she wasn't there, but she was. Her wrinkled lips pressed together and she blinked several times. "I have something in my eye."

I readied myself for what she was about to do. Her glass eye would pop out when she rubbed it and she'd say, *Oh no, I lost my eye again.* But she didn't rub it. She rubbed the real one, and it fell from its socket to hang from its optic nerve.

"Oh no, Heath, now I've lost my other eye."

My stomach turned inside out. Since coming here, I'd seen plenty of gruesome things. This wasn't the worst, but it was still a nightmare.

I buried my face in my hands and rubbed so hard the skin could have slid off my bones. When I lowered my arms, I almost didn't look up. But I did and I saw a very pale man behind a nearby tree with his eyes on me. I couldn't look away. I said nothing and didn't move. For what seemed like forever, we focused on one another. Then he moved toward me. I started to advance as well, but then stayed put, watching as he observed me. I tried to keep in mind he wasn't real.

He crept toward me, waddling a few paces until he stopped half an arm's length away. "Dustan. My name is Dustan."

"Heath," I said thickly.

"You're the first one I've ever spoken to."

I could swear he was speaking in an accent that wasn't American, but I couldn't distinguish the nationality. Then again, I didn't really try.

"I like it up here," Dustan said. "But it's frightening. One day, I'll stay here with the trees and rain and never go home."

"Why would you want to stay here?"

"It's far better than where I live."

"Anywhere is better than here," I grumbled. I couldn't believe I was arguing with a hallucination.

He snorted. "I wouldn't say that." He waddled back to the trees and vanished into the darkness.

I couldn't take any more after that. I stood and went back to the fire. Khenan kept his casual position against the tree, watching the fire and holding his pistol at his side. Eric still talked to himself and Point-Blank never moved from his Michael Myers pose. Other than Eric's mumbling and the crackling fire, everything was eerily quiet, motionless. I didn't see the spinning shapes anymore but the colors remained. Acid bubbles bloated my gut. I looked into the flames. They swirled in pink, blue, and bright green, and relaxed me.

"Da fire is wicked, yeah?" Khenan said.

"Yeah. Are you seeing colors too?"

"Yeah, mon."

"What's happening to us?"

"Dun know, but we need to keep our 'eads 'bout us an' stay put fer a while."

"He's wrong, dude," Gavin said urgently. "You need to go. Now!"

I looked around but didn't see him. "Do you think we should wake Travis?"

Khenan didn't answer. I don't even know if he heard me.

"Heath!" Gavin shouted. "Move your ass.

They're coming!"

Behind me came heavy footsteps. When I turned, three short but well-built men wielding axes and swords emerged from the thicket. One had a large club.

"Shit," I said.

"Run, dumb ass! Run!" Gavin yelled.

"Vikings!" Khenan exclaimed, firing off a shot.

When he did, I thought the Viking closest to me had shot me.

"You haven't been hit," Gavin reassured. "Go! Go!"

I nearly tripped over myself trying to get away. The Viking with the axe swung at me but missed. I leapt over the fire. Khenan was gone but Eric sat unmoving.

I heard another shot from the tent. Travis came out and cocked his rifle back. The faster everything moved, the more blurry it all became. Travis called for me but I couldn't understand him.

"He's telling you to get your gun," Gavin barked. "I'm telling you, you need to run!"

Again, I ignored him. Instead, I clasped Eric's arm and tried pulling him to his feet. He pushed me away. The Viking with the axe came at us. I told Eric to shoot him, but he just sat there and let the Viking lop his head clean off.

Travis fought two Vikings at once. My vision was hazy, but it appeared as if he used his rifle to block the blades. I took a step toward them, aiming to help, but the Viking with the axe came at me again. He swung and somehow I avoided getting sliced.

I didn't have any weapons but I had my fists, and I used them to punch him in the face. I think his nose cracked. I kneed him in the crotch for good measure—

anything to keep him from swinging that lumberjack weapon.

With my attacker doubled over, I had time to race to Travis's assistance. I didn't go alone. Khenan came out of nowhere and together we ran toward him. One Viking managed to stab Travis in the back as he was distracted by the other.

"No!" I heard myself scream seconds before I leapt onto the back of the Viking who'd stabbed him. I punched the Viking viciously in the head, trying to render him unconscious. I had no idea how I could fight like this. It had to come from pure adrenaline.

The second Viking charged Khenan when he stopped to take aim. He was close enough not to miss. A shot rang out but I didn't see what happened afterward. The man I was on threw me off, tossing me on top of the tent. I clambered to my feet, stumbled, fell, and scrambled to get up again as another Viking came.

"Run!" Gavin screamed.

This time I listened. Another gunshot blasted behind me as I ran toward Point-Blank. I tried taking one of his knives, but he swung and sliced me on the forearm. He didn't attack but I wasn't going to get a knife from him. That distraction gave the Viking with the axe enough time to catch up to me. He swung his weapon and I leapt back. I lost my balance and went tumbling down the incline. That was when I blacked out.

Gavin spoke to me. His voice said my name seconds before I opened my eyes. "Don't move an inch."

I didn't understand but I listened. Above me, tree branches and leaves pressed against the gray sky.

"Don't move," Gavin repeated. "And don't get spooked when you can see again."

"See what?" I asked, sliding my eyes down my body. When I'd rolled down the hill, I'd struck a wide tree. Right beside me was the Viking. I wanted to get up immediately.

"If you move him, he'll haunt your dumb ass," Gavin warned.

I had a horrid, bitter taste in my mouth that made my words stick when I spoke. "He's dead?"

"Yep. You fell and rolled till you hit the tree. This moron went after you, but slipped and broke his neck."

The body was right up beside me but wasn't pressing.

"Did he fall against me?"

"No. He stopped before he touched you."

I took a long breath of relief.

"Just ease on outta there," Gavin instructed.

"Where are you?"

"Hiding outta sight. You're seeing things. I didn't want you freaking out seeing someone as fucked up as me in the state you're in."

"How do you know what's happening to me?"

"You told me."

"When?"

"When you came out of the tent. I asked what was wrong and you told me you were feeling strange. Then you started talking to someone who wasn't there, right before that crazy ghost man showed up."

"What crazy ghost man?"

"Never mind that right now. Let's work on getting you out of this mess."

"Jesus, Gavin, you saved my life back there."

256

"Don't mention it. But next time I tell you to run, do it."

I returned my attention to the dead Viking. He stank worse than any human I'd ever smelled before. I suppose the years living with insanity kept the thought of cleanliness at bay. He was on his back, his head twisted toward me, and I could see the swollen section of his neck where the bone had broken. His long, matted hair draped part of his face. I wished it covered him entirely. His pale wide eyes were locked directly on me like scud missiles. He had a long beard with twigs and dirt in it, which made him appear old, yet his eyes weren't that ancient. He couldn't have been any older than twenty when he'd landed on the island.

It was some messed-up luck we'd fallen so close to each other, but things could have been worse. Neither his arms nor legs lay on me, just a human skull and some smaller bones hanging from a surprisingly modern-looking leather belt. He must have gotten the belt from one of his victims.

The bones on my leg didn't worry me. They weren't part of him, so moving them shouldn't curse me with his soul. I cringed at the thought of having a crazed Viking following me around forever.

I slowly shifted myself onto my side, creating space between us. I was so close to him that my pounding heart could've rocked him.

"Shit," Gavin cursed suddenly. "Watch yourself."

"I am!" I snapped. "Shut up and let me do this."

I feared if I touched him it would be enough to draw another spirit like Gavin's to me. I stayed still for a long time, feeling my heart bang against my chest. I moved my shoe ever so slowly, gritting my teeth the entire time. Once my foot was safely away, I used my arms to lift me up. Then I stood.

"That's it, dude, now side-step out."

I moved like I was on the ledge of a high building. With my back against the tree, I tip-toed beside the Viking, then leapt away.

"Dude, my heart would be pumping if it could still beat," Gavin remarked. "D'you think you're in the clear?"

"Not sure," I said nervously. "Would you have to deal with him if he showed up?"

"Dunno. I'm new here too. You should've seen how many ghosts he had with him."

"What ghosts?"

"The ones following him. Jeez, he must've killed a bunch of people."

I almost forgot that ghosts could see each other. "Did they say anything to you?"

"No, didn't give me the time of day. I think they were in a hurry to leave."

"You mean they're not here now?"

"No. When this asshole died, they just wandered off into the fog. It was like they were free."

Just like Darwin. I wondered if the dead were able to leave the island if they had no living person to latch onto.

A sharp pain erupted from my arm. Looking down, I remembered the slash from Point-Blank's knife. The cut was pretty deep and I needed to get it wrapped.

"You better get back to camp," Gavin said. "Your friend needs you."

I didn't understand what he meant by that but I headed up to the campsite anyway. Things still shifted and jumped about, but my hands felt oddly numb. I was ready to get off this trip.

Point-Blank was the first to catch my eye when I made it back up the hill. He remained in place, holding a knife in each hand.

"PB?" I said, slowly approaching him. Ever mindful of his knives, I crept around him. I let him know I was there as a friend. "It's me, Heath. Are you all right? Talk to me."

As I came around to face him, it was like looking at an entirely different person. He appeared old. No, not old, more like he'd been drained of all his bodily fluids. His face was completely sunken and his lips were chapped and bleeding from constantly licking and biting. He rocked slightly from side to side, his eyes darting around as if he could see something I couldn't. My blood stained his knife's blade.

"Point-Blank, talk to me," I urged.

"I wasn't talking about him," Gavin said somberly.

I turned in the direction of his voice but saw no one. "Who do you mean? Damn it, show yourself, Gavin. I'm not going to freak."

Gavin suddenly stood beside Point-Blank and I jumped with a girlish yelp.

"You said you wouldn't freak!" he snapped.

"You popped out of nowhere," I said.

"Heath?" came a weak voice near the tents. "Is that you, mate?"

"Travis?" I said, rushing over. When I reached the campsite, several creatures scampered away. They'd been eating the corpses. Travis was on his side near a soot pile that used to be our fire. He looked pale.

"I thought you'd gone round the bend, lad," he said with a feeble grin.

"Let me help you up," I offered, kneeling beside him.

"No, leave me. I'm dying."

I didn't want to believe it, but there was a bone handle sticking out of his lower back.

"I've been bleeding for hours now. It hurts so much. And worse, I've got two Viking bastards taunting me."

I spotted the body of a Viking behind the tent. He was face-down with a bullet wound to the back of his head. The other Viking lay near Eric's decapitated body.

"Khenan is a lousy marksman," Travis said. "I had to finish the bugger off."

"Travis," I whispered pitifully.

"He needs your help," Gavin said.

"How?"

"Pull this bloody blade outta me. Let me die faster."

I shook my head. "No, I can get you out of here. You can live."

"I've been bleeding for too long, mate. Carrying me down the mountain won't do me any good. Just put me out of me misery."

"Do it, Heath," Gavin said. "Give the man his peace."

"If I do this, you'll be stuck with me for eternity," I said.

"No, lad, you didn't kill me, the Viking did. We killed each other. Only that bastard beat me to the punch."

He shook horribly and was as pale as ash. He was going to die sooner or later and it was up to me to decide which.

"All right," I said. I reached around and took a firm grip on the handle.

"Don't give up hope, lad," Travis said just above a whisper. "Keep searching and set us all free."

"I will," I promised.

He smiled. "Good man."

I ripped the knife out. The blade had stopped most of the blood in the liver, and when I yanked it out, it was like pulling a cork from a drain. Black blood poured from him. I stayed by his side until he passed away.

Chapter Twenty-six

I knelt beside Travis's body for a long time, until my foot fell asleep. When I came to terms with what had happened, I sat on the embankment overlooking our disastrous campsite. I found a first aid kit in Eric's bag and cleaned and bandaged the gash on my arm. I checked the old wound on my hand, still fresh underneath the smear of salve. At least that kept it from hurting so much, just like Travis had said it would. I briefly wondered how people had discovered that. Then again, how did ancient Europeans come up with the idea of making musical strings from animal intestines? It's just one of those discoveries, I suppose.

"Gavin," I said weakly.

"Yeah."

"I think I'm gonna lose it, man. Tell me something about yourself. You know, normal stuff. I need normal right now."

"Um, all right. I was born in Nassau, Florida thirty-two years ago. I like fishing and sports, and um . . . I dress up in women's clothes sometimes."

I glared at him, perplexed.

"Kidding, dude. I mean, I did dress once in drag for Halloween."

"Why did you want to take up flying?"

"It was something new and exciting, I guess. Thought I could fly back to my little town in Baker County and brag about my new skill before soaring off into the unknown. Just a stupid fantasy, y'know?"

"I don't think it's stupid," I said quietly.

A soothing silence settled like dust on a recently disturbed road. Finally, he said, "He was right, y'know? Travis, I mean."

"About what?" I said, rolling the gauze around my arm.

"You shouldn't give up searching."

"I need to get Point-Blank back to South Village."

"He ain't gonna let you touch him. Have you forgotten who gave you that little love mark on your arm?"

"I've caused the death of so many people already. It's time to call it quits."

"You ain't caused no one to die. If it makes you feel any better, you're all alone now. Ain't no one in danger of dying around you."

"Touching," I said mildly.

I cut and tied the bandage off, securing it snugly around my arm. A rustle in the woods drew my attention.

I slid my hand over the pistol sitting beside me when a Neanderthal woman emerged from the thicket. She wore ripped, well-worn denim shorts and a T-shirt. Whatever image was imprinted on the shirt had long since faded beyond recognition. She was extremely dirty, with bright red leaves stuck in her long tangled hair. She was a powerful looking thing, with almost the same amount of muscle as me. I bet she'd be awesome in a bar fight.

The animal skin wrapped around her feet had muffled her footsteps, concealing her approach. She was armed with a bow, an arrow fixed in the string, ready to fire at me Robin Hood-style. Her posture was hunched and her sharp eyes never left me. I didn't move, hardly breathed. I think I held my weapon just as tightly as she held hers, both our knuckles stretched over the bones.

She was one of the Ancient Ones. I'd seen her on the beach when I'd first come to the island.

"Jeez, I know I got no room to talk, but she's got a face not even a mother could love," Gavin put in.

She halted and her fuzzy unibrow rose.

"Holy crap, did she just hear me?" He cupped his hand around his mouth. "Hey! You hear me?"

It wasn't his shouting that had caught her attention, it was my gun. Whether she knew what it was and what it could do, she clearly recognized it as a weapon. I didn't want a confrontation just because she felt threatened.

I took a chance and let the gun go, placing my hand on my knee. She already had me pegged with the arrow anyway. I'd have to raise the gun, take aim, and pull the trigger to hit her. All she needed to do was let go of the string. Even if I could fire, I didn't want to kill her. I hoped she understood the consequences of taking a life.

She had several arrows in a skin quiver strapped to her back, and some knives as well. I guess she was a hunter.

She moved on, looking at the bodies on the ground, careful not to disturb any of them. She seemed wise to the otherworldly rule, but it wouldn't matter if she moved them, since they'd killed each other.

Her expression went wide at the sight of the dead Vikings. She craned her head to Travis, then back to the Vikings. She made a fist and hit her chest a few times, then glided her hand over Travis's body in a smooth motion. I imagine it was a salute of gratitude.

She must have figured out that Travis had been the one who'd shot them. Her delight in their death didn't surprise me. I'm sure her tribe must've had many unpleasant encounters with them throughout the years.

She went over to Point-Blank next. She came around him, took one look at his body, and nodded with a grunt.

Gavin approached me. "She knows what happened to him."

"How do you know that?"

"Simply observing, my dear Watson. I've gotten good at it since I can't do a whole lot of anything else. Like while you were fighting for your life last night, I was observing. I had the chance to catch details. That's how I knew Travis was in trouble."

I said nothing. Not because I was ignoring him, but because I didn't want to startle the girl. I watched as she glanced down the embankment where the other dead Viking lay. My heart sped up as she approached me. She no longer held her bow defensively. That eased my anxiety slightly, but not enough to dismiss the gun from my mind. I sat frozen as she leaped over Eric's headless body and a Viking to reach me. When she came close, I noticed the scars on her body. Her pale eyes had dark circles around them. She must've been tracking the sound of gunshots all night.

She offered me the same salute and grinned. At least I think she grinned. Her thick upper lip curled upward, showing the worst set of teeth I'd ever seen. No dentist alive could repair that grill. Travis would have been happy to see teeth worse than his.

She waved for me to follow.

"Let's go with her," Gavin suggested excitedly.

"I told you, I have to get Point-Blank home."

My response caused her to take a step back. She cocked her head sideways with a puzzled expression.

"And I told you, you can't do anything for him. He ain't going anywhere," Gavin said. "Focus on the agenda. Follow the ugly chick."

I looked at my wounded arm. The only way I'd get Point-Blank to South Village was if I knocked him out, tied him up, and dragged him down the island. Considering his fragile state of mind, if he took a hard enough hit on the head, it could cause him more damage. I remembered the last thing Travis had said to me. *Keep searching and set us all free.*

"Jeez, you can come back and get the psycho statue later," Gavin groaned.

I shifted my eyes to him. The girl grunted, drawing my attention back to her. She spoke in what sounded like a deep husky baby speech. Again, she signaled me to come with her. Reluctantly, I stood, grabbed my bag, and left.

We walked for what seemed like a lifetime. The higher we climbed, the worse the humidity got. The dense forest made the hike atrocious. I used Eric's machete to hack away the mess. The girl kept swiveling her head back to me with a look of envy. She'd been climbing through the shit with nothing but a dinky knife she might have made herself. Finally, I lent the machete to her. After all, she was leading the way.

After a while, we stopped for a break. I took a drink from my canteen and handed it to her. I felt a little bad for drinking first, but I only did so to show there was nothing harmful in it. I didn't want to risk losing the rest of my water if she turned the canteen upside down or slit my throat, thinking I was trying to poison her.

She seemed savvy enough, easily catching on. Perhaps it was millions of years' experience or she was naturally smart, but she gulped it down. Then she plucked some red leaves from a nearby brush, the same kind that were in her hair. I'd seen those scattered about. The bright red color made it look like the biblical burning bush. She rubbed a couple of them on her hairy arms, neck, legs, and face. I thought it was a weird grooming ritual. She yanked more off and tried handing them to me.

"No thanks, I like to use soap."

She snatched my wrist and started grinding the leaves against my arm.

"Okay!" I shouted, taking them from her. "I'll do it, damn it."

She didn't move or take her eyes off me until I'd scrubbed the leaves over every inch of my naked skin. The leaves caused a strange tingle.

When we caught our second wind, I decided to ask her a very important question I'd refrained from asking before. "Where are we going?"

She looked at me, confused. I repeated the question more slowly, as if uttering the words cautiously made them more understandable to someone who didn't speak my language. I tried pantomiming my meaning by pointing at her, then to me. "Where are we..." I did the walking man with my fingers. "...going?"

I should've tried asking her back at the campsite, but in the midst of my grief, I simply hadn't cared if she was leading me into a black hole.

She stared at me for a good long while, then took a stick and drew a circle in the dirt. Not a perfect circle, but hell, how many people could do that? I studied it, then raised my chin to her. She grunted, stood, and walked on before I could ask her about it.

For the rest of the way, we went across the island instead of up it. She led me somewhere I hoped wasn't to her tribe. Cannibalism came to mind. I wanted to reach the top of the island. Maybe up there, I could see some open gateway out of this place.

I kept my mouth shut—mostly to save myself from dehydration—and followed her. To my relief, we came to a stream. I washed the sweat off my face and filled my canteen. Maybe the stream was the reason we'd come in this direction.

Once we'd refreshed ourselves, she continued along the same route. Again, I said nothing. My feet ached from struggling to maintain my balance against the steep embankment. The sticky humidity got to me. If we'd kept going up straight, we would've reached the top by now.

"All right," I finally said in frustration. "I've had it with this shit."

I started upward but didn't get far before she grabbed my wrist. Not just grabbed, but held it so tightly it felt like my bone was crushed into a fine powder. I would've hated it more if she'd snatched my wounded arm. "Ow, Jesus!"

She grunted loudly, followed by other incomprehensible noises. It made me wonder if this was what teenagers sounded like to their parents when they talked slang to them.

"Let go," I protested, trying to pull my arm free. "I don't want to follow you anymore."

That didn't work. In fact, she yanked me down to the hacked trail she'd created and spoke again.

Whatever she said, it sounded urgent. I'll admit, she scared me.

She let go, scratching me with those long jagged fingernails of hers, then pointed forward with the machete and began hacking through the vegetation again. I decided it was best to cooperate.

It was another fifteen minutes before she stopped. She spoke to me in her gibberish again. I raised my head while wiping sweat from my tired eyes.

"What the...?"

At first, I believed the heat played tricks on my mind when I saw an alien aircraft protruding from the rock wall. I knew in an instant the thing hadn't been manufactured on Earth. The object was identical to the description people had recounted about their encounters with Martians. It was a silver sphere, at least two hundred feet wide. It looked as though it had crashed right onto the island, hitting so hard the rocky mountainside had devoured it. The undercarriage was scratched and badly dented. Nature had nearly consumed it. Thick vines hugged the machine's every curve. Moss had made a home on the roof with flowers and other plant life sprouting from it.

I stood there, stupefied, until my trance broke when the girl climbed on top of the craft.

"Ah," I managed to say. I feared the aircraft would loosen from its rocky bed and fall over, transforming into a sliding whirling disk of death for anyone in its path. But it didn't budge, even as she walked all over it.

"Take a picture, Heath," Gavin said. "Ain't no one gonna believe this."

The girl pointed to the other side of the ship. I walked around it and between the vines was a foot-wide line of glass surrounding the craft. The half that wasn't supported by rocks stuck out vertically. I could hide under it for shelter, if needed. At the rear—at least, I think it was the rear—where the glass line was, were five diamond shapes lined up side by side. Two of them were broken. They appeared to be bulbs, most likely the kind of lights spotted from the sky. Hanging from the undercarriage was some kind of landing gear. Not a wheel, but three metal poles with a flat end, almost resembling suction cups. The craft wouldn't have rolled over the ground like an airplane, but hovered down for landings.

As I came around, the girl crouched at the ship's edge and pointed to a platform leading into an opening.

"Ooh, go in," Gavin urged. "Go in, go in! I wanna see what's inside."

I debated it. I wished the girl could explain things to me, like why she'd brought me to an alien spacecraft and what was inside that she wanted me to see.

I approached the platform and stopped at the bottom of it, where I took out my gun and aimed it at the ground. The girl objected. She grunted, shook her head, and jumped onto the platform. She was built like a gladiator and took a huge leap to land with ease on an uneven surface. It made me a little jealous.

She waved me forward and went inside. I didn't holster my gun, but followed.

I expected it to be pitch-black inside, but as we entered the craft, everything was as transparent as if we'd entered a glass room. The only thing not translucent was the floor, which was made from a glossy metal. The gripping vines, moss, and everything else outside were visible. From the outside, the ship's exterior appeared to be solid steel, but the inside told a different story. The front of the ship was totaled. Broken equipment littered the floor. Earth and rock spilled through a large hole caused by its impact. I couldn't identify anything. What looked like switches could have been something else. Hell, I didn't even know how they'd steered this thing. There were no chairs, only a cracked glass counter that wrapped around the wall. When I studied the counter top, I found faint symbols imprinted on it.

The girl's grunt caused me to turn to her. She waved me over, and I approached another platform leading into a hull. Unlike the rest of the ship, it was dark. The girl held a small torch and a lighter. Where she'd gotten the lighter, I'll never know, but after lighting the torch, she descended into the hull. I went with her.

I almost expected some mystical being living on the ship, a being with the answers to all my questions, but the hull was empty, completely and miserably vacant. The empty space might have been used to hold supplies, all of which had been taken by the aliens who'd once manned the ship.

"Why are we down here?" Gavin asked, as if I knew. He walked ahead, following the girl, and his hunched silhouette reminded me of Igor. "Jeez! Heath, take a gander at this."

I joined the girl where she stood by a pile of bones. They looked like the complete skeleton of a large animal. Then I noticed the skull. Kneeling, I picked it up and examined it. It felt spongy, like foam rubber. It had small eye sockets, two tiny holes for a nasal cavity, and toothpick-like teeth. It also had a large crack at the base, revealing how the creature must have died.

I was in awe. I mean, damn, I was holding the actual skull of an extra-terrestrial. No one on Earth I knew had done that except for those who'd found the ancient Incan tribal skulls and suspected they were alien. But that wasn't what I was looking at. This was the real deal. I wanted to take it back with me but I didn't. Instead, I placed the skull back in its original spot with the rest of the skeleton and left the ship with the girl.

She wanted to show me something else and I followed without argument. After coming across the spacecraft, I could only envision what other wonders she knew about. We left the spaceship and this time headed up.

We came across more trees covered in slimy, smelly goo. These trees had grown on top of huge boulders sitting close together. I had no intention of touching one, but as we closed in, the girl suddenly stopped and whipped around to face me. She made a series of loud urgent noises, pointing to the trees, shaking her head.

"I don't think she wants you touching them," Gavin said.

"I gathered," I retorted.

Why not, I wondered, then figured it out. The trees made you lose your mind.

It made sense. Nearly all of us had touched the sap on the trees hours before we'd started seeing things. My hallucinations had worn off because I'd only gotten a little on me, unlike Eric and Point-Blank, who'd gone nuts after they'd been doused with the shit. I wondered if Khenan was still alive and if he'd ridden out his nightmares like me.

I nodded to the girl, letting her know I

understood, and we moved on.

The journey past the boulders and trees was unnerving. It was like walking through a dangerous labyrinth. I did my best not to touch the gooey sap-covered roots that smothered the rocks. When squeezing through tight spots, I started to perspire, and it wasn't because of the heat. The rotten egg stench was overwhelming. I nearly vomited.

After passing through the field of doomsday boulders, we continued on. When we reached the top, we were again on solid ground. The next leg of the trip lasted until we reached a two-story house. A nice house, I might add. One made of logs and stone, with a chimney—though when it was ever cold in the Bermuda Triangle, I had no idea.

The house sat in a clearing, with the logs likely coming from the surrounding woods. The owner had an actual yard and a garden, and that was where I spotted a woman. The girl made a loud noise to get her attention and the woman turned. She seemed surprised.

"Abby?" the woman said in an English accent. "What are you doing?"

Without a word, the girl ran away and vanished down an embankment, taking my machete with her. I stayed in place as the woman approached. She cradled a basket against her hip. As she drew closer, I caught more details about her. She appeared to be in her late thirties or early forties, and wore green Capri pants and a sleeveless shirt. She wore no shoes, and like Carlton, her skin was cocaine-white.

"Why did she bring you here?" she asked hotly, never breaking her steady stride. "Who are you?"

"Heath Sharp. And I don't know why she brought me here. Maybe it has something to do with the dead

273

Vikings."

The woman stopped abruptly. "Dead Vikings? Have those bastards finally been killed off? Who's the poor hero who has Viking blood on his hands? You?"

"No, a good friend of mine shot two of them. He's dead now."

"Oh," she said with sympathy. "I'm so sorry." She took off her dirty gardening gloves and extended a hand to me. "I'm Doctor Calla Newbury."

I was about to shake her hand when she quickly withdrew it. She sniffed at me. "You haven't touched the purple sap have you?"

"No."

"Good. That bloody stuff really stinks." We shook hands. "What happened to your arm?"

"I got sliced by a knife," I answered, glancing at the red seeping through the gauze around my arm.

"It seems as though it needs to be treated. No worries, I have plenty of salve here. So, tell me, Mr. Sharp, what brings you to my home?"

I told her about my mission and the people who'd died along the way. I explained that the girl, the one she called Abby, had led me to an alien spacecraft where she'd shown me the occupant's bones.

"Really?" she said, surprised but not all that astonished. "You saw Hector? Would you like to meet his sister? She's in the house playing Mouse Trap."

Chapter Twenty-seven

It didn't fully register what she said even as we approached her house.

"Did she say sister?" Gavin asked, walking beside me.

"I can't believe Abby brought you to me," Calla said. "It's quite odd. She's never done that before."

"Does she come here often?"

"Once in a while. I give her vegetables for her tribe."

"So why did she run off like that?"

"She's probably hunting. Bringing you here must've interrupted her."

I had so many questions for this woman, I didn't know where to begin. I decided to start with the basics. "How long have you've been trapped on the island?"

"Seventy-four years."

"Plane or ship?"

"Boat," she said as we reached the door to her house. "I'm probably the only one who deliberately trapped herself here."

"Why?"

She scraped her bare feet over a mat, moving like a chicken. "Would you mind taking off your shoes? I keep a clean house."

I sat on a small bench beside the door and unlaced my dirty sneakers.

"I'm a researcher. I study strange occurrences around the world. At least I used to. When my husband died, I went out on a mission—perhaps a suicidal mission—to study the Devil's Triangle."

I slipped off one shoe and unlaced the other.

"I wanted to know why ships and planes were vanishing. What caused them to drop off the face of the Earth. I rented a boat, brought my notes, and sailed into the Atlantic. Needless to say, I found out."

For good measure, I removed my grimy socks. "What did you do, then?"

"I lived in North Village. South Village wasn't really built like it is now. Not until the World War II chaps arrived and Worley had enough men to build it. Come in."

I followed her inside.

"I wish Amelia Earhart had crashed here. She would've been grand to talk with. She and I are alike, both women who ventured into men's fields."

It was a very clean and picturesque house. The main section had bookshelves not only filled with books, but other items, like ship parts, landing wheels, and brass compasses. On the wall hung portholes and life preservers.

We came into the kitchen with a dinner table between where the kitchen ended and the rest of the house began. The chimney suddenly made sense. Set in a space between a kitchen counter was a small fireplace where an iron kettle hung over a fire. The makeshift stove had a few pots cooking. Calla placed the basket of vegetables on the counter next to a bowl of water and a jar filled with dead insects.

"I stayed in the village and studied plants, wildlife, even the people who'd been here long before me." She explained while taking out the vegetables and washing them in the bowl. "I took notes, but without any kind of scientific equipment, I couldn't do any real experiments. One day—I think it was in the fifties—I left the village to explore the island, despite the dangers. I'd been looking for answers, after all."

"What did you find?"

She dried her hands on her pants, leaving the vegetables on a cutting board. "Ruby."

I followed her through the main section of the house and up a spiral staircase, where we came to a door. Calla knocked on it.

A strange sound came from behind it, like keys scrapping over a jagged piece of metal. I turned to Gavin and he only shrugged. Calla turned the knob and went inside—or outside, I should say. We stepped onto a large deck with small tables in every corner, sheltered by patio umbrellas. On the tables were objects I couldn't make out through the mosquito netting hanging from the umbrellas.

"She likes to be outside," Calla explained.

"Who?"

"Holy moly!" Gavin exclaimed. "That can't be real."

I craned my neck to see the far end of the deck where the alien stood. It was eight feet tall and had a slender neck and an overly large head, the same shape as the skull in the spacecraft. Its body reminded me of a lizard, with a broad chest and skinny waist. I mean anorexic to the point where a young starlet would be jealous. It also had bony hips and long limbs.

The alien stood by a table, where it dropped a silver ball into a red basket. That began a chain reaction in a game of Mouse Trap. The metal ball rolled and clanked against the plastic components. My attention wasn't on the ball, but on the creature from another world.

"Ruby," Calla called, "we have a guest."

The thing grudgingly turned its head from the game to lay its beady gray eyes on me. It walked toward us, its posture perfectly straight, which made it seem much taller and frightening. I took a step back, every nerve in my legs twitching to make a run for it.

"Relax," Calla said. "Ruby isn't a monster. She's a highly intelligent being with perfect social skills."

Her claim didn't sell me, especially after seeing the alien get its jollies off on a child's board game. "How do you know it's a girl?"

"She, not *it*," Calla snapped. "And I know because she told me."

"Beeesides," Ruby said in a voice like tearing Velcro, *"can't you ssseeee my vaginaaaa?"*

My eyes focused on her stilt legs. What appeared to be two milky-white flaps of skin hung between them.

"Jeez, porn stars have privates tighter than hers," Gavin chortled.

"You speak English?" I asked, quickly shifting my eyes up her body. Ruby's hands and feet were large and bony, with long black nails curled in short spirals.

"I speeeeak hundreds of languagesss. Ssseverrral are yoursss."

"She taught me a few of our other languages," Calla said. "German, French, Portuguese, and Spanish." She said something to Ruby in Russian. It sounded like a question.

"Nnnyet," Rudy replied.

"See?" Calla said.

"I . . . I think I need to sit down," I said, glancing around for a chair. There were none.

"Ruby's kind doesn't sit," Calla said. "Come with

278

me back downstairs. I'll make you some tea."

I followed her downstairs and Ruby came with us. Calla offered me a chair near a window.

"You're in luck," she said as I slowly lowered myself into the cushy seat. "The water's boiling."

She went to the fireplace in the kitchen, while Ruby stayed with me, standing nearby, watching me with those waxy eyes of hers. They had no pupils. Her ashy skin was mottled and had protruding veins over her body. She wasn't grotesque, just not what I expected to find when I'd regained consciousness this morning.

"Youuu have questionsss," she said, her words tearing the air. When she spoke, her lipless mouth hardly moved.

"Many, starting with—"

"Meee," she cut in.

"Yeah," I squeaked.

"Weee were explorersss, my brrrother and I. Our plaaanet isss twice assss large asss yoursss and one hundrrred fifty millionnnn light yeeearsss awaaay. Our ship and twooo othersss came herrre when wee crashed."

"How can you breathe this air?" I asked stupidly.

"The air heeere isss acceptaaable to everrrry living thing. Did yooou not notice the air differsss from yourrrr own?"

I remembered the tightness in my chest when I'd first arrived.

"Are you educated in history, Mr. Sharp?" Calla asked, returning with a tea set. She placed the tray on the table in front of me.

"I know some things. Call me Heath."

"Did you ever read about Christopher

279

Columbus's claim of lights in the sky while sailing across the Atlantic?"

"I saw something about it on the History Channel once."

"The History Channel?" she questioned, pouring tea into two cups.

Again, I needed to remind myself where people like her had come from. I didn't feel like explaining, so I simply said, "Yeah, I heard about it."

"Those lights were from Ruby and Hector's party." She handed me a cup.

"My brrrother died in the crash. He wassss in the storrrage hull jussst beforrre the storm caaame upon usss. He haaad no time to come up befoore ourrr ship slammed into the island."

Ruby became quiet and turned her head away. She spoke in some weird language to something that wasn't there.

"Who's she talking to?" I asked.

"Hector," Calla replied and casually sipped her tea. She didn't need to explain the details. I understood.

"What's she saying?"

"I don't know. Their language is far too complicated for me to comprehend. That's why I call her Ruby and her brother Hector. I can't pronounce their real names to save my life."

After Ruby finished speaking to her brother's spirit, she turned to me. *"I saw the otherrr shipsssss circling around. Theirrr lightsss pieeerced the black sky after the storrrm clouds clearrrred. I don't eeeven think they sssaw the island. Eeeventually, they left and I wasss alone."*

"Why did you come here to begin with?"

280

"Toooo ssstudy the enerrrgy moooon frrragment."

That took me by surprise. "The energy moon fragment?"

"They call it another name," Calla said. "One impossible for us to pronounce."

"Oh. Okay, what's an energy moon?"

"It'sss a moooon made of high quaaantiteees of pure enerrrgy. It wasss your planet's sssecond mooon. It collided wiiith the moooon yoooou knooow of today."

"What? The Earth had two moons?"

"Indeeed," Ruby said. *"Two moooons once orbited your planet millions of yearsss after the other plaaanet collided with Earth. The farthest and smaller moooon had stored much of what the Earth needed to start life—waaater. Asss time passssed, water began forming oceansss of powerful and dangerrrous energy."*

What she said about this other planet colliding with Earth took me aback. But then I remembered the theory of a Mars-size planet called Thea that had supposedly crashed into Earth, sending rocks orbiting around until they clumped up to form our moon...or moons as I just learned.

"And you said this energy moon collided with our bigger moon?" I asked in awe.

"Yesss. We believe the energy moooon targeted Earth and pulled itself toward Earth'sss gravitational field. When it did, it caaame into the paaath of the larger moon and collided with it. Fragments of the collisssion maaade it all the waaay to Earth."

"We were lucky," Calla said. "The fragments that penetrated our atmosphere were small and didn't cause

281

much damage."

"Whoa, whoa, wait a sec," I said, putting a hand up after I set my cup on the table. "What are we exactly talking about here?"

"I'm talking about luck," Calla said. "If the fragments of this energy moon had been larger when they'd struck, there may not have been an Earth for us to evolve on."

"No, that's not what I'm asking. I'm . . ." My questions got tangled up in my head and I didn't know which to ask first. "You both said fragments? Meaning more than one?"

"Yes, one landed off the coast of Japan, another crashed in Alaska. The third landed somewhere in the ocean and eventually ended up here."

"How do you know that?"

"Ruby told me," Calla said, smiling at the tall alien. "She was part of a research team. Their mission was to locate these fragments, study them, and bring samples back to her home planet."

"You're saying we're sitting on a moon fragment?" I asked in disbelief. "I hate to tell you, but this place isn't a fragment."

"That'sss becaussse it greeew," Ruby explained. *"The sssalinity in the waaater awaaakened itsss energggy. Yourrr planet isss verrry fertile."*

"As the Earth's continents broke apart and shifted, this particular fragment followed an enormous land mass that later became America. Eventually, it settled on top of an underwater volcano. The fragment merged with the molten earth and slowly matured into this island."

"It grew?"

"Like a seed," Calla put in. "It's the energy that

kept the fragments alive."

"Alive?"

"Yes, moons can be living things too, depending on the situation. What's unique is that the fragments remained alive so long after the energy moon was destroyed."

"The fragment had much of itsss own waaater storrd within it."

"What about the one in Japan? Has it grown into an island?"

"Nooo," Ruby said. *"It never did. The fragment maaay ssstill be down there. I've been trapped here for a long while."*

"What about the reports of alien aircraft coming out of the water over there?" I asked, remembering the segment on the History Channel.

"Humansss haaave claimed to haaave seen shipsss?"

"All the time," I said. "There are reports from all over the world."

She snorted. *"That shooould not surprissse meee. Other life formsss haaave visited thissss world since the—"* She uttered something incomprehensible. *"—discovered it twooo million yearsss agooo."*

"The what?"

"The other aliens," Calla clarified.

"It'sss only out of curiousity, you underrrstaaand, that other speeecies come to yourrr planet. Our thirst for knowledge is insaaatiable."

I considered asking about experiments on humans but I really wasn't in the mood to discuss anal probing with her, so I went with, "Those other aircraft spotted in Japan are just explorers studying the other fragment?"

"Most likely."

"No weird alien space station down there?"

"Nooo."

"What about Alaska? People go missing more up there than they do down here, and there isn't any island. "

"That's because it's part of the land now," Calla said. "The fragment can grow and shift in Earth's soil fairly easily, since it had come from here anyway. In a way, it's like the fragments were returning home."

"Where are the people who're trapped up there, then?"

Calla shrugged. "I don't know. I've never been to Alaska."

"The energggy isss very much here. It pullsss in other energggies."

"Other energies?"

"Us, for instance," Calla said. "The fragment feeds off our energy to survive."

"Is that why we're trapped here? To feed this damn island?" Was that why so many of us had been taken from our lives? It made me sick to my stomach.

"Yes, the more inhabitants there are, the stronger the fragment becomes. It even sucks the life from batteries."

Ruby's comment about the hungry energy moon suddenly made sense...well, sense enough for this weird conversation.

"And the dead?"

"Our soul—or whatever you wish to call it—is pure energy and that's what the fragment needs. It uses its own energy to hold the souls of the departed to their bodies, but only by a thread. When that thread is broken by a disturbance, it causes the soul to awaken.

In a way, it's like a second chance at living. The body decays but its energy latches onto the one who disturbed it, like a magnet."

Gavin sat cross-legged on the floor, listening intently. He'd been strangely quiet since we'd come downstairs.

"Even the souls of the dead are needed?" I asked, feeling odd.

"Yes, but the dead don't supply as much energy as the living. They're like an appetizer before the main course."

"Why can't anyone else see the ghosts?

"When the spirit is attached to someone, it becomes part of that person, like an outside thought."

"Sort of like an imaginary friend?" I said. She seemed confused by that, so I said, "A make-believe friend no one else can see."

"I suppose, but their imaginary friend is real. I've come to the conclusion that the fragment didn't deliberately make spirits invisible to other people. It just turned out that way."

"What you're saying is that the meat and soul are attached even after death, like a teetering glass on a table's edge, and anyone who tips the glass over has to clean it up?"

"That's a very good analogy," Calla said. "The fragment keeps us immortal to feed it. When it needs more nourishment, it simply waits until it senses energy, sometimes from miles away, and pulls the unsuspecting soul in by creating a storm."

"If the island needs more energy, it should let people have children."

"The radiation after we cross into the fragment's boundaries seems to sterilize men and women, keeping them from ever conceiving children."

"Then what about needing to eat? If we're preserved the way we are, wouldn't we stay full or hungry, however we arrived?"

"Energy needs fuel to survive. We can't go without restoring our spent energy, the same as the fragment must. It's just the way it is."

"What about the ships and planes?" I asked, picking up the tea cup. "Don't tell me they have souls too."

"It'sss the water. It holdssss so much of the fragggment'sss power that it can keep inanimate objectsss untouched by time."

"And the wildlife? Did the island make them?"

"Kind of. It was lucky for the fragment that it landed on such a habitable planet. Trillions of tiny organisms surrounded it. Things began to evolve with the fragment's influence. They became whatever they were going to be elsewhere, but with some differences. They would have developed into creatures you and I know now if not for the fragment's mutations."

"But what about the people? Why aren't there any humanoids running around?"

Calla laughed. "Humans? That's hilarious, isn't it, Ruby?"

Ruby nodded, letting out a piggish snort.

"Why is that so funny?"

"I often wondered what Homo sapiens would be like if they evolved with the fragment's influence. What kind of help they could offer the people here. The things they could accomplish if they just set their minds to it."

She went silent, turning to the window. Her face came aglow as her expression tightened. I almost said something, but then she turned back to me. "It's all well and good there aren't any people here. If they weren't friendly, I can imagine what kind of damage they could do. Native living things of the fragment aren't cursed with the souls of our dead or the dead of other native things."

"Why? Aren't the living things giving out energy, as well?"

"Aye, and in the beginning, the fragment fed off those organisms. But as time passed, those organisms merged with the fragment so much that the fragment could no longer absorb their energy without doing damage to itself. The fragment may be many things, but it isn't a cannibal. It now needs outside sources of energy to survive.

I saw her point and shuddered, then asked a question I'd once asked Inglewood. "How is it that no one has found this place? Not even by satellite."

"The reeesearch teeeam before ussss supposssed the energggy moooon had a unique deeefenssse mechanisssm that allowsss it to camouflaaage itsssself."

"Like a chameleon?"

"A what?" Calla asked, confused.

"A chameleon. You know, a lizard that changes colors." Who the hell didn't know what a chameleon is?

"Oh," she said, then changed the subject. "The fragment is powerful but not as strong as when it was a whole moon."

"What's that supposed to mean?"

"A lot of people here don't know where their planes or ships are. We think it's because people are more easily taken."

287

"Maybe that's why there's wreckage outside the island's borders," I offered.

"Is there?" she asked.

"Yep, ships and planes are found all over the Bermuda Triangle, but not many bodies."

"Ah," Calla mused. "Even so, I wouldn't blame it all on the fragment. Ships sink and planes go down all the time. That's just the way it is."

"Before the moooon'sss destruction, a frrrigid cold compleeetely shielded it. Ourrr best theory wasss that the moooon wasss a verrry warm plaaace and it usssed the cold to manifest sssuperrr ssstorrrmsss to capture annnny life formsss within range."

"That explains the weird coldness outside the junkyard," I said. "So, the moon once did what the island does now?"

"Yesss. The VezQuu's*—the first onesss to have discovered your solar sssystem—had ships vanish when they neared the energy moooon. They kept records of their disssappearanccces. At first, it wasss believed the moon stole shipsss when it felt threatened. Now we see the fragment does what it does in order to survive.*

"You said the native organisms aren't stuck with the souls of our dead if they kill us. What keeps them from eating the corpses?" I felt like an interviewer now, asking questions for the scoop of the century. "Aren't they an easy meal?"

"It depends on where the body is located. The higher the corpse is on the fragment, the more of a chance that something will scavenge it. The Shark Eaters will eat anything they can get a hold of in the warm area of the ocean. But down at the beach, there aren't a lot of predators—except for the stingrays—

that'll go after the dead because of all the people around."

"The fleasss have deterred most from going too far up the island," Ruby chimed in.

"Fleas?" I asked. "What about the fleas?"

"Little bastards carry a powerful hallucinogen that'll mess your head up if enough bite you," Calla said.

"Wait, *that's* what makes people go insane here? Fleas?"

"They're mostly in the more humid parts of the forest and are practically invisible. To keep them away, you have to smear red leaves all over yourself. The sap acts like a pesticide."

"What about bug spray?"

"Bug spray will do the trick, but it's not as effective."

Now I understood why Abby had offered me the leaves. Bugs had bitten me all that day. Apparently, the bug spray I'd used helped keep the attack to a minimum, unlike the soldiers, who'd used none of the spray and had been eaten alive.

"I thought that purple tree sap was the culprit for driving them crazy."

"No, it just smells bloody awful."

"How did you find the fragment?" I asked Ruby.

"My kind didn't discover it," she admitted. *"It wasss the* VezQuu *yearsss after their discovery of Earth."*

I caught a few phonetic sounds this time. A "v" and a "q" maybe. I usually have a pretty good memory but not with that word.

"Five thousand years ago, those others aliens discovered this fragment by accident, while studying

289

our planet," Calla said. "They knew they'd come upon something odd when their equipment went wild. After searching through their records, they found out what it was. At the time, the fragment couldn't pull in something as powerful as their ship and they could study it."

"But it caught yours," I said to Ruby.

"Because the fraggment haaad more strength by then."

"But these other aliens landed here?"

"Only once," Calla said. "They took samples and did studies on the living things here. Once they left, they couldn't find the island anymore."

"Mosssst likely, the fragggment kept itssself hidden from them after theeey left."

"But that didn't keep them from trying to find it for years afterward," Calla said bitterly, as if what they'd done was personal to her. "Finally, they gave up and continued on with their research of Earth. Ancient people apparently noticed the alien's documents of the fragment and were told stories about it. In time, people began building replicas of the fragment."

"Pyramids?" I guessed.

"Exactly."

This was a shitload to take in. It was more than I'd expected to find when I'd set out on my mission. I decided to ask the million dollar question. "What about escaping?"

Calla displayed her most baffled expression yet. "Escape? Have you tried?"

"I'm looking for a way. Why does a storm keep people from sailing out?"

"The fragment senses when someone is heading for its boundaries and triggers a storm."

290

"Why?"

"It needs us to survive. It has to feed off our energy to live."

"Keeping us trapped here like zoo animals?"

"Zoo animals?" Again, Calla's apparent lack in knowledge of ordinary things took me by surprise.

"Yeah, y'know, locked up."

"Oh."

"Are yooou hungry?" Ruby asked. *"I maaake an exccellent casserrrole."*

I was hungry—very much so. "Yeah, actually. Need any help?"

"No, I prefer to cooook alone."

"She's a very good cook," Calla said as Ruby left for the kitchen. "She knows Julia Childs's recipes by heart."

"Why did you bring cookbooks with you?"

"I didn't, but someone on a yacht had them. Over the years, I've scavenged through the junkyard for supplies. You'd be amazed what you can find out there."

"I've seen plenty. No one ever said anything about you in the village, not even Eleanor."

"I like to keep to myself. I told Eleanor that I was heading up the island for answers. Since I never came back, they must've thought I'd died. I intended to go back, but then I found Ruby and decided not to return."

"Why?"

"She needed me as much as I needed her. She's been alone for over five hundred years, living on the fragment. She survived the Vikings by planting those smelly trees. The Vikings were afraid of them. Even so, I'm shocked she's lived this long."

"How come? Can't she defend herself?"

291

Calla shook her head. "Ruby may appear intimidating but her body is very soft. She succumbs to injury very easily, which is why I have plenty of salve around."

I was reminded of the alien's spongy skull.

"Her level of intelligence is something we can never reach, but her physical features are as brittle as rotten wood."

"When did you find her?"

"Fifty-three years ago," she said with accuracy. "While I was out exploring, I came across her ship. That's where I found her. Like you, she scared me, and I scared her, but eventually, we started communicating. She was so lonely. She'd had no contact with anyone other than her dead brother. The Neanderthals are terrified of her. She saw me as no threat, though. Since then, we've studied the fragment together. Two scientists from separate worlds, working side by side. With my strength, I could gather samples she couldn't, giving both of us a chance to find out more about this place than we could ever have done alone." She laughed softly. "I suppose, in this case, I'm the brawn and she's the brains."

"And you've never found a way out?"

She expelled such a long sigh I thought she'd never stop exhaling. "I've studied this place long enough to know there's no way out. My advice to you is to accept the fragment as your home and stop this fruitless search before you end up dead—or worse."

A flush of disappointment spread through my entire body. After some time, Ruby called us in for dinner. I ate, and Ruby was right. She did make an excellent casserole.

Chapter Twenty-eight

The casserole was delicious but it rested heavily in my gut. Calla's discouraging news left me feeling completely hopeless. I could've eaten a cream puff and it would've sat like a brick inside my stomach. If a scientist slams the door on any possible escape from the island, that's a wrap. After all, I've never heard a report of someone describing a gloomy island surrounded by a museum of lost ships. Hell, there were people trapped in the Bermuda Triangle dating back hundreds of thousands of years. Nobody had gotten out—nobody. Why would I be any different? All I wanted was to find a way out, but maybe I had delusions of grandeur. Maybe I aimed to achieve where others had failed, leading the way to freedom for future generations of Bermuda Triangle prisoners.

No, it wasn't that, I was simply in denial. I longed for home, longed for something familiar—the sight of the sunset from my back porch, the welcoming feeling I got from my friends' faces, and the sound of my mother's laugh.

After dinner, I put salve on both my cuts, then went outside, put my shoes on, and admired Calla's beautiful garden. I'd offered to help with the dishes but that was a task Ruby preferred to do alone. She hadn't eaten what she'd cooked, but she'd enjoyed a salad with vegetables and dead insects from a jar.

"I'm glad you came by," Calla said, joining me. "You caught me up on current events."

During dinner, I'd answered her questions about

the outside world since 1947. Her last contact with anyone had been the WWII soldiers who'd helped build her house. Ruby had remained hidden in her ship until they'd left.

"Before you leave, I must ask you for something."

"I won't tell anyone about you or Ruby," I promised.

She gave me a grateful smile. "Are you sure you want to leave so close to dark? Ruby makes a wonderful omelet."

"I have to take someone back to South Village before something kills him."

"I see."

"Why do you think Abby brought me here?"

Calla shrugged. "I haven't the faintest idea. Perhaps she hoped I could tell you the way out of this place. I think she tried asking me once years ago, after she realized I wasn't going to hurt her."

"Were you able to get her to understand that there isn't any way off the island?" I hated to sound so dead serious with the question, but it made me realize the bitter truth.

"No, I wanted Ruby to speak to her. Ruby only needs minutes to learn any language. But Abby has always been afraid of her."

My disappointment dropped to an all-time low. It seemed even the Ancient Ones wanted out, and Abby, so desperate to find answers, had delayed her hunt to bring me here. Travis, Eric, and Phil were dead. Khenan was missing and Point-Blank had lost his mind, all because of my stupid quest. I should've gone alone. I might have died but it'd be better than carrying such a heavy sack of guilt around for eternity.

"You see that bush over there?" Calla asked, pointing to a shrub with fiery red leaves. "Pick some leaves and rub them on your skin. Keep yourself safe from the fleas on your way back."

Calla invited me to come back the next time I was in the area. I thanked her for her hospitality and waved goodbye to Ruby through the kitchen window, then headed to the campsite, rubbing the leaves all over myself.

My body felt heavy. Maybe it was the strain to keep my feet from slipping out from under me as I descended the decline. Gavin stayed close but said nothing. I didn't mind. I wasn't in a talkative mood. At that point, I didn't care if I fell and broke my neck. I felt lower than shit. Lower than any level on Earth that shit could sit on. My friend, possibly two of them, were dead, along with two good-hearted soldiers, all for nothing.

As I descended, Abby appeared. Her many years of sneaking up on her quarry had given her the ability to come upon me like a shark in water. She startled me but I didn't show it.

She grunted and made her usual cryptic sounds. I could do nothing but shake my head with a dreadfully long face. She bowed hers low. I wished I could tell her that she and her family would be happier on the island, especially now that the Vikings were dead. The outside world had changed so drastically, it would be impossible for them to adapt to it. She and her tribe would most likely end up in a laboratory, prodded at. How could I make her understand that?

I turned to leave. With a bone-fracturing grasp only she could apply, she gripped my arm. Her sudden hold nearly sent me off-balance, forcing me to grab a

295

tree to keep from falling on my ass.

"What?" I asked sharply, steadying my feet.

She tugged on my arm and made guttural noises. She wanted me to go in the opposite direction.

"I have to get someone," I explained—hopelessly. "He's in danger and it'll be dark soon."

There was blood on her hands—dried blood, but I still didn't want her touching me. But she pulled on me, dragging me in the other direction by force. I decided it would be best to follow.

We went down the island slope, past the smelly trees, and a little farther, until we came to a small cave. Abby put a finger to her lips, indicating that I should remain quiet, and slowly approached the mouth of the cave.

I glumly followed her. A cool breeze drifted from the cave like an air conditioner.

"Whoa," said Gavin, "look at this dude."

Sitting on a short boulder was a man. His hair reached the small of his back and his long beard reminded me of Dusty Hill from ZZ Top. His clothes were tattered and his hands had scabs on them.

"Hi there," I said, not caring if he freaked out on me.

He didn't. Instead, he raised his chin and said, "Can you help me get back? I don't like it here."

"Where are you from?"

"Originally, Boston. I got stuck here during the war. We were building a village on the shore, I think, but me and some pals came up here and it all became a blur."

"Did you help build a house on top of the island?"

He shrugged. "Don't remember. I don't

remember much of anything. I've been—what's the word—in limbo? I've tried heading back to shore but I kept coming back here."

He was most likely one of the sixteen who'd helped Calla build her house. The six at the village had somehow managed to find their way back. The others had probably been killed by Vikings.

"How have you survived all this time?"

He turned to Abby and pointed at her. "She brings me food once in a while. Rubs red leaves on me every day. I think she's tried taking me back, but she'll only go so far before she leaves. I end up back here again. I don't like it here. I hear them whispering."

That caught me off guard.

"I wonder how many fleas got to him," Gavin remarked.

"Hear who?"

"Dunno. I never see them, but I hear them at night inside the cave."

I studied this so-called cave. It didn't appear deep. The jagged walls were in view from where I stood. The hanging moss swaying in the cool breeze indicated that something was hollow behind the wall.

Gavin peered in, then turned to me and shrugged. "Looks safe to me."

"Mind if I go inside and take a look?"

"Go ahead. Just wipe your feet first."

Honestly, I couldn't tell if he was joking or not. I decided it was best to act a little silly and wipe my feet rather than start some unnecessary drama by not respecting his wishes.

Once I scraped the mud off my shoes, I stepped into the cave. The cool breeze became more forceful.

The cave wasn't so much a cave as it was a

shallow indentation in the island. The low ceiling forced me to duck, and after two steps, I reached a back wall. The hole was enough for a decent shelter from the rain, but I couldn't imagine trying to sleep on its hard floor.

I followed the breeze with my hand, which brought about an odd sensation that ran up my arm, raising the hair on it like an electrical current. A few openings between the stones were near the ceiling and hanging moss blocked the majority of the pale light coming in from the outside, allowing shadows to claim most of the upper territory. One opening was large enough for my hand to fit through. Inside, it was bumpy and I slid my entire forearm in before I reached a dead end. There must be a hollow space beyond the wall but not enough to indicate that it was a tunnel. The whispering was the man's delusion. Other than that, there was nothing worth investigating. I stepped back out.

The man turned to me and said, "Hello, can you help me get back? I don't like it here."

He told me his name was Henry and followed me back to the campsite. Abby had split while I'd been in the cave and I had no idea if I'd ever see her again. Gavin helped keep an eye on Henry, and at times, I had to backtrack to keep him from heading back to the cave. Every time I had to, he forgot who I was and asked me to help him get back to the village. It wouldn't have been so bad if we headed straight for the shore, but I had to get to the campsite and collect Point-Blank. I was glad Abby had brought me to Henry, though. Helping him back to his friends gave my life meaning.

When we reached the campsite, my heart lodged

298

in my throat. Both Travis' and Eric's bodies were missing. The place reeked of decay from the dead Vikings. Animals had already torn into them, while thousands of insects had burrowed into their flesh.

After learning about the island, I wondered if it also fed from the energy of decomposing bodies. I was sure if it did, it wasn't as plentiful as living energy.

"Wow, look at that," Henry said. "I remember having a rifle like that."

I turned my attention to him as he picked up Travis' WWII rifle.

Where had the bodies gone? I wondered. I didn't believe animals had dragged them away, although in a place like this, anything was possible.

I looked over to where Point-Blank had stood. He was no longer there. I checked on Henry. He was rummaging through Eric's bag, unconcerned with the blood he stood in.

Gavin gave me a thumbs up. "I'll watch him."

Confidant that Henry was safely occupied, I searched for Point-Blank. I found nothing, although the ground where he'd stood was disturbed. The leaves had been kicked up, exposing footprints in the dirt. It seemed like he'd been dragged away. I saw no blood, just the remnants of a struggle. I kept my fingers crossed that whoever had taken him and the others had been friends.

Fat raindrops fell in the blink of an eye. Between the oncoming darkness and the muddy trek down, it was a very tricky journey. Henry followed me. I brought the vine rope we'd need at the drop-off, but lowering Henry was no easy task. He couldn't descend the rope himself, which forced me to tie it around his waist and ease him down. Once my own feet touched the ground, I caught him staring into the thicket.

"Come on, we need to keep moving," I said.

"Do you think she needs help?" he asked.

I was in no mood to go along with his hallucinations. The downpour had never let up and I was completely drenched. But when I opened my mouth to speak, I saw her. It was the little Viking girl, Sassy. She watched us unblinkingly, holding her doll tightly against her. I became unsettled, aware of what she was capable of.

"We ought to go," I whispered.

"Wait," Gavin said beside me. "Somebody's with her."

"Who?" I asked, my heart racing.

"Some guy in a Hawaiian shirt."

Inglewood. His soul now followed her after she'd murdered him.

"What's he doing?" I asked.

"He's talking to her."

"What's he saying?"

"He's whispering something like, 'Shush, Sassy, don't be afraid of them. Let's move on.' Sassy? What kind of dumb name is that?"

Good, I thought, with Inglewood there to calm her, maybe she wouldn't attack us.

Gavin waved, then said that Inglewood waved back. After a brief standoff, Sassy moved on, vanishing into the thicket. The only evidence of her presence was the crushing of leaves under her feet.

"I think you're clear," Gavin said. "Whatever he said to her, he must've let her know you weren't going to hurt her. I'm surprised he could talk, though. His throat was torn wide open."

We moved on. Darkness came and the rain

continued. We finally made it back to South Village, where a few soldiers took Henry off to tend to him. Soon afterward, I found a familiar face.

"Khenan!" I exclaimed happily.

We went to the village's pub and had a much needed drink. He explained that they'd had a funeral service for both Travis and Eric after the bodies had been brought down. I hoped whoever had gone up to get them had drenched themselves in bug spray.

"Jeez, mon, I t'ought you'd died," Khenan said.

"I thought you were dead too." I was giddy with delight. "How do you feel?"

"I 'ad a bad taste in my mout' since da ot'er night, but I ain't seen any more bullshit. You?"

"The same. I guess we were the lucky ones."

"I'm sorry 'bout ditching you back dere. It's just . . . I never been so scared in me life. Not even when me ship got caught in da storm. What we experienced was a different kind of fear. A psychological fear dat tore into my soul. Shit, I was so scared I couldn't go back to show da soldiers where to find da campsite. I just couldn't bring myself to do it."

"None of this is your fault. It's mine. I shouldn't have dragged any of you with me. Now Travis is dead and I'm right back where I started." Of course, I didn't tell him about what I'd found at the top of the island.

"I miss me son," Khenan said somberly. "I miss me family."

"I know."

His eyes lifted from his mug to me. "We all went up dere fer our own reasons, mon. It was wort' trying. We might've lost a great deal, but if we didn't at least try, we might as well shoot ourselves in da head an call it quits, eh?"

301

We stayed the night in the village and in the morning, we headed back to our own. By the time we got there, the dock was complete. The only thing left was to bring in the ships.

The dock was magnificent, reaching three hundred feet out to sea and ten feet wide, with twenty extended piers on either side. It looked as though it could hold the entire village population and then some.

I avoided everyone who tried to talk to me, even Marissa. I did tell Carlton to ask the soldiers at South Village to help assemble the ships at the docks. I then expressed that I was tired and I'd tell him everything he wanted to know after I got some sleep. It wasn't a lie by any means. I was exhausted and drifted away on the floor of my hut the second my head hit the ground. I needed to get some furniture.

By the time I woke, night had come. I drew my aching body up and went out to the front porch. My stomach grumbled. As I looked out into the dark void, wondering how I was going to eat, a very dangerous thought came to mind. With everything that had happened, losing Eleanor and now Travis, I couldn't face spending eternity homesick and miserable. I decided on a suicide mission.

Chapter Twenty-nine

I now understood why people with a serious intent to kill themselves never said anything. Maybe they dropped hints here and there, but they usually didn't convey their intentions verbally. It made sense. I mean, why tell people? They'd only try to talk them out of it, most likely put them on suicide watch, delaying the inevitable.

I said nothing to Carlton, or even Khenan, who joined us at Marissa and Tammy's place for dinner and drinks. Khenan and I spoke about our frightening journey and what had happened to the soldiers. A lump formed in my throat when I talked about Travis and what I'd had to do to give him peace.

"Don't take none of it so hard, boys," Carlton said. "People die. It's just the way it is. Those boys lived very long lives, especially Travis."

"Did you make it to the top?" Tammy asked before slurping her soup.

At first, I didn't realize she'd spoken to me. But as I filled my belly, my mind focused more on my agenda. "Sorry? Er, yeah, but I didn't find anything."

I told them about the fleas, which I'd also told Worley about before we'd left South Village. He could spread the word. Everyone at the table could do the same. I wouldn't be around to do it myself.

"Fleas, huh?" Marissa said. "Ain't that something?"

"I can't believe those damn Vikings are dead," Carlton said. "With them gone and an explanation for

303

what makes people go mad, at least you boys didn't go through hell for nothing."

"We haven't told them any of our news yet, "Marissa said. "While you were gone, a woman from the Obsoletes came over and told us that Doctor Chancier killed everyone in the village before he killed himself."

My jaw hit the table.

"Wah?" Khenan said. "Why?"

"He just up and lost his mind, is all," Marissa said. "Couldn't stand the sight of his wife's hanging body every day. He wanted her back but not as a ghost."

"Gnarly," said Gavin, sitting on a nearby empty chair.

Marissa stole a long glance at Tammy. It made my own mournful heart bleed a little more. She returned her attention to me and Khenan. "After two hundred years, he finally blew up in the worst possible way."

"What about the woman who told you this?" I asked. "How'd she escape?"

"She didn't," Carlton said. "She claims he let her live. Said she woke to the sound of the doc hacking at her husband's face with a meat cleaver."

"Jesus Christ!" I exclaimed.

"What 'e let 'er live fer?" Khenan wondered.

"To tell everyone what he'd done. Then he put a pistol in his mouth and *bang*!"

"Now she lives with us, poor thing," Carlton said.

"How big was the village?" I asked.

"It wasn't as populated as ours or South Village, but it did accommodate quite a few people. He waited until everyone was asleep before he went at them."

"Some of us went over there to investigate," Marissa said.

"Yeah, I wish you weren't so curious," Tammy complained.

Marissa rolled her eyes. "Anyway, I'd never seen such a bloody mess in my life. I've seen some shit, but I nearly lost it over there. We buried the victims and left the good doctor where he died. Maybe we'll clean the houses up and some of us can move over there someday."

"This sort of thing has happened before throughout the years," Carlton said. "People lose it one way or another. It's our price for immortality."

* * *

The following morning, I stood on my front porch, waiting for the sunrise. When it did, the little mysterious dot appeared on the horizon. I heard Dominic say, "Do you know what that is?"

"Another island," I said without turning to him.

"It is the Somers Isles, or Bermuda."

"How do you know?"

"We are facing north. That is why this is called North Village. A map and compass tell you plenty. I like to come out once in a while to look at it before the fog comes. We're so close to the outside world and yet we can't reach it. It's like being imprisoned on Alcatraz."

"Alcatraz?" Gavin said, bewildered.

I knew what he meant. Alcatraz prisoners had suffered the torture of seeing San Francisco through their windows. The city and inmates had been separated only by the bay. Prisoners had reported

305

smelling coffee and hearing loud parties across the water, some of life's little pleasures only a short distance away.

"If you breathe deep enough, you can smell their rum cakes baking," Dominic said. He sucked in a deep breath, exhaled, and looked at me. "You have that look in your eyes. You are going to do something stupid, yes?"

"I'm going to try sailing out," I said unexpectedly. I couldn't explain it, but I felt like I could trust Dominic enough to tell him my intentions.

"You're gonna what?" Gavin said beside me.

Dominic only nodded and said, "Before you go, let's eat some breakfast. You can't face your possible end on an empty stomach."

He cooked strips of stingray meat with slices of fruits. We didn't talk. Once we'd eaten, I thanked him for the food and set out into the junkyard, taking the same life raft I'd yet to return.

I reached the boundary within a couple of hours. By then, I'd grown accustomed to navigating through the dangerous terrain. As I neared the edge, I took a moment to gaze out beyond the boundary. Did I really want to do this?

Remembering the bitter cold beyond the junkyard, I'd brought a coat Dominic had lent me. It was an old flight jacket. It would keep me warm enough.

The fog was thick by now, making it difficult to see anything ahead of me. If Dominic was right about Bermuda, the distance between us wasn't very far. If I could make it past the island's boundary, I could easily reach it.

Well, maybe not easily. Bermuda seemed a good

fifteen miles away.

Ice chunks floated over the midnight blue water under the fog, into warmer waters, instantly melting. Some bottles, with notes inside, floated around as well. I put the jacket on and took a breath before rowing on.

The frigid cold stole the air out of my lungs and left my chest burning. And no, the coat didn't help much. The cold seeped through the leather and wool, latching onto my flesh like leeches. My hands became numb as I rowed. I'd mentally prepared myself for this. I'd dealt with extreme cold before, but living in Florida had spoiled me. Even so, I kept a steady pace, not fast enough to wear me down and not slow enough to allow the cold to dominate me. I wished the water had frozen over. It was cold enough for it, but maybe the two warmer bodies of water surrounding it kept ice from forming into a solid floor I could simply stroll over.

Luckily, there was no wind. Not just because of the cold, but because it meant no dreaded storm.

"Do you really think this is going to work?" Gavin asked, suddenly appearing in the seat in front of me. I'd become used to it by now.

"I . . . I don't know." My breath gusted from my mouth as dense as the fog around us. "I'm not h-h-holding much hope f-f-for it. S-s-so many others have tr-tr-tried this stunt already and n-n-n-nobody's m-m-made it."

"That's right, bring on the sunshine," Gavin said, his voice steady and unaffected by the cold. "You expect to die out here, huh?"

"I'm j-j-just trying to g-g-get home."

Gavin sat quiet for a moment. Then, "If you die, I wonder what'll happen to me."

It couldn't have been more than five minutes but

it felt like five hours. My joints stiffened as if the cold had glued them in place. Gavin was kind enough to give me updates about my physical appearance.

"Damn, dude, your face is really red. Wipe your nose, will ya? Wow, I think ice is forming in your hair."

If I didn't get warm soon, I'd turn into the abominable snowman.

A breeze gently whisked by. It started as a calm flow that gnawed at me and I shivered. Nothing but fog surrounded me and it began to swirl in spirals, like many little tornados. The wind gusts picked up and the boat started to rock. Within the gray fog, sparks of blue and purplish light popped, then crackled with thunder. Static electricity sparked under my skin.

"I think this is it," Gavin said, gripping the edge of the raft with one hand, as if staying on really mattered. "Row like hell, dude!"

I did. The storm grew and I thought it best to move quickly. The wind became fierce enough to rip the oars from my hands. I could do nothing but hold onto the sides of the raft and brace myself.

The raft lifted completely from the water and spun. I kept my eyes shut the entire time. I would've screamed but my heart had wedged itself in my throat. I don't know how long I stayed in the air, spinning around like Dorothy's house, but before I knew it, the raft slammed into the icy water and threw me out. Cold, biting waves doused me. I couldn't breathe. My lungs tightened into knots and no air seemed to flow in. The water and wind paralyzed me to the point that I became nothing more than a floating cork. I would've gone under if not for the waves pushing me around. The cold was too much for my shocked body to withstand. My heartbeat pulsated in my head, pounding against my skull. Another waved rushed at me. It was the last thing I remember.

* * *

"Heath, wake up, damn it!"

Gavin was saying my name but my mind was on the warmth that embraced me. Liquid warmth.

Lifting my eyelids was like retracting the curtains of an out-of-focus movie. I blinked several times to sharpen my vision. My face lay on some kind of steel object. I lifted my head to discover it was the wing of a plane. Gavin was crouched down on it.

"Whoa, that's a ride that ought to be included at Universal."

Every nerve in my body tingled. The tropical water lapped against my back.

"Watch for the bodies," Gavin warned.

I craned my neck to the side to find two bodies floating face down near me. The waves had brought us at least twenty feet into the junkyard. The fog was now light enough to see that much.

"You all right?" Gavin asked as I found my footing on the uneven ground.

"No," I said. My mouth was dry from the saltwater and my throat felt scratchy, as if I had a cactus stuck in it.

The wind kicked up again and the sky turned into a light show. Thunder boomed like a cannon blast.

"Another storm?" Gavin said over the howling wind. "Is this place trying to kill you?"

The wind wasn't as fierce as before, but it made the boats rock and planes creak. Thunder clashed seconds after the blinding flashes and raindrops the size of my fist poured down. Even over the racket, I heard the sound of something very heavy falling.

My eyes turned toward the sky. Between a few clear patches within the fog, I witnessed an airplane crashing. It was difficult to tell, but it looked like a Sukhoi Su-31M. There was no engine noise because every electrical function would have failed, just like mine had.

"I think the spider caught another fly," Gavin said, watching it as well.

The aircraft wasn't far. I could see the pilot eject from the cockpit. Wind blew under the plane's wing, spinning it in wide circles. It spiraled down to the junkyard like a leaf in a whirling wind. Had that been the way my plane had gone down?

"There he is!" Gavin shouted. "See him?"

I did. A red parachute with someone hanging at the end sailed through the sky, toward the silhouette of a large vessel.

To the pilot's good fortune, the storm dissolved as rapidly as it materialized, allowing him to glide safely down. I guess once the island captured its victim, the aggressive weather was no longer necessary.

Adrenaline kicked in and I climbed onto the wing, ready to find the pilot. My whole body ached and I was nauseous from the saltwater I'd swallowed. At one point, I stopped to puke.

Gavin warned me about sharks as I leapt onto a floating longboat set adrift from a nearby galleon. The life raft I'd brought was lost and I didn't bother looking for it. This vessel had one oar and was built to accommodate ten grown men. I wished I'd found a dingy instead. A laundry basket floating nearby would have been easier to maneuver than this thing. If only Gavin could help me row.

Even so, the boat's heavy body acted as a shield from the sharks' constant banging. The storm had stirred them up and they were trying to tip me over. With every knock, I shuddered, especially when their heads emerged and my oh-shit expression reflected in their black eyes. Luckily, I didn't have to go far before I reached a cluster of wreckage.

I wedged the longboat between the cockpit of a F9F-2 Panther and the tail of a Cessna. Using the rudder to hoist myself up, I got away from the hungry beasts. When I felt safe, I continued across the junkyard, now following the pilot's desperate cries.

"We ain't far now," Gavin stated. "Come on!"

I did my best to quicken my pace. The pilot didn't call out much, but with Gavin's guidance, I made my way over the wreckage and came to the stern of a slightly tilted yacht. A capsized cargo ship sat before me with a thirty-foot-wide expanse of water between us.

"Where is he?"

"Up there."

I looked around.

"Higher, idiot," Gavin said.

I lifted my eyes and spied the pilot dangling from the freighter's crane eighty feet up. I couldn't make out any details of his face.

"Best tell him not to cut himself loose," Gavin warned, staring down at the water.

I turned my attention to where his was. Fins pierced the murky water's surface. "Damn it. I bet those are the same sharks that followed me."

"Don't cut the cords!" I shouted up at the pilot. "There are sharks down here and the water isn't that deep!"

The pilot turned his head in my direction. "Yeah! I can see them. I'm gonna try swinging over and climbing down!"

I knew that voice. "Starr?"

Again, the man looked at me. "Sharp? Is that you?"

My grin stretched from ear to ear. I should've thought as much, seeing his Sukhoi Su-31M. He'd bought it junked and had it restored like he'd done with most of his other planes. It was the only one in his collection with an ejector seat.

"Jesus, it is you!" I said. "What the hell are you doing here? Actually, hold that thought. Let's get you out of this mess first."

"Sounds like a plan," Starr said in his casual manner.

I needed a boat to get to the freighter while he climbed down. I thought about going back for the longboat, but I searched the yacht instead and found another life raft. The rubber was thick but would it withstand a shark bite? I doubted it.

I told Starr to hang tight—no pun intended—that I'd be back soon to fetch him, then hurried through the wreckage, wondering how long it would take to row around it. The cluster consisted of three small yachts, two fighter planes, and the Cessna I'd lifted myself onto. A mess for sure, but not very wide around.

I found another oar and brought it back to the longboat. When the boat had become wedged in the wreckage, I'd failed to notice a hole one of the sharks had made in it. Water swallowed the boat in a long slow gulp and I had the pleasure of watching it go under.

"Shit."

Starr shouted for me to get back and I did.

"My chute is tearing," he said. "Every time I swing, it tears."

"Then stop swinging."

"I'm gonna fall, man!"

Without a choice, I pulled the cord on the life raft and let it inflate on the yacht's deck. I needed some kind of weapon to defend myself against the sharks and remembered a flare gun and ammo in the captain's helm. Whoever had owned the yacht had no common sense about using their survival gear. Stupid for them but fortunate for me.

I aimed the flare gun at the water where the sharks circled. They were close enough to the surface for a kill shot. Remembering what had happened the last time I'd done this, I fired. I nailed one on the back and it thrashed around amid a blinding red and white fireball. I almost felt sorry for the damn thing. It went under with its buddies following. A violent battle ensued as the sharks attacked. While they did, I slid the raft into the water, took a deep breath, and jumped into it. With the sharks distracted, I had time to row out to the cargo ship and plant myself under Starr.

"Cut yourself loose!" I called to him.

I worried that once he landed, the raft would burst and we'd be at the mercy of the sharks. But we had no other choice. Starr couldn't get himself over to climb down and I couldn't climb up to help him.

Starr sliced through the parachute cords. I turned my attention to the water, watching for any sign of a shark. I reloaded the flare gun and aimed at the water, hoping for two things—the sharks to fill up on their friend and leave us alone, and that Starr wouldn't land on me. I couldn't say which ranked higher on my list.

"Geronimo!" Starr cried.

I whipped my head up as he plummeted. Right then, my plan went to shit. He fell as hard as a sack of cement blocks. The instant before he landed, I realized he wasn't going to land on his feet, but on his ass. That shouldn't be too bad.

What happened next reminded me of when I'd been a child playing in an inflatable bouncy house and bigger kids bounced me right off my feet. Starr sent me up, out, and into the water.

Sharks! Oh, God, sharks! That was my immediate thought.

In a panic, I fired the flare gun, unleashing another fireball into nothing. The dirty water prevented me from seeing anything more than a foot down, but I didn't remain in the water for long. I must've been a trout in my past life the way I leapt back into the life raft and landed halfway in.

"Pull me in! Pull me in!" I shouted hysterically.

Starr grabbed the back of my collar and belt and hoisted me into the raft.

"Row! Row!" I yelled as I flipped over on my back and sat up.

"With what?" Starr asked.

"Hey, I know that guy," Gavin chimed. "I've seen you talking to him before we went out flying. Should'a rung a bell when you said his name. I've never been good with names, though. Faces, voices, that's what I recall."

I only half listened to him. I was too busy looking at the oar that had bounced out with me, floating in the water, too far for me to reach.

"Hands," I said. "Use your hands! Come on, we gotta get back to that boat!"

Both Starr and I paddled. My only thought was the fear of losing one of my hands or having a shark chomp down and pull me under. I feared the same would happen to Starr. That terror kept me paddling through the shadowy water without stopping. I had no idea if the sharks came for us or not, at least not until we were safe on the yacht.

"Jesus, man, you're alive," Starr said, catching his breath.

I looked into the water, where the raft rode on the small waves we'd created.

"I told 'em," he said in his Alabama accent. "I told them idiot Coastguardsmen you didn't crash."

I looked at him. "I did crash. Come on, I'll tell you all about it on our way home."

Chapter Thirty

The saliva in my mouth dried when I used the word *home* to describe the island. It sickened me because I finally realized it was true. Starr, on the other hand, thought I meant Miami.

"Wait," he protested, "I want to explore this place before we go back."

I shook my head pitifully. It was sort of shitty to throw a heavy word like home at him. After all, I'd just come to terms with my own defeat. "Were you searching for me?"

"Yeah." His eyes traveled around. "Jeez, look at this place. Where the hell are we?"

"In the Bermuda Triangle," I answered grimly. "The storm that brought your plane down was manifested by a fragment of our second moon that grew into an island."

Starr craned his head over to me with an are-you-serious expression. "Sharp, have you lost your mind?"

"I did, a little," I said mildly. "How long have you been searching for me?"

"For us," Gavin said irritably. "You weren't the only one who went missing."

"The first week you were missing, the Coast Guard and rescue pilots searched. All us guys at the airport went out looking. Then a month went by and it dwindled to just us pilots. After the second month, it came down to me and a few others guys. We thought you were dead, but every weekend, we still combed the area, hoping to find some trace of your plane. What the

316

hell were you doing flying near Somers, anyway?"

"I wasn't anywhere near there," I said, surprised.

"We received your mayday call and tracked the signal approximately sixteen hundred kilometers southeast, buddy."

"It takes three hours to reach Bermuda." I pointed out. "Gavin and I were in the air barely an hour."

Starr considered that a moment. "You're right. Our records show you took off seventy-two minutes before your mayday call. You vanished from our scope seconds afterward." He looked at his torn chute hanging like tissue paper off the cargo ship. "Maybe there was some kind of glitch in our system that day."

"No," I said thickly, "there was no glitch. The island used its power to suck us in like ants through a straw."

I knew he thought I was crazy. I'd been in his shoes when I'd first arrived. Hell, if I'd had a straightjacket, I'd have put it on Jean Laffite when I'd first met him.

"You're scaring me, Sharp."

"I think it's best you come and see for yourself."

We found paddles on the yacht and rowed through the junkyard on the life raft. I let him take everything in and answered any questions he had along the way. He asked about the old ships and planes. I told him but he didn't believe me. Then we came across the jet plane where I'd discovered the pilot's body and showed him. I thought that would help get it through his head what this place was.

"Holy shit!" he said when he saw George. "How long has he been sitting here? And why is he wearing a World War II pilot's uniform?"

"He *is* a World War II pilot. He's been in this

317

plane for the last sixty years."

Again, his expression changed to an are-you-trying-to-pull-a-fast-one look. As if I had freaking built everything around us just to pull a prank.

"I'm serious," I said with as much strength in my voice as I could afford. "When people die here, their bodies don't rot unless they're killed or the body is disturbed. If that happens, their soul follows you forever."

"Forever?"

"Yeah, the island allows us to live forever. There are people who've been trapped here since the prehistoric age. The island feeds off our energy. It needs us and won't allow us to leave. Got it?"

He casually rubbed his chin. I'd never seen him surprised before, as if fighting in the Gulf War kept him from ever being caught off-guard. I'd hoped for the laid-back version of Starr, rather than the in-your-face screaming one. I even worried he'd shake the dead pilot. Deep down, I didn't expect him to. Starr was a man in his late-forties, filled with life experience, not some naïve teen who enjoyed testing the boundaries of a warning. Instead, he moved his head this way and that, studying the ships and planes that were within eyesight. It seemed like I was slowly getting through to him.

"Where do you live?" he asked.

"In a village. There are three of them. One is South Village, another is North Village—where I stay—and there *was* one on the other side of the island, but the people were butchered a couple days ago."

He gave me another peculiar look. Again, not one of surprise, just a peculiar one. "Show me the island."

The fog had grown more opaque as the day

318

dragged on. I'd wanted Starr to see the island at a distance to absorb its full effect but I had to settle with a close-up view. When we reached the beach, I realized how hungry I was.

"Come on," I said. "It's getting late. We need to get back before the stingrays come out."

"Stingrays? The pussycats of the sea?"

"They're more like bloodthirsty cougars around here."

It had been a long day and I couldn't believe how anxious I was to get back. During our walk, I kept myself occupied by telling him everything I knew about the island, about its rules and the strange wildlife. I even told him why I'd been in the junkyard when he'd crashed. He listened and asked questions, but never seemed shocked by anything. His acceptance of everything disturbed me. The only thing I withheld from him was what I knew about Calla and Ruby. I'd promised to keep them a secret and I intended to honor that promise.

A mix of emotions came over me—sadness that he, too, had gotten caught by the Atlantic Pyramid's trap, but also happy to have him around again. Any suicidal intentions I felt after returning from the forest left me just from him being there.

I told him the villagers would hold a Welcoming party for him, giving him a chance to meet everyone. I knew he wouldn't mind, he'd always been a social person. To mingle with the Bermuda Triangle crew would be a real treat for him.

We had an hour left of daylight by the time we reached the village. I noticed the population had grown. I recognized several faces from South Village, even Worley. I asked Carlton about it as he stood by the newly-finished docks.

"They've come to help bring ships in, just like you suggested."

I'd completely forgotten about that. The soldiers had already cleared away many of the small fishing boats and brought them up to shore to make room for the yachts and other larger vessels.

"It's going to take time to disassemble and reassemble the mess," Worley explained. "You want to help?"

I volunteered myself and allowed Starr to make up his own mind, which he agreed to. I couldn't tell if he grasped the entire situation or not. With him, it was always hard to tell until it was too late.

Carlton said they planned on having a feast with the soldiers and the other people from South Village who'd come to help. Throwing together a Welcoming for Starr would be no trouble.

When I brought Starr up to my hut, he noticed Tommy Pine's body beneath the back porch. "There's a guy down there."

"I know. I haven't gotten around to covering him up yet. Don't worry, he's dead."

"Jesus," Starr said, stepping back inside. "Got any other demonic lawn ornaments I should know about?"

"I don't think so. I've decided to live by the docks if I can find my own ship. If you want this place—"

"No way," he said, shaking his head and waving his hands. "I've got no desire to share a room with a dead guy whose brains are all over the place."

"We'll need to find your plane so you can collect any supplies you have."

320

I wanted to keep myself busy with anything I could think of, especially now that I'd accepted I'd never leave the Triangle. I couldn't stay still and think about that without it driving me crazy. I needed to ease into that cold hard fact, allow myself to slip comfortably into my prison before there was nothing but living to do.

"Yeah, I do have some things I should get," Starr said. "Maybe my radio will work."

"It won't. This place drains electrical devices. Not even batteries work."

"Damn, that means I can't play my MP3?"

I grinned.

* * *

Starr set off to explore the village while I changed into clean clothes and took a nap. I was beat and my head swam. My chest tightened with sickness as I lay down. When Starr woke me, my symptoms were worse. I coughed and my muscles ached. I sucked it up and joined him for dinner. I had soup there. I didn't care what was in it. I just needed something hot. I spoke to Doctor Sam West about how I felt and he instructed me to eat what I could and get some rest. In the morning, he'd bring me crushed leaves to ease my headache and syrup from a plant root for my cold.

I took his advice. I ate the soup and left Starr at the table. He didn't mind. He was sharing war stories with the crew of Flight 19. Starr was much more interesting than I'd been at my Welcoming. I went back to my hut and lit a candle on the single table.

"I need to tell you sssomethiiing," Ruby said.

My soul nearly slipped away from fright. "Ruby,"

I said after collecting myself, "what are you doing here?"

"I need to tell youuuu sssomethiiiing. It's imporrrtant."

As she spoke, shiny clear fluid ran down her arms, chest, and legs, and dripped on the floor.

"Are you hurt?" I asked.

Her waxy eyes dropped to her arm. *"Yesss. Coming all the waaay here hasss wounded me."*

Her feet were the worst. I took a step toward her. "I'll mix up some salve for you. Do you need to sit for a while?"

"I don't sit," she reminded me.

"Oh, right."

I offered to get her a damp cloth to clean up what I guess was blood from her body and she accepted. As I searched my survival bag, hard rain dropped from the sky.

"I should have told youuu thisss when youuu came to ussss," Ruby went on as I pulled out a washcloth from the bag. *"Calla didn't want youuuu to knooow."*

"Know what?" I asked, walking out to the back porch to dunk the washcloth into a water bucket. I wrung it out and handed it to her.

"Youuu must understaaand when I tell youuu that Calla only wantsss to protect meee," she explained while cleaning the wounds on her chest.

"What?" I said before my ears caught the shouting of people below.

Alarmed, I went out to the front porch and looked across the village to see everyone scrambling for cover. A storm had slowly swept over the island and only then reached the people at the feast. I turned my attention to Ruby. She now stood on the back porch, quenching herself in the rain.

"What do you know?" I inquired.

"Weee told youuu the islaaand isss a fragggment from a living mooon and there is no waaay to leeeave. That may not beee entirely so."

I stumbled back a bit. "Whoa, wait a minute. *Not* entirely so?"

She gave a slow nod. The rain slid off her large cranium like off a balloon. *"The fragggment has a life sourrrce. The energggy can beee felt beneeeath my feeet. I belieeeve this life sourrrce may lie underground."*

"Underground? How far?"

"I don't knooow. I've never been able to explore any caaaves by myssself."

I pounced on the word. "Caves? Jesus, of course, the holes in the ground. The hole Phil fell in. Why didn't I . . ."

I'd never given much thought to the strange holes around the village, the ones we used as toilets. Not even when the breeze in Henry's cave had made the nerves in my arms tingle. How could I or anyone else have missed it?

Footsteps pounded toward the hut. Minutes later, Starr rushed in, sopping wet. "Wow, does it always rain like this?" His voice trailed away to nothing when his eyes locked on the eight-foot alien standing on my back porch.

"Starr, don't freak out," I said, rushing to the door to close it. "She's a friend. She won't hurt you."

"I caaan't hurt youuu."

"It . . . talks?"

Now he was surprised?

"*She* talks," I corrected sternly.

He flashed me a wide look. "It's a female?" he whispered.

"Can't you see her vagina?" I said.

I didn't expect him to look, but he did.

"Damn," he said, going back to his casual tone, "looks like she gave birth to an elephant."

"I've neverrr givvven birrrth," Ruby returned.

She and Starr were getting off on the wrong foot. "Ruby, this is my friend, Starr. Starr, this is Ruby. She's an alien."

"Ruby? Ruby the Alien?"

"Just Ruby," I said. "And she risked her life to come here to tell me something."

"Why is she standing in the rain?"

I sighed. "Don't worry about that. Listen, she was telling me there might be some kind of underground life source for the island."

"Okay," Starr said slowly, "what's that mean?"

"It means if we can find it, we might find a way out of here."

"How?"

"By destroooying it."

"All right, if it's destroyed, then what?"

"The fragggment will die," Ruby answered. *"Everrryone will beee freee."*

I turned to her. "You should stay the night. We can escort you back in the morning."

"Thank youuu," Ruby said.

"We?" Starr chimed in.

I pulled him aside. "You don't have to go with me, but I have to look into this."

"Do you even know where to begin?"

I held my breath on the question. I did know

where to start but it wouldn't be pleasant.

"I do," I answered. "But first, I have to get Ruby home. It's the least I can do for her."

Starr leaned in close to whisper, "Y'know, you didn't tell me about meeting a goddamn alien."

"I couldn't. I made a promise not to say anything."

"Calla maade youuu promise, didn't sheee?" Ruby said. *"Sheee is sooo protective of meee and herrr home. I no longerrr care for my own wellbeeeing. I just waaant this to beee overrr."*

"What do you mean? What will happen to you if the island dies?"

"I will go with it," she said bluntly. *"If the fragggmeeent dies and the boundarrrries break, the air of your worrrld will enterrr. I cannot breeeathe Earrrth's oxygen. My kind hasss known thisss since weee first caaame to thisss planet."*

"Are we breathing alien air?" Starr asked, startled. "Is that why my chest hurts?"

"Yesss, but alsooo your own air. It's the perfect mixturrre to keep all life alive."

"Ruby," I said, taking a step forward.

"Do not concern yourself with meee. I've discusssed thisss with my brotherrr and weee concurrr it's for the best. I have lived through too many lifetmes and cannot bear another. I used tooo beee an explorer. Now, I'm just standing still. Life has nothing to offerrr meee anymorrre."

Deep down, I knew exactly how she felt.

Chapter Thirty-one

Later, when we were trying to sleep, somebody cried out in alarm. When I opened my eyes, Starr had a man by the shirt collar in the hut. I leapt to my feet just as he slammed the intruder against the wall, cupping his hand over his mouth.

"West?" I said.

I looked back at Ruby standing on the back porch. The rain had since stopped and I'd left the back door open to make sure she was all right. I'd closed the front door, though, which meant West had either walked in on his own or Starr had answered the door. Thankfully, the doctor's screams hadn't awakened Ruby.

Starr held West firmly against the wall. West's bug eyes nearly popped out of their sockets. They shifted to Ruby outside and then to me.

"West," I said soothingly, "it's all right, she won't hurt anyone. She's a friend. Understand?"

He nodded.

"Sorry," Starr said to me. "I heard him knocking and answered without thinking."

How he could forget about Ruby was beyond me. Then again, it's not every day he helped hide another life form.

"Starr will let you go as long as you don't flip out," I said.

West gave another nod of understanding.

"Good," I said in the same calm tone.

As Starr removed his hand, I held my breath.

326

West didn't scream and Starr wiped spit off his hand.

"What the hell is that thing?" West whispered loudly.

"She's an alien," I explained. "Her name is Ruby."

As I spoke her name, a series of harsh coughs arose in my throat. I turned away and hacked into my fist. My lungs burned.

"I brought your medicine," West said, holding up a cooler.

Wiping hot, stinging tears from my eyes, I took the box. "Thanks."

"Can I . . ." he began. "Can I have a closer look?"

I turned my attention to Ruby. Her bowed head and closed eyes indicated she was still asleep. I didn't like the idea of showing her off like a circus freak, but if I allowed West to get an eyeful, perhaps I could convince him not to talk. I wasn't aware of how far I'd go to secure Ruby's safety, but it wouldn't be pretty if West threatened to expose her.

"Sure," I said, clearing the junky buildup in my throat. "Just don't disturb her."

Starr slid his hand off the man's chest. We watched as West crept over to the back doorway, slightly hunched over like he was about to pounce. I clenched my teeth, imaging Ruby's frightened reaction to a stranger staring at her if she woke. I could almost hear her letting out a loud, glass-cracking scream, and West running for the door, shrieking for help.

West edged closer, stopped and stood for a long moment. Ruby never woke up.

"Incredible," he muttered. "Where did she come from?"

"I can't tell you," I said. "And you can't say

anything to anyone about her."

He turned to us. "Why is she here?"

I opened my mouth to answer, then snapped it shut. In a split-second, I decided against disclosing what Ruby had told me. I didn't want to risk getting anyone's hopes up about returning home if it turned out to be nothing. "She's just visiting. Like I said, she's a friend."

"Are there more of her?"

"No, just her. Do you promise not to say anything?"

"Yeah, sure, I give you my word—if you tell me the truth."

"What do you mean?"

He crossed his arms. "I mean, what's she really doing here? Does it have anything to do with the island?"

Hope flickered in his eyes. I sensed he wanted me to tell him I'd found a way out.

"Are you hiding something, Heath?" he asked in earnest. "It wouldn't be fair if you've discovered an escape route and didn't tell the rest of us about it."

"It's not like that. Listen, we—"

"We need rope," Starr cut in. "Lots of it."

West grew confused. "Why?"

"Ruby told us there's something weird underground and we're going to check it out."

"Like a cave?" West inquired. "Did you find a cave when you went up there, Heath?"

"Something like that," I grudgingly admitted. "I didn't want to say anything until I explored them. I swear I don't intend to sneak out and leave everyone else behind."

West considered this. "I can help you get rope,

but I want to come too."

I saw no harm in letting him tag along. Where we were going, an extra body could come in handy.

"All right. Starr, go with him and collect the rope. I'll get Ruby indoors before anyone else sees her. Then I'll get us some supplies."

When they left, I went out to the back porch. Ruby suddenly raised her head, sending me leaping back. The island had certainly made me jumpy.

"Maaaybe youuuu should haaave closed both doors."

"You're awake?"

"Yesss. Thaaat screaming humaaan woooke meee."

"Yeah, sorry about that."

"It'sss not yourrr fault."

It felt good to hear someone say that. "Come inside. I have to get some stuff before we go."

We needed supplies—lights, helmets, machetes, and perhaps a gun or two. Travis had all those things, and Khenan had taken the liberty of clearing out most of his belongings from his hut, leaving the rest for anyone wanting them.

People were on the beach getting ready to go out and dismantle their first ship. They'd held a lotto game to determine whose vessel would be first. I felt shitty for promising to help, only to dip out on the first day. I guess I'd lose my chance to live on the docks.

When I arrived at Khenan's, he was sitting at his outside table, smoking a cigarette. He'd never smoked before, but I guess after what had happened, he decided a little tobacco couldn't hurt. I joined him at the table and told him where I was going and why. Dread reflected in his eyes.

"I can't," he said, his voice trembling. "I can't go back up dere."

"I understand."

"I saw t'ings," he said.

"I know, I saw things too."

Khenan lowered his gaze to the table. His hands shook and his eyes watered. "I seen me son dat night after da Vikings attacked us. I went to 'old 'im when 'e burst into flames, just like me brot'er. Me wife appeared, screaming at me dat is was me fault."

"It wasn't real," I assured him.

"Sorry, I canna 'elp you."

Khenan gave me protective headgear—a fighter pilot's and a football helmet. Since we didn't know how long we'd be underground, he included food and cooking supplies. He offered flare torches, a few knives, two machetes, lighters, and a first aid kit. He even handed me a pair of pistols. Once I had everything bagged up, I said goodbye and headed back to my hut. By the time I returned, Starr and West were waiting with loads of different types of rope.

"Think this will be enough?" Starr asked.

"I have no idea," I said truthfully. "We'll find out once we get there."

Before leaving, West suggested I take more medicine. The syrup tasted like cold coffee. The crushed leaves, mixed in with the syrup, crunched between my teeth. I asked how this remedy and the other for cuts had been discovered, and he said someone had discovered it long ago and passed it on.

I told them about the fleas and what they did. We found a red leaf bush and rubbed it over ourselves. For good measure, we also sprayed ourselves with bug repellent. I offered the leaves and repellent to Ruby, but she informed me the fleas didn't affect her.

We headed up the island after sneaking Ruby out the back. Starr and I hacked through the thick greenery, while Ruby stayed between us. It was like escorting a moving glass figurine. To my surprise, her wounds had healed overnight after I'd applied the salve, giving her a healthy body to make the steep climb. I even tied cloth around her feet to keep them from getting sliced up. Everything went fine for the first thirty minutes, until Calla crossed our path.

"Ruby!" she called, hurrying down the incline with a tall walking stick in her hand. "Thank goodness you're all right. I've been searching everywhere for you."

I thought she'd hug Ruby, but instead, she stopped and looked up at her with relief. She then shifted her eyes to me. They weren't the windows looking in on a happy soul. "What's the meaning of this? What are you doing with her?"

"Before you start, Ruby came to *me.*"

Calla's expression loosened. She switched her attention back to Ruby. "Why would you risk your life to see him?"

"To tell me things *you* failed to mention when I asked about getting off the island," I cut in snidely.

"What are you talking about?"

"The holes."

"Oh, those. They're nothing more than death traps."

"What do you mean death traps?" West asked nervously.

"People have gone into them and never come back."

"What?" Starr said. "They vanished?"

331

"Worse. Throughout the years, people have found holes here and there. Before I found Ruby, I helped assist some lads into one. I advised them not to go but they were headstrong. Like you, Heath. Once they went down, they never returned."

"No one ever mentioned that," I said. "Not even Eleanor."

"Since the arrival of sailors, men have wandered up there, searching for answers, only to vanish or be killed by the Vikings, or lose their minds. Eventually, they stopped going up the island and remained near the shore. Eleanor knew nothing about the dangers until five men from North Village and I discovered a hole. Their disappearance still haunts me. I warned Eleanor about it and we made a pact to never let anyone know about them. It really wasn't a problem. Most people were frightened to venture too far beyond the shoreline. Even Worley knew better after his banishment from his own village. What happened to him only perpetrated the fear."

"Why didn't you go into the hole with them?" West asked.

Calla's cheeks lit up red. "I'm highly claustrophobic. As a child, I got locked in an old ice box playing silly games with my siblings. Ever since, I've been deathly afraid of enclosed spaces. But that phobia saved my life."

"If you didn't go with them, how do you know they're dead?" Starr asked.

"I can't imagine what else could've happened. They've never reappeared anywhere else on the island, and I can't imagine there's any food or light down there for them to have survived this long."

"You should've told me about them," I said

peevishly.

"I was only trying to protect you and the others from facing the same fate." She turned to Ruby. "You shouldn't have told him. *You,* more than anyone else, ought to know better."

"Something isss down there," Ruby said. *"There is a power thaaat mussst be discovered."*

Calla kept silent a moment. Then, with a deep sigh, she said, "All right, if you really think there's something of importance down there, let the idiots go. Come on, Ruby, let's get you home."

"I am going with them."

"Whoa, what?" I said.

"You can't go into the holes," Calla protested. "Your body—"

"There'sss nooo doubt I'll be injured, but my injurrrieees heal verrry fast. Until Heath caaame, there was nooo one elssse but youuu who I could contact about explorrring the underrrground. He isss willing to risk hisss life to find a waaay out, and so am I."

"Ruby, even if there is some way off the island, you'll die," Calla pointed out.

"I don't waaant to gooo on anymorrre," she said in her reptilian tone. *"I usssed to journey among the staaarsss. Nooow, I've been grounded foreverrr. Even my brotherrr agreees thaaat thisss isss the time to seizzze the opportunity."*

"You never said anything about how miserable you are," Calla said weakly, on the verge of crying.

"I care for youuu," Ruby said, placing her long hand on Calla's shoulder. *"I didn't wish for youuu to think I did not by expressing my desirrre to leave."*

"We should go," I interjected. "We have a long

hike ahead of us."

"Indeed," Calla said with a sniff. "There's a hole up near the top on the other side of the island, near my home. I can lead you to it, but we won't get there until nightfall."

I shook my head. "I know one that's much closer."

The way took some time only because of our pace. Cutting through dense, clawing foliage and dealing with biting bugs bogged us down. I warned both Starr and West—who amazed me by sticking around—that if Sassy crossed our path to let her be. Finally, we came to the hole where Phil had fallen in.

"You mean there's going to be a badly damaged body down there?" West said when I told them. "I . . . I think I'll stay up here."

"Aren't you a doctor?" Starr commented. "Haven't you seen dead people before?"

"I don't want to go down there, all right?" he said petulantly.

I believe he just didn't want to risk getting killed. "It's fine. We'll need an extra pair of hands to help lower us down."

Calla took one look at the black pit. "I can't go, either."

"I wasn't excepting you to." I dropped my bag of supplies. "I need you to help West get us down safely."

I wasn't too thrilled to have Ruby come with us. I had no idea what lay underground and I wasn't sure if I could protect her. Even so, she and everyone else trapped on the island had every right to risk their lives to escape.

I decided to go first. We tied every rope together until we had a four hundred-foot line. Starr helped me tie one end around my waist and two separate pieces over my shoulders and between my legs, making a harness, then tied those to the main rope. We both knew what we were doing. On weekends, he and I used to fly north to Georgia for camping and mountain climbing.

"You ready?" he asked.

"As ready as I'll ever be," I said, putting on the fighter pilot helmet.

Once we checked the security of the ropes, I was set to go. I'll admit, I had second thoughts as I leaned over the hole's edge.

Starr, Calla, and West held the rope and began lowering me as I rappelled down against the jagged wall. I wanted to drop a flare to get an indication of how deep the hole was, but if it hit Phil's body and burned it, would that count as disturbing it? I didn't need another soul following me around.

Still, I wasn't willing to face anything I might encounter down there in total darkness so I pulled out a candle as I descended and lit it, hoping the steady breeze wouldn't blow it out. The dim circle of light above me shrank smaller and smaller. The air made me shudder, even though it wasn't cold.

I soon saw something. The grotesque sight seized my heart and kept it from beating. I couldn't breathe, couldn't scream or make any kind of sound. It was the sort of thing found in a haunted house, only it wasn't made from latex, food coloring, or painted with oils. It came from an actual person. Chunks of skin and clumps of hair stuck to the wall, glued by thick trails of dried blood. No doubt it had been Phil. On his way down, his body must've slammed and scraped against the rocks, shredding him like grated cheese. I only hoped the impact had killed him instantly.

When my voice returned, I called for West and Starr to stop, giving me a chance to warn them about what waited down here. Then I continued to descend.

There were more gory bits. Apparently, Phil had ping-ponged off the walls as he fell, leaving pieces of himself on both sides. The gray circle of sunlight at the top of the hole diminished to the size of a coin and the candle became my only source of light. I worried about many things, such as the hole narrowing in on me, preventing me from going any farther, or being submerged in a massive body of water. Such thoughts drove me to take a chance and drop a flare.

I hollered for Starr and West to stop. My voice echoed upward but my descent halted. They yelled down to me but I was too far to understand them. Most likely, they wondered why a red fireball had suddenly ignited. I dropped the flare and watched it fall. The light quickly narrowed to the size of a thimble and still kept going.

"Shit."

It eventually hit the ground. Though the flame looked more like a distant star, I could still see it. I called for West and Starr to keep lowering me. Blood and skin plastered the wall, but I ignored it. After a long ride, the hole opened up. I came through the ceiling of a wide hollow space. When I touched ground, I untied myself. Once free, I tugged on the rope, letting them know I'd hit the bottom.

I picked up the flare. It gave out enough light to show me that I was in a vast chamber the size of a basketball court. But my amazement dried up when I noticed a trail of blood on the ground. Phil's body had been dragged away.

Chapter Thirty-two

I picked up the torch and followed the blood trail as the rope rose back up to the opening in the ceiling. The trail led to a small cave. I thought to investigate farther but decided it would be best to wait for Ruby and Starr.

What the hell could've dragged Phil's body away? It had to be some kind of animal, maybe a large underground cat.

"What do you think?" I asked Gavin.

There was no answer.

"Gavin?" I called, panning the torch around, expecting to see him, but he was nowhere to be found. "If you're trying to mess with me, it's not funny!"

No response. I didn't know what game he was playing but there was nothing I could do about it, so I waited.

It was a long wait. I carved the skin off the vine and mashed it in a small bowl before mixing it with seed juice. I knew Ruby would need it. The flare fizzled out and I had to relight my candle. Ruby took a long time to descend. When she finally reached the bottom, she had cuts carved into her flesh. Once I untied her, I brought out the first aid kit to clean her wounds in order to apply the salve as Starr worked his way down. Her moist skin felt grimy, like loose soil. I mentioned nothing to her about it. I'm sure my skin felt strange to her.

"I have a spirit who's attached to me," I told her while checking her wounds for any sign of Phil's

337

blood. I had no idea what would happen if human blood came in contact with hers.

"What isss hisss naaame?"

"Gavin Cole. He was my flight student." I paused to take a breath. "You said water holds a lot of the island's power and in turn has kept the ships and planes from disintegrating, right?"

"Yesss."

I then told her about Gavin's illusion after the crash. The muscles of her face stretched when I told her how I'd been duped into burning his body.

"Ahhh, he died in the boundary. When someone touches a body out there, it givesss the fragggment easy access to manipulaaate the mind," she said gravely.

I took out a roll of gauze from the first aid kit. "Why would the island want me to disturb his body all the way out there?"

"To ussse the enerrrgy. When someone diesss in the boundary, their life sourrrce—itsss soul—isss idle and producesss no enerrrgy for the island to absorb. Afterrr people becaaame wissse about the dead and ssstarted to leave them alooone, the fragggment found a waaay to trick the living into awaaakening the dead in the boundaries."

"Really? The island can send an exact replica of dead people to pose as them? How is that possible?"

"The fragggment recorrrds the traaaits of an organnnism as it diesss and sendsss out imagessss of the dead to deceive the living."

"The false Gavin came just before sunrise and vanished shortly afterward."

"That makes senssse. The image can't laaast long. It drains tooo much of the fragggment's own

338

strength. So it choooses a time when a person isss resssting to approach, making it easier to coax them into doing what it wantsss them to dooo."

"Is the island that smart?"

"Perhaaaps."

I wondered if that was what had driven Irving to slit his wrists in jail. Constantly being awakened by the dead and cursed at would cause anyone to go mad after a while.

"Why is it that when you ignore these fake spirits, they eventually vanish?"

"You mussst have ssspoken to Jean Laffite. Calla once spoke to him about it when sheee learrrned it frrrom aaanother humaaan."

Travis. I thought.

"The illusssions the fragggment producesss responds to actions. Where there'sss an action, there'sss a reaction, and when anyone givesss thessse illusssions attention, they unknowingly let off a charggge of enerrrgy causssed by their acknowledgement, allowing the illusssion to return. When ignored, the impossster lossesss that connnnection."

"Have you found out how the island can draw fake spirits to someone?"

"Yesss. When a sssoul isss asleep, it taaakes a certain amount of disssturbance to awaaaken it, such asss moving the body or shaaaking it hard enough to rouse it."

"Like waking up a sleeping person?"

"Yesss. The fragggment hasss figured out how to connect the illusssions of the dead to the living by waaay of alternating currents to laaatch onto our own enerrrgy sssource."

What she said reminded me of those plasma globes I'd seen at novelty stores, the ones with the neon currents that were attracted by the touch of a person.

"What about the urge that Lafitte talked about? The one that drew him to his first mate? I had the same experience with Gavin."

"Once the fragggment hasss you within itsss boundaries, it hasss waaaysss to control you. Not completely, but in smaaall waaaysss to get you to dooo whaaat it wantsss, such asss usssing the connection the perssson already hasss with a deceasssed companion."

"Sort of like installing an addiction in someone?"

"Yesss. The clossser a perssson gets to the body, the lesss connntrol they haaave to resissst."

"Lafitte said the island is changing and trying to communicate with us about a means to an end. Like it's ready to die or something."

"He isss half-right. The fragggment is weakening."

"Weakening? How?"

"I'm not suuure, but I've noticed the changesss mysssself. Something isss causssing it turmoil. But it'sss not trying to communicate, it only wantsss an endlesss supply of nourrrishment."

"Meaning it wants to bring in more people as others die off," I surmised, wrapping the bandages around her arm. "Like an entire cruise ship?"

"Indeed."

"If the island stays, it'll swallow up more people."

"Yesss. Itsss appetite hasss become more dangerousss. It'll continue taking in living organisms for asss long asss it existsss."

340

I pondered that for a moment. It hurt to think about all those people yanked from their lives, only to serve as a dish for some hungry moon rock.

"Now that the island is weakening, it's the perfect time to find its sweet spot and stab it, right?"

"Yesss."

I still had a long way to go in tending her wounds, so I asked, "What's your kind like?"

"Currrious," she said. *"Passionnnate and peaceful. Our race yearrrns to learrrn and explore."* She seemed to laugh a little. I couldn't tell. *"I think we're like the fragggment. We must absorrrb everything we can in orderrr to surrrvive."*

"I think all living things share that nature," I said, cleaning a gash across her back. "How smart do you think the island is? How far would it go to protect itself?"

"Like anything that valuesss itsss life, thisss plaaace will do what isss necessaaary to staaay alive."

I came around to clean and smear salve on her chest, meeting her eyes.

"And the deeper we gooo, the more dangerousss I fear our search will become."

* * *

When Starr touched the ground, I showed him the blood trail and the cave it led to.

"Damn," he said, peering into the tunnel with his own candle. "What do you think happened to the body?"

"An animal, I'm guessing. We should be careful."

The large chamber had several openings to other caves, some reaching as high as the ceiling, others low enough for only a peek inside. Each cave varied in size, some small enough for only a toddler to fit through. We discussed briefly which one to enter, since splitting up wasn't an option.

We snuffed out the candles and lit torches before entering the mouth of a fourteen-foot cave that descended into the cool unknown underground. The temperature dropped significantly and a breeze increased the farther we went into it. An odd sensation took over. Each nerve in my body tingled and every strand of my hair rose as though an electrical current traveled through me. I felt charged, my senses sharpened to a fine point, and I was more aware than I ever remembered being. Starr expressed that he experienced the same sensation and that even in his prime he'd never possessed this kind of energy. Ruby healed instantly and tore off her bandages.

The ground wasn't exactly smooth but was carpeted in dirt, making for an easy trek. Then the cave started to close in on us. There were entrances to other passageways, and when the ceiling dropped a little too low, we slipped into another tunnel.

"This place is a labyrinth," I said. "We're going to get lost if we don't mark where we've been."

"Don't worry," Ruby said. *"I have a superrrb memorrry. I can retrace our stepsss."*

We walked through the tunnels for hours, stopping only to eat.

"It's odd that we haven't run into any dead ends," Starr pointed out as I stirred a pot of soup over a fire. "It's like this place is completely interconnected."

"We arrre in the islandsss' lungsss," Ruby stated.

"Come again?" Starr said.

"We're in the lungsss of the fragggment," she explained.

"Are you saying this place breathes?" Starr challenged.

"Haven't you noticed a pattern of airflooow?"

She was onto something. The air came in one way, then went out the other in a rhythmic pattern, as though somewhere in the caves something inhaled and exhaled. The air that was pulled in felt more intense than the air going out.

"Do you really think there's some kind of life source here?" Starr asked Ruby.

"Yesss."

"How will we know when we find it?"

"I'm thinking it won't be hard to miss," I said. "The question is can we actually destroy it?"

"It dependsss on what we're dealing with," Ruby said.

We ate and moved on, traveling through another cave with a high ceiling and narrow walls. My shoulders scrapped painfully against either side, forcing me to walk canted to one side. Ruby had to do the same. She had a thin frame but her shoulders were wider than a football player in pads.

Starr led the way through the narrow passageway. I wanted his place but he'd won the coin toss. I just hoped the tunnel didn't narrow down any more, forcing us to turn back after coming all this way.

"Hey," Starr said, stopping, "do you hear that?"

In the silence, a faint but steady roar, like heavy traffic, echoed in a distance.

"What is that? Water?" I asked.

"Probably."

"Where there'sss waaater, there'sss life," Ruby

put in.

I swallowed my nervousness. What kind of living things would we find down here?

"Let's move," Starr commanded.

As we pressed on, the roar grew louder, until I could identify it as a waterfall. I became more alert and prepared for any creatures we might face. Ruby's comment knocked ten points off my courage card. I was glad Starr had won the toss to take the lead after all.

Paranoia kept me glancing over my shoulder, to the point my neck ached. But the pain disappeared the moment the floor beneath Ruby and Starr caved in. They dropped from sight in a heartbeat. I'd been close enough to nearly fall in with them, but I managed to stumble backward as the ground crumbled like dry clay underfoot. I fell back, landing on my ass, but on solid ground.

I picked up my torch and leaned over the edge, calling out to them. They weren't there. Instead, a fifteen-foot drop into rushing water went by as fast as white water rapids. The roar of the current drowned out my voice.

It didn't matter. They were gone and I had no idea where they were headed. I envisioned the river led to a pool somewhere, possibly back outside.

"Gavin!" I screamed. "I need your help! Where are you?"

He never appeared.

Finding the life source of the island dissolved. Finding my friends was my new priority. My first dumb thought was to jump in after them, but I refrained from doing so. If the current happened to fork, I could go the wrong way. If I cracked my head on a rock, what good would I be to them—if they were still alive. I worried for Ruby the most. Starr, like me, still wore his helmet, but Ruby's body wasn't equipped to withstand much abuse.

I hated it, but I decided to continue through the cave and search for them on foot.

"Gavin, where the hell are you?"

I panned my torch around, expecting him to appear in the fiery light, but he never showed. I didn't know why he wasn't here but I had no time to stand around, waiting.

I sucked in my gut and leapt over the opening, imagining the floor caving in the moment I landed on the opposite side. It didn't and I moved on.

The tunnel inclined drastically and my feet started sliding. The ground got very slippery. Fat water droplets dripped from the ceiling, annoying me whenever they landed on my shoulders. The waterfall sounded closer. I guesstimated it to be somewhere to my right and the stream that had taken Ruby and Starr came from it.

I kept a hand on the damp wall, giving myself as much balance as a tightrope walker in a high wind. Eventually, I crouched and skidded on my feet over the incline. The torch's flame withstood the extra breeze until the ground left my feet and I dropped into four feet of water. I didn't even see the drop-off coming. A tunnel of darkness was the only thing visible and my entire body was soaked. A perfect setting for a horror scene—moron caught in the dark, regretting every decision that had led him to this point.

I stood up and groped the air blindly with one hand, while holding the now useless torch in the other. I found a ledge and hoisted myself out of the water. As

I stood in the pitch blackness, with the sound of drops striking the floor, I flicked my lighter. Only small sparks flashed from it, the flint too wet for a flame. Yet sparks were a good sign. Time, however, wasn't on my side. I had to find Ruby and Starr. Even if they were dead, I had to know.

I didn't worry about finding my way out. I'd pretty much gotten lost the second Ruby and I had separated. With no light to guide me, I took the course slowly.

To my good fortune, the floor leveled out and I could walk without the fear of slipping. Falling was another story. I had no idea if or when the ground would cave in beneath me. That it had collapsed so easily when Starr and Ruby had walked over it made me realize the island *was* getting weaker. The island's distress would be sweet if not for being deep in its bowels.

I hummed as a distraction and flicked my lighter until my thumb throbbed. After a while, a flame sparked to life. I wanted to jump for joy but I restrained myself and kept going.

It wasn't long afterwards that a raunchy stench burned my nostrils and made me gag. I'd smelled it before but I couldn't remember where.

The tunnel opened up and a gust of wind blew my lighter out. I stepped into the quiet opening, no longer feeling the walls around me, and stopped. I wasn't completely in the dark, though. Above me were thousands of glowing pale green lights, each the size of a tennis ball, blinking like oversized fireflies. They amazed me to no end.

The smell persisted and was something I could have done without. I tried flicking my lighter, only to have the flame extinguished by the breeze. I decided to try my last flare. I brought it out and ignited it. Big mistake. If only I'd known what those beautiful lights were and recognized that horrible stench, I would've crept through the darkness like a rat looking for a hole to scamper into.

The chamber lit up in a bright flash of red and white as thousands of bats went mad. When the flare erupted, they screeched and flew frantically around. Some dropped to the floor into mounds of their own guano.

Even having a heart attack, I refused to backtrack. I swatted at any creature that came near me as I ran toward the nearest exit with thoughts of my limbs being bitten off. My feet didn't stop even when I was well into the throat of the other tunnel.

My heart pounded against my ribs and I shook like a Chihuahua. I tried to collect myself until a strange scratching sound caught my attention. It was accompanied by chirping and hissing. The cave's walls, ceiling, and floor were covered in millions of insects, some as large as my face. I hurried on, ignoring their crunch under my feet.

I went through the cave and exited into something extraordinary. It was the largest chamber yet and the energy from it was overwhelming. Bugs no longer crunched under the soles of my shoes. Instead, I stepped on soft moss. Sprouting from it were flowers, tall mushrooms, and small trees no higher than my waist. In the center of the stadium-sized chamber was a pool of dark water.

My flare fizzled out. I wrapped what was left of the first aid gauze around the head of my torch and flicked the lighter to set it ablaze. I staked the torch in

347

the soft earth beside a wide rock column and knelt beside the pool.

The water bubbled like a hot tub. The wind entered it for a moment, then flowed out again, escaping through hundreds of holes in the ceiling and passageways. Curious, I held my hand over it, feeling every hair stand on end. Blue electrical currents shot into my arm and fingertips, causing my heart to skip a beat.

I snatched my hand away and fell back on my ass, holding my wrist. It occurred to me that this was the water the fragment had stored within itself and I might have found the island's life source.

Where there is water, there is life.

I picked up the torch and straightened to my full height, ready to search for Ruby and Starr. Instead, I turned and found myself face to face with a ghost. Only it wasn't Gavin.

"Who the bloody fuck are you?" the ghost asked, pointing a sword at my chest.

I raised my hand that held the torch and gave him a fake smile. He was the oddest thing I'd seen. His skin was so pale he glowed. He had black hair and eyes, with a shade of gray around both. He wore torn pants with a sleeveless shirt and no shoes.

I reached slowly for the pistol tucked under my belt. "Just someone who took a wrong turn."

A sharp point pressed against my back. "Don't do it, wanker!" shouted another voice behind me.

I raised my other hand after my weapon was taken from me.

"Is it a gun?" the man in front asked. Their British accents threw me for a loop.

"Aye, should we fire it off?"

348

"No, idiot, save the bullets. It's not every day we get a loaded gun, eh?"

The other person finally walked around to face me. He, too, looked like a corpse, only his hair was dark red. He wore no shirt, just a pair of ratty brown pants and one sock on his left foot. In his hand was also a sword.

"What's that thing on your head?"

"It's a helmet."

The redhead demanded that I give it to him, and I did. He put it on. "What should we do with him, eh?"

I threw in my two cents. "Let him go?"

"Quiet, you," the black-haired one ordered. "You have no rights anymore. You belong to us now."

"Let's take him to see what Killian wants to do. He might think we have too many of these as it is."

"Too many of what?" I asked, already forgetting the order to keep quiet.

They didn't yell at me. Instead, the black-haired one actually answered me. "Other aboveground buggers like you. Killian might decide we have too many. And if so, you're in real trouble."

Chapter Thirty-three

We journeyed beside the pond and past other wide columns. My head was bloated with questions and concerns. Not concern for my own wellbeing, but for my friends. I said nothing about them. If they were alive, I didn't want these people searching for them. They weren't friendly and I had no idea what they were capable of.

My torch was what must have drawn them. I was allowed to keep it only because it seemed they didn't need light to guide them. We walked around the pond and through another cave, where a tunnel inclined upward in a spiral.

"Where are you taking me?"

"Shut it," the redhead snapped. "You'll bloody well know soon enough."

"Are you from England?"

"I said shut it. We don't like your kind coming down here, sniffing about."

"My kind?"

"Frankie!" exclaimed the black-haired man, "stop chatting with him."

"He's the one who won't bloody shut his trap, Amos."

Amos whipped around to face me, jabbing a finger at my chest. "Listen, boy-o, you're ours now. From here on out, you don't speak unless you're spoken to. You don't ask questions unless you're given permission to, got it?"

"Got it," I grunted.

We continued through the cave until it opened up to reveal a dark village. This chamber appeared to be the same size as the one below us. Stairways carved into the walls spiraled upward and led to hollow spaces that appeared to be homes. Tall poles were staked in the ground, burning blue and green flames inside glass lamps. My own torch was taken away and tossed to the side.

We stepped into what looked like a marketplace on the ground level, passing shops made of wood. Other ghostly figures glared at us. In the center of the market was a small stage where costumed children performed.

"What slew none and yet slew twelve?" a young boy said to a girl dressed like a princess.

"A raven ate from a dead poisoned horse and died from it. Then twelve robbers ate the raven and died from that," the princess said.

The boy laughed. "Ha, ha, ha! You have not solved the riddle but merely sought the answer while I slept."

"And what proof do you have?" she challenged.

The boy beckoned three other boys over to him. Each carried a robe. "Your robes, my lady. Each one found in my bedchambers. And this one . . ." He pointed to the robe in the middle. ". . . will be embroidered in gold and silver and be worn on our wedding day."

"Look what we found," Amos announced loudly.

Everyone within earshot stopped what they were doing and turned to us. A cold shudder vibrated through my bones when their eyes fell upon me. They started muttering to each other as we walked to the staircase, then climbed it.

My guess that the hollow spaces were homes was right. Every so often, I looked into a window or open doorway to get a quick peek inside. They had furniture, hanging ornaments, and wall paintings. They even had pets. Blue lizards the size of small dogs sat on everything, mostly clinging to the walls. They perched on people's shoulders, while smaller ones encircled their owner's arms like bracelets. More glowing bats hung upside down in cages.

We kept climbing. People asked me why I was here or why we—meaning us aboveground people—couldn't stay in our own territory. I gave no reply.

I could only imagine what they'd do to me if I answered honestly. Each spoke with a British accent like Amos and Frankie. I was dying to know who they were and why they lived underground. They couldn't be from England or anywhere else from the outside world. Like the Shark Hunters and man-eating stingrays, these people had to be native to the island. If I ever saw Calla again, I'd throw that in her face.

We reached a cave at the top of the staircase. The door was half open and Amos knocked on it. "Killian, are you in there?"

"Aye," came a voice. "Come in."

Frankie shoved me into the room. Many candles set the room aglow in a range of sapphire and jade. The cave had many creatures inside. More lizards rested on furniture and walls, while shiny silver fish glided along in a large crystal bowl in the center of the room. Moss and short vines hung from the ceiling with small hairless rodents crawling through them. I became so engrossed in the décor that I failed to notice a pale man lying on a bed in the far corner of the room.

"What is it?" Killian asked in a raspy tone.

"Begging your pardon, sir," Amos said, stopping at the foot of the bed. "We captured another intruder."

Killian lay on his side, reading a book, oblivious to me until Amos spoke. He was the palest one I'd seen yet, with gray hair thinning around the bald area on his bumpy head. What little hair he had was knotted and shoulder-length.

He craned his neck to look at me and his electric blue eyes glowed in the dark. "What's your name?"

"Heath Sharp."

"What are you doing down here?"

"Just exploring. I found a hole and—"

"I don't need a full explanation!" he cut in.

His sharp tone agitated his throat and he coughed into a cloth. It got to the point where it sounded like he was choking. When the attack subsided, he wiped tears from his bony cheeks and sat up. Beside him was a table with a jar of leaves and a bowl of syrup. I recognized it as the same kind of medicine West had brought me that morning.

"Come closer," he ordered, dipping a leaf into the bowl.

I stepped to the foot of the bed where he sat Indian-style. He shoved the leaf between his teeth and chewed it with an open mouth. We made eye contact for a long moment; or, at least, what I took was a long moment. I wanted answers, but these people had a low tolerance for disobedience and I'd been told not to speak.

"You look strong," he said with a mouth full of chewed leaf. "You'll become very useful around here."

The hell with that. "Who are you people?"

"Don't bloody speak unless you're spoken to, worm!" Frankie shouted.

"And why the hell do you speak with a British accent?"

Amos grabbed my arm, about to pull me away, when I snatched it back. His hold was weak compared to mine.

"I want some goddamn answers!" I exclaimed angrily. I'd tried going with the flow but I couldn't take it anymore. I was ready to fight off both Amos and Frankie. Frankie still had my gun but he seemed to have forgotten about it. Instead, they pointed their swords at me.

I thought to grab Amos' weapon and use it to fight my way out, but that wasn't such a sound plan. Even if I seized the weapon and got out of Killian's home, I still had a horde of others to deal with.

In any case, I never got a chance to make a daring escape. I was struck in the back of the head with something hard enough to bring me to my knees. When I was down, I saw that Killian had a small stone statue in his hand.

"Next time you bring me these things, make sure they're bound."

"Yes, sir," Frankie said. He brought out my pistol and whacked me across the head with it.

* * *

I woke in another low-light cave and found I wasn't alone.

"Are you all right, lad?" a man asked.

I rolled my head over to find him sitting beside me.

"You people are assholes," I grumbled, slowly sitting up.

"No, lad, we're not them folk."

I studied him in confusion. His complexion wasn't as pale as the others and his dull eyes spoke of a long hardship. "Who are you?"

"I'm Captain James McCarran. I've been trapped in this Godforsaken place since 1688."

"You've been down here all that time?"

"Mostly. Me and the crew explored the island and came across a cave on the side of the mountain, near the shore. We got lost in its maze of endless tunnels. Eventually, these demons found us and brought us here."

I scanned the cave we were in. It was relatively large, set on the ground level of the village, segregated by bars. I counted thirty people, if not more, locked in with us, some women, but mostly men. They sat around in a circle, staring at me.

"Are you all from the same ship?" I asked.

"No, only myself is left," the captain said soberly. "The rest of my men died throughout the years, either by their own hand or killed trying to escape."

"Sixteen eighty-eight?" I said, rubbing the knot on my head. "I don't remember any record of a ship gone missing that far back."

"Probably wouldn't, since we were pirates. I doubt there's a record out there that even says we existed."

"Oh."

"We've been here since 1940," another man said, pointing to six other men.

"You were with Calla Newbury?"

"That's right, sport," another one in the group said. "Did she talk you into coming here?"

"No. Actually, she didn't want me to come at

all."

"Really? She was all gung-ho about sending us down here. She was too afraid to come herself but wanted us to return and report what we found. You should've listened to her and stayed out."

"I'm starting to see that now," I said grimly.

"The rest of us," someone else spoke, "come from other times. Some of us have been here since the eighteen hundreds, the latest, since the eighties."

"What's your name, son?" a man with sandy blond hair asked.

"Heath."

"I'm Jack." He pointed to another young man with a scar on his chin. "That's Ernest."

"How's it going?" Ernest said with a New York accent.

"I'm Clint," a young man said in a deep voice.

"David."

"And I'm Jeff."

Everyone went through roll call, though I only remembered the first five names because my mind wandered to something I wanted to know. "What are these people doing underground?"

"They've always been living under the earth, I suppose," Clint said. "The captain told us they've lived in this village since he was caught."

I turned my attention to McCarran. "Really?"

"Aye. When they captured me and my crew, they were fascinated by us, but also afraid. They kept us locked up like livestock for weeks. Eventually, we began talking to them, and they listened. We taught them to speak English."

"Do they live forever too?" I asked, noting the children I'd seen when they'd brought me through the

356

village. I wondered if they'd all been born here.

"No, they are as mortal as we once were," McCarran said. "I've seen many generations come and go in the course of my long imprisonment."

"They took my Brothers Grimm storybook," complained a young man. "I should like to have it returned someday."

"They once spoke their own language," McCarran went on. "But, in time, they converted to English, even adopted our inflections. We tried befriending them but they never allowed us to leave. Once in a while, one of my crew managed to slip away, only to be killed by their hunters."

I remembered Ruby and Calla telling me how the organisms on the island were altered by the island's own DNA, creating weird and aggressive versions of the original. It seemed the same thing had happened to these people. They were like us, but because they'd evolved within the island's boundaries, they'd somehow become underground dwellers. I doubted any of them, especially the kids, had ever seen sunlight.

"What do they make you do?"

"Cleanup, mostly," Jack replied. "Repair work or anything else they don't want to do themselves. The other day, a hunter found a body and took me and Clint to the spot where it was. They made us drag it off and bury it. Y'know, get it out of sight."

Phil, I thought.

"They made you disturb the body? Who touched it first?"

Jack and Clint looked at me in confusion.

"I did," Jack said.

"Can you relay a message for me?"

"Relay a message to who?"

"To the dead man. I want to tell him I'm sorry for what happened to him."

I could hear the footsteps of an insect scampering by, it was so quiet. Eventually, Jack spoke. "What are you talking about?"

"Oh!" a woman pounced in, "he's talking about that thing with the dead."

Jack turned back to me. "That shit doesn't happen down here."

"Really? Why not?"

He shrugged. "Got me. I have to say I'm grateful for it. When we lived on the surface, we had a few fellas claiming the souls of their dead chums followed them around even after they'd buried them. It wasn't a pretty sight watching them go through that."

"Have you guys seen that strange pond below us?"

"Yeah," Ernest said. "What about it?"

"I think it's what keeps this island alive."

"You mean the fragment," Clint cut in. "Calla said its part of some other second moon that once orbited our planet."

"That's why I'm here, to see if it's true. If it's destroyed, the island might die."

"What would happen then?" Jack asked.

"I don't know."

For some reason, I turned to McCarran, who'd seldom spoken. He looked at me with those broken eyes of his and gave a slow shrug. "Can't do anything about it now. Once they have you, there's no getting out. They don't fancy intruders. They've even killed the ones they've caught when their leader decided there was no use for them. I think they're scared. They're curious but too damn afraid to coexist with those living aboveground. I suppose they view us as dangerous invaders, untrustworthy foreigners. Long ago, their ancestors asked me if my crew and I came from the ships with lights that used to fly around the island."

I thought about the other aliens Ruby and Calla had mentioned. Had the ancestors of these underground dwellers once seen them hovering in the sky?

"I've been imprisoned for four centuries and their arrogance hasn't changed. We're trapped here forever and there's nothing we can do about it."

* * *

A couple of hours went by. I stood by the bars, watching the villagers. A guard stood off to the side of the cell, armed with a sword. Once in a while, a villager glanced at me as they passed, saying nothing.

I watched the stage play. This time, they performed a scene from *The Wolf and the Seven Young Kids*. A woman wearing a goat mask pretended to cut open the stomach of a man in a wolf outfit in order to free the children he'd eaten. Kids in goat masks crawled out one by one from the oversized costume. The woman then filled the belly with stones.

I was sick of stumbling into unsolved mysteries. Ever since I'd come to the island, I'd been trying to escape, only to end up digging myself in deeper. When I finally found a possible way out, I got locked in a cage. This sucked.

"You're a real dolt for coming down this way," the guard whispered to me.

"What?"

He looked over his shoulder. I recognized him. "Dustan?"

"Aye, you remembered. See your wits returned, eh?"

Dustan hadn't been a part of my hallucinations after all. He was just a curious youth who'd had the courage to speak to an outsider. Now he was my prison guard.

"Dustan, get me outta here," I pleaded.

"I can't do that. I'd be killed if I let you escape, and I don't know you well enough to sacrifice so much. Sorry, chap."

A gunshot exploded. People screamed. Everyone in the cell raced to the bars.

"Where's my friend!" Starr hollered. "I know you have him!"

Starr stood at the main entrance to the village and he wasn't alone. Amos was in front of him, his hand slightly in the air.

"Starr!" I shouted as loud as I could.

He turned in my direction. "There you are."

"Starr, get out of here! Go get help!"

Knowing he was alive gave me hope. It also filled me with dread. If there was any chance for freedom, he was it, unless he got locked up too. Or worse.

Ruby appeared. The villagers stood like statues at the sight of her.

"What is that bloody thing?" Dustan asked, clutching his sword.

"Don't try to fight it," I said. "You'll only make it angrier."

I didn't like calling Ruby an it, but referring to her that way sounded more fearsome.

Starr tossed Amos aside and approached my cell.

Ruby made strange hissing sounds to keep everyone at bay. Starr aimed his gun one way, then the other, ordering everyone to stay back.

"What goes on here?" Killian bellowed.

I peeked around as Killian stepped down the stone stairs. "Starr, he's their leader! Grab him!"

Starr rushed over and seized Killian by the collar of his robe. He jabbed the gun under Killian's chin and said, "Order your people to unlock that door or I'll have my alien friend infect your village with a painful life-threatening illness!"

Mean, I had to admit, but effective. Captain McCarran was right. These people's nerves were as frail as tissue paper. They had no idea what Ruby was or what she was cable of doing, and that scared color *into* them.

Killian ordered Dustan to unlock the cell door. When he did, I told everyone inside to leave. They all did, except for McCarran.

"We have to go," I urged.

He was apprehensive, too afraid to move. I grabbed him by the arm and pushed him forward.

"What the hell is that?" Clint asked, looking at Ruby.

"She's a friend of mine. And she's helping us, so don't be a dick to her."

Starr came up to us, dragging Killian with him. "Let's go."

We headed toward the cave's entrance with the villager's eyes following us. To make certain no one interfered, Ruby let loose with a loud screech, sending them into a panic. They ran for the safety of their homes and never came out again.

"Where did you two come from?" I asked as we

hurried down the curvy tunnel.

"I'll tell you later," Starr said, pushing Killian on. "Did you notice that pool below us?"

"Yeah. Is it—"

"The life sourrrce," Ruby cut in. *"Yesss. We havvve found the fragggment's weakness."*

Chapter Thirty-four

We traveled down the coiling tunnel toward the energy pool by the light of the torch I held.

"Let me go, you bloody bastards!" Killian cried, then coughed harshly.

"Why do you people sound like you're all from England?" Starr asked, shoving our hostage forward.

Killian caught his balance and brought himself back to full height. When he turned to face Starr, he had a hateful expression I hadn't seen since I'd jokingly told an ex-girlfriend her butt looked big in her new dress.

"Easy," I said, stepping in, "he's not a POW."

"We need to get baaack to the surrrface," Ruby urged.

"Holy cow!" someone shouted. "You talk?"

"She speaks dozens of languages," I said. "And not all from this planet."

"What should we do with Contagious here?" Starr asked.

"Bring him," I said. "We might need to use him as leverage if his people come after us."

Luckily, the journey wasn't far. I kept hearing the racing steps of Killian's people echoing behind us, while Ruby screeched intermittently to scare them away. If it weren't for their fearfulness, we might have already been killed.

The salt of the ocean scented the air as we came to a low tunnel. At the end was a small crawl space where the sweet smell of freedom became stronger.

"This opening should be closed off," Killian said angrily. "People must have been leaving the underground again. I'll have them killed for this!"

I waved for the previous prisoners to go ahead. They didn't have to be told twice. There were lots of them, some crying, others shoving. Waiting for them to crawl out only intensified the suspense. McCarran, though, stayed in place.

"Get Ruby and Killian out," I said to Starr, taking the torch from him.

"Those freaks are right behind us," Starr argued.

"Just go."

Thankfully, he didn't protest, but helped Ruby into the crawl space. As he shoved Killian in after her, I took McCarran by the arm. "Don't be stupid. Do you want them to take you prisoner again?"

"It's been four hundred years since I've breathed the ocean air," he choked out tearfully. "I've forgotten that smell."

I tried seeing things from his perspective. He'd been kept in captivity for centuries. He'd become institutionalized and most likely from the length of his incarceration, he'd never recover. Even so, I had no time to pull therapy out of my ass before a bunch of merciless executioners dragged us away.

"Move it, you scurvy dog!" I shouted in pirate lingo. I didn't know what else to do. Shouting at him was the first thing that came to mind. "The enemy is upon us! Get moving or we're all dead!"

I didn't wait to see if my tactic worked. I shoved him into the crawl space and ordered him to go, go, go! He went in. I was ready to follow when someone grabbed me and pulled me back.

"Release Killian, you sod!"

I recognized Frankie's voice and remembered that he had my gun. I snapped my body around, throwing my fist back. Gun or no gun, I wasn't going to let them lock me up again. My knuckles struck his hard white cheekbone, knocking him sideways. Immediately, I saw a fleet of ghostly faces behind him.

Grabbing Frankie, I whipped him around and held him against me as a human shield. The others came at us and I waved the torch vigorously at them, ready to burn the face of anyone who got too close. Since the firelight was bright, it hurt their eyes. They screamed and hid their faces. That was when I pushed my hostage into the nearest ones and bolted into the crawl space.

"Heath, quit fooling around in there!" Starr yelled.

The moment my head poked out the other side, someone grabbed my ankle. I tried kicking with my free foot but my other ankle was seized too.

"They got me!" I cried.

Someone yanked me backward, forcing me onto my stomach. The impact hurt like hell. The floor was rough stone, as were the walls, cutting into my skin.

Both Starr and Jack snatched my wrists and pulled in the opposite direction. Having double the strength worked in my favor, though being tugged back and forth over jagged rocks made me feel like I was being gutted. Finally, with one solid heave, Starr and Jack yanked me out of the crawl space, back onto soft sand again.

"Ignite your flare!" I hollered.

I had no idea if Starr had any more flares after his life-threatening water slide adventure, but, to my relief, a blaze of red and white exploded to illuminate our surroundings. I shot to my feet, snatched the flare from him, and threw it into the crawl space. "Run! Run!"

Everyone ran like marathon competitors down the beach. Although we booked it, Ruby was already a mile ahead.

"Wait up!" I called after her.

She didn't seem to hear me and was soon out of sight. We kept going at full speed, not because of our pursuers, but because the stingrays came after us in a horde of tail-cracking fury. We leapt over them and ran until everyone followed me into the forest.

"We shouldn't stop," Starr said as we caught our breath. "Those people could come out of anywhere."

"They want me back," Killian bellowed. "Let me go and they'll leave the rest of you be!"

I grabbed him by his robe and yanked his face to mine. "Stop fucking yelling. If you draw them to us, I'll slit you from forehead to foreskin."

I really wouldn't, but it sounded good.

"Where should we go?" Clint asked.

"Let's stick to the forest's edge," Starr suggested. "Till we reach a village."

None of us spoke during the pitch-black trek. We needed to stay as quiet as possible. Walking through a blanket of black, bumping into trees and nearly falling over everything in my path, I started to miss the full moon. I missed countless things I'd taken for granted only months ago. At the moment, it was the metallic glow of the moonlight.

We didn't know exactly where we were going or which village we'd end up at first. We just went in the direction Ruby headed. After a long hike through the wild, we finally saw a light ahead. The sight of the fiery orange glow excited us, yet we approached with caution.

"It'sss saaafe," Ruby called out. *"There'sss nothing here excccept a dead hummman."*

Right then I knew where we were. We'd reached the abandoned village of the Obsoletes.

Like damned souls, we headed for the fire. When we stepped onto a wooden walkway, I let out a sigh of relief. Relief that was sweet and bitter.

"Who the hell are you?" Jack asked, looking at nothing beside him.

"What?" a woman said, turning to him. "Who are you talking to?"

"He's got himself a soul to deal with," Gavin said beside me.

I craned my neck around. Gavin was casually leaning against a walkway railing.

"Where the hell have you been?" I asked before stopping myself. Everyone's attention then turned to me.

"It's that guy who fell into the hole," Gavin explained. "What's his name?"

"Phil," I said. "Jack, it's okay. His name is Phil. He was a soldier like you."

"He says hi," Jack said, turning back to the ghost. "This chum says he's sorry for what happened to you." There was a pause before Jack said, "He says he knows. He heard you while we were underground."

"He's been with you this whole time and you haven't seen him?" Clint asked.

"It wasss the fragggment's high quantity of enerrrgy," Ruby put in. *"Thaaat wasss why we felt so alive in the caaavesss. Lower quantities of enerrrgy, such asss spiritsss, are absorbed by it."*

"Then how did Gavin come back?" I asked,

367

imagining how we looked to the ones listening to this.

"Enerrrgy can never truly die. We maaay not haaave ssseen or heard them, but thaaat didn't mean they weren't there with us."

I turned to Gavin, who only shrugged.

"He's really messed up," Jack said shakily. "Like he went through a meat grinder."

"Let's get inside," I suggested. "We need to get our heads straight to figure out our next move."

"I beg you," Killian pleaded, "let me go back to my people."

To tell the truth, I wanted to let him go. The last thing I'd wanted to do was kidnap somebody. Unfortunately, cutting him loose wasn't an option. No doubt, he'd go back to send his people after us.

Starr was thinking along those same lines. "Don't think we're stupid enough to believe you'll just go home and not send the cavalry. Now get inside."

Jeff took the torch and led everyone into the nearest house. I heard a harsh rasping that didn't come from Killian.

"Ruby," I said, placing a hand on her shoulder, "is everything all right?"

"You haaave to find a waaay to destroooy the fragggment."

Then she insisted on staying outside, which I knew she would, being the outdoor type. Besides, we could use a lookout.

When I went back in, Starr approached me. "I know you don't have a weak stomach, but I don't recommend going into the bedroom."

I'd already heard the story about Doctor Chancier's gruesome attack on the people in the village. And since I'd come to the island, I'd seen

368

plenty of carnage. The dots of blood on the floor leading from the door to the bedroom's threshold, along with the dead man in the bed with a bullet hole in his head, didn't affect me much. No doubt it was Chancier. Blood and chunks of flesh from his last victim slathered the pillow and sheets.

Not surprisingly, no one wanted to stay the night there. I took it upon myself to search for a house without too much gore in it, and Starr went with me.

"Where did you and Ruby end up after you fell through the floor?" I asked.

"Our little trip didn't last long before the water calmed enough for us to grab hold of something and pull our way out. Did you know she can see in the dark?"

"She can? Right about now I wish I could."

"Do you have any ideas how to bring this place down?" Starr asked as we went inside the house next door.

"No clue. Whatever we do, we need to consider the people living underground."

His hand gripped my shoulder, stopping me dead in my tracks. "Are you out of your mind? Those freaks locked you up and almost killed us."

"They're still people, with families—children. They might be aggressive but that doesn't mean we should commit mass murder."

Starr said nothing as we investigated the house. It seemed vacant enough. I found no bodies in the bedroom and Starr announced that the other two rooms were clear, as well. It wasn't until I came across a desk near the bedroom door that I realized whose house we'd stumbled onto. On the desk was a journal. I read the page the book was opened to.

I would write a date if I only knew what it was. It's been countless years since I've written in this book. I like to believe it's 1864 and the world outside is as it was when we first arrived. However, too many lost souls who have become trapped here have given testimony otherwise. Alas, as the years stretch like a monotonous nightmare, my hope of escaping has dwindled to nothing. The world, my world, has changed. This I have finally come to realize, much to my displeasure. Nothing, however, has pained me more than losing my Eleanor. I held out hope that she would come to her senses and return to my side where she belongs. Today, a rude young man strangely came to inform me that she has taken another suitor and possesses passionate feelings for him that I daresay she should have for me. I am at my wits end. If Eleanor cannot see that she is mine and mine alone, then I must go on the morrow and show her. It's now time for her to fulfill her destiny to be with me for all time.

Darwin Bradford

Bastard.

There was nothing more written after that. It was the last thing he'd written before he'd left the village to destroy her. It would've been worth having his soul attached to me forever just to have killed him before he'd acted. So far, keeping myself occupied had kept me from breaking down whenever I thought about her. Then came those pockets of dead time when thoughts of her resurfaced in my mind.

I closed the journal as Starr entered the room.

"All clear," he reported. "Think we found a

370

winner."

"Cool," I replied weakly. "Let's get everyone inside."

I turned, only to have Starr slap his hand against my chest. "I want you to know, I thought about what you said."

I was relieved, which was stupid, since there were two ways to interpret that. The good way being, *I thought about what you said and I agree.* Or the bad, *I thought about what you said and I don't give a shit.*

"You oughta know that I have no intention of staying here forever, especially if there's a way out," he said.

"I agree," I replied, removing his hand. "I'm just saying we need to do so without hurting others."

I headed for the door, but then stopped when he said, "Would you rather stay trapped on this depressing spit of land?"

"In war, if you were given an order to complete a mission and the only way to do it was to blow up an entire village filled with innocent civilians, would you do it?"

He didn't answer. In truth, I didn't give him time to offer one. I left. I was afraid of what he might say.

Once everyone moved from the crime scene to the clear house, I went out back to take a breath.

"What a quandary, huh?" Gavin said.

I jumped a bit.

"Stay here forever or risk killing a bunch of people."

My blood turned from ice cold to boiling. "Goddamn it, I just want some peace," I said indignantly.

"Sorry, I'll keep outta sight and shut my trap,"

371

Gavin said.

The instant after my outburst, I regretted my words. "No, wait. Stay. It's been an ass of a day."

"Yeah, I've had those. Like one day, this guy blew up my dead body and the next thing I know, I became a walking, talking stick of beef jerky."

I glared at him but he didn't seem to notice. "Where were you today, anyway?"

"With you."

"The entire time?"

"Every step, dude. Guess down there, we disembodied souls become like we do on the outside. Invisible." He started making scary ghost sounds.

"Funny," I said.

"I screamed my lungs out, trying to warn you about those sneaky people while they were creepin' up on you."

"I bet you did," I said sincerely. "You're a good friend to have around."

"You're a good egg too. Can't think of anyone else I'd rather have my crispy spirit stuck to."

"Thanks. I think."

"Except my old high school math teacher," he added bitterly. "I'd love to make every second of his life painful. I'd tell him I was a demon waiting for him to take his final breath so I could pull him into the darkest pit of Hell for flunking a wonderful young man like Gavin Cole."

"Wow," I said mildly.

"Talking to your mate?" someone said behind me. It was Captain McCarran. "I have thirteen it turns out."

"Thirteen? How . . . ?"

"My shipmates," he explained. "Whenever those

underground dwellers killed one or found their bodies, they got me to dispose of them. In those days, they were afraid to touch us."

"Why?"

"Superstitious, I suppose. As a sailor, I can relate. They eventually realized touching us wouldn't hurt them, but they made us move the bodies, anyway."

"You witnessed many generations come and go down there, huh?"

"I have."

"Do you hate them for what they did to you and your crew?"

"I used to. But over the years, I reckoned they hadn't done any worse than the rest of the human race has done to each other. They're a lot like us."

I gave what he said some serious thought. Although none of us had any real plan of how to kill the island, this obstacle still remained. Any one of us could argue that we hadn't asked to be on the island, and neither had they. They were human beings like the rest of us and we had no right to take their lives, no more than they had the right to take ours.

* * *

The night stayed calm. In the morning, I went outside to where Starr knelt beside Ruby.

"Jesus!" I cried, falling to my knees beside her. "Ruby?"

"I think she's dead," he said, quickly grabbing my hand and yanking it back before I touched her. "Look."

She lay on her belly. Deep gashes on her back and arms spilled glassy blood on the walkway.

"It looks like she passed away not long ago," he observed. "Just settled down, closed her eyes, and let herself bleed to death. No one heard her fall."

Ruby's death devastated me. I remembered the things she'd said about how she'd used to travel among the stars, only to end up marooned on an alien planet. She'd wanted her freedom and I believe that was the reason why she'd never asked for help. I asked Gavin if he could see her brother.

He shook his head. "Guess he left too. It seems when us ghosts have no one to latch onto, we're free."

"There's a woman over there," Starr said, pointing.

I followed his finger to the back of a house, where a woman hung from a tree.

"Don't worry about her. Let's get ready and go."

Both Killian's and McCarran's eyes were too sensitive for the light, though the day was more overcast and foggy than usual. We blindfolded them and led them over the beach. On the way, I spotted Dominic's freighter, *The Anita*. She was the closest ship to the shore.

The walk to North Village was a long one, yet no one complained. I was sure each of us had different things going through our heads. I'd been worried McCarran would freak out over his long dead crew mates now around him, but he neither said nor did anything erratic.

When we reached the village, the soldiers joined their compatriots, while the others scattered about. I got one of them to take McCarran to Miller's Tavern for a drink before I hurried Killian to my hut, while Starr fetched Carlton.

"What are you planning to do with me?" Killian

asked as I removed his blindfold.

"We're not going to hurt you, if that's what you're worried about. Stop acting so dramatic."

"That monster said you know how to destroy the fragment. What fragment? What are you planning to do?"

"I don't know. Whatever we decide, it could endanger your people. They might have to evacuate from the underground."

"Evacuate? To where? The light hurts our eyes too much."

"We'll think of something. You have to understand, there are hundreds of people who want to go home. Now that the secret is out, there won't be anything to stop them from finding a way to destroy this place. I'll do what I can to make sure your people aren't hurt, but you're going to have to help."

"It'll be war," he said. "My people will stand against yours."

"And you'll lose," I said harshly. "Think about it. We outnumber you. Most of the people we have are actual soldiers with real combat experience. If you so much as try anything, they'll go underground and smoke each of you out like rodents. Is that what you want?"

He kept his focus on me for a moment, then bowed his head. I was glad he understood. I didn't want to deal with his obstinacy when I was trying to save his people.

"People have always adjusted to their surroundings," I said in a more sensitive tone. "Maybe your people can adapt to sunlight."

"I know we can."

What he said surprised the hell out of me. "You .

. . what?"

Starr stepped inside with Carlton.

"Hey, Carlton," I said. "I didn't know who else to tell about this."

"Yeah," he said, giving me a nod. "Mr. Starr told me everything." He approached Killian with his chubby hands on his waist. "Well, cat's outta the bag. Things are going to change, my brother."

Chapter Thirty-five

Some surprises can be fun. Others, not so much. And some are just bizarre. Finding out Carlton was Killian's brother turned my brain inside out.

"You're brothers?" I gasped. "I thought you were a chief of police from Texas."

"No," he admitted, sounding completely British now. "The man I stole me identify from was. Years ago, the real Carlton Malone went underground and got caught by our people. I was a prison guard then. I talked to him and he told me his life story. One day, while doing repair work, he tried to escape and got killed. Not by me, mind you."

"Why did you take his identity?"

"I didn't want to live underground anymore."

"Too good for us, he is," Killian snarled.

"Shut it, big brother," Carlton snapped. "At least I had the guts to come to the surface. Unlike you, coward."

"So, it's true," I cut in before a sibling feud broke out. "Your kind can adjust to the light."

"Of course we can," Carlton said. "It takes time, depending on how old we are, but we can adjust."

"Speaking of age, how long have you been living up here?"

"Ten years. Since the real Carlton lived in South Village, I came to North Village, where no one knew him. I kept to myself while I practiced my southern brogue. I always thought whenever I got old enough for people to take notice, I'd claim I was sick."

"We know how to destroy the island," Starr interjected. "If your people want to live, they need to get out of our way."

"An evacuation will take time, my boy," Carlton explained. "We're talking about moving an entire society."

Carlton was right. Below us was a small town. Getting them onboard for a major change would be time-consuming and delicate work.

"Get them ready or they can die with this creepy place," Starr said before storming out.

"Forceful little shit, isn't he?" Carlton said.

This was the in-your-face Starr I didn't want coming out. "I'll talk to him. Killian, I don't want to hold you against your will anymore, so I'm asking you to stay. The lives of your people depend on it."

Killian sighed and rolled his eyes, like a lazy roommate being asked to take out the trash. "I'll stay, but not because you ask me to. It's because I'm sick. You've probably killed me bringing me up here."

"Stop your complaining," Carlton said. "You've always been such a whiny little cuss." And to me, he said, "I'll watch him."

I hurried to catch up with Starr as he ran down the stairs. The rain fell like tiny stones on my shoulders. "Starr, wait up!"

He stopped, and when he turned to me, I said, "What the hell, man? You can't throw your weight around like that. We got to plan things out before we make a move."

"I'm the soldier here, not you," he fired back, water and spit flying out of his mouth. "We need to act on this right now, before those things attack us."

"Those *things* are people," I reminded him. "And

378

I don't think they're going to try anything."

"You don't know that. We're in a critical situation right now and there's no time to piss around."

I hadn't fought in the Gulf War with Starr. I'd never fought in any war. But it seemed to me his instincts as a soldier had kicked into high gear. He considered the underground dwellers a threat that needed to be controlled.

"What exactly are you going to do?" I challenged. "Do you even have a plan to destroy the island?" His blank expression told me he didn't. "All right, then, go to the bar. Have a drink and clear your head. We'll talk in the morning."

As I headed up the stairs, I hoped he'd take my advice. For as long as I'd known him, he'd been a straight-up guy. I'd seen him fist-fight someone at a bar over something stupid and then have a drink with him. Maybe if he had time to relax, he'd return to an understanding, cooperative guy and not an alpha dog with rabies.

When I rejoined Carlton and Killian in my hut, I had questions of my own. "Is there anyone else in the village like you two?"

"Some," Carlton replied. "I won't give names. You should just be grateful we're living among you. We've shown your people how to use plants for medicine, among other things."

"How long has your kind been doing this?"

"We didn't start until the turn of the century, when a band of our youngsters left to experience the world above. Except they were killed after they came back. Still, most who live underground wanted to come up, but because the traditionalists…" He stared at his brother. "They portray the surface as being overrun

379

with death and monsters. Only so many of us try making a living up here."

"Well, *everyone* down there is going to have to adjust pretty damn quick after word spreads about this," I said.

"Are you really going to try to destroy the island?" Killian asked.

"Yes."

He snorted. "You're mad. How are you going to destroy an entire island? Get pickaxes and break it apart?"

Again with the critical question how. It seemed to be the question of the day, yet I had zero time to think about it.

I asked Carlton to take his brother back to his hut. I needed some time to think. I wished Ruby was here. We could have collaborated on a solution.

"Ruby," I lamented to myself.

Shit, I'd forgotten about Calla and West, where they were and if they were all right. I doubted after the time we'd spent underground they'd stayed by the hole. I couldn't search for them now, though. I needed time to think.

I lit some candles and stretched out on the floor. "Have any ideas?" I asked Gavin.

"About what?"

"About the island, how we can destroy it."

"Got me. I skipped the whole 'How to Destroy an Entire Land Mass' course in college."

My chest rose with the breath I took. While I slowly exhaled, Gavin said, "Ruby said now that you've found that weird pool, you guys could kill the fragment."

"Right, that pool is the life source."

"Isn't there a way to, I don't know, drain the pool?"

"I doubt there's a cork at the bottom."

He appeared and paced back and forth by my feet. "That place was weird, huh?"

"Yeah, it was. Especially the breeze."

"What breeze?"

I'd forgotten he could no longer feel anything. "The breeze that came in and out. It was caused by the energy pool."

"'Cause it was breathing, like Ruby said?"

"Yep, it . . ."

I sat up, my heart pounding hard and my palms sweating, like I was about to ask the head cheerleader to the prom. "It *is* breathing."

"A breathing island," Gavin snorted. "Weird."

"The holes scattered all over the place must be the island's nostrils."

"Okay, even stranger. What should you do? Go around stuffing up the holes to suffocate the damn thing?"

I went back to what Killian had said about how the crawl space we'd escaped through should have been sealed off. For years, these underground dwellers must have been sealing the caves, cutting off the island's airflow, slowly suffocating it.

"Suffocation. That's it! If we can cut off the pool's airflow, the island won't be able to breathe."

"Great," Gavin said, giving me a thumbs up. "Stuffing holes it is, then."

"No, we need to do something more extreme than that."

"Like what?"

I thought about it. The answer came to me when

Gavin's smart-ass remark abruptly resurfaced in my mind. *Like one day, this dude blew up my dead body and next thing I knew, I became a walking, talking stick of beef jerky.* And then what I'd said to Starr inside Darwin's house. *In war, if you were given an order to complete a mission and the only way to do it was to blow up an entire village filled with innocent civilians, would you do it?*

Two key words were in both sentences—blow up. I felt like Michael Bay conjuring up a movie script.

"I got it," I said, raising my eyes to Gavin. "I know what to do."

* * *

I went to Carlton's hut. When I got there, he was giving his brother something to drink.

"This stuff is bloody bitter," Killian complained. "Have you just poisoned me?"

"It's tea, idiot. Jeez, use the honey with it." Carlton turned his attention to me. "Thought you needed time to think."

I stood dripping water on his floor. He didn't seem to mind. "I did, and I came up with a something. We blow the island up from the inside. The explosion might cause it to cave in on itself and fill the pool with large sections of stone."

"And what will that do?" Killian asked with a sniff.

I didn't want to go into everything I'd learned about the island, about how it was really a living fragment of a collision between two moons, so I said, "It'll kill the island. If it dies, the people might be able to go home."

"Killing the island might also kill everyone living on it," Carlton said bluntly. "Ever think of that?"

I hadn't.

"And where are you going to get enough explosives to blow up a small mountain?"

"John T. Shubrick."

Carlton let out a hearty laugh that reverberated against my eardrums. "Shubrick? The ole' loony sea king?"

"Yep. He has barrels of gunpowder and crates of TNT."

Carlton's face turned grim. "You're really gonna do it, aren't ya?"

"It's our only shot. And I won't be the only one who'll figure this out. I propose that Killian goes back underground to get his people ready to leave. You and I should hold a meeting with everyone and explain everything to them."

"Where are we supposed to go?" Killian asked.

"There's an abandoned village on the other side of the island," I said. "Go there after dark. In a few days, I'll come by and fill you in. You may have to go into the junkyard in case there's a landslide."

"Landslide?" Carlton bellowed. "How much explosives are you planning to use?"

"All of them."

I'll admit, I was leaning more toward setting off explosives rather than dealing with the responsibility of the people underground. I wanted them to stay alive, that was no lie, but I was going to be juggling other problems too. First, Killian needed to talk to his people while Carlton and I brought everyone else up to speed. We needed to get organized before anything drastic happened. Then I thought about the Ancient Ones.

How was I going to find them and get them to understand what was going to happen?

As I left the hut, I spotted someone running down the stairs. I assumed it was Carlton's next door neighbor willing to get drenched for a drink. I needed to relax.

Calming my nerves, I went to Khenan's hut and told him everything over a drink.

"You tink it'll work?" he asked.

"I hope so. Tomorrow, we'll get everyone onboard. My only concern is Starr. He could stir up a lot of trouble if he wants to."

"You said 'e doesn't know 'bout your plan. I'm sure someone else won't tink up da same idea right away. Dat'll give dem people below time to leave."

That put my mind at ease. I relaxed and drank a few more beers before passing out in his armchair. Now, looking back on it, I wish I hadn't let my guard down. Every concern I had turned into full-blown realities.

Chapter Thirty-six

A banging came from the door. It felt like a nail being driven into my brain. Khenan rushed past me just as I opened my eyes to the darkness. He swung the door open. Whoever the visitor was held a lantern and stood against a black backdrop.

"Jeez, mon, wah is it?"

"Is Heath here?" Calla asked.

"You got a visitor," Khenan said with a deep yawn.

Uh-oh. The drinks from earlier made my body ache.

"Hey, Calla," I said as she stepped into the hut.

I was in for the scolding of a lifetime. When I received it, I knew my head would explode. I prepared myself to tell her the bad news about Ruby. Like ripping off a Band-Aid, I decided to go ahead and tell her.

"Ruby's dead," she said as I opened my mouth to speak.

"How do you know?" I asked, dumbfounded.

"I just came from the village on the other side of the island and found her. She was badly cut up. What happened?"

I told her how Ruby had gotten wounded as we'd escaped the underground. I also explained that Ruby had said nothing about her injuries. I didn't want Calla thinking I was an asshole for not trying to save her, which I would've if Ruby had allowed me to.

Calla bowed her head. "She didn't want to live anymore. I've known that for some time but I ignored it because I wanted her to stay with me."

That sparked an important question. "You didn't—"

"She's free now," she said abruptly. "At least I hope."

"What about West?"

"You mean that crybaby? Jeez, I've never heard a grown man complain so much. He wouldn't stop whining or go back to the village alone, so I took him there."

Night had descended but I didn't know how old it was. People ran past the doorway, although I hardly paid it any mind. "When did you get here?"

"Just now. I took a shortcut through the mountain."

"*Through* the mountain?"

She gave me a hard stare and something suddenly occurred to me. "You're one of them. All that shit about being a researcher is a lie, isn't it?"

That would explain why she hadn't known what a chameleon or a zoo was, and why she didn't want anyone going into the caves.

"Yes," she replied. "I took the real Calla's identity and everything I knew about her past, even that bit about being claustrophobic because she'd been trapped in an ice box." She chuckled. "I don't even know what those are. But that was why I didn't tell you about the holes. Not to save my people, but to keep you out of their cages. Then Ruby decided to sneak away to see you. She saw something in you."

"What?"

"Courage. She thought it was a sign you'd come to us when you did."

"You mean while the island is weakening?"

386

"Yes. She and the real Calla told me that when the three of us lived together. They'd asked me about the underground, but it wasn't until Calla . . ." She trailed off, grief-stricken. I gave her time while she gathered her thoughts. Finally, she said, "I told them about my people and that they were dangerous."

"Why didn't you tell them about the pool under your village?"

"What about it?" she demanded. "Is that what Ruby was looking for?"

"Yes."

"I never thought too much about it."

"That's why you didn't want to go with us. You didn't want to run into your people. Why?"

"I ran away thirty years ago. I never returned because they'd kill me if I went back. I can't live the way they do. Hardly anyone down there lives past forty. They either die of disease or in childbirth."

"What keeps them down there?"

"The elders tell horrible stories about flying lights that took people away and brought them back broken. Ruby confirmed the abductions were true."

Holy shit! Was it those aliens before Ruby that had run experiments on the island? They'd taken the people too?

"Still, that was hundreds of years ago. Yet the elders continued to describe the world above as a wild and dangerous place, infested with pain and death. They believed people marooned on the island weren't people at all, but savage hunters, which was true when the Vikings arrived. Killian helped keep that fear alive, like his mother and father before him, and his grandparents before them."

"What about the soldiers? Why did you tell them

387

to go underground if you knew what could happen to them?"

"They'd been imprisoned before I was even born. The real Calla told them to go because she was claustrophobic. You see, when I left, I met the real Calla Newbury. Ruby was with her even then. They took me in, helped me adjust to the light. Later, I told Calla about the men. She thought they'd died down there. After they helped build her house, she told them about a cave nearby and wanted them to go in. When I told her what had happened, she died going after them. I was leading her when she slipped and fell. She cracked her head open. I took her identity, and ever since, Ruby and I have lived together."

"Why didn't you tell me this sooner? It would've saved me a hell of a lot of trouble."

"I didn't think you'd find anything, and I didn't want to give away my true identity. Anyway, you had Ruby with you. I knew my people would be afraid of her."

"Well, believe it or not, the life source does exist. It turns out to be that pool you failed to mention."

Outside, people kept rushing back and forth. Finally, I went outside to see what all the ruckus was. People raced to and from the docks, some carrying barrels.

"That's my powder!" a man cried from the new docks. "You never asked my permission to seize it!"

"Hey," I said to someone rushing toward the water, "what's going on?"

"Some guy found an underground world and we're gonna blow the hell outta it!"

"Whoa, wait a sec," I said, catching his arm when he tried to leave. "Who are you talking about?"

He shrugged. "Don't know the man. He just said it might get us outta this shithole."

My heart fell like a stone inside my stomach. "Goddamn it, Starr."

"Wah is it?" Khenan asked.

"Starr managed to come up with the same plan I did, but he's going to go through with it before we get those people out." My eyes came in contact with Calla's. "I need you to lead me to your people's village before the explosives are in place."

"I know a shortcut. Come with me."

"Wait," Khenan called. "I'm coming wit you dis time."

We hurried across the pier, about to head into the forest, when Carlton called to me. "They took my brother! That friend of yours and some other sods."

"Why?"

"He said he needed Killian to guide them to the pool to blow it up."

"When?"

"Not too long ago. I've been trying to find you."

"Damn it. How did he come up with the same idea?"

"He didn't. He had a tail on you after he left. His spy must've heard you telling me and Killian about your plan."

I remembered the man I'd seen running down the stairs after I'd left Carlton's place. *Touché, Starr.*

"Hi, Carlton," Calla called.

The old man squinted at her.

"Kathy? Oh, it's Calla now, is it? It's been ages. Look how you've grown! The last time I saw you, you were barely a teenager."

"We have to go," I urged before they started

389

reminiscing. "I'll take care of this, Carlton."

"Good luck."

Calla took Khenan and me on a short journey into the wooded hillside, then through a slim crawl space under a rock protruding from the mountainside.

"It took me a while to move these rocks out of the way," she said, motioning to the rock pile inside the cave. "I think someone moved them before me and put them back."

"Did your people seal off every cave entrance big enough for people to fit through?"

"After the Vikings came, our ancestors sealed off the caves to keep them from venturing underground." She crawled inside on her belly and vanished into the darkness. "It's a tight squeeze, lads."

I gave Khenan a lantern and went in after her. After squeezing through a space just a hair short of rib-cracking closeness, we headed through a tunnel. Calla's shortcut got us to the energy pool twice as fast as the last time. When we got there, everything seemed quiet enough.

"Good, we beat them here," I whispered. "Calla, go warn everyone what's about to happen. Khenan and I—"

"Warn us about what?" came a voice out of the darkness.

Frankie came into view of our lamplight. He held my gun trained on me. He wasn't alone. With him was Dustan and Amos. They looked pissed.

"'Im be da whitest man I've ever seen," Khenan whispered.

I noticed several more faces appearing in the light.

"Kathy," Frankie said, "looks to me like you've

spent too much time living on the surface."

"It's Calla now," she returned. "And you should try living up there. I look much healthier than you."

Frankie snorted and set his sights on me. "I didn't expect to see you after your daring escape. Where's Killian?"

"On his way right now. He's guiding a bunch of outsiders to this very spot."

He looked baffled. "You're lying."

"No, I'm not. They're bringing explosives to blow this place. I strongly advise getting your people out of here."

"Put the gun down," Calla ordered. "We have work to do."

"But . . ." Frankie stammered, "they can't. This is our home. Why do you people want to hurt us?"

This was the very reason why I'd wanted to take things slow. There were so many questions to answer, so much preparation to do. We needed to hold a meeting, set the stage before performing this play. Rushing an evacuation of scared, confused people could cause many unpleasant turns. If they decided to stand and fight, things would get messy. I imagined many horrible things happening, like an accident involving explosives. Unless they went peacefully, nothing good was going to come from this.

"This place isn't home anymore," Calla said. "It's time for our people to walk in the light where we belong."

"We'll go blind," Frankie said, his tone wavering.

"No, I'm proof we won't. We haven't lived in the pitch blackness. In time, our eyes will become accustomed to the light. You have to trust me."

"We should fight!" Dustan yelled. "We have the

element of surprise."

"You don't have shit!" I bellowed, fed up with the whole thing. "If you don't go right now, you risk getting killed. You want your children to end up crushed to death under tons of stone because you're too fucking busy being dead to get them out of harm's way?"

What I said led to muttering. I thought I was getting through to them. Then Starr yelled, "He's right. You don't have shit on us."

I looked back as he and a group of others emerged from the mouth of a cave. With him was Killian and what looked like five of Killian's people.

"Those are our best lookouts," Frankie muttered in disbelief. No doubt, the sight of their finest held captive shocked him.

While Frankie was distracted, I snatched my gun from his hand. He almost lunged at me, but I held up a fist and gritted my teeth in warning, and he stayed put.

"Help me," Killian pleaded to his people. "Please, someone get me away from these beasts!"

"Let him go, Starr," I said.

Amazingly, he did. "Go on, shoo," he said, shoving Killian. "We don't need you now."

Killian stumbled away, his hand on his chest as if he was suffering a heart attack. Amos came to aid him.

"And the others," I said, stopping an arm's length from Starr.

"Don't try to stop us," he growled.

"This isn't the way to do this. You don't need to hurt anyone."

"They locked us up for sixty years," Clint hollered from behind Starr. "We did nothing to them and they put us in cages like animals!"

"Are you willing to make the next generation pay for what their ancestors did?" I challenged.

He didn't respond.

"Heath," Starr said calmly, "we just want to go home."

"So do I, but killing these people won't help." When I saw that he wasn't completely won over, I added, "Going on a killing spree will only delay detonation. Think about it."

He glared at me. Then, with a grin, he said, "You're a manipulative asshole. All right, you have till we set up the explosives. That should give you practically the whole night."

"Sounds great." I held out my hand to shake in a truce. After the shit he'd pulled, I really didn't want to, but I needed to keep the peace as long as possible. "Don't mess this up. We only have one shot at this."

We shook. Just as I was about to let go, he yanked me toward him and whispered, "And don't let any of those sons of bitches attack us or this place will become their burial ground."

I kept eye contact with him, my expression as serious as his. Eventually, he let go of my hand and said, "Good luck to you."

I wanted to break his nose but I stood in place as he ordered the volunteers to release the prisoners. After the five were cut free, we hurried up the tunnel to the village above.

* * *

At least the evacuation went well. Once Killian's group told everyone what was going to happen, no one tried to resist. There were a few mild protests but those

393

people eventually listened to reason. I did feel bad about their situation. They were given the choice of leaving everything behind or getting blown up. I tried to see the bright side. I saw Calla as a strong, healthy woman in comparison to her people, even the youngsters. She was right. They belonged in the light like the rest of us. Some wouldn't adapt right away, and others might never adjust, but, in time, the majority would ease into it and thrive. They'd learn new things and grow as a community.

I remembered what Ruby had said about how anything that values its life would do what was necessary to stay alive. Was it solely the fear that kept these people from venturing aboveground or had this island provoked them to evolve where they had to protect its life source? Not all plans work. These people weren't warriors. They lacked fighting experience, and worse, because of small-minded fear mongers like Killian, they lacked the knowledge of those they considered to be their enemies. No matter, eventually someone would have figured out the island's secrets if I hadn't.

Hours went by before everyone gathered what they needed and headed down the cave. My nerves were wracked as we entered the energy pool chamber. From the additional light, I spotted dozens of wide, rocky columns. They seemed to support the floor to the chamber above. People were busy stacking gunpowder barrels and bricks of TNT everywhere. With all the torches moving around, it amazed me that no one had blown themselves up already. What irked me were the hard stares we received as Calla, Khenan, and I led the line of these soon-to-be-homeless underground dwellers around the pond. It would only take a few cross words to ignite a conflict and bring us to an explosive confrontation. But no one said a word to each other and we slowly trailed out.

"Will you get them to the village where Ruby's body is?" I asked Calla as we journeyed through the narrow passageways.

"You think it's best to keep them away from North Village?"

"For the moment, yeah. There's that cargo ship pretty close to shore. I think you should gather everyone onto it. Being on land might not be the safest place to be with the amount of explosives they're loading down there."

"Good idea. Where are you going?"

"Back to North Village." Then I added a lie. "To collect my things."

We resurfaced in the wooded area between North Village and the village of the Obsoletes. Khenan and I parted from the pack and headed home.

"Wah if it doesn't work, mon?"

"I'm trying not to think of that. When we get back, you should pack up everything you want to keep and tell everyone to get to the docks."

"I'd be very upset if it doesn't work."

"You and me both."

The sky began to brighten by the time we reached home. I realized how late in the night it was, or early in the morning, I should say.

Marissa and Tammy asked us what was going on. I told them to tell everyone to pack their things and get down to the docks, then I headed up the stairs alone, only I didn't stop at my hut.

When I reached the boarded-up door, I took a moment to ask myself if this was what I really wanted.

Was I prepared to take the next step? The only way to know was to go in.

The boards nailed over the window had just enough space between them for me to slip my hand through and yank them off. I threw them off to the side and climbed inside. My lantern lit up the dark house. Its warm glow illuminated my way to Eleanor's body.

Nothing had changed since the day I'd said farewell to her. She remained on the floor, untouched by decay, resting in a pool of dark blood, her hand clutching the gun. I placed the lantern near her head and knelt beside her.

"Are you gonna do what I think you're gonna do?" Gavin asked.

"What if . . ." I said, my lips dry when I spoke. "What if there's a landslide and it crushes the house? What do you think would happen to her soul, then?"

"Couldn't say. Nothing might happen. Just, whatever you do, consider her more than yourself."

"I am."

"Then here we are."

Here we were. I'd made a dumb promise to let her be. What right did I have to force her to be around me forever? If the plan worked and we could return to the outside world, would the rules of the dead still apply? Or would souls move on to some other place? This could be the only time I'd have to tell her goodbye face to face. Who wouldn't jump at the chance to speak to a departed loved one, one last time?

Without putting too much thought into it, I lifted her and held her against me. The sunlight crept through the window, sweeping a bright golden glow throughout the entire house.

"Heath, darling," she said, "what took you so

long?"

Chapter Thirty-seven

She stood in the sunlight. The morning glow had turned most of her hair white; the rest was clumped in red. Blood dripped from her jaw line, onto her shoulder, sliding down her arm and chest. Having her stand there made me almost forget I was holding her dead body.

"How do you feel?" I asked.

"Fine, I suppose. I've been cooped up in this house for so long."

"Did you see us after you shot yourself?"

"I saw everyone. You looked so sad."

"Is Darwin with you?"

"No," she answered with a pleasant smile. "He had no choice but to leave when there was no host to attach himself to."

That was the best news I'd heard in a while.

"Now we can be together, darling."

"For a little while, at least. We're blowing up the island today."

"Really? How exciting!"

She looked at me a moment, then shifted her eyes to her corpse. "You should put that down. It's useless now."

"I thought I'd bury your body properly."

"If the island is going to be destroyed, why bother? I'm not attached to the thing any longer. Leave it here."

She approached me as gray light cast a gloom over the golden morning. I looked up at her from the

398

floor as if she was my queen and I was her humble servant. She reached for my face. I couldn't feel her touch, even though her hand was on my cheek.

"It's all right, darling, leave it behind."

I placed her body on the bed, folded her hands over her chest, and covered her with a blanket.

"Let's go outside," she said. "I don't want to miss the excitement."

I crawled through the window. Everyone was headed for the docks.

"Oh, they finished it," she observed.

"Yep."

"I wasn't able to see its completion after they boarded up my windows. I couldn't even leave the house."

"Really?" That depressed me. "I wished I'd known. I would've come for you sooner."

"I wish you had. But the docks look perfect."

"Except now it looks like they're going to be used as a safety plank instead of a floating suburb."

"Everything is done for a reason," she remarked.

We walked side by side down the stairs. I wished I could hold her hand.

"It's good to see you again," I told her. "I've missed you."

"I've missed you too. And whatever happens from this point on, I'm glad to have had this time with you."

Her words relieved me. I worried she'd be upset at what I'd done but her eyes told me she was content. I was thrilled to have her by my side again.

Those who'd gone underground to set up the explosives were returning to the docks. I looked forward to finding a secluded place with Eleanor so we could watch the island fall apart.

"Everything's set," Starr said.

I turned around and found him standing at least a dozen steps above me. "Good for you," I said flatly.

"Want to come with me for a final sweep of the place before doing the honors?"

"You totally screwed me," I returned harshly. "Do it yourself."

"We found the critical answers together. It seems only right to end it together."

"What, we're best buds again, now that you got your way?"

"What's past is past," he said. "What matters is here and now."

He turned and went back up the stairs. The rage I felt for him made my stomach tighten. Granted, the chance to blow up an island didn't come along every day, but I'd rather hang out with a mass murderer than go with Starr.

"Let's go," Eleanor's lovely voice chimed in.

My head fell sideways onto my shoulder, my eyes rolling over to her. "I'd much rather spend time with you."

"It'll be exciting," she encouraged.

In truth, I'd had enough excitement to fill the life of a stunt double. But when those big blue eyes of hers latched onto mine, I couldn't say no. We followed Starr.

Once again, I journeyed underground. The three of us came to a cave entrance with dozens of boulders piled around its mouth. Eleanor hummed sweetly beside me until her voice and image faded.

"I just want to tell you I'm sorry for the shit that went down," Starr said as I followed him through a tunnel thin enough to force us to walk slightly sideways.

"Save it," I returned sharply. "I thought you were cool, but you're really just a dick, running high on testosterone."

"True," he concurred. "This place freaked me out in the worst way. I don't understand how any of this can be real. It's a lot to take in."

"It was a lot for me to take in but I didn't flip the fuck out."

"In my defense, you've been here longer than me. You had time to adsorb it. I got shit thrown at me like an angry monkey."

"The hell with you. You have no idea what I've been through. You were willing to kill people to get to this point."

He said nothing to that.

"Whatever," I said. "By the way, I quit."

We came to the energy pool chamber where others stood by the edge of the water.

"Lafitte?" I said in surprise.

Beside him was his crewman, Judson, also an underground dweller. That's why he'd spotted me in the dark when I'd first found *The Pride*. He had great night vision. I wondered if Lafitte had known or just found out.

Lafitte held a glowing lantern in one hand, a lit pipe in the other. "*Bonjour, Monsieur* Sharp." He turned to Judson. "*Merci* for guiding me, *mon ami*. You should go and reunite with your kind."

"Aye, aye, Captain," Judson humbly said before darting off into a nearby tunnel.

"They're at the village on the other side of the island," I shouted in case he didn't already know. He didn't answer back.

"What a wonderful day to blow up an island, *non?*" Lafitte stated.

"If you don't put out that pipe, we'll be included in the show," I said as Starr and I approached. "What are you doing down here?"

"Shubrick came to my ship ranting about how people came to his kingdom and stole his gunpowder. Naturally, I was curious, so we wandered over to see what the fuss was all about."

My eyes snagged on the sword under his leather belt. "Why do you have that?"

Lafitte glanced down at his weapon, then raised his eyes to me. "A smart man always arms himself when traveling into potential danger. Guns are too risky since killing isn't wise. There is more control with a sword."

"You've never been down here before?" Starr asked.

Lafitte, being the gentleman he was, answered as politely as he could. "If I had been, something like this would have been done ages ago."

Starr grunted. "Let's get to it."

The three of us went up to the underground village. Seeing it vacant with TNT bricks piled on the stage and the smell of gunpowder in the air shot a dose of eeriness into my spine. I became numb. We were like invaders ready to destroy what we'd conquered in order to mark our victory.

"You set explosives up here too?" I asked Starr.

"You were right about having one shot at this. If we put enough TNT here to bring the floor down, the ceiling above us might cave in also."

Something clicked beside me. Lafitte lit a pipe

with a lighter. I couldn't speak for him, but I was painfully aware of what sat very close to us. The only thing I could say was, "Really?"

"When the columns under us blow, the village floor should cave in," Starr finished explaining.

"How do you plan to set all these off at once?" Lafitte asked before taking a drag.

"There are gunpowder trails running through two tunnels that lead outside. One down there, one up here. In order for the explosives to go off simultaneously—which is the only way this is going to work—we need to time the ignitions just right. Heath, you'll light the trail below. You'll have an easier time getting to safety rather than running your ass down the mountainside before it comes down. I'll light the one up here."

That was Starr, a pure asshole one minute; the next, he was ready to throw himself on a live grenade to save his fellow man.

"How are we going to communicate?" I asked. "Use two cans and a long string?"

"Like I said, idiot," he retorted, "we need to time it right. Since we don't have walkie-talkies or working watches, we're going to have to use our math skills."

"I have a pocket watch," Laffite said, slipping one out from his pocket. "It is already wound."

I stared at the silver watch dangling from its sterling chain. Its low ticking made me realize that even in a land of immortals, time ticked on.

As Laffite handed it to me, Starr grabbed it. "Thanks. It's gonna be more dangerous on my end." To me, he said, "Can you count to a hundred and eighty?"

"I'm so going to break your face."

"From the tunnel where the gunpowder trail

starts, it'll take you exactly twelve minutes to reach the outside," Starr went on. "Walk a steady pace. Don't stop until you get to the end. When you get there, count to a hundred and eighty. That's three minutes."

"I know," I grumbled. "Okay, let me guess. The three minutes will give you time to get to your place."

"Right. It'll be enough for me to crawl through the tunnel and get to the end of the trail outside. If you ignite your end in fifteen minutes and I light mine in ten, the explosions will go off together."

"Sounds like a plan," I said.

Starr led us back down to the pool and showed us which tunnel the trail was laid out.

"All right, give me twenty seconds to run back to the village," he said. "Good luck."

It seemed like one of those moments where I should say something, like *See you soon, buddy*, with the subliminal message of, *I forgive you* woven into it. But I didn't think he was looking for forgiveness. Just in case one of us got killed, I shook his hand and said, "You too."

He took off toward the village while I kept count in my head. When I reached twenty, both Laffite and I walked through the tunnel.

"If this works," I said, "what will you do?"

"I must confess, *mon ami*, I never thought about it. After three hundred years, the hope to sail the sea again has dimmed."

What he said got me thinking about everyone else whose times had long since passed. How would they adjust to the changed world around them? How would the rest of the world accept them? With so many people trapped in the Bermuda Triangle, someone was bound to spill the beans. John T. Shubrick had proclaimed that if he ever got out, he'd complete his mission and deliver the Dey of Algiers Treaty to South Carolina. When that happened, I'd be miles away. With all the walking, talking antiques to marvel at, I'd be the least interesting.

We kept up our steady pace and emerged from the four-foot hole where the gunpowder trail started. I began counting down in my head.

"Lafitte!" someone yelled.

We both turned to a one-armed man training a gun on Lafitte.

"Saxon," Lafitte said calmly, despite the gun. "What an unpleasant surprise this is. Here to check on your arm? I assure you, it's doing just fine. I think it prefers my company over yours, though."

"They say a plan to destroy this wretched place is in effect," Saxon said. "If that's true, I see no reason *not* to kill you."

Saxon fired three shots into Lafitte.

"No!" I cried, catching Lafitte as he fell back.

Saxon tried firing another shot, to no avail. When he realized his gun was empty, he tossed it away.

"Now it's finished," he said in triumph.

"You're an idiot," Lafitte weakly retorted, rising from my arms. "When you plan to take me down, make certain your pistol is fully loaded."

The first few seconds of Lafitte's reincarnation stunned both me and Saxon.

"You devil!" Saxon exclaimed. "Is this a trick?"

"Not in the least, you thick-headed swine. It is but a bulletproof vest." Lafitte slid his hand over his chest where the bullet holes were. "I always wear one when on land, just in case our paths cross." He pulled his sword. "I think I'll collect that other arm now."

405

Saxon darted down the mountainside with Lafitte wielding his sword after him. I laughed at the sight, until I remembered what I needed from Lafitte.

"Wait! Your lighter!"

I took up the chase after them. Doing so, I lost count and had no idea how much time was left. Without the lighter, it wouldn't matter. Luckily, the pursuit was short lived when Saxon tripped and tumbled down the mountain.

"Laffite," I called, "give me your lighter!"

"Oh," he said, tossing it to me. "Here you are."

As Laffite chased after his quarry, I darted back up the hill. When I stopped at the end of the gunpowder trail, I tried to calculate how much time was left. If I ignited my trail prematurely, we could lose the TNT stacked in the village when the ground collapsed. If I was too late, the floor above would collapse and wipe out the bricks strapped to the columns. Either way, the job would only get half done.

I flicked the lighter and sparked a flame. "I guess it's now or never," I muttered to myself.

"No, you have thirty-two seconds left," Eleanor said, standing by a nearby tree.

I jumped. "You scared the hell out of me."

"Thirty seconds."

She must have overheard Starr and kept count on her own. I couldn't help but smile. She stood so beautifully by the tree, I didn't even care about the blood dripping off her head.

"Get   ready,"   she   warned. "Six…five…four…three…two…one."

I put the lighter to the line and the flame kissed it. Sparks flew as the flame traveled into the tunnel and vanished.

"Better get to the docks," Eleanor urged. "We have only two minutes."

I ran until the joints in my knees ached. I hoped Starr was doing the same. When I reached the docks, everyone was packed together on it. Some had found shelter on nearby ships and boats. I searched for Starr but didn't see him.

Since every inch of the docks was taken up by people and their bags, I dragged one of the beached fishing boats into the water.

"This is exciting," Eleanor said, sitting beside me. "I have missed so much since I've been dead."

I looked at her but her attention was drawn to the island. "I can't believe you're here," I said quietly.

She turned to me. Her lips rose pleasantly. I didn't think anything could tear my eyes away from her but the explosion did the trick. A loud boom rumbled within the island. Rocks, earth, and soot shot from holes, and shock waves reverberated like an earthquake, stealing the balance from beneath dozens of people on the dock. Waves rocked my boat.

Honestly, I hadn't expected the magnitude of the blast to be so thunderous. Sections of the mountain broke apart and tumbled inward. Just as I had worried, a massive landslide happened, trees and boulders tumbling down, crashing into huts and smashing them to pieces. The grand finale came when the top of the island collapsed and fell in on itself, sucking in trees as it went. The movement stirred up a heavy fog, swirling it around in a funnel. A cloud of soot wafted into the sky like volcanic ash. It sounded like hundreds of cars dropping from the Burj Dubai building. I covered my ears.

A second landslide finished the demolition job.

Chunks of the mountain rolled right over the village and onto the beach. North Village was taken out by what seemed like endless clumps of boulders and trees, erasing it from existence. This had better work or everyone was going to be homeless.

I'd predicted the villages would get pulverized but not the entire beach getting buried. Nor had I imagined the panic that broke out in the crowd. When the rocks crushed the village pier, it rumbled the docks, provoking people to push against each other like they were in a mosh pit. To save myself from being crushed, I pushed against a column holding up the dock and shoved the boat away. Just as I did, a woman dropped into the water where I'd been. I helped hoist her into the boat as other people worked to get themselves to safety.

Eventually, the rocks stopped toppling and the ground grew still. The sky was dulled by the dust cloud.

Hours after the blast, several of us made the bumpy climb to where the top of the island had caved in. It was a long hike. I was hungry and tired, but I wanted to see. The air was completely different from the last time I'd ascended the mountain. Instead of a thick, bug-infested forest to battle through, fallen trees, rocks, and loose gravel had become the new obstacles.

At the top, I saw where the island had fallen in on itself, a low pit of rocks closing it in. There was no way the energy pool below us hadn't been buried. If any air got in, it wouldn't be enough to keep the island alive.

"You did wonderfully," Eleanor said, standing beside me on a stack of boulders.

"Did it work?"

"Too early to tell."

I looked around at the mess that used to be North Village. My blood boiled when I realized what we'd lost. Thanks to Starr, we had no contingency plan.

"If this doesn't work, we're going to be in big trouble," I said. "Most of the food and shelter was on the beach. Starr is such an asshole for not listening to me."

"What a mess," Laffite said.

I raised my chin as he approached. "You made it. What about Saxon?"

"He fell. Let's leave it at that, shall we? Have you found your friend?"

"No," I said somberly.

Laffite patted me on the shoulder. "It's early yet. I'm going back to my ship. If you need food and a place to sleep, you're welcome to stop in."

"Thanks."

* * *

As the day wore on and the impact of what had happened sank in, everyone began to ask questions. Many were confused about why the island had been blown up.

I finally found Carlton and told him it'd be a good idea to hold a meeting and explain the situation in full detail. I hoped he'd also tell them to make a contingency plan in case nothing we'd done had had any effect.

I left that up to him. I was beat. The thought of organizing a gathering to face the confused islanders gave me a headache. I didn't have the strength. Washing my hands of it, I left to take Laffite up on his offer.

Eleanor kept me company. We chatted, and after a while, I forgot she was dead. I clued her in on what had happened since her death. I told her about Gavin and going into the forest. Then I explained how Travis had died. I told her about how one of the Neanderthals had taken me to the top of the island, where I'd met Calla and an actual alien named Ruby. Eleanor wagged a scolding finger at me when I told her how I'd tried crossing the boundaries.

"I wish I could've been there with you. Being dead all alone is dreadfully boring."

"Everyone told me not to disturb your body."

"I can't blame them for that."

Not every part of the mountainside had been buried under rock. A line of trees here and there had survived. Boulders and many other smaller rocks had settled on the beach.

"Sharp!" Starr called from a short distance off. He was climbing an eight-foot-wide trail down the mountain, where boulders had rolled over trees and whatever lay in its path.

Seeing him, I let out a long breath of relief.

"I just came from the top. Looks like we did it."

"Yeah," I said flatly, remembering in my relief that I was royally pissed at him.

He reached the beach and approached me. "How long should we wait before making a break for it?"

"Don't know. I've never assassinated an island before."

"Where are you going?" he asked.

"I need time to myself."

"Mind if I tag along? I think I could use some downtime too."

"Actually, I do."

His face scrunched up. "Damn, are you still ticked?"

"Look, you went and did things your way instead of waiting a few days to get everything straight like I wanted. I think it's only appropriate that you go back and sort it out. Right now, Carlton is calling for a meeting. You ought to help clean up the mess you made. We're done here."

I left him there on the beach.

I stayed the night on *The Pride* with Laffite. I ate a good meal and slept soundly. I woke in the afternoon, refreshed and ready to deal with the aftermath of the explosion. During a late breakfast, I told Laffite I was going to the other side of the island to check on Calla and her people. When I returned, I'd help him figure out what kind of occupation he might be interested in if the island was, in fact, dead.

I washed up the best I could and set out down the beach. People were cheerful in South Village. Worley ran up to me and told me the morning sunlight had lasted five minutes longer than usual. It was uplifting news but I didn't take it as proof that the island was dead.

"Darling, look," Eleanor said an hour after we left South Village.

Following her finger, I spotted a patch of brightly colored flowers at the forest's edge.

"They're wilting," she said.

I knelt to examine them. Each flower was shriveling, their petals dry like autumn leaves.

"These flowers are harder to kill than the living dead," I said, remembering when Eleanor had shown me their durability after she'd stomped on them.

411

We continued on. The Shark Hunters flew overhead. They soared in a scattered formation, as if disorientated. Halfway through our journey, we came to the cruise ship *Ramón*. She lay capsized in the distance. Seeing her massive body gave me hope that even if the island wasn't completely dead and was still able to keep us within its boundaries, it might be too weak to keep itself camouflaged from the rest of the world. Eventually, someone from the outside might spot the wreckage.

The cool gray sky turned to a warm steely gray by the time I reached the village of the Obsoletes. Surprisingly, it had been spared by the landslide. That's where I found Calla standing on the walkway in front of a house. As I approached, two men emerged, carrying out Chancier's corpse.

"What are you doing?" I asked.

"Removing this eyesore, including the one hanging in the tree," she said. "We had to wait until dusk to bring everyone out to dispose of this unfortunate sod before making this village our new home."

"Where are they taking him? And aren't you afraid of —"

"That doesn't apply to natural born beings of the fragment, remember? We're burying the body in the woods with the others." She dropped her head. "Yesterday I burned Ruby's body on the beach."

"What's your next move?"

She raised her chin to eye me thoughtfully. The brightness in her face returned. "We're going to move forward. Everyone who's lived on the surface is going to help the rest of us adjust. It's going to be thrilling."

On the beach, a group of children ran around,

laughing and playing. Among them was the little Viking girl, Sassy.

"She came to us," Calla said. "She hasn't left since. I think she likes it here."

"What about Abby and her tribe? Have you seen them around?"

"They made camp on the beach not too far from here. I saw them while we were taking Ruby's body away."

"Do you think it worked? Is the island dead?"

"Only time will tell, I suppose."

Night came and Calla got everyone inside before the stingrays went on the prowl. I stood on the walkway alone. Calla was teaching the children the song *Knick Knack, Paddy Whack, Give a Dog a Bone* in the house behind me.

"If the island is really dead," I said to Eleanor, "what will happen to you?"

"I won't leave you, darling. You might not see me anymore but I won't go anywhere."

Her hand rested on the railing. I placed mine over hers but it went straight through.

"What about me?" Gavin chimed in. "Aren't you concerned about what might happen to me?"

"Where the hell have you been?"

"Thought since you brought your lady friend back, I'd make myself scarce to give you two some privacy."

If my body wouldn't go right through him, I would've hugged him.

"However long we have left," Eleanor said, drawing my attention back to her, "I'm thankful for it."

"Me too."

It was hard to accept that I'd not only been part of

a mystery, but I'd helped tear it down. Maybe with the island dead, no one else would suffer for its needs. No more tormented loved ones not knowing what had happened to them.

"Darling, look up. God, it's been so long since I've seen them."

I lifted my chin to the sky. There, embedded in a crisp indigo canopy were thousands of gorgeous wonders—stars.

Michelle E. Lowe is the author of *The Warning*, *Atlantic Pyramid*, *Cherished Thief*, the action adventure/fantasy steampunk novel, *Legacy*. Children's books, *Poe's Haunted House Tour*, and the three part adventure children's series, *The Hex Hunt*. She's a mother, wife, and painter. Her works in progress are the continuations for *Legacy*. Currently, she lives in Lake Forest, California.

Website: www.michellelowe.net
Facebook: Facebook.com/michelleloweauthor
Twitter: @MichelleLowe_7

CALL TO ACTION!!!!

If you've enjoyed this author's work and would like to know more as well have an inclusive updates of Lowe's other projects, visit www.michellelowe.net and join her mailing list!

Read on through the first chapters of Michelle Lowe's next novel, *Legacy,* now available!

Legacy

"The world as we know it is standing on the pivotal edge of change! An evolution is taking shape. This is the climb, my friends! The climb up towards the peak of the Industrial Revolution! I say unto thee, we must contribute to thrive. Contribute to the Age of the Machine!"

—Professor Raphael Brooke

The Contract

Sinai Peninsula, Spring, 1636

Thooranu had arrived in the Blue Desert late that evening, but already he'd slain many jackals. After his last kill, he built two fire pits in the sand and gutted the beast. He always ate his final kill, or at least the one that proved hardest to bring down. This particular jackal had been both.

He'd taken the beast with bare hands, wrestling the animal until he'd broken its neck. The jackal had gotten in a few good bites, rending deep gashes into his back and crushing sharp teeth through his arm. But the jackal had sensed its attacker was otherworldly and had known it would eventually fail. Nonetheless, that hadn't prevented it from putting up a good fight.

After tossing the lungs, liver, brain, eyes, tongue, balls and heart into a blackened iron cauldron to boil, Thooranu skinned and beheaded the animal, then put the carcass on a skewer to rotate over a second fire.

With most of the work done, he sat and wiped his hands clean. His wounds had already healed. From a rough hessian sack, he brought out a bottle of wine, pulling the cork free with his teeth. He breathed in deeply, the wine's earthy aroma giving clues to its origins. It was old, bottled before his birth. Italian. He poured some into a glass and sipped. It tasted like the beginning of everything.

He leaned back, eying the heavens and the myriad stars, a smile flickering over his lips. Then it vanished. Someone was nearby.

"Mind if I join you?" a male voice asked.

The stranger's abrupt approach startled him, which was difficult to do. It must be the human part of him, he thought. But the stranger could not be human. No mortal could survive this far into the desert without a camel. He wasn't even dressed for the harsh conditions.

The man appeared to be teetering between wealth and poverty. His slashed doublet was a shiny red, embroidered with black skeletons, but his cape was ragged along the hem. The boots were the most sensible thing he was wearing, although they were still too heavy for the day's heat, and a ridiculous hat sat upon his head.

Thooranu breathed deeply, trying to sniff the stranger out. There were many scents. Was he a demon too? A punk? Or perhaps a ghost? Whatever he was, Thooranu sensed no threat.

"Please," he said, gesturing for the stranger to join him.

The flamboyantly dressed man took a seat by one of the fires and poked at it with a shiny black cane. He removed his rabbit fur hat, sporting lively ostrich feathers, and set it down beside him. He was handsome, if a little on the feminine side, with dark hair, a carefully trimmed mustache and beard, along with a charming smile and perfectly shaped eyes that captured the flickering firelight like jewels.

"You've built a couple of nice fires here," the stranger complimented, stroking his beard. He sniffed the cauldron. "Is there a heart in there? I do rather enjoy a good, tasty heart."

"Would you care for some?" Thooranu asked.

"I would, indeed, and perhaps a glass of wine? If you don't mind, that is."

Thooranu did not, for he could obtain wine anywhere with little effort. He poured his guest a glass that he manifested with a gesture of his hand from the sand and fire.

"Ah," the stranger said, accepting the drink. "Thank you kindly. You are a good host."

The stranger didn't speak with any accent, as though he belonged to no particular region. Then again, neither did Thooranu.

"I'm Jack Pack," the man said, extending his hand.

"Thooranu."

They shook hands then Jack Pack settled back, taking another sip of wine.

"I knew a Thooranu once," Jack Pack admitted. "He was an incubus."

"My father."

"I see." Jack Pack looked him up and down. "It appears that you took after your mother. Human?"

Thooranu smiled. "I suppose I did. And yes."

"That's good for you; for as I said, I've met your father, and I wouldn't curse my worst enemy to inherit his looks."

Thooranu laughed, for he couldn't agree more. "And what of you?"

"Oh, I'm no one special, really. Just a wanderer. A lost soul, if you will. I journey around the universe, seeing what's out there, what trouble I can get myself into, that sort of thing."

"Sounds a bit like me," Thooranu said, looking up again at the star-glittered sky. "Have you ever visited the outer planes?"

The wanderer shrugged. "Sure, a few times. The worlds beyond are interesting enough, but not like this one. Even the best miss the little things that complete this world. I like it here more than most places."

Thooranu nodded. "I concur."

They sat in silence like old friends. Steam curled up from the cauldron. Thooranu glanced at the stranger. Jack Pack had made an impression on him. He hoped the man wouldn't take his leave too soon. It had been a while since he'd had any company.

Thooranu noticed a coil of braided hair pinned by a jeweled brooch onto Jack Pack's doublet. "Whose hair is that?"

Jack Pack raised the braid and looked at it, a wistful smile forming. "It was a gift. It's Guinevere's hair. Fascinating creature."

"Lancelot's Guinevere?"

"The very same. Those two were a good example of how fun mortals are to toy with."

"Oh?"

"Indeed." A shrug. "It passes the time."

"How so?"

"Many years ago, a Trickster, a Dökkálfar and an Adlet beast made a bet on who could find a certain relic that had been hidden; the Holy Grail."

Thooranu's eyes narrowed. "The Grail, huh?"

"Yes, yes, I know; we've all heard stories about the fruitless quests to find it. Not many know how the whole thing got started, though. It's a story wrapped within a story."

"All right."

"Contrary to what many believe, the Grail started out as nothing more than a fallen star. A servant of the Fisher King found it and brought the stone to a

421

craftsman, who carved it into a dish. The humble servant then brought the dish to the Fisher King. The king declared the dish to be a grail and kept it for many years until he could no longer carry on with his duties as king. As his kingdom fell into ruin, the Grail passed on to Joseph of Arimathea, who had it made into a cup; and shortly thereafter, it became known as the *Holy* Grail after Christ's crucifixion. Later, the elderly and dying Joseph passed it on to Elaine of Corbenic, and she became the Grail's keeper."

Jack Pack stared into the fire, a wistful look on his face. "Elaine of Corbenic fell in love with poor ole Lancelot. To get him to sleep with her, she twice tricked him into thinking she was Guinevere. She even gave birth to his child, one Galahad by name. When Guinevere discovered this, she cursed Lancelot and he went mad with grief."

"I know the story," Thooranu said. "Later, Elaine finds Lancelot in shambles in her garden. To cure him of his insanity, she lets him drink from the Grail."

"Indeed. Rumors of that spread. In order for Elaine and Lancelot to have a life together without being badgered by those wanting the Grail, Elaine handed it over to a holy court, who hid it away."

"And that's when the Trickster, the elf, and the beast bet on who could find it first?"

"They made the bet long before any of this happened. Each of them was aware of the relic, and when the three attended the funeral of the Fisher King, it became a conversation piece. They knew the Grail would eventually become hidden or lost, as most relics do, and decided that when it did, they would race to find it. The challenge was, however, that they had to only use mortals in their search."

422

"Interesting," Thooranu admitted. "I am intrigued. What happened?"

"When he became a young man, Galahad went to King Arthur, offering to serve him. The king put him to the test."

"The old sword in the stone, eh?"

"Indeed, another legend. Now, here is the reason the stories cross paths. A wizard came to Arthur years before and showed him the stone, which was nothing more than a simple boulder by a river. The wizard then presented a sword made from steel that had come from another world. The hilt was wrapped in the hide of a creature that no longer existed, and set inside the pommel was a jewel that once resided far within the earth's heart. The wizard claimed the sword had come from God." Jack Pack took a deep draught of his wine, sighing in appreciation of the vintage.

The wizard sheathed the sword in the stone and said that only the worthiest knight would be able to pull it free, and that knight would serve Arthur well. Arthur, believing that the sword was indeed a holy relic, held an annual ceremony to find that worthy. Once a year, knights would come to pull the sword free. Legend of the sword spread throughout the lands. No one, however, could get the sword out, and after a while, Arthur stopped holding the ceremony."

"Then one day, Sir Galahad showed up," Thooranu surmised.

"Yes, but he wasn't a knight then, not until he pulled the sword free."

"What made him worthy?"

"Ah-ah, wait," Jack Pack said, wagging his finger. "The king proclaimed that Galahad would become one of the Knights of the Round Table. Shortly afterwards,

Arthur had a vision about the Grail and ordered a search for it. The king sent three knights: Galahad of course, Sir Bors, and Sir Perceval. The Trickster, the elf, and the Adlet beast had to choose which of the knights would find the Grail. Whoever's knight found the relic would win the wager. The elf chose Sir Perceval; the Adlet beast chose Sir Bors, and the Trickster chose Galahad."

"How did they determine who got which knight?" Thooranu inquired.

"They went by rank. The Trickster was a god, you see, and being the most powerful, he chose first. The Dökkálfar went next and then the Adlet beast."

Thooranu nodded. It made sense.

Jack Pack continued. "The knights went on with their quest and spent years searching. Then one day, the Trickster became distressed when Sir Bors saved Galahad's life. To show his gratitude, Galahad traded the sword he'd pulled from the stone with Bors."

Thooranu leaned over to pour more wine into his guest's glass. "So what? After the sword had proven Galahad to Arthur, what other purpose did the thing serve?"

"Don't be impatient," Jack Pack said, holding out his glass until it was full. "The Trickster needed the sword returned to Galahad and he found an opportunity for that to happen. After some time apart, the knights reunited when they came across Perceval's sister. She brought them to a ship bound for the Wasteland. When they landed, they continued on their journey together. On the way, the Trickster came to them, masquerading as a holy man and said that in order for them to cross the Wasteland, they first needed the blessing of the sick lady. They went to the sick lady's castle, where the custom was for one of her choosing to drink her blood from a silver dish." Jack Pack paused for a moment, savoring more of the fragrant wine.

"What the knights did not know was that anyone who drank the blood would die. The woman chose Bors. Perceval's sister, who was aware of this custom, offered to drink the blood in his stead. The sick lady allowed it, and when the sister drank, the lady revealed that Perceval's sister would die and that Bors now owed her for her sacrifice. Bors took it upon himself to uphold the dying sister's request to be brought back to the city of Sarras. The sick lady then said that because he had allowed this to happen—even though he'd been unaware of the fatal consequences—he no longer was deemed worthy to hold onto the sword from the stone. Guilt drove him to give the sword back to Galahad."

"You're saying that this Trickster had a hand in her death?" Thooranu asked, amazed. "How could he do that? Did he make a bargain with the Fates?"

"He didn't. Only if the Fates are absent from their realm can the laws of death and life be changed. However, the Trickster was one of the gifted few who had the ability to bend rules."

"I see. If that is so, then why kill Perceval's sister? Why not let Bors drink the blood?"

"It would have suited the Trickster just fine except that Bors might have been buried with the sword that had been given to him. It was customary for knights to be buried with their swords and shields. The Trickster had to make certain Galahad got his sword back."

"What if the sick lady hadn't chosen Bors?"

"She didn't *choose* at all. The Trickster had made a deal with her."

"And the sister couldn't just warn Bors?"

"They had been forbidden to leave until a sacrifice was made—a payment, if you will. Until then, they were bound within the castle walls forever."

Thooranu nodded cautiously and gestured for Jack to continue.

"The sword was returned to its rightful owner and Bors left to take Perceval's sister's body back to her homeland," Jack Pack went on, "leaving only Galahad and Perceval to continue the search for the Grail. After years of adventures, the pair finally came to the court of King Pelles and his son, Eliazar. These two holy men were the Grail's keepers. They told the knights that only a blessed man, a man of pure heart, could see the Holy Grail. Galahad then presented the sword he had pulled from the stone."

"Wait, I thought it was the Sword of David, the one given to him on the ship of faith."

"That's one version of the story, but it's not true. It was really the sword that proved his salt to King Arthur. The Trickster then won the contest the moment Galahad showed the king and his son the sword."

"What?" Thooranu said. "How is that?"

"It was rather simple, actually," Jack Pack said with a mischievous smirk. "It was the Trickster who had come to King Arthur with the sword. The wizard presented the sword that he, himself, had forged. In telling the lie that it had come from God, it helped to get the tale out into the world, where it was eventually brought to the attention of the holy court."

"Why go through the trouble with the sword?"

"Well, because of the love affair between Lancelot and Guinevere, Arthur was reluctant to allow the son of the man who stole his woman's heart to join his

426

circle of knights. The sword convinced the King that Galahad was the knight he needed."

"Why did the Trickster want Galahad to be chosen to look for the Grail? Wouldn't any knight do?"

"No. Even with the sword, no mere human could be allowed to even see the Grail, which had become so much more than just a fallen star. The sword was designed to release itself from the stone only by someone with a special bloodline, which Galahad had."

"Did this Trickster have a hand in Galahad's birth?" Thooranu asked, sensing a deeper history to this god's involvement.

"Very good guess, young man," the wanderer praised. "He most certainly did. To win the bet, the Trickster needed a mortal with an edge over the other two knights. He decided to use the love that Elaine had for Lancelot as a means to bring forth said mortal. He'd portrayed himself as a servant girl and told Elaine that if she wanted Lancelot to lay with her, she needed to give him wine and to wear a certain ring. The wine and ring were utterly useless, merely a ruse that gave her the confidence to go forth with the plan. It was the Trickster who'd led Lancelot to believe that it was Guinevere he was laying with. When their son was born, the Trickster made the sword and presented it to King Arthur."

"Then the Trickster was pulling the strings the entire time? Why?"

"To win the bet, my boy."

Thooranu snorted. "Not much of a challenge if he was going to cheat."

"Oh, but it was. The bet wasn't just about winning; it was a way for the Trickster to test his scheming

427

skills, and what better way to do that than with a fixed wager?"

"Huh. So Galahad saw the Grail for himself. What happened then?"

"Not much; he died."

"And who gave Arthur the vision?"

Jack Pack smiled. "The Trickster, of course."

"And the Dökkálfar and the Adlet beast never suspected?"

"*That* was the real challenge, being able to do all of that trickery without getting caught."

"You mean all that backstabbing, it seems."

The wanderer shrugged. "No one said that Tricksters were honest."

Thooranu raised his glass, and gave a wry smile. "Well played."

They both drank.

"Who gave you Guinevere's hair?" Thooranu asked.

"The Trickster. It was the only thing he requested of her when she asked him to convince Elaine to kill herself, which wasn't hard seeing how she was utterly heartbroken. Lancelot never stopped loving Guinevere, you know."

"So you met the Trickster?"

"I did, indeed." Jack Pack took a long drink of wine and turned to Thooranu. "Now, let's have some of that heart."

They spoke for hours on many topics: the places they'd seen, women they'd seduced, and mischievous deeds committed. Several bottles of wine and one jackal later, they were conversing on matters that Thooranu had never discussed with anyone. As the sun began to rise over the sandy hills, Jack Pack told him that he was going to explore the moons of Jupiter and invited him along.

For the next few years, the two were inseparable. They traveled together, sharing adventures that Thooranu hoped would never end. He felt he'd found a true friend in Jack Pack.

One hot summer's day in Greece, they were enjoying coffee at a café when Jack Pack offered a proposal. "Have you ever thought about running a business?"

"Pardon?" Thooranu said, setting his cup on its saucer. "A business?"

"I've been flirting with the idea for quite some time now. I was once an architect, you know."

"An architect?" he chuckled. "Why?"

"Sometimes I like to grow roots. It's a change of pace. I like to keep myself busy, and what better way than running a business, eh?"

Thooranu's curiosity was piqued. He had never tried such an endeavor. "What sort of business?"

"I was thinking of a tavern and brothel."

"Where?"

"Here, in Athens. I've already picked out a place."

Thooranu leaned back in his chair. "A brothel, eh?" he said, rubbing his chin.

"We'll only employ the finest women," Jack Pack added slyly.

Both the human and incubus side of Thooranu liked that idea and he grinned. "Where is it?"

Jack Pack took him to an abandoned brick building in Piraeus. Fragments of pottery lay everywhere, and a couple of amphora stood against one wall.

"It used to be a warehouse," Jack Pack explained, walking farther inside. "Until last year, when the owner committed suicide after he lost two of his ships."

Thooranu imagined how it might be, not as the hollow forgotten place it now was, but as a fully stocked tavern, filled with people drinking and singing. He smelled cigar smoke and heard music. There would be blood on his face from a fight. Once in a while, he'd sneak off with one of the whores for a good fucking. Seeing everything so clearly got him excited. What did he have to lose?

"What say you?" Jack Pack asked. "Are you game?"

"Sure. Why the hell not. We can just walk away from it when we're bored."

"Ah," Jack Pack said, coming back. "That is so, but we need a signed contract for the building."

Thooranu's eyebrows knitted together. "Why?"

"To make it legal, of course." He reached into his inside coat pocket.

"I don't understand. It isn't as if it matters if we lose money. I sure as hell don't care. Why sign a contract?"

"As you pointed out, we can leave the business anytime we wish. The contract is simply a formality to the owner of the property. It's meaningless to us, but the mortal I leased the building from needs it." Jack Pack brought out a rolled up piece of paper. "Have a look and see."

Thooranu took the paper and unrolled it. He had never read a legal document before. The single sheet was indeed a lease for the building, the price paid for it each month, and other legal jargon that bored him. Jack's name was already scrawled in black.

"How come you've already signed it?"

"I want it," Jack Pack said. "Do you?"

Thooranu thought on that for a moment, then turned his eyes back to the contract and to the blank line next to Jack's signature.

"You can sign it later, if you want," Jack said. "I don't want us to be late for the matinee."

Seven against Thebes. Thooranu had nearly forgotten about the play. He checked his pocket watch. It was already one-twenty-three.

"Got a pen?" he asked.

Jack Pack smirked and handed over a quill. Thooranu took it and carefully signed his name. Instantly he felt woozy, suddenly weak.

"What is it?" Jack asked.

"I'm not sure," he muttered, almost falling, catching himself against a support beam at the last second. "I feel off somehow."

"Oh?" Jack crossed his arms. "Do you feel a bit hollow, as if you've just lost something?"

Thooranu did not like the tone in his friend's voice. Nevertheless, what Jack Pack had said captured his attention. Something was terribly wrong. He felt a sense of loss.

"What have you done?" he asked fretfully.

"It's not what *I've* done, per se; it's what you just did."

"What?"

"Look at the contract."

Thooranu did so—immediately—as if obeying Jack Pack's command. He read the contract again, only it wasn't a deed to the ownership of the building they stood in, but a deed to ownership of *him*! Thooranu's name was printed before a statement that he had surrendered his freedom to whoever's name was on the deed. The other name was none other than Jack Pack.

431

"I . . . I don't understand," Thooranu stammered. "This isn't what I just read."

Jack began jumping up and down, clapping his hands while laughing. "I got you! I did it! I caught a demon!"

Reeling from what was happening, Thooranu shifted his wide eyes up to him. "Why have you done this?"

"Why?" Jack said, stopping his excited jumping. "Because I wanted to. Because I've never done it before. You're my property now, for an entire year. Until the contract expires."

Thooranu's face was stone. He looked at Jack Pack through slitted eyes. When the deed finally expired, he would tear his betrayer to bits.

"Oh, but you won't," Jack Pack said, catching his thoughts. "All I need to do is sign my name again."

Thooranu was still holding the contact. He tried to rip it to shreds, but his arms locked up. No matter how hard he struggled, he couldn't tear up the piece of paper.

"You're not allowed to do that," Jack Pack said with a wagging finger. "If you read on, you'll see why. Also, if the deed is destroyed, you will be forced to destroy yourself in the most painful way that a demon can die."

Thooranu lowered the paper. His whole body was numb with shock. "How did you do this?"

"Well, first I had to gain your trust," Jack Pack said, taking the paper from Thooranu's hand. "Then, when the time came, I drew this deed up and put an illusion over it that kept you from seeing the real meaning."

"An illusion?"

Jack Pack winked. "Yes, just like Elaine and Lancelot."

"Fiend! *You're* the Trickster!"

"Indeed. And I have succeeded in my scheme."

Being a demon, emotions usually didn't penetrate Thooranu's cerebral cortex. Yet the human side of him felt the sting of betrayal that this *thing*, this petty god, had inflicted upon him.

The Trickster lost his smile. He leaned in closer, his face now only inches from the demon's.

"I have you, Thooranu, you're mine. Until I sell you to the highest bidder."

Chapter One
Mother of Craft

Spring, 1843

Mother of Craft's garden smelled like new life in the fresh afternoon air, growing everything from local to exotic plants; from peas to poppies, orchids to onions, daisies to dwarf apples. The plot was vibrant with its variety of colors, a wonderful little spot in the world overlooking the sea. Her garden was a place where life began. And sometimes where it ended.

Tarquin Norwich rode up the lane toward the modest cottage. For years, he had come to Mother of Craft, seeking guidance. Today, he'd come with a special request.

He dismounted. The roan was shiny with sweat. He started for the front door when he spied Mother of Craft on her knees, at work amongst the flowers. She didn't greet him, continuing to weed. Norwich was allergic to pollen, a fact she knew, and no doubt was why she was waiting for him in the garden. She smirked as he approached, as if she sensed his discomfort.

"Mother of Craft," he said, clearing his throat loudly.

"I'm not deaf, Tarquin Norwich," she retorted, pulling weeds from amongst the chamomile.

Norwich sighed, then sneezed. "Mother of Craft, *please*." His tone hardened.

She rose and examined him. Norwich's eyes were red and glossy, like freshly spilled blood. But despite his sniffing and heavy breathing, he stood arrow straight, head high like a proud, albeit sick, lion.

"Let's go inside," she said, heading for the back door, a bouquet of white chamomile in her hand. "The water will be boiling by now."

As she knew he would, he hurried to follow.

Her home felt like an ancient memory, an echo of a past life. A few glass plated daguerreotypes of her and her daughter hung on the dark blue wall, along with oil paintings of forested landscapes and abstracts of cities. Twisted vines cradled glass lamps in their green fingers. Inside, living plants thrived, nurturing in the low glow of the lamps' light.

Norwich hung his coat and hat on a rack, then went to the kitchen and sat at his usual chair. It was the most inviting room in the small cottage. Freshly baked biscuits sat within a small wicker basket, giving it a homey aroma. Through a wide window above the counter was a view of an endless ocean.

While she removed her sun hat and loosened the ribbon around her long coquelicot colored hair, Norwich took out a handkerchief and blew his nose.

"Tell me, Tarquin," Mother of Craft said, tearing flower pedals from their stems, dropping them into a small bowl, "what is it you seek?"

"The Toymaker," he said, his voice clear now. "Can you help me find him?"

"Indigo Peachtree, eh? Has he gone missing?"

"Yes," Norwich admitted. "In truth, he escaped from me last night."

The iron kettle hanging over the range began to whistle sharply. It was sculpted like a short twisted tree with roots snaking its body, with a branch for a handle. It was half covered by small tesserae with tea-leaves painted on. She dumped the bowl of petals into a matching teapot, then grabbed the kettle with a cloth and poured in the steaming water. She smiled wistfully, breathing the heady aroma as she stirred the brew.

"No," she said, pouring the tea into a cup.

"No?" he exclaimed, his face reddening. He slapped his hand down on the table.

"Don't you be hitting anything that belongs to me, Tarquin Norwich!" she admonished fiercely. Although her anger was feigned, it was enough to put him in his place.

Norwich was deemed an important man. He was also power hungry, ambitious, cruel, and deadly. Mother of Craft helped him because he played a vital role in her plans.

Norwich's face softened and he looked away, not meeting her gaze. He cleared his throat as if to say something, but no words were forthcoming.

"I don't know where to find Indigo Peachtree," Mother of Craft said. It was a lie, but he could not know that. She placed the teacup down before him. "But"—she hesitated, relishing the little torment it gave him—"there are those who do."

Norwich leaned over his cup, wafting the steam up with his hands, breathing deeply. He spoke in a casual tone, that barely masked his profound interest. "And who might they be?"

"The Landcross brothers."

Norwich sat bolt upright. "Landcross," he gasped. "How can that be?"

"The two have crossed paths with Indigo."

436

"I see," Norwich said, nodding solemnly. He took a sip of tea. "Do you know how to find them? Either, I don't care which."

The sun vanished behind a mass of grey clouds, a warning of oncoming rain. Mother of Craft lit candles inside several yellowing glass lanterns that she placed upon the table. "Not just one, but *both* of them."

"I only need one," he replied, taking a biscuit from the basket. "The one who will best cooperate, that is."

"You'll find that both will cooperate in their own way," she said.

"Why do I need both?" He chewed the soft biscuit, letting its sweet taste lighten his mood.

"The oldest knows where to find the Toymaker. However, the younger knows where to find an important item you seek."

She looked him in the eye, but he turned away. Her unusual violet eyes unnerved him.

"The journal?" Norwich asked in a whisper. "He knows where it is?"

"Indeed. As well as the masks. You'll need those, too, Tarquin. Do not misjudge their importance."

Norwich could not hide his excitement. "And you can locate them?"

"Yes, I believe I can."

She left the kitchen with the teacup in hand, walking over to a bookshelf in the other room. "They're many miles distant, but not for long." She stopped in front of a map of England painted on a burlap canvas that hung on the wall like a ragged curtain.

"Are they together?" Norwich asked.

"No," she said, planting her finger on the map. "One is here."

437

He stood up and came over to her. "Bristol? It'll take me a week to get there and back. "

"That's why you'll wait a week until he arrives here," Mother of Craft said, sliding her finger down to the forest area of Ampfield. "On this road, at Pagan Tree Dressing Church, you'll be able to capture him when he and his gang of highwaymen try to rob you."

"Which brother is it?"

"The oldest."

"Right," he huffed. "Where's the other one?"

She sipped her tea, then turned to face him. Just mentioning the younger brother boiled her blood. The years she'd invested in that boy! It kept her awake at nights.

"He's in France, on his way to Le Havre. You'll find him in an inn by the sea."

"How is it that you can tell me exactly where those two are, but not Peachtree?" His tone conveyed more than simply suspicion; there was a threat there too.

"The brothers were touched by the supernatural many years ago, and that allows me—and any good witch or warlock—to sense them. I have an insight into their futures."

What she told him was only half of the truth. Indeed, the Landcross brothers had the cloak of craft over them. Like most enchanters, she was able to look into the kaleidoscope of someone's future and see the many different outcomes in their life. Contrary to what many believed, there was no such thing as destiny, only random acts that kept the future constantly shifting. Consequently, one's future could not be told in a single path. The only certainty was death, the time of which was determined before birth.

Mother of Craft was a talented witch. Like most with magical blessings, she did not need a lot of paraphernalia to use her power. It simply resided within her like a vital organ.

And she didn't mind the term witch. She was who she was, and she had no quarrel with that. After all, she had let herself die in order to become an enchantress. After that, other concerns seemed petty.

"How will I know him?" Norwich asked. "The one in France."

"He has a scar across his throat. This is common knowledge so he will try to hide it, concealed under an old scarf. He also wears a Greek coin on a chain around his neck; a stater. When you find him, he'll be eating soup."

"Eating soup?"

She nodded.

"Is he not in Le Havre now?" Norwich asked with a dash of impatience in his tone.

"No, Calais. He arrived after a narrow escape from the royal guards. He will be heading south to Le Havre." She went back to the kitchen and poured herself more tea. He followed slowly, with a last lingering look at the map.

"These are the closest locations that the brothers will be to you. Try not to be impatient. Let them draw themselves in on their own." She turned her eyes up to him. "Besides, do you not have business at your summer estate?"

His look betrayed his thoughts as he frowned. "Ah, yes. I do, indeed."

Norwich drained his last drops of tea, and Mother of Craft poured more for him. "Another shipment coming in, yes?"

He snorted. "I confide too much in you."

He was obviously feeling better now.

"And for good reason," she replied. "If you had not confided in me about what Indigo told you, I could not have explained what I knew—and the power that could be gained from what he has. You're crossing dangerous ground, dove, and you need all the help you can get."

"I'll be fine."

She raised her chin. "Just in case, I will give you something."

She headed to the spice rack, with him following closely. She could feel his strength whenever he was near, and not just his physical might. His willpower was an unbreakable force. His stony grey eyes matching his salt and pepper hair, set within his majestic warrior's face. Physically, he was a handsome man, yet he was a hardened soul who had not even mourned the death of his lovely wife when she'd taken her own life.

But, however strong, Tarquin Norwich was an automaton, a mindless machine for her to use.

She took a small, pink vial from the rack. She popped the tiny cork and poured out the fine anise seeds. She moved over to the counter near the window and lifted the lid of the largest of the matryoshka nesting dolls lining the wall. From it, she brought out a round, midnight blue jar. After twisting the cap off, she poured what looked to be black oil into the vial. She pressed the cork back and placed the pink container in front of Norwich. "Use it well."

Norwich picked it up, studying it, his face scrunching in distaste. "What is it?"

"Demon's blood."

He laughed, thinking it was a joke. But when she didn't join him, he fell silent.

"Mix this into something when you give it to someone. It'll be easier for the individual to drink it if they don't know what it is. Afterwards you have complete control over them."

He nodded. "The color of the bottle makes me half believe it's a love potion."

She snorted. "*That* doesn't exist. Otherwise, I would have sold you some to use on your wife."

He grimaced and placed his cup on the counter. "I must go. It's a long ride to Southampton." He set a coin purse down next to his teacup and headed for the coat rack.

"One more thing," Mother of Craft said, paying no mind to the purse. "It would be best to send all three of your children out to find the brothers."

Norwich turned to her as he donned his coat. "Archie? He's a weak imbecile. Useless on all fronts. And Clover? She's a ten-year-old girl. Just as useless."

"Trust me," she said earnestly. "You'll need them. And if you think so poorly of them, send them after the easiest one to catch."

He didn't seem convinced, yet she knew that his trust in her would outweigh his doubt.

She saw him out and watched him ride down the lane through the sprinkling rain. As she did every time he'd come to seek guidance, she thought it was funny that he never asked if he would succeed in his plan. It wasn't fear that kept him from inquiring. Tarquin Norwich simply had too much damn self-confidence. A flaw, for that blinding buoyancy would be his undoing.

Vela, Mother of Craft's daughter, emerged from the woods in time to see him leave. She carried two limp, dangling hares. The mirror image of Mother of Craft, but at only eleven, she still had a lot of growing to do. She also shared some of her father's features, like his wild heart and slender build. Mother of Craft had to admit she missed him sometimes.

"Was that Norwich again?" Vela asked.

"Aye."

"What did he want this time?"

"He wants many things, as most men do. None of which concern you."

"Yes, Mother."

"I will say this, child," she added. "This may well be the last you'll ever see of him."

Legacy is available at Amazon.com, Barnesandnoble.com, and Norldlandpublishing.com

Michelle Lowe